THE TALES OF ZREN JANIN

WAR AND WRENS

BOOK 3

M. L. DUNKER

Publishing Services provided by Paper Raven Books LLC
Printed in the United States of America
First Printing, 2022

Hardcover ISBN: 979-8-9850536-4-7
Paperback ISBN: 979-8-9850536-5-4

*Dedication: For the ones who do not wait to be asked
to change the world.*

"If you are asked to do something and you choose not to,
how are you part of the solution?"
- Daniel Dae Kim

THE WRENS: (OLDEST TO YOUNGEST)

Oro – Says he's twenty, but Ngahuru is not convinced. A Matasi name on a Viklander/Kereki face. There's a story there, but only the Orphan Master knows for sure. He was never one of Ngahuru's Wrens, but she recognizes a *titiro mai ki ahau* when she sees one.

Falan – The nineteen-year-old daughter of the owner of the Red Cup, a wealthy gambling den in the Sinner's District. Began working with Ngahuru years ago to save Josef from her father's greed. Shrewd and sharp, she wears her anger like a favorite dress. Reads and writes Keresh.

Callis – A tailor in the Sinner's District. Strong, smart, and kind, able to read and write. At eighteen, Callis knew her father could only protect his three daughters so long without marrying them to men who were stronger than he was. Following Ngahuru to the war was better than that.

Linna – The daughter of a wealthy shopkeeper in the Flower District. Linna gathered secrets overheard in her father's shop and passed them along to Ngahuru. When she turned eighteen and her father didn't agree with her choice in love, she used Ngahuru's offer to escape to the frontier.

Nelo – At seventeen, he has been running Lost Girls and Lost Boys since he was barely older than they were. He has distinctive white-blond hair with a scarred face. He can't read in any language. He understands Kereki metal poisoning very well. He keeps his promises…and his secrets.

Arden – Arden has a dog named Mother who some say is smarter than he is. He says he is only a Kereki thief from the Flower District, although he is as sun-dark as Kid. He may have said once he was sixteen, but he also says he cannot read or write. He says he is not clever or brave. And yet…so much of this cannot be true.

Josef – Bought by Falan's father when he was only a toddler. A very beautiful child, he was dressed as a girl and taught to prance and coo and sing about the gambling tables as a distraction. Now fifteen and still beautiful, his greatest talent is pretending to be anyone other than himself.

Kid – Kid has perfect recall and an ability to remain so still he seems invisible. He was hired by the Harbor Master in Dockside to overhear and repeat conversations between ship captains and the men of business. He also sells secrets to others who profit from his information. He can read, write, and understand much more than Keresh. Only fourteen, he has carried a man's responsibilities on his boyish shoulders for years.

Dica – One of Nelo's Lost Girls until she grew too old to earn the pity of passersby. Nelo taught her to be a pickpocket, and Ngahuru taught her to be an 'eye.' Now thirteen, she is very clever, and as fearless as Falan. Her father was Conrosan, although no one knows who he was.

Jenny – Ngahuru's favorite of Nelo's Lost Girls. At twelve, she is small and thin for her age. In Kerek City, Falan and Josef passed gambling losses and Kid passed shipping information to Nelo's Lost Girls to give to Ngahuru for blackmail and bribery. Jenny is brave beyond her years.

Ross – Turned out on the street by the Orphan Master. But at twelve, Ross was too young to survive long without a protector of some sort. Ngahuru saved his life. Whether his stubbornness allows him to keep it is another matter. The other Wrens don't trust him.

Tyra – The youngest and smallest of the Wrens. With her pixie face and quick smile, she was one of Nelo's most successful Lost Girls in bringing home enough coin to keep them all fed. The frontier may be no place for a tiny eleven-year-old Matasi girl, but neither is Lowertown.

THOSE AT MANUMINA

Piffik Qanaq – A Conrosan who supported most of Manumina before the war as a furniture maker. The Wrens call him *Padro Morto* (Father Death) because he drives a coffin wagon to rescue Viklanders and on some of his delivery routes. A pacifist, he still prefers to talk his way out of a dance with Trouble, but now carries a short bow on his wagon to defend the Wrens.

Siba Namikk – A Conrosan healer who taught Zren to live beyond childhood. She sees the Wrens for who they can become, not as the throwaways they appear to be. Teaches the Wrens to read and write a little Keresh in the Academy of Treason. Siba and Piffik are best friends.

Rygee – The only Kereki survivor from the Battle at the Bridge. He deserted the Kereki army, stayed at Manumina and became a baker. He married Siba Namikk and took her family name. He is the Farm Manager and face of Manumina during the war, allowing the others to hide behind his knowledge and hard work. Perhaps the best *titiro mai ki ahau* of all.

Zren Janin – Dragged to the other side of childhood by all of Manumina. He is nineteen, but because of his damaged childhood years in Kerek City, he thinks and acts far younger. He is loyal and fierce and will do anything he thinks is necessary to protect his home at Manumina and the people he calls his family. He loves stories, food, and sleeping late.

Rell Huena – a Viklander bowmaster and healer. She is everything Zren admires, and he thrives in her affections as her little brother. She remained behind at Manumina when asked to return to the Diplo. She should be considered a Vikland deserter, but things are not always as they seem.

Tiju Tia – Ngahuru/Willow/Will. Zren thinks she came to Manumina to answer his call for help. Falan says she came for revenge on the Kerek King for her ambassador's murder. The Wrens wish she came back to save them from Kerek City. "But if wishes were horses," Ngahuru always says, "we would all ride behind the King." Perhaps all of this is true…or not.

Lou – a cheesemaker and army deserter from south Kerek. A man who so desires a safe place to live, he deliberately chooses not to see what is right in front of him. Lives outside of the Manumina stockade and keeps out of the way of everyone to sustain the illusion.

THE VIKLANDER SOFTFOOTS AND ACCOMPLICES

Bima Ritwik – Considered Vikland's greatest Softfoot, Bima is willing to use anyone, sacrifice any secret, and be only an occasional acquaintance of Truth and Honor in order to serve Vikland. He is capable of great generosity and greater cruelty. You can ask him to tell you the rest of his secrets, and then spend the rest of your life looking over your shoulder for a dance with Trouble.

Rani – A softfoot known for his ability to stay calm in deadly circumstances. He survived an attack on the Northern Track, and is now softfooting near the Kereki great houses—strong allies of the Kerek King. He holds Piffik in high regard and considers him the mastermind behind the network of Wrens and their hideouts. Friendlier than Bima, but just as ruthless.

Lomes – Softfoots through the battlefields and wears whatever maskovesto is required, does whatever is needed. While Tiju Tia and Lomes are both dual souls, Lomes uses the pronoun 'they' and Tiju Tia prefers 'she.' Lomes suspects Tiju Tia is the true runner of the Wrens, and more than just another Kereki unhappy with the current King. Keeps their suspicions as their own secrets.

Kern – Kern came back to the Diplo and her life as a softfoot when her spouse Ceri came back to fight in the war. Kern's talents as a 'look at me' are not as useful in war as they are in embasados. She spends most of her time in Juisiti training in new softfoots and then guides them to their roles in Kerek. Works with Nelo and Inezi to move soldiers from Fortika to Vikland.

Inezi – the Gamekeeper's daughter at Fortika. Disregarded by her father who is embarrassed by her Matasi face, underappreciated by Bima who is frustrated she cannot read or write, the Wrens see her true talents as only they can. A lifetime of rejection has impacted her reasoning. She tests Chul's prototype of a compound bow by practicing on those who would do her harm.

Therin – Somewhere between eight and ten, Therin is an occasional scrub boy in the kitchens with the ability to roam freely throughout Fortika. He can memorize long conversations and news from Tyra and the household to share with Inezi or Nelo. He knows how to care for horses out of sight of the stables. Nelo likes him. There are very few people Nelo likes.

TABLE OF CONTENTS

KEREK
COLD MOUNTAINS
Regno
Evensong
Fortika
Earles
Nelo's House
Josef's House
Balza
Hur
Southern Farm
Northern Track
Cloa
Sary
VIKLAND
Manumina
Ishes
To Juisiti

CHAPTER 1

A PLEA FOR HELP

To: Ngahuru, daughter of the Tailor to the West Islands King and sister to Koanga, Storyteller of the West Islands.

From: Zren Janin of the Conrosan settlement of Manumina, Kerek.

My dear Ngahuru,

As I look back on this Wet Season, I think to myself it has been over two years since I last saw you in Salisport, Matasi. That I should wait so long to write to my name giver, and the person who set me on a path to a life I did not know could be mine, is a sin even the Lost God of Matasi could not forgive.

When you were given this thick packet of paper, you must have wondered, 'What could Zren Janin have to say that I would want to sit down in my busy day to read so much?' But it is only I have written the same gratitudes, news, and requests in both Conrosan and Wester. I am not confident I can be understood in your beautiful language, and so I write to you in my mother tongue as well.

First of all, the fool I was in Salisport is not the man I am today. I want you to know all you have taught me.

The greatest gift I have learned from you began with the heading of this letter. A person of great power does not need to announce their power to the world. I see now the lessons you tried to teach me all along the Coast Road and through Matasi. I only wish I would have understood them then, so I could thank you in person.

One of the hardest lessons I have learned is the difference between friendly and friendship, kindness and love. To a child who has grown up in the streets of Kerek City, any act of decency and goodness can be misconstrued. You warned me and saved me from making a grave error with your brother. You were not there to guide me with Miyamoto Suki, and we parted as less than friends. But time and forgiveness can wash away pain and mistakes like footprints at low tide.

I did not accompany Miyamoto Suki and the others all the way to Vikland, but I know he reached there safely. We were attacked by bandits before Sary, and our wagon train of nine people did not emerge unscathed. We six survivors were rescued by Conrosans, yes, Conrosans. I have stayed with them and learned to read and write in the language of my unknown parents. Also left behind was a Viklander healer named Rell Huena. She and I share a house, and she has tried to teach me Wester. At first, she was afraid to live because others had died. But she has healed many here at Manumina, and I believe her purpose has been restored.

I have a purpose as well. At the beginning of the Wet, the Kereki army came and took away all our livestock to feed their soldiers and burned our remaining fields. We are a small settlement and too few to defend ourselves. We sent emissaries from our Council of Wisdom to the Kerek King to demand recompense, but they have not returned, nor have we had word of them. We survived the Wet season on the grains, fruits, and vegetables already harvested.

Ten days ago, as soon as the Northern Track was dry enough, we loaded all the wagons with our remaining food and packed bags. The Council of Wisdom took all but a handful of us on an exodus to Vikland. They are refugees once again.

Those of us who remain have a different purpose, and here Ngahuru, is where I beg for your help. I need to learn of your skills with pots of paint, hiding in plain sight, and softfooting to help those who helped us. I know the West Islanders are neutral in this war, as are the Conrosans, but Kerek and Matasi have betrayed Vikland. The Kerek King willingly sold away parts of his country from the southern border to the Old Fort Road. He sits in his Kerek City with his wheelbarrows full of Matasi coin to buy soldiers, food, and supplies to fight Vikland.

Matasi now refuses to allow Viklanders to use the Silver Mountain passes, and charges those found within their borders outrageous coin for accommodations, travel passes, and freedom of movement—all those injuries once done to the Kerekis as we ourselves fled through Matasi ages ago. Only now do I see the injustice of it. Vikland's supply routes have been interrupted for the last nine years and cut all together for the last two seasons. We desperately need people like you, Ngahuru, to teach us how to survive.

I dare not say more in this letter, except for this: Names have power. To bear the name of a Conrosan folk hero in the Manumina settlement brought a smile to everyone who met me when I first arrived. You smoothed the way by the grace of your wisdom and foresight. When the settlement children learned who I was, their eyes would grow round with wonder. Perhaps now they are safe from danger in Vikland, I will not disappoint them any longer.

Please share with me any wisdom on how I can keep my people safe from harm.

I remain, today and always, your devoted friend,

Zren Janin

CHAPTER 2

HOW IT ALL BEGAN

Two years since Salisport, and a war that Vikland thought would be over in a season. But that's the way of it isn't it? The elders blather and the youth bleed.

The Council of Wisdom said we would remain neutral. That we would be a friend to all. But from the very beginning we were forced to see the conflict outside the stockade gates.

I remember when I learned war had been declared.

The Empress of Vikland had sent emissaries to Kerek City to open the Northern Track, the Vikland Road, and the Old Fort Road from the Kerek City port to each of the three Vikland border crossings. The Empress wanted the treaties honored, to keep the roads free of bandits and outlaws, and allow supply trains to pass through unmolested and untaxed. The Kerek King had replied he had been alive for forty years and King for fifteen and never once had he met one of these fabled bandits and cutthroats.

The emissaries pointed out the King's own Kereki army had not been paid in ages because the army paychests were stolen and the Kerek guards and paymasters murdered before the coin could be delivered to the far-off military garrisons.

The King had replied he was sure it was Viklanders who had murdered and stolen, or perhaps other dishonorable foreigners such as the Matasi or Spice Islanders. Perhaps if they were all removed from his country, there would be no more bandits. And then he had laughed.

The next day the Viklander emissaries had returned with Ambassador Lalsy, escorted by First Soldier Joon. They presented their demands again, stating the King's father had honored the treaty from his great grandfather's time. The King yawned and claimed the Viklanders were boring him.

And so it was, the King was presented with the Declaration of War.

I learned of this from Bima Ritwik, Vikland's greatest Softfoot, who was in Kerek City when all this took place.

On the first day, the emissaries came back to the embasado and told those in the Diplo and those soldiers assigned to Kerek City and the embasado of the King's behavior. The Ambassador and Secondo knew war was coming, and there would not be enough time to get everyone through Kerek along the Northern

Track or the Old Vikland Road, so they sent most of the staff and soldiers on every ship in the harbor to the West Islands, Spice Island, or Matasi. Only the softfoots remained, pulling in their last secrets, releasing their information sources, paying their street runners enough coin to disappear. Within decons, the Vikland Embasado of Kerek City was nearly deserted.

On the second day, when Ambassador Lalsy accompanied the emissaries, the King had seemed amused when the Ambassador stated the Viklanders would take the Northern Track and all the land to the Cold Mountains if negotiations did not begin to reopen the tracks to safe travel.

"Planning to raise sheep, are you?" the Kerek King had jested, "That's all that land is good for." Then he had waved his hand, and said, "Let the war begin." He said any Viklander still in Kerek City at dawn the next day would be arrested and hung…or burned… or buried at sea…or anything else he could think of. When the emissaries and the Ambassador had stood there in shocked disbelief, the King had merely said, "What are you waiting for? Run, you little rabbits, run! You are at war with Kerek!"

There were no ships in the harbor that second day, so as soon as Ambassador Lalsy had told him the news, Bima had gathered the remaining softfoots. A Spice Islander, a woman with fingers so light she could whisper any document into her pockets, had been in the embasado delivering information when war was declared. Bima knew she was from a family of thieves. He also knew her life would be stolen if she left the Viklander embasado alone, so Bima had taken her along with them to Aldi. There the six of them waited in a West Islander's print shop until a plan and an escape could be made.

The printer and softfoots decided the Spice Islander thief had a better chance to live another day if she would stay in Aldi. From there, she could send news to her family she was safe. The printer assured them he could create the false traveling papers she would need, and could get her to Matasi, where she could sail to the Spice Island and bring the rest of her family home. Bima gave her the coins in his pocket for her to care for herself. As for the Viklanders, the printer knew they could be hidden in a farmer's wagon traveling the Vikland Road to Ahni. From there, Bima thought they could find another way to a crossing into Vikland.

Just past Pagta, the driver of the wagon was overtaken by soldiers racing to the military garrison at Nadon. They shouted at the driver that Kerek was at war with Vikland, and they were on their way to make sure none of those long-haired fools tried sneaking into Kerek. The soldiers shot off again in a cloud of dust, whooping and hollering. The driver was shaking so badly from the close call that he pulled far off the road and let the Viklanders out of their wooden crate for Bima to come up with a new plan. Now that the news of the war was ahead of them, traveling on the Old Vikland Road to slip past the guards at the Kerek-Vikland border was no longer a choice.

The driver knew of two roads intersecting the Old Vikland Road, he told Bima. The Heartland Trail was behind them, he said, but there was the Huntsman's Trail which ran straight north from Ahni to the Northern Track and then to a military garrison called Earles. The driver had heard rumors the Earles garrison had been abandoned by the Kerekis and taken over by Viklanders, but he wasn't sure. He thought it was probably only wishful thinking of those who hated the bandits. He also knew of a little used breakaway running past a Conrosan settlement close to the Vikland border. The driver didn't know much about the Conrosans at Manumina. He had never met one personally.

"And that, Zren Janin, is why we are sitting at your table, with no supplies, no food, and no way into Vikland." Bima had given me a tired half smile.

I had looked around the table at the faces that would be fighting this war; they were young—all of Bima's softfoots were young—tired and hungry. They had been running for their lives for the past five days.

"It's been a while since you have been here, Bima." I pushed myself from the table, went into the kitchen at the back of the house and from the cold box I brought smoked meat and cheese, bread and butter, fruit and nuts and set them on the table. "Eat this. When you have finished, I will take you to Salik Oqina and the Council of Wisdom. They will offer you the guest house inside the stockade. It has five bedrooms with washtubs and running water. Wash, sleep. You are safe here." I thought about the driver of the wagon who had barely stopped long enough to let the Viklanders out of the crate before turning and heading home. I wondered if he would be going all the way back to Aldi or if he would find a place to fade away along the road.

"Piffik is making a delivery to Cloa. When he returns, he'll know what to do and how to get you to Vikland. For now, your only concern is to eat and rest. Again, you are safe here."

I remember then how the fear and the tension in the room dissipated.

"Thank you," said Bima, gratitude and relief evident in his lines of exhaustion. "Thank you."

*****

But that was two years ago. I think back then how easy it was to reach for food—if not in the cold box, there were always the gardens, the bakery where Rygee worked, or the dairy shop. Now we had sent most of our food stores on the wagon train to Vikland for we did not want our families to arrive without means.

There were two journeymen and three manabouts who stayed behind to help us plant as much as we could in the fields and create a stockpile of Piffik's most wanted woodworkings.

But once their work was done, it would only be the five of us, Piffik, Siba and Rygee, Rell, and me who had volunteered to stay behind and stretch what we had left until harvest.

Tomorrow, Piffik and I would be traveling all the way to Aldi to deliver a crate large enough and sturdy enough to box up a printing press. Our West Islands printer who had saved Bima and his softfoots all those seasons ago was now sailing for his own home in the West Islands. His livelihood and his family had been threatened, and he didn't want any part of a war that was not his.

When the printer had commissioned the packing case, he had agreed to carry our letters as well. I was grateful my letter to Ngahuru would not languish somewhere waiting for a traveler to go to the West Islands. However, there were others I wished to hear from.

I had no idea where anyone was—the Viklanders moved from battlefield to home and back again too quickly to have any letters reach them. So even though I finally had a reliable means to reach someone, I had no idea where to reach Solkka, Miya, Bima, or Kern. My world had shrunk to Manumina.

Piffik had hopes of some letters reaching his brother Zadah, a sailor on the seas for a Spice Islander *kapene* named Buku Pramana who had washed up in Manumina—as unlikely as that could be. We had letters from him in the past. He wrote of marvels, and stars, and distant islands, and thanked his brother in every letter for the gift to be himself. But to send a letter *to* Zadah was not so easy, for a ship on the seas does not stay in one place.

We were sad to see our printer go home, but we wished him and his family peace and prosperity in the West Islands. We told him of our news—Manumina evacuated and the Conrosans now refugees in Vikland at the mercy of the Empress. The ones remaining, a handful of us, would keep the settlement from falling into disrepair and neglect until the Conrosans could come home at the end of the war. The printer cautioned us from sharing the news farther. It would be too easy for a Kereki band of smugglers to take over Manumina for themselves, he said. He sent us on our way with seeds, food, and items too fragile to survive a sea crossing.

There is no direct route from Aldi to Manumina. But with the Northern Track a battlefield between the Kereki and Viklander soldiers, and the Vikland Road clogged with refugees fleeing the war in the north and those who had sold their farms and orchards to the Matasi in the south, there were few good choices. Piffik had found a little used trail, little more than wagon tracks, coursing diagonally through back country. With two nights of camping rough and very early starts, we could be home late the third day.

We had an easy friendship, Piffik and I. We could be silent or speak and be at peace with both. He said he was not yet thirty, but he looked older than the Viklanders I knew. He was doing a man's work when he was still a boy because his father had been sick and died young. His face was lined about his eyes, which crinkled when he smiled or squinted as he drove his delivery wagon of furniture and coffins and other woodworkings. He had been kissed by the sun so much his skin stayed sun-dark even in the Wet season. He had the kindest eyes I had ever seen on anyone ever.

Piffik was quiet for a while and then, "I noticed you didn't have many letters to post."

I shrugged. "I know where my friend, Ngahuru, is. At least, I think I do. But the Viklanders could be posted anywhere." I paused. "Many of them could be fighting. A letter from me complaining about weeding vegetables or grinding flour wouldn't make much sense to them."

"Ah," Piffik was quiet.

After I couldn't wait any longer for him to continue, I asked, "Ah, what?"

"I just thought you had spent a lot of time learning Wester this past year."

I cocked my head and glared at him. It would have been much more effective if I wouldn't have had to look up to do it. "The letter I sent off today was written in Wester," I reminded him.

He turned away and hid a smile. "I was there, Zren. I took Bima Ritwik and Solkka Ulani to Cloa to rejoin their soldiers. This Viklander soldier all but lays down at your feet and you say, 'Well, yes, goodbye and all that.'"

Now I scowled for real. "Piffik, it wasn't that easy. I made a terrible mistake wanting Koanga who was only offering a traveling friendship, and then, following Miya like a Lost Girl because I thought he would make me a prince just as refined as he was instead of…"

I gave a heartfelt sigh. "Then Solkka comes along, and I want him too. I mean, I think I do, but I don't want to go through that pain and humiliation again. I thought I would see him as quickly as the next season. Now a year has passed, and I spend each day wondering if Solkka is safe, if he still thinks of me, when I will see him again, and how do I feel about all that? I hate this war because he is not free to come here, and I have no idea where he is to go there."

Piffik listened silently and then sighed. "I know, my friend, it isn't easy for anyone. If only the Kerek King wasn't such a fool and the Empress of Vikland so proud. Now the world pays the price."

My next words were as bitter as my feelings. "The world— bah! Actually, Matasi and the West Islands seem to be doing quite well. They shake hands with the two troublemakers and say they'll stay out of it, yet both are making coin selling everything they can make, grow, or transport to both sides. Did they think no one would notice? Only the Spice Islanders seem to honor their words to stay out of the conflict. Since the Kerek King's wife is a Spice Islander, I imagine there are angry words in the King's bedroom as well."

Piffik shrugged and we ambled along in silence. I was watching the scrubland on both sides, Rell's crossbow at my feet. The only good thing from the war was now banditry on single travelers was nearly non-existent. Why would they? A raid on a Kereki army patrol or Viklander scouts would yield weapons and food and possibly maps and plans to be sold to the enemy for coin. Settlers like us just barely scraping by? Hardly worth their time.

I let my thoughts drift. Piffik was right, I had pestered Rell to teach me to read and write and speak Wester. She had been standing with me waving goodbye to the Viklanders when Solkka Ulani had turned back his horse and told me, "*Whala te iti kahurangi kit e tuohu, koe me he maunga teilei.*" I had finally learned its meaning, "Seek the treasure you value most dearly, if you bow your head, let it be to a mountain." He had said, "You are my mountain," and had turned to catch up to the others.

Growing up on the streets of Kerek City had not given me a sense of who I was. I didn't know I was a Conrosan. I didn't know I had others like me living in Kerek. I didn't know it was possible to eat whenever I wanted, or until I was no longer hungry. I could remember only ever being called, 'Red.' Even my name, Zren Janin, had been bestowed upon me by Ngahuru, the West Islander who found me on the road to Aldi.

But worse than that, a child who grows up without love seeks it everywhere. What is only human kindness to one person becomes a desperate declaration of affection to one who has never known it. And that was the emotional wreckage I swam through to reach Solkka.

CHAPTER 3

A CHEESEMAKER NAMED LOU

"Whoa!" Piffik pulled back on the reins, and I finally saw what he did. A bundle of sand-colored clothes, man-shaped, half a furlough or so away from the track. I scouted the flat landscape for bandits in hiding, a glint of sunshine off a long glass, a slight movement in the scant cheatgrass, anything to tell me this was a trap. The track was open pastureland smooth enough to drive a cart over, no trees or waterways to interfere with a wagon traveling cross country. There was nowhere for bandits to hide.

I jumped down, grabbed a water flask and a riata, those rubble-filled Kereki ties that could bring down a bird in a tree or a cornered rabbit, or check if a soldier or bandit was dead or just slyly waiting to harm and rob me.

A little ways away and I gave the riata a lazy loop over my head and let it land on the body just above the legs. It twitched. Alive then. I swung wide so I could come around by the head. I heard a groan.

"Where are you hurt?" I hollered. I heard mumbling and then a cough. I took a step closer. "Turn over so I can see your hands." One of the legs pulled up and then stopped.

I blew out a noisy breath trying to decide what to do. "I am carrying water and a Sailor's Curse. Don't make any quick movements and I'll help you." I moved in slowly and toed him over. It was a Kereki soldier. Far older than Piffik, with a shirt covered in blood and one hand holding his ribs. His nose was certainly broken. I could hear the labored breathing, and one eye was swollen shut. I looked at Piffik and shook my head. He lowered the crossbow while I picked up the riata.

I dropped to my knees and tipped up the water flask with one hand and held up the soldier's head with the other so he wouldn't choke. He drank for a long while. I wetted one of the ends of the riata and tried to wipe his face. He cried out when I brushed his nose. It was definitely broken.

"How long have you been here?" I looked around for horse tracks or signs of a fight or ambush.

"Dunno. Yesterday sometime."

"Are you a scout? Advance patrol?"

"No. Ten of us sent to join the garrison at Earles. Jumped by bandits wearing Kereki army uniforms. We thought they were another group coming to join us." He licked his chapped lips. "More water."

I let him drink his fill and thought about what he had said. We wouldn't be crossing the Huntsman's Trail for another decon at my reckoning. This soldier was a long way from where he was supposed to be. I took a closer look at the surroundings. I didn't see broken cheatgrass, churned up dirt, or horse tracks. There hadn't been an ambush.

Piffik walked up and I gave him a mischievous grin. "Are we taking him with us? Or should we save Rell the trouble and kill him here?"

The soldier stiffened, and Piffik smiled at him. "He's not serious. Our healer is very good."

I looked at Piffik. "He says he and ten others were ambushed on the way to the Earles garrison." I kept my voice as neutral as possible because I knew Piffik would see what I had.

Piffik looked around and took a few steps in a circle about us. He looked at me and the soldier, and his eyes narrowed. So we both knew we had been lied to, but why?

Piffik shrugged. "Let's get him up in the wagon."

We probably weren't as gentle as we could have been, but he was finally arranged to Piffik's satisfaction. Piffik took the reins, and I straddled the wagon seat so I could keep one eye on the surrounding landscape for a trap and one eye on our soldier.

We reached the intersection where our faint track crossed over the Huntsman's Trail. The road was empty in both directions and Piffik hurried us over.

Our passenger was either asleep or unconscious, so I whispered to Piffik, "Deserter?"

He shrugged. "Most likely. But getting thrown from his horse wouldn't account for that much damage."

I paused a long time before speaking, "Rell is not going to be happy."

"I know," Piffik sighed. "But no one else would have passed that way. Leaving him there would be the same as murder. You can tell her I was giving you a lesson in compassion for those not like us."

I gave him a sly grin. "Maybe he will repay us with information we can share with the Viklander garrison."

Piffik snorted. "So much for compassion." He looked back into the cart. "Maybe he can cook."

***

Rell was not happy. In fact, she was so not happy, she was furious.

"You want me to save this soldier's life? This Kereki soldier who may have slaughtered all my friends?" she shouted at me and Piffik as we dragged in the soldier, hanging between us, his arms pulled over our shoulders.

We eased him into a chair, and I took a critical look at him. "Well, I don't think you need to save his life," the soldier jerked his head up, "He doesn't look like he's going to die. Just patch him up a bit. So we can talk to him and see if Trouble is coming to dance with us."

Rell crouched down in front of his chair. "Answer me truthfully, have you ever shot a bow, or pulled a knife on a Viklander?"

"I've never even seen a Viklander, I mean, until now. I didn't know you all were so pretty," he blurted out.

"I'm the Viklander, not them!"

He jumped. "I meant you. They're not as pretty as you. I mean, they're boys, er, men."

"How old are you anyway?" Rell stood up abruptly and started gathering her supplies.

"Forty-four."

She stopped what she was doing and gave him a long look. "What did you do before you started marching for your King?"

"I was a cheesemaker in South Kerek, just north of Diempf. My family had a dairy there for six generations. We had caves and springhouses for aging the cheeses, and I made the sheep and goat cheese. My mother's family is famous for their cheeses." He fell silent.

"And Matasi bought all the land from the border to the Old Fort Road," Piffik said gently. "Your new landlord?"

"Many people work the orchards in South Kerek. Families know each other for generations. Workers come to work the same estancias, children work for the children of the previous generations. The Matasi think we are going to revolt and take back our lands and our country. So people are watched. Workers who migrate with the crops, or with shearing or butchering, are escorted from estancia to estancia, and after the day's work is done, they are locked into the bunkhouses at night by the new Matasi landlords."

"Creating fear and distrust where none was found before," Piffik mused.

The soldier shrugged. "I was out visiting friends at a neighboring estancia. I have known them all my life. We were drinking. It got late. I was found after curfew by Matasi guards. There is no appealing to a Matasi guard's better nature. They have none. They beat me and made me run behind their horses all the way to the garrison at Neblin. The Kereki commander thanked them for his newest recruit. There was already a group of soldiers headed to the Earles garrison. I was stuck on a horse and told to stay with them." He stopped when Rell started to wash his face. She was gentler, I noticed, about his broken nose than I expected.

"There were no Kereki bandits, were there?" Piffik asked.

The soldier said nothing, and then slowly shook his head. "No. I knew I was moving to the front of the war, and I don't know how to do anything except make cheese." He licked his cracked lips. "So when I heard we were less than a day away from Sary, I decided to make a run for it. But I've only ridden plow horses. This one was skittish and threw me once we got out alone in the scrubland. It's how I hurt my ribs, I think." He touched them tenderly. "I thought I was going to die out there. I was so cold last night. I didn't know it got so cold at night."

"It's why all the citrus is grown in the south of Kerek and in Matasi," said Rell crossly. "Now hold still, I'm going to set your nose." She packed the nostrils with wadding and pinched all along the bridge. He yelped, or maybe I did. Rell never believed anyone should have time to think about what she was going to do to heal them.

She went out and brought back a clean basin of water and soft rags. As she set it down in front of him, she told him to strip and wash everywhere, she was going to go out and talk to Rygee for a bit. Once she was gone, Piffik and I washed the soldier's back and ribs where some very heavy bruising had set in.

"Who's Rygee?" The soldier winced as I accidently brushed against a deep bruise.

I made my face as serious as possible. "He's our resident Kereki. She's going to ask him if he thinks your story is true, or if she should push one of these cracked ribs into a lung." I felt him stiffen his shoulders, and Piffik gave me a long-suffering look over his head.

"So you deserted the Kereki army," Piffik started slowly. "That means if you go back, they will put you in jail and hang you, or if you are lucky, send you to the battlefields."

"I'm not going back," he said fervently.

"Well, you can't go back home. The Matasi guards will just pick you up again and give you another beating," Piffik said pleasantly. I recognized that tone of voice. Piffik used it on me when he wanted me to reason something out that would agree with his own plans.

The soldier thought for a moment. "Do you have a dairy here?"

"We did, but the Kereki army came just before the Wet and took all our livestock with them to feed their troops. Our goats are gone."

He considered Piffik's answer. "Do you have springhouses or caves to store the cheese to age and a manabout to tend to the goats and sheep?"

I wrinkled my nose at that, and Piffik laughed out loud. "Are you willing to get our dairy up and running again in exchange for a place to sleep without fear and food in your belly?"

"Yes." He was still thanking us when Rell came back.

"Do you have a name?" she asked.

"Lou."

"Lou, fine. These two will take you to Rygee. If he offers to feed you, say yes. He's the best cook we have. And then I am done with you." She went back and found an old shirt for him to put on. "Burn the uniform," she said sharply. "We don't need to be found with that about."

As Piffik led him out to find Rygee at the bakery, Rell put her hand on my arm to keep me behind.

"He can't stay with us, Zren, I mean it. Not in our house. I can't do that."

"I'll see if Piffik will take him." She gave me a sharp look and bit back her response. "Look, Rell, I know it wasn't easy. But you saw it yourself, he doesn't want any part of this war either. And if he can get the dairy back up and running, then there will be coin coming in. We won't have to rely only on Siba's and your potions and Piffik's woodworking coin."

"I know, I know. Just… how do we know he's not a softfoot for Kerek?"

I thought about it for a moment. "We put him in charge of the livestock."

***

One thing you could say about Lou—he was trainable. He became Manumina's newest manabout. He would show up when asked, do whatever he was shown to do, and work until the work was done. When he had time, he cleaned out the dairy, reinforced the springhouses farthest from the stockade, and drew pictures of the casks and cases he needed Piffik to make him out of white oak to store and age his cheeses, butters, and other products.

He didn't live with Piffik. He chose a house on the east side. Piffik still lived on the south side, next to the journeymen's house, and Rell and I had the west view towards the breakaway and closest to the gates. With the three manabouts living on the northside, it made Rell uneasy to have Lou so isolated. When Rygee asked him why the east side, Lou looked surprised and said his choice was closest to the springhouses. Rell was still suspicious he was softfooting for Kerek.

Lou and Rygee went all the way to Huk to a goat farmer that Lou's family had heard about and came back with eight does, one buck, and a wether. Piffik and I had fixed the fencing on the pastures while they were gone. Then when they had driven all the goats into the two gated areas, we four just stood looking at them over the gate. We had had goats before—Salik Oqina and his family raised them. But Salik and his family were in Vikland now, and his goats had been taken by the Kereki army.

Siba and Rell drifted out of the stockade and stood with us while we watched the goats explore their new surroundings and crop the roughage that had been allowed to grow since our own livestock had been driven off.

"They're cute," Rell admitted.

"And profitable," acknowledged Lou. "Provided I can keep the predators away. What do I have to worry about here anyway?"

"The Kereki army," Rell responded quickly. Both Siba and Rygee leaned back to give her a long look.

Rygee answered, "We can drive them into the stockade for the night and stable them with the horses for a while if it would make you feel better."

Lou didn't answer him. "I'm going to need rennet. Is there a butcher shop nearby or do we need to raise our own calves?"

I stared at him. "I grew up in Kerek City. You are going to have to explain that entire last thought to me."

So he did. In graphic detail, Lou explained animal rennet comes from stomach linings and how it was used in cheese making. After all of us were staring at him with appalled looks and dropped jaws, he casually mentioned there was vegetable rennet as well, but he would need someone else to grow the cardoon thistle, artichokes, and nettle.

Siba and Rygee exchanged a look, and Rygee said he would see if he could find the seeds in Sary the next time he went, or he would stop at the butcher shop. We wouldn't be raising calves.

CHAPTER 4

JUST WHEN YOU THINK YOU KNOW SOMEONE

I felt uncomfortable with how much Lou's history mirrored my own. Found by the side of the road, cared for by strangers, and working to learn any task set before him because he had no skills of his own. He spoke only Keresh. He had none of the other many languages: Vik, Conrosan, Wester, and some Mata, those I lived with knew. One night, when I was home alone with Rell, I tried to explain how he made me feel. She listened carefully—it was one of the many, many things I liked about her.

She had been quiet for a while after I finished pouring out my worries. At last, she tipped her head to the side.

"I think I hear what you are not saying, Zren. You think we do not trust Lou because he is a stranger, a Kereki, and if we ask him to leave, then we are going to look around and see you. You worry we are going to tell ourselves, 'Here is Zren' we know nothing about him either, and maybe he should leave us as well. You are concerned we are going to open the gates of Manumina and throw you out to Kerek where the color of your skin and your small size will make you a victim of anyone who passes by—just as you were in Kerek City."

I sighed. I had said a mouthful of other things, but Rell had heard my heart and not the words that had fallen from my lips. I nodded, but I didn't risk saying anything more.

She began slowly, "When you and Piffik brought Lou to me to heal, I could not see beyond his Kereki uniform. To me, he was the enemy, and nothing else. That was my blindness, not yours.

"Rygee did not, does not, trust him because Lou is unfailingly honest. But Lou is honest because he doesn't know when to shade the truth, when to withhold information because those in Sary do not need to know. I have learned, Lou isn't smart enough to deceive anyone. And for Rygee, that means Lou could jeopardize all of our lives here by telling the wrong people we are so few here at Manumina. Lou could mention we have Viklanders—me— here without realizing the consequences to my life. He may boast there is always coin for our needs without understanding others may wonder how we earn it." She paused, gathering her thoughts.

"I think he was a cheesemaker in his family's business because it was something Lou could learn to do, and his family could shelter him from those who would do him harm. Piffik and Siba are Conrosans. Their belief in non-violence is bred to their very being. They may worry Lou will betray them, yet they would not harm him, nor cause others to harm him by throwing him out. They believe his life is as valuable as their own. You are also Conrosan by birth, but you have the heart of a Viklander and the mind of a Kereki. You and I, Zren, have promised to protect those who need our protection. That means Manumina as well as those who live within its walls. I needed to learn this again." She paused and smiled at me.

"I learned it again from you. When we traveled the Northern Track together, you were a fierce boy who knew only violence and fear as a way of life. And yet, you protected us in the only way you knew how.

"Zren, I hear your fear, but no one is going to be cast out of Manumina. Lou will only leave Manumina when he chooses. As for you, you have lodged in my heart as completely as any of my brothers whom I left behind in Vikland. You do not leave Manumina without me." She bobbed her head. "Or at least without telling me." She gave me a lopsided grin.

Rell was a bowmaster of Vikland. I had seen her practice her crossbow almost daily, thudding quarrel after quarrel into the straw until the centers of the targets were shredded. I had heard her drag her wounded legs up and down the stairs of our home many times a day and night, until they worked again the way she wanted them to. She had taught me to speak and read and write Wester, because I had asked her, and because she had known Solkka Ulani from her own days in the Diplo and said he was a man worthy of me. She had lived in the House of Nations with me, and Chul, and Rygee. She had known Rygee and me as orphans of the heart and treated us as younger brothers until our hearts were no longer broken by betrayal and abandonment. Rygee had moved out to live with Siba Namikk, and Chul had returned to Vikland. Still she and I lived together in peace.

She was fierce and strong and everything I admired and wanted for myself, and she very nearly had said she loved me too. The truth of her words slammed into my heart. I left her in our sitting room and went up the stairs to my bedroom. I laid down on the bed and wept with relief and happiness.

***

In the abandoned dairy, Lou found Chul's inventions—the self-churning butter churns, the waterbath cheese paddles—and considered them remarkable. He found us in the stables and asked more about the person who had made them. I started to tell him about Chul Swyler and how he made life better for everyone in Manumina, but Piffik abruptly cut me off and just described Chul as a Matasi traveler passing through Manumina who had given us the inventions as payment for a horse and wagon.

Lou had just looked back and forth between the two of us and then headed quietly out the door of the stockade to his vegetable gardens and his goats.

"You've been prickly to Lou since we found him along the track," I started slowly. "It's not like you, and that tells me I am not seeing something very important right in front of me."

Piffik said nothing but stopped putting feed out for the horses. Finally, as if it hurt him to say it, he asked, "Has Rell said anything to you?"

"About Lou?" I put down my pitchfork. "Only that she doesn't think he is very smart. At first, she wondered if he had an injury to the brain when he was a child. But now she says his world was just so small—cheese, and his family, and south Kerek. When I said I didn't know anything when I first came to Manumina, she said 'maybe.' But she said I was smart enough to drag myself to the other side of childhood and no one had done the same for Lou."

Piffik blew out a breath. "And my world is woodworking and horses and Manumina. Thank you, Zren, you're not helping." He started to say more and then hit the wooden gate with his open palm.

"Let's get the coffin wagon loaded tonight. I leave at first light for the garrison at Ishes, and this way I won't have to wake you tomorrow morning. I never knew you had such a soft life in Kerek City. You'd sleep in until the sun was fully over the horizon if I gave you a chance."

I snorted and followed him to the woodworking shop. We had the journeymen help us load the coffins. Their jokes and gallows humor made us groan and guffaw, and soon Piffik seemed his old self again.

I had always imagined a war within Kerek would put the entire country in turmoil, but I was wrong. Only the Northern Track and north to the Cold Mountains were battlegrounds. The rest of the country seemed rather unconcerned about it all. Even with the war, Piffik's business continued to grow. He made sturdy moving chests, coffins, and traveling desks for the garrison, settlers, and armies north of us. He made fine furniture, wardrobes, and other objects for the wealthy landowners south of us. Lou's stories about south Kerek were more about the Matasi merchants buying the estancias and the inconveniences of their lives, and no stories about the Viklanders dying to demand Kerek honor its treaties.

The handful of manabouts and journeymen who had stayed behind with us worked hard to restore the damage done to the buildings and barns by the Kereki army before the Wet. At first, we had posted lookouts everywhere. Rell and her crossbow on the top floor of houses outside of the stockade, and roving manabouts on horses and foot. The rest of us planted and tended the fields and orchards.

But we were too few to maintain this for long. Once the others left for Vikland we were reduced to one person on horseback circling the stockade to give us a warning of visitors and vagrants instead of invaders. Rell told us the stockade would have to stand in for a regiment of soldiers. Siba had wrinkled her nose at that but had said nothing.

We heard nothing from Vikland. We knew the war was far to the north and west of us—as far as Vingt and Balza. Occasionally, Piffik and Rygee would pick up something overheard in the shops of Cloa and Sary and share it with those remaining within Manumina. We knew the war was not going well for the Kereki army. Drafted, kidnapped by impressment gangs and crimpers, or enlisted, it didn't matter. The soldiers received a year's pay in advance because the paymasters wouldn't see another paychest from the King. With so much coin in their pocket in the first days, there was no incentive to remain and soldier. Desertion was high. Everyone knew robbery and death by outlaw was as likely as death by Viklander.

But Vikland didn't have the easy victory it expected. They had thought the Kerek army was the enemy, but they were wrong. Landowners would fight for farms and towns that had been their homes and livelihoods for generations. The town militias and landowners' guerrillas were wearing down the Vikland forces, not the Kereki army. They knew the countryside and Viklanders separated from their units had a low survival rate.

After the fields were planted and the last of the journeymen left, Rygee had taken over the baking for all of us that remained and began selling more in Sary. With only Piffik, Rygee, Siba, Rell, and I, we combined our households and ate together. It helped Rygee and Siba were the only decent cooks among us. Even so, Lou said he wanted to cook and eat by himself.

Supplies continued to get more difficult to find, and more expensive when the supply wagons actually could get through the battles and blockades to Sary. When Rygee could no longer get flour and sugar, he came back from the shopping with an assortment of plants and seeds I had never seen before. He cleared another section of an empty field with the horses and plow. He taught all of us how to plant the red oats, yams, and a tuber that he said could be boiled and mashed for sweetness.

Siba and Rell dressed in the clothes of Kereki boys and weeded with us outside the gates. Lou protested, saying a Kereki woman would never be found working in the fields or wearing men's clothes, and the women were not acting like women should.

Rell had narrowed her eyes at him but before she could bite back a retort, Siba had stood up straight and said, "We all eat, we all work. That is the Conrosan way when all things are held in common. This is a choice you must accept to live here. I am not going to change who I am to fit your thoughts of who I should be."

Lou was silent but took his hoe and his basket and worked on the other side of me, as far away as possible from the women. Rell caught my eye and smirked.

One evening, Rygee and I were walking about the outside of the stockade before we closed the gates against the night.

"This reminds me of our watches on the Northern Track." I smiled at him. "Remember how we would circle about the dying fire? I always hoped I had first watch, because then Kern would let me sleep in until I smelled first meal. Meals sure got a lot better once you and Chul took over the cooking." I chuckled. "Miya was smart not to have me or Mouser cook. I never learned how, and Mouser would have poisoned us so he could escape with all the Kereki payroll and Vikland chests of West Islands steel."

Rygee stopped. "That's such an odd name. And I know it was not his own, although he claimed it on the Track. Why did you call him that?"

I paused and gathered my thoughts together. "You did not know this, Rygee, but when First Soldier Joon and Miyamoto Suki asked the Kerek King for an escort on the Northern Track from Kerek City to the Vikland border, they did not expect the request to be honored. It had not been granted in the past. It was only a formality, Miya told me, so the King could hear the Viklanders beg. It was said the King would mock them for being Warriors who could not defend themselves on a country road against nothing more than scorpion stings and dust devils.

"I never told Mouser why I called him so. But he took the name as his, rather than give us his own. Miya said he always planned to desert with the paychest and if we did not know his true name, then no one would be able to find him." I sighed. "As for why I called him Mouser, this is the story I told to Miya and the others while you were burying Bitterboots.

"I grew up in Kerek City, which you know, but in Lowertown down by the docks, which you did not know. I grew up loved, and then one day I was not, but I do not remember how it happened. Before I came to Manumina, I could neither read nor write in any language, although I spoke Castle Kerek rather than the rough language of the streets. I think now, I must have been protected until six? Maybe seven?"

I paused, wondering why I still couldn't remember what had happened. Ngahuru had said my mind was protecting me from the horrors of my life and perhaps I would never know. Or maybe, she said, when I was an old man and the grief would not overwhelm me, I would wake up and remember, or fall asleep and dream of it. But today? I still remembered nothing.

I continued my story, "In those Lowertown streets, there was a pirate who would lurch down the alleys and byways on his cane in the name of Trouble. He would grab the little children—the pickpockets, the pretty ones pretending to be lost children, the street runners and messengers for the taverns, shops, and shipmasters—and drag them in the alleys. Sometimes he stole their coin, sometimes their food, and sometimes their hope in a just world. If a child screamed for help, the adults nearby would look away, and we children would sigh in relief, 'Today was not our day.' We called him Mouser because he was like a cat who pounced and preyed on the little ones."

Rygee carefully avoided my eyes and looked out into the distance. "What happened to him?"

"Even in Lowertown, where food was in short supply and trust was even shorter, children grow up. There was a Matasi girl a handful of years older than I was. She had been raised in the faith of the Lost God before she had been abandoned on the streets and left to make her way. She gathered us all together and told us he was one man, one cane, one knife. If we all worked together, she said, 'We could be avenging angels with many knives bringing Justice to Lowertown. We would be the Fist of God.'"

I sighed. "Rygee, she told us a pretty story. She gave us hope. I didn't know what an avenging angel was, but I did know what a fist was. A 'Fist of God' sounded very much like something that could hurt Mouser as much as he hurt us.

"She had three daggers and four Sailor's Curses. I have no idea how she was able to lay her hands on so many weapons. She handed them out to the bigger children and told the rest of us to find rocks and sharp scraps of metal or anything that could cause pain. She asked for a Lost Girl to be the one to lure Mouser into the alley where the rest of us were to stand absolutely still. When she gave the word, we would take away his cane, and hit him with rocks, and cut him with our knives and Sailor's Curses.

"We waited one night outside the tavern where he liked to drink. When he came out, Lilly ran across the sidewalk in front of him and Mouser knocked her down with his cane. We stood motionless in the dark as he dragged her into our alley. Before he had untied the rope about his pants, we had swarmed him." I paused, wondering what Rygee was thinking.

"Children who have been made to feel powerless and hopeless are not compassionate creatures. By the time we heard more steps coming from the taverns and stopped our frenzy, the alley was drenched in his blood. We were pulled off the body, but when the adults saw the remains of who it was, they just told us to run to our hiding places and tell no one." I turned to Rygee. "I was maybe…eight years old?"

I heard him suck in a big breath, but he said nothing.

"Rygee, when I saw Mouser watching Rell at the fire that first night on the Northern Track with that hungry look in his eyes, all those feelings of powerlessness came crashing back. It's true, I deliberately hunted your fellow soldier. I did not expect it to be Bitterboots, but he grabbed Rell's cloak with me in it. He was not innocent." I considered my next words carefully.

"Did I misjudge Mouser because of how I grew up? I don't know. When he went after Song, she was so confident in her power and her skill she beat him to the ground, but she left him alive. I am not sure I could have done that. Until I came to Manumina, I do not know that I ever understood what the word 'mercy' meant. But you use your knowledge of farming, your talents in baking and cooking and preserving, to keep us all alive. I am trying to do the same, but my skills and talents are nothing like yours."

Rygee was silent for a long time, and I began to grow uneasy.

"Huh," he said at last, and turned back towards Manumina's gates. "Mouser told Nebs and me that Miyamoto Suki deliberately chose you to murder Bitterboots the first night to show us you were the littlest and weakest of all of Miya's travelers, and still completely without a conscience. He told us if we did not desert at the first chance we had the Viklanders would murder us all. I had told you a long time ago I was afraid every day of that journey. What I didn't say? I was afraid of all of you."

CHAPTER 5

OLD FRIENDS AND NEW WRENS

The Dry season had been the right mix of sun and dew, and Chul's irrigation ditches had been untouched by the Kereki army. All of us had been able to plant and keep alive enough crops to be able to survive ourselves. We were maybe five days away from harvest, and Rell and Siba had again joined Lou and me in the field. There were four of us weeding the rows of red oats. Rygee was circling the stockade on horseback with a crossbow. Piffik was picking up supplies in Sary. Rygee said he felt awkward riding while Siba did fieldwork, so we teased him we hadn't washed all the Kereki out of him yet. Siba explained we all had to take turns—it was the Conrosan way. Since she had no idea how to fire a crossbow, she had a better chance of living to see the next day if he wielded it instead of her. She always knew what to say so people could lose the argument with their dignity intact.

We were joking about the delicacies Rygee would be able to make once the red oats were harvested and had been ground into meal and flour. Rygee responded only those who could hit the side of the goat barn with the crossbow would see one of his oakcakes with jam. He looked pointedly at Siba.

It was the dust we saw first. Coming from the north on the Huntsman's Trail, one settler wagon piled high with goods and three outriders on slow-moving horses. It was too far to see who they were, even for Rell. When they turned and took the breakaway to Manumina, Siba, Rell, and Lou drifted inside the stockade to bar the gate. Rygee had tried to give Rell the crossbow, but she had told him to take out as many as he could, she would pull her larger crossbow hidden in the infirmary and defend us from the lookout, and from within if the strangers breeched the gates.

Rygee and I waited to greet our visitors, and I hoped it wasn't my last day on earth.

The outriders reached us first. One of them had a black dog trotting alongside, knee-high to the horse. They were all dressed in shapeless brown and grey clothes with bright colored Kereki ties about their calves and ankles. From Kerek City then. An old woman drove the wagon, hunched about with clothes mismatched, her white hair frizzing about her head and peeking out from the hood of her traveler's cloak. A young man, tall and slender, with oddly cropped black hair, was sitting on the bench seat beside her, holding a short bow nocked in his lap. It would only take a moment for him to pull and fire.

I took a deep breath and walked out of the oat field towards them. I heard Rygee nock the crossbow behind me. I stood just far enough away I wouldn't need to shout.

Then I addressed them as Piffik had taught me, "Welcome to Manumina, a Conrosan settlement neutral in the battle between Kerek and Vikland. Can I help you find your way?"

One of the outriders approached and turned his horse sideways to me. He was fair-haired—so fair his eyebrows did not show, giving his scarred face an odd open look. He had the too-thin look of Lowertown, but I had never known any of them to have ever ridden a horse.

He held his hands palms out, empty, and to his sides. "I carry no weapons. We are far from our home and seek sanctuary."

A Matasi girl peeked over the side of the wagon and was pulled down by an unseen hand. I cocked my head to the side.

"How many are you?"

No one spoke, and the old woman slowly climbed down from the wagon. Her cloak was faded and dusty and the hood was pulled so far forward it hid her face. Bent over with age, she shuffled toward me. Rygee brought up his crossbow. The young man on the wagon seat brought up his bow and the outriders moved in closer, surreptitiously reaching in their own cloaks for their weapons. I knew the blond boy had been lying. They were all armed.

I could smell the stink of fear sweat on me but pushed as much command in my voice as I could. "We are two; you are many. We are not so foolish, Rygee and I, to think we would prevail. Put down your weapons."

The woman stopped a body's length away from me and straightened. She pushed back her hood and before my eyes she became a young woman barely thirty with a West Islands face and the pale skin of the Kereki. She still didn't reach the height of my nose.

She smiled. "How many do you need?"

"Willow!" I crossed to her in three strides and picked her up and hugged her. "I have never been so glad to see someone! Rygee, this is the woman who saved my life on the road to Aldi. And now she comes to save us again! Oh, it is so good to see you!" I knew I was babbling, and my face hurt I was grinning so hard, but she was such a welcome sight. I hugged her tightly again, and she patted my arm to put her down.

"You had us worried when we came close. I thought you were being guarded by a Kereki soldier and your settlement had already fallen in the war. Otherwise, we would have hailed you sooner," she explained.

"Come inside! We have water for you and your horses." I reached for her hands and saw the left sleeve of her Kereki shirt sewn shut over the end. "No!" I snapped my eyes up. "What happened?"

"We can talk later. For now, know it is not what it seems. Besides, who looks closely at an old woman except to see if she has valuables worth taking at the end of a knife?"

The stockade gates swung open. I turned to see Siba and Lou at the gates and Rell casually holding her crossbow at rest between them. *They must have noticed the friendly greeting from the lookout*, I thought.

Willow looked at Rell and her crossbow and smiled. "By the size of that bow, and the black braid of honor down your back, my Viklander, I know my friend, Zren Janin, is not so helpless as he claims to be. I am Tiju Tia of Kerek City with friends to you and yours." She waved the wagon forward to follow Rygee, still on horseback, inside. The outriders formed a wedge to the front and sides of the wagon as they all moved into the settlement.

Willow and I followed behind, still talking.

"I thank you for your wisdom in calling out, 'Willow.' Your

Viklander must never know who I am. This is bigger than you and I. Do you understand what I am saying, Zren?"

I nodded quickly, and she continued, "I had to pick up my little Wrens in Kerek City." She sighed and looked away for a moment. "Some of them are gone now. Lowertown is nothing more than a place where Trouble dances. I was forced to flee too quickly before. I did not take care of my Wrens as well as a softfoot should. But near the embasados, I still found some of my street runners and others who were ready for a new adventure in exchange for a place to call home."

She pulled me back still further. "There is one that I do not know from before. One of my Wrens brought him, he was on the wagon seat beside me, and just drove the wagon inside your gates. He tells me this: he remembers living in the West Islands as a child, and he knows how to use our short bows. He remembers sailing to Kerek and being sold to the Orphan Master. He speaks some Wester and Keresh." She paused. "Formal Wester, street Keresh. He says he is twenty. I think he may be younger. He has Kereki features but you can see the Viklander in him with his black hair. He says his name is 'Oro' which means 'gold' in Mata." She gave me a broad smile. "You see why I could not leave him behind? A puzzle such as this?"

She slid her right hand in mine. "I am so glad you sent me that letter, Zren. I knew when I received it, I could not risk a letter back but could only make the journey myself. My King and I agreed I could only be called Tiju Tia. I can never be seen or known as Ngahuru until the war is over or the Kerek King is dead. I am here as your friend, not as a West Islands softfoot. My head still has a price on it, and the West Islands still pretend to be neutral in this war."

I agreed quickly. "Tiju Tia," I tested the name on my tongue and nodded. "I know you risked so much to come here, but for the first time since the war began, I have hope."

***

There were ten of them, in addition to Oro and Ngahuru. I showed the ones crowded about me the guesthouse and told them there were five bedrooms and washrooms.

"Leave one for Tiju Tia," I said. When I tried to assign rooms, Tiju Tia just patted my arm. "Let's not be so concerned about labels. We can let them sort themselves out. Some of them know each other from before and some do not. They are capable of deciding who will make them feel safe in their room."

Rygee and Siba came over to the guesthouse carrying baskets of food. I left them cooking in the back kitchen while Oro, Tiju Tia, and I went to unload the wagon. Without the Wrens in the cargo area, it was not as full as I first thought when I saw it coming down the breakaway from the Huntsman's Trail. I am not sure who had taken the horses and wagon to the stables, probably Rell, but the five horses had been rubbed down, fed, and watered. They were content.

Ngahuru—Tiju Tia—described what she had brought, "All the West Islands steel I could get my hands on. Which wasn't as much as you would think. For a country which claims to be neutral in this war, our foundries are running at full capacity, and yet nothing can be found in the shops. I also brought short bows and arrows. I see now you have at least two Viklander crossbows. I thought West Islands bows and arrows won't give you away if you are forced to lie for your life in front of a Kereki soldier."

She pulled out some bulging leather packs and large burlap bags. "I also brought my pots of paint and had Koanga make costumes we can switch from inside to outside. He made dagger pockets that can be tied on and hidden under clothes, soft leather knife sheaths for boots, and padded tunics for fighting." She quirked a smile at me.

"He said to tell you to be careful. He did not take away his time from making gowns and dresses for those who visit with the King to make these gifts for you and the Wrens to be only worn once." She paused. "This is his way of saying he is sorry about before. We understood so little of what your life had been before we met you on the road to Aldi. We both would like to see you visit the West Islands as our friend, and not as a Conrosan to be paraded about to show off to our family and others."

She was quiet and when I nodded my thanks because my throat was too full to speak, she went on briskly, "I think my Wrens and I can help you the most with information. We are not so skilled with fighting as we are with survival." She sighed. "Although any child in the depths of Lowertown, Dockside, or the Sinner's District who doesn't know how to fight with a knife has lost the will to live."

There was nothing I could say to that. Until she and her brother Koanga had rescued me, I had been one of those children in Lowertown surviving on my speed and my wits to live another day. Back then, I had thought myself seventeen or so—not many birthdays are celebrated in Lowertown—but in the years since I had left had been a lifetime of understanding just how narrowly I had escaped.

She switched to Conrosan, a language I could see Oro didn't know when he narrowed his eyes at her.

"My friend Raumati owes you a life debt. She and I both know this. Her family paid for all the goods on this wagon. They are that grateful you returned her safely to them."

I tipped my head up fast to keep the tears from spilling over and running down my cheeks. We stood there silently, Oro watching me, wondering what she had said to cause a man tears, and Tiju Tia watching the wagon until I could compose myself.

I cleared my throat. "Raumati had many friends who wanted to see her safe at home. The Viklanders gave her food, shelter, and paid for her passage home. I could do none of that."

"But the Viklanders did it because it benefited them, and it did, my King rewarded them. But you did it because it was the right thing to do." She switched back to Keresh. "Now where do you want these chests?"

Piffik drove his wagon and horses into the stable. "Ah, so this is why the gates of Manumina are hanging wide open and the fields are deserted. I thought to myself, I had just gone to Sary and back, I could not see Manumina falling so quickly to an enemy who leaves our fields intact and our goats in the pasture." He spoke Conrosan to give me a chance to say if those in front of him were friendly or not. Ngahuru smiled and introduced herself, also in Conrosan, as Tiju Tia. He quirked an eyebrow and stepped down from his wagon.

"There are ten more in the guesthouse," I explained, switching to Keresh so Oro could also be a part of the conversation. "Rell is getting them sorted out and explaining the plumbing. Rygee and Siba are making food for them."

He grimaced and explained to Tiju Tia, "We are a few days

away from harvest. At the beginning of last year's Wet the Kereki army drove off our livestock and tried to burn our fields. We did not have much in the settlement for food today before I went to Sary to get supplies," he waved at his wagon, "but if anyone can multiply twigs and grass into a meal worth eating, it's Rygee."

He handed each of us a basket full of vegetables, eggs, rice, and shifted a large bag of flour over his shoulder. He smiled at the look on my face.

"I don't know who brought it through, or where it was meant to go, but I bought it before it was even unloaded into the store. Rygee will be beyond pleased."

The four of us walked silently to the guesthouse. Inside, Siba and Rell were putting bowls of soup and plates of unleavened bread in front of the children. That's really what they were. Once the dust and sorrow of the road had been washed away, their faces and voices had returned to the look and sound of children.

I looked across the table at Rell. "I know," she said sadly. "These are Vikland's allies." I started to protest, but I realized Rell was looking at the Wrens with the eyes of a Viklander. She had grown up on stories of warriors and monsters, gone to the academies in Juisiti to be a healer, and trained to be a bowmaster. She had served her three years in the military and joined the Diplo. What she knew as her truth was far different than what these children had known.

I, on the other hand, had grown up as these children had, running faster than Trouble, hiding where those bigger and stronger could not find us, and stealing food to keep from starving. These children weren't meant to be soldiers and masters of their weapons. They would steal documents and maps, hide and listen to secrets, and find help for injured Viklanders. These Wrens, Ngahuru's network of street children in Kerek City, were exactly what we needed.

"And finer allies could not be found anywhere," I stated firmly. "My name is Zren Janin, and I call Manumina my home. Someday, Tiju Tia may tell you of my travels, but for tonight, eat as much as your bellies will hold, sleep as long and deeply as you want, and tomorrow is another day. You are at Manumina, a place where you will wake up unhurt and unafraid." I gave them my biggest smile. "It is the best feeling in the world!"

***

That night, Piffik, Rygee, and I sat on the porch swing in front of my house. The stars were out scattered like sparks from the Smith's forge. I tilted my head back and watched the sky as Piffik and Rygee talked of the settlement.

"The oats will be ready first, but not until after the next Rest Day, and it could be as long as a fortnight before the orchards are ripe for picking," Rygee began.

"It's not that we can't afford the food in the shops in Sary, it is that there is nothing to be had," Piffik explained to him. "According to the gossip and rumors, Matasi is taking all the harvests from the south of Kerek and bringing them into her borders. Food and goods from Vikland are certainly not going to flow west to Kerek. The West Islands ships are full of steel and weapons. The Spice Island ships refuse to even come into the Kerek City harbor, instead taking their trade only to the West Islands and Matasi."

"And now we have a dozen more mouths to feed." Rygee sighed.

"Silly men. You drag me from Kerek City just to do all my work for me. I might as well have stayed in bed." Ngahuru emerged from the darkness, and I was surprised we all didn't yelp in fear. I had no idea she had been there.

"How long were you listening to us?" Piffik demanded.

"Long enough, you would all be dead if I was so inclined." She pushed the head of her cloak back. "As long as we are all up, let's go inside and listen to what I have to say."

***

Ngahuru had made her plans from the moment she had gotten my letter. She had talked to the West Islands King for advice and coin and the role she should play, her brother Koanga for costumes, and the other West Islands softfoots for contacts outside of Kerek City and their connections and codes to get information to where it would do the most good.

She had made other plans once she was on the ship to Kerek City, for the King had provided a military escort only from the time the ship would sail in until it sailed out on the next tide. She had half a day to find her Wrens, buy horses and a wagon, secure her supplies, and be hidden in Kerek City out of Trouble's embrace. Her guards had been up for the task. By the time they had marched back to the ship for its middle of the night sailing, she was settled in at the camp of refugees at the edge of the city, attached to a wagon of Matasi missionaries who visited Lowertown with food and prayer, and found Dica, one of her old 'eyes' standing on the street looking for coin and charity from market goers.

Dica's eyes had gone wide when she recognized Ngahuru, and she jumped in the Matasi missionary's wagon to learn the how and why of the Softfoot's return. Ngahuru had talked and listened for nearly a decon learning who was about, who had disappeared, and where it was safe. Ngahuru gave Dica coins to share with the others if they needed food or clothes or shoes. Dica would tell the ones she knew, they would tell others, and whoever appeared by midday the next day in the street of the embasados, Ngahuru said, would be the ones to go to Manumina.

There had been fewer than she had hoped. None of them had weapons beyond a few Sailor's Curses. None of them could ride a horse. She had her two plow horses and a wagon, and one horse for an outrider.

"You will be pleased to know, Zren, I learned from your own travels across the Northern Track." She smiled at me. "From the time you and I parted at Salisport until the day I landed in Kerek City again, I learned to ride a horse."

She told me each day on the Northern Track she would teach the oldest ones to ride. When they were tired, sore, or the horse was done with them, she would be the outrider with her short bow for the rest of the day, and the wagon would be driven by the others.

On the way out to Manumina she had noticed many postings on the market crosses. In the shops and elsewhere, Patrons were hiring for those who were willing to work in trades and towns and farms. So many had been conscripted in the army, she said, there were places where a stranger could slip in, and no one would take too much notice. As they traveled, she had started to plan where she would try to place her information gatherers to do the most good.

Once inside my house, Tiju Tia settled herself into a chair at the table.

"My friends, I have already spoken with Rell and Siba. My Wrens need to learn to use weapons, and to mend soldiers and softfoots, of course, but also how to work for pay and barter, how to live in a village, and not attract attention. You have a settlement that needs more people to do everything to be done in a day. Decide among yourselves who will teach what, but beginning tomorrow morning, the Academy of Treason will be in session."

Piffik choked and Rygee coughed. Tiju Tia merely raised an eyebrow. "This should not be a surprise to you. You see it as helping the Viklanders who helped you, who have taken in your families into her borders, but if any of these Wrens are caught, Kerek will see it as treason committed by Kerekis. Think on that, if you are ever tempted to be lax in your training because you think they are just children or too busy to talk to someone who needs your advice and help."

The room was silent for a long moment as Tiju Tia let the words settle in. Finally, she said briskly as she stood up from the table, "I am off to my bed then. We have a plan, hope, and willing hands. This is what friends do for each other." She opened the door and Piffik offered to walk her back to the guesthouse.

Rygee and I followed them out the door and stood on the porch while they walked back into the side door of the stockade.

"I don't know where you find them, Zren, but I sure do like your friends."

I smiled at him in the dark. "I am glad to count you among them." I clapped him on the back and turned to go back inside. "Tomorrow looks better already. Goodnight!"

CHAPTER 6

THE ACADEMY OF TREASON

The Wrens and I must have been the only ones who slept the night. The next morning, Rygee had already made fluffy biscuits and Lou brought over cheese and fresh butter before disappearing into his springhouses. There were eggs and vegetables and a few early wild plums Siba had gathered at daybreak east of the stockade.

As the Wrens filtered into the dining room, Rell and I would hand them a plate full of food and smile in pleasure as their eyes would go round as noodle bowls. The room was silent as they ate, and I could hear Rygee talking softly with Tiju Tia in the kitchen. Rell brought out a smaller bowl for me, and she and I stood against the wall, ate our food, and watched the room. Piffik brought out more biscuits and set them in the middle of the table. The children looked at them, and then looked at each other.

"Piffik brought them out for you to eat. If you just look at them, you'll hurt Rygee the baker's feelings," Siba said as she walked out of the kitchen. Hands grabbed for the basket, and I burst out laughing. Siba looked at the overturned basket and the guilty faces all holding a bun in their hands. "Well, that went as well as I should have expected," she added drily.

When I finished my food, I started clearing the empty platters in front of the others. Tiju Tia came out of the kitchen with Rygee and Piffik. She asked all the Wrens to stay seated where they were. She wanted to talk about the days ahead. Rell helped me take away the pottery, but we came back out to the room instead of starting the washing up.

"You have skills the Vikland army needs," Tiju Tia began. "You answered my call in Kerek City, and now you are here to gain other skills to be a gift to those who need you. Those people standing about the walls will be using the next days to teach you some means of supporting yourself. This will provide you with a *maskovesto*, a disguise for those who are too lazy to see beyond what they want to see. When you leave here, people will see you through a mirror of respectability—as manabouts, healers, shop girls, and apprentices. This will allow you to perform as softfoots and guides. No one will suspect you.

"There are others who will be teaching you to mend a broken bone, to care for the wounded you may encounter, and administer poisons and potions. Don't get them mixed up." She looked pointedly at an older girl with short chopped off hair.

"You will be trained with crossbows and bongs in case you come across Viklander weapons, also short bows, and West Islands daggers—"

"And riatas," I interrupted.

Tiju Tia nodded and went on, "I will teach you to change your face and hair with pots of paint and colors and plants you will find in the woods.

"There is not enough time to teach you all to read, but we will learn enough words so that you know what documents are important, how to read maps, where to find someone from a written description. Siba will teach you. I don't fancy losing any of you to the hangman because you stole a list of wants from a general's wife to pick up at the toggery."

A giggle from one of the youngest children, the Matasi girl with a delicate pixie face.

"If you like something you are learning, say so. We need to find posts for you in stables, and houses, and shops. I would much rather you work at something you like. Your paypackets are your own. We will provide the costs of what you need for Kereki clothes for the Viklanders, your housing, and the food which you need to hide in the places for Viklanders to find. Let me say this again, your paypackets are your own. No one here will steal or demand your coin at the end of the day in order for you to sleep unharmed." She waited and let her words sink in.

"I will be driving a rag and bone wagon through all of your locations. This means I will only see you every ten days or more. Piffik here," she pointed to Piffik, "drives a delivery wagon of furniture and coffins. He will be picking up your lost Viklanders. Rygee conducts the business of Manumina with the rest of the country of Kerek. Use him only to pass messages. His Kereki face is too valuable to us to use him as anything but a maskovesto to hide behind."

She pointed to Siba and Rell. "These are Manumina's healers and defenders. They will teach you to save a life and save yourselves. Listen closely to them. Zren Janin is the manabout of Manumina. He is responsible for animals, the fields, and orchards. When we need him, he may drive a cart, but if you see him on the Northern Track make time for him. He has a face that cannot lie, so I will not risk you, or him, unnecessarily.

"Lou is the cheesemaker here at Manumina. And he is your first assignment. You must never let him know what you are. For the next few days, we are refugees from the war north of us, helping with the harvest in exchange for our food and shelter. Be convincing. He is only the first one you must deceive on who you are and what you are capable of."

She smiled at all of them and then at us standing around

the walls. "I have sat down with Siba and Rell and Piffik and we have set your days. We will tell you the day's work and training schedule at first meal every morning and then write it on the wall in this room. It is an incentive to learn to read your own name and those whose lives you may someday hold in your hand." She pulled out a worn piece of paper from a fold within her dress. "Stand when I say your name, those standing against the wall must learn who you are."

"Nelo." Ah, the fair haired one with the scar on his face. Taller than me, but clearly younger. "Falan." A girl, older than Nelo but not by much. Her brown hair was chopped short, and she had the wary look of one who was always on the edge of danger. "Tyra." The small Matasi girl with the delicate face. She looked much younger than she probably was. I guessed she played the part of a Lost Girl for coins in Kerek City. "You three will start with Siba in the infirmary."

"Josef." A beautiful face—too beautiful to be safe in Lowertown. He was the tallest of the Wrens except for Oro. Josef had a smile like Kern's and the bluest eyes I had ever seen on anyone. His face still looked innocent, so he wasn't a fancy. His Protector must have been fierce indeed. "Linna." A sweet looking girl, she stood primly in her grey dress looking shyly about the room. *If she was from Kerek City,* I mused, *she must have been a shop girl with a big man for a father and a bigger cudgel at the door to his shop. Why was she here?*

"Kid." A boy just younger than the three who had played the role of outrider yesterday. He held himself so still I knew immediately his talent in Lowertown was to hide and gather information for the information brokers or the gang bosses. A rich life—for Lowertown—but a short one. I had known some of them. Paid very well until the day they were discovered and killed by those whose secrets they stole and sold.

"Dica." The first one to see Tiju Tia in Kerek City. Ngahuru had said she had been playing the part of a Lost Girl. But I knew better. She was already too old and plain for that. She would have been a pickpocket. And if she wouldn't have been a good one, her future alternatives would have been even worse. "You four go with Rygee. If any of you have a talent for cooking and baking, we will try to find positions for you in one of the great houses of the north." Tiju Tia smiled at them and looked back at her list.

"Arden." The boy with the dog. He was all lean muscle, brown eyes, and long brown hair worn loose rather than clubbed or tied back. Plain-faced. Like Kid, a stranger's eyes would pass right over him. I thought they might be Spice Islanders—they were sun-dark, but Arden and Kid didn't wear any rings in their ears or on their fingers like the sailors I saw in Dockside. Of course, if they lived in Lowertown, they wouldn't be alive if either wore his wealth so boldly.

I had never met anyone who had a dog of their own except

for the ones who used them as guards for their shops or in the fights. This dog seemed different somehow. It was calm, not crowding about Arden, not anxious or threatening around the other people. I wondered if Arden might have been a pickpocket in Lowertown, using his dog as a *titiro mai ki ahau*—a distraction. I smiled to myself. I had played that role for Ngahuru once. At the time, I didn't understand how important such a role could be.

"Callis." Broad shouldered and strong looking, Callis stared about the room as if she dared anyone to challenge her. She wore her brown hair tied back like a boy. Like most of the others, her face and skin reflected the immigrants and travelers crowded into Lowertown, Dockside, the Flower Market, and Sinner's District. She wasn't sweet looking like Linna, or as wary as Falan, or even as pretty as Josef. In Kerek City, to be unremarkable was a good thing.

"Ross." A boy. Too small to run in the gangs, and too big and too old to be a Lost Child in Lowertown, Ross's days in the streets were probably already numbered. I wondered if Ngahuru knew she saved him from almost certain death. "You three learn the manabout role on a farm with animals with Zren. You could be placed in a stable, a settlement, or a great house."

As a group, the Wrens looked to Oro. They had been paying attention on who was where and had noticed he had not been chosen. Tiju Tia noted their attention, "I have asked Oro to ride to Ishes today with Piffik to exchange some West Islands steel for Viklander crossbows for you. Oro needs to learn to barter and buy to make deliveries and push packages and gather notes. He will be our contact with the Viklander garrisons within Kerek—Ishes, Earles, and the other forts—as they are captured for Vikland."

The Wrens were not the only ones paying attention to who was doing what.

I hissed at Rell, "Why aren't you teaching?"

She smiled slyly. "This morning I learn to shoot a West Islands bow from Tiju Tia. This afternoon, I amaze you all with my skill. I shall shoot a perfect circle about your arrow, Zren Janin, even if it is in the side of the goat barn instead of the straw bales." She laughed at my scowl. "You should be happy, look at all the help you have for your chores this morning. You might even have time to join those who are learning to cook." She pushed off from the wall and followed the others outside.

Tiju Tia may have called it the Academy of Treason, but to me it just seemed like the first seasons after I had arrived at Manumina, when Siba and Piffik had taught me to abandon my feral past and find myself on the other side of childhood. There were classes in reading and writing in Keresh. In counting coins and the value of things. In buying and selling in Sary and

Ahni and the military garrison at Ishes with Rygee and Piffik. Rell taught us all enough Vik to understand and give simple commands, offers of help and assistance, and directions.

There were also lessons with weapons. The Wrens would fight with riatas and daggers—weapons of Kerek—wearing their padded tunics and as many pants as they could walk in. We all became a fine hand with a needle mending the results. "Not the face, not the face!" was the morning chant before every training bout.

Then they would use the short bows of the West Islands. Rell was right; even after only one morning of lessons, she was better than anyone else—even Oro who had known the skill from growing up on the West Islands. Rell taught the crossbow on the four new crossbows Piffik brought back from the Viklander garrison at Ishes. She also taught short and long bong defense using scraps of wood from Piffik's woodworking shop.

"You might be trapped in a barn," she said, "with two wounded Viklanders and no crossbow in sight. But if the Viklanders have a tahn or a jeong bong with them, or if you can find the stem of a pitchfork or a hoe, you can still live to fight another day."

Callis was the best on the bongs. I liked to watch her spar with Rell and the others. Rell showed us the forms and defensive moves but admitted she would only use a bong if no crossbow was in sight. She didn't have the gracefulness I had remembered from Song Yao. But Song had been a bongmaster of Vikland before she had died saving all of our lives at the Battle at the Bridge. I missed her still.

The groups shifted and shrank and grew as the Wrens found their talents and tasks they enjoyed. The three oldest women—Falan, Linna, and Callis—slipped easily into the roles Tiju Tia planned for them. They could all read and write in Keresh, count change, and tote numbers in their head. Linna and Falan had worked in their family businesses. Callis had been a tailor, ready to hang out her own shingle. All had a sense of what it was to work for wages. The three women could cook a little and had all lived in houses growing up and understood how to care for one.

Although Kerek wouldn't let them live alone, Tiju Tia and Piffik agreed they should be the main contacts along the Northern Track. They would try to get positions in the dry goods store, the toggery, or other shops of the towns, with healers or others. The three would be in the best position to hear news and pass along documents and maps.

It was Rygee who suggested they have another Wren as a "younger brother" and live in their own places. It would give them more freedom of movement than boarding with other households. So Piffik and Tiju Tia looked at the next four Wrens: Nelo, Arden, Josef, and Kid, who stair-stepped in age. Nelo thought he was maybe seventeen or eighteen, Kid estimated his own age at thirteen or fourteen. His voice had changed during the last Wet, he thought. No one knew for sure. None of them remembered celebrating a birthday. They only remembered what other people had told them.

Although they were among the oldest, neither Nelo nor Arden said they knew how to read or write Keresh. But they were willing to work in the woodworking shop with Piffik while he taught them their letters. Both said they preferred to work outside and would listen carefully as Rygee taught them to harvest the orchards and care for the animals of Manumina.

I had been close in my guess. Tiju Tia told me Arden was a thief for her in the Flower District and his dog a part of it. He reminded me of Buku Pramana, and one day while we were feeding the chickens, I asked if he was from the Spice Island. He gave me a long look and showed me his long narrow fingers without any rings.

"Too poor to be a Spice Islander," he said. "I am just another Kereki thief, Zren Janin. I know there are so many of them, you would not have remembered meeting me." I realized he hadn't truly answered my question and wondered why. I also knew he had lied to me: I knew I had never met him. But every time I saw him and Kid together, I knew there was a puzzle there. I wondered if I would ever be smart enough to figure it out on my own.

Nelo never admitted to anything in his life before coming to Manumina. But he was strong and smart and comfortable with hard work. It was agreed, he and Arden would try to be manabouts and try to find positions where it would be easy for them to reach out to Viklanders and gather documents and maps to pass on to others.

Josef loved the beauty of horses, but he had no past connections for the buying and selling of them, and no desire to clean up after them. He knew his letters—barely, but had a keen sense of coin and the value of things. His true talent was in mimicry, entertaining us with his cheery personality, pretending to be someone else from the Kerek King to Wester sailor, Matasi missionary to the haughty Viklander patrols we had all seen in Lowertown, just after the West Islands Ambassador had been murdered.

I wondered if he had been one of those traveling players who entertained the Kerek King, but when I asked him, he just laughed and said he had been bought to be a distraction in the gambling halls, sometimes male, sometimes female, and always out of reach of anyone who wanted to buy his beauty for the night or even just a decon or two.

He had sobered then, "But Falan told me of Tiju Tia's offer just in time, Zren. I could tell the day was coming when a man who liked fresh faces, or a group of soldiers, would offer my owner more coin than he would refuse." At my look of horror, he clapped me on the back, and japed, "And now, I get to know the great Zren Janin, and ride horses to my heart's ease!"

Kid's talents were so rare and so valuable, Tiju Tia wasn't sure where she wanted to place him. He wore his hair short like a Matasi and wore better clothes than the other boys. But most importantly, he could read and write, so well we would often come across him reading a book, or pamphlet, or newsprint he had discovered about the settlement. He said he had worked for the Harbor Master in Dockside, listening in to conversations and deals between ship captains and the men of business or the gangs of longshoremen. It was a rich life, he smiled thinly, for one bit of information could be sold many times. But for those who were not careful enough, life tended to be short.

To amuse himself, Kid would hold himself unnaturally still and would often listen in to conversations and then repeat them word for word at mealtimes. He could imitate Piffik's Keresh with the rolled 'r' sounds, swear in Vik in Rell's tone of voice, and whisper back secrets in Conrosan. If someone took offense, he would shrug his shoulders and claim he had been standing in plain sight. They should have asked him to leave if it was meant to be private. He claimed he didn't know any other languages; he said he didn't need to. He only repeated what he heard to the Harbor Master, and it was up to those who paid him to have someone there to translate the words.

In the end, Kid told Tiju Tia he wanted to be a servant in the great houses of the north, under the Cold Mountains. He had heard some of them were strong allies of the Kerek King, and he thought he could practice being a good softfoot there.

"There is no practice," Tiju Tia had sputtered. "If you are caught, you will be hung." Kid had only given her a long bland look.

"I have read in books of such things as a footman or a valet. I would like to try that," he said calmly. "I think I would be much better at that than tending animals."

Tyra, Ross, and Dica, were still young enough—eleven to thirteen—they could be placed as apprentices learning their positions.

"I know it doesn't sound like much because you will be at the bottom and people can be cruel," Tiju Tia consoled them, "but your wages are your own and you will be in some of the best places to hear the news to save us all." She paused. "You will learn a trade to support yourself when all this is over."

Because she was a Viklander in a land at war with Vikland, Rell had only left the stockade and the immediate fields once in the years since she and I had been taken in at Manumina. But she was by far the best horse rider among us, and the Wrens needed to know how to ride well enough to flee for their lives or to cover long distances to pick up and drop off anything and anyone of value throughout Tiju Tia's territory.

So with the Wrens as part of her maskovesto, Rell would twist up her long black hair like a Conrosan married woman would wear. She would take her bows and the Wrens out east of the settlement walls and teach them to ride on the floppy Kereki saddle, a Viklander saddle with pommel and loaded with sheaths for the bongs, and bareback. They learned to ride double, with another Wren, or a flour bag full of sand for injured or dead. She would force them to ride flat out with her pursuing and shooting dulled arrows at them to teach them to keep their head down and their wits about them. She taught them to lead the target and shoot the short bows with both horses moving. To use the bongs to fight off those on foot and from horseback. And to hunt.

For the first time in a long time, there was meat in our stew pots again. And when one small group was recovering from her lessons, she would laugh and take another group out until they were all comfortable—if not accomplished—on every horse in the Manumina stable.

She threatened to take Piffik out as well, "and turn you into a proper horseman," but he would just smile at her until the lines by his eyes would crinkle, and say he was too busy trying to keep the Wrens from sawing off each other's limbs in the woodworking shop.

There was food without fear, sleep without watches, and

a purpose to our lives. We may have planned to overthrow a corrupt King, but for all the time at Manumina, I watched the Wrens lose their hunted looks, gain in weight and height with all the food they could eat, and learn the value of themselves.

We were happy.

CHAPTER 7

THE STORY BEFORE MANUMINA

Tiju Tia wasn't content with the Academy of Treason as a gift to the Viklanders. She was grateful for their help getting her home without Matasi or Kerek knowing her whereabouts after the death of the Ambassador and his wife, Hana, the sister to her King. But she felt she had abandoned her network of street runners and information gatherers when she had been forced to hide the Ambassador's children and flee out of Kerek City. She wanted their time at Manumina to give them hope and coin and skills for the future.

She knew they would need work they could learn and a place to live. Tiju Tia wanted Manumina to support them so the Wrens could keep all of their paypackets, not just the portion left after supporting themselves. We weren't rich enough for that, Piffik argued, and as Tiju Tia had looked about the settlement she could see for herself it was true.

But that night while Rell was out watching the Wrens care for the horses, I had taken Tiju Tia to my room on the third floor and showed her the soldier's bag Miya gave me. I spilled the coins across my blanket.

"Tiju Tia, on the last night Miya was here, I had told him I would not return to Vikland with him. He gave me this, 'two years' salary for a soldier,' he said. Enough coin so I wouldn't be a burden on Manumina, but instead, a Conrosan who had found a home with those from a homeland I don't remember, speaking a language I had never learned."

I paused and ran my hand through the coins. "I've hardly touched it. I bought a few clothes when I started growing out of my other ones. A gift or two when someone has done me a kindness. But in Manumina, all things are held in common, and I have given them my labor as a manabout, and they have given me a roof over my head and food in my belly. I understand, probably more than anyone here, what you are trying to do for your Wrens. If we can use this coin so they can be returned to themselves just as I was," I looked at her and smiled tentatively, "I would think it would be a good thing to spend it on."

"Oh, Zren. Just when I have decided you are what I see in front of me, you open your hand and show me another gem of goodness." She laid her hand over mine. "Thank you. You know I am telling the truth when I say this may save their lives."

I nodded and started sweeping the coins together and pushing them back into their hiding place. Tiju Tia sat on the bed next to me.

"I'd like to tell you a story, Zren, and I would like you to tell me one as well. Tell me the journey of Miya's thirteenth crossing, and I shall tell you of my first time across the Northern Track. Because there are things between us, Zren, we must know before we jump off this cliff together in the days and seasons ahead."

She started by telling me she had seen Viklanders between Balza and Huk. "You know how the Huk River flows close to the Northern Track there? I was driving through in the middle of the day trying not to arrive so late I would be forced to stay where I could be easily found. This was still when I had only one outrider horse, and the Wrens could barely sit the saddle for a decon at a time."

She told me how she had caught a movement in the trees and whistled up the children. They all popped their heads over the sides of the wagon with West Islands bows and short pikes, and she told them to look fierce. "I wanted to warn whoever was going to give me trouble we wouldn't go easily," Tiju Tia explained.

"'Grandmother,' a female voice had called. 'I beg your aid and no harm will come to you and yours.'" Tiju Tia gave me a mischievous look. "Who knew, Zren? Here I was trying to hide

I am merely thirty and my hair's lack of pigmentation, and not a lack of days left on the earth, and lo, I am so good at what I do I am called Grandmother!"

She continued her story, "I asked her to step out of the woods, and we would not fire until we were fired upon. She stepped out with her hands out to her side and empty. She did not recognize me, but I recognized her. It was Ven Wila from Salisport. Do you remember her, Zren? She had traveled with me and Koanga to the West Islands as an honor guard, or so she said then. But you and I both know, she and Solkka Ulani were sent to see for themselves if the Ambassador's lost children were safe in the West Islands.

"In Salisport, I had been wearing my pots of paints and she had seen a West Islands diplomat, brown as a koa tree and built close to the ground. She had seen me dressed in my finest at the Vikland embasado reception. Upon my return to the West Islands, she had seen me greeted by my father, the tailor to the King. She heard my brother, a great Storyteller of the West Islands, stand in the King's Hall and tell two great stories—one of the Traveler, a favorite of the Constellations, and one new story of three adventurers who had nothing but trust and time. And before she, Solkka, Bima, and Raeshon had sailed back across the sea, they had seen with their own eyes the Ambassador's children safe in their homeland and now part of the King's household."

"*Titiro mai ki ahau*," I said softly, "on the Northern Track, you were your own *titiro mai ki ahau*."

"Ah, you remembered!" She clapped her hands together. "I was. She did not expect to see Ngahuru the Softfoot on the Northern track, pale as a Kereki, as old as the Cold Mountains, with a wagon full of children. And because she did not expect to see me there, she did not.

"They had stumbled on a camp of thieves, Ven Wila had said, and while the bandits would no longer hunt me and mine, she said two of theirs had taken grave injury. She asked for honey and bandages, so I said I had medicinals if she would take me to them.

"She hesitated, as any good commander would. I had asked her if she wanted my help or no. I was an old woman, and she could see all the children in my care. She finally nodded.

"So I pulled the wagon off the track about two furloughs and followed her down the riverbank until we reached their camp, and the wagon was completely hidden from view of the main track. The soldiers about the fire jumped up with crossbows cocked before Ven shouted 'weapons down.' Then Solkka Ulani came out from the trees and demanded to know what was going on. He was the only other one I recognized.

"I said, 'You may not remember me, Solkka Ulani, prince of Vikland, but once you did a kindness for my family, and I am here to return the favor. I am so insignificant, I know you have forgotten my name, I am Tiju Tia of Kerek City,' and I curtseyed as if I was before my own King." Tiju Tia heard me suck in my breath, but she ignored it and continued, "He looked startled that I would call him by name, and then he looked closely at my face and his eyes dropped to my left hand where I was wearing my black glove. He gave me a large grin." Tiju Tia shot me a thoughtful look. "Now why would he look at me that way?

"'Tiju Tia of Kerek City,' he had repeated slowly. 'I do remember you,' he said. 'You were introduced to me by your friend Zren Janin, who has since become my friend as well. You and your children are welcome at our fire.'

I blew out a breath. Solkka Ulani was soldiering in Kerek, and he was unhurt. Two years ago, he had confessed his interest in getting to know me, and I had skittered away like the lost boy I was. My heart and my head had not known what I wanted, and then I had crudely assumed he had wanted to trade my body for keeping a secret. Now I knew better, and while I cringed on the memories of that visit, I also wished for us to meet and speak again. Ngahuru had just told me he still considered me a friend. He had also kept his word, for while he knew Ngahuru's secret—or part of it anyway—no one else at the soldier's camp had recognized the great Softfoot of the West Islands.

They had taken her to their injured. Ngahuru had done what she could, but she was no great healer. Oro had helped her cut out the broken tip of an arrow from a leg and held a man down while she reset a broken arm. All the while, Ngahuru had told the Viklanders of what she had seen in Kerek City and beyond for Kereki troops, supplies in towns, areas that could possibly hide danger, or provide shelter. Neither Solkka nor Ven had said anything of their own plans. She didn't expect them to, she was a softfoot providing the information they needed.

As she was packing up her supplies, Ven had asked Oro his name. When he told her, she had responded, "A Matasi name on a Viklander face, found in Kerek City. There must be a story behind that."

Oro had stiffened and merely replied, "A story too private for someone I just met, a friend of Tiju Tia's or no." Ven Wila took the rebuke lightly, and Ngahuru had sent Oro to take the medicine chest back to the wagon. Solkka asked to take a walk with her.

He told her they had lost their healer four days ago in a skirmish. They were not fighting the Kereki army where they were, but taking out the lawless, trying to convince the local people that rule under Vikland would be safer than what they had currently under the Kerek King.

"The Kereki army comes through without supply wagons. They take without asking, they eat without paying." Solkka had been frustrated. "We had been tracking these outlaws for days. But there must have been a local man or woman involved, they were ready for us."

Solkka had looked at her. "When your local economy is based on the stolen goods and coin from Vikland wagon trains for the past years, and the people who say they want to help you have a different language and skin color, and when their women do and say and dress as they please and do not cringe before their husbands, fathers, and brothers, such as the Kereki women are forced to do, well, then it becomes too much change." He paused. "Even if we see it as change for the good." Another pause. "We may have to pull back. But that is Ven's decision. I am not her best soldier, but I am her most experienced one. That does not bode well for this patrol."

Ngahuru was silent for a while, letting me take comfort that the people I cared about were alive and still determined to win back passage from Kerek City to the Vikland border.

Ngahuru reached for my hand. "I made a decision, Zren. I did not know what I would find at Manumina. Your letter had arrived a season ago. I did not know whether your settlement had fallen, or whether you were fighting for your lives and desperate for the supplies I was bringing. But in your letter, you said Matasi had betrayed Vikland, and so I thought we were in agreement. So I told Solkka if we could stay under their protection and their watch for that night, we would provide food and supplies in gratitude. He said that was Ven's decision to make, not his, but he would be very glad not to have a meal of watercress again.

"We cooked a hearty meal for them and made stonebread for their packs. We opened the chest of West Islands steel and gave everyone water flasks, daggers, and West Islands bows and quivers of arrows. They had two horses who no longer had riders, and we accepted those as gifts against the day when my Wrens could sit a saddle all day.

"I asked if they could use a street runner, a Kereki face to go into towns and buy supplies or send messages to a rag and bone woman who would be traveling along the Northern Track now and again. Ven had said yes immediately, and I asked for volunteers, thinking Oro would leave me to join them. Instead, one of my favorites, Jenny, begged to stay. She is perhaps twelve, but in the way of all children with not enough food to eat, small for her age. In Kerek City, she could gather secrets for me by soliciting coin as a Lost Girl. She's so very clever and quick and I was beyond sad to see her go. Ven must have seen my dismay because she immediately told Jenny she would be welcome for her large heart and small size which could still slip into the villages without catching the eye of those who distrusted strangers. Solkka said nothing, but he fisted his hand over his heart, and I knew he would protect her with his life."

Ngahuru sighed. "You need to know this. I told them I was on my way to you and why. I know it was not my story to tell, but they needed to know the brave and loyal hearts of Manumina were going to be more than a safe haven. I asked them to take a good look at the faces they had welcomed about their fire and to know if they encountered those faces again, they only needed to say the word and there would be help and assistance."

I looked at her and smiled. "That was exactly your story to tell. You and I are from neutral countries, but we are not neutral hearts. I want my Vikland friends to know there is a plan, willing hands, and hope for them." I smiled, or rather smirked. "A wise woman once told me, that is what friends do; they bring hope." She laughed.

I sobered then and told her of Miya's thirteenth crossing and how we came to Manumina. I explained how I hunted Mouser but killed Bitterboots when he thought I was Rell taking the night watch alone. How the Kereki soldiers overcame our disdain for them and our calloused bynames of Farm Boy 1 and Farm Boy 2 and became Nebs and Rygee. How Nebs died at the Battle at the Bridge when we were overrun by children wielding knives. I cried as I told her of Song's death, Chul's burns, and Rell's brokenness.

I described my first sight of Manumina, and how Piffik had offered us sanctuary outside of the butcher shop in Sary. That all of Manumina—the entire settlement—had taken us in and gave us time and space to heal. How Bima and Solkka had come back a year later looking for other lost Viklanders. How Chul said they were really gathering information and drawing maps before war was declared. I explained Chul had made invention after invention for Manumina, even though his hands were too damaged to draw, and he used his bastono to get about. When Bima had asked him to return as a fire master to Vikland, he agreed only if Piffik's sister, Aajan, would accompany him and be educated at the academies, a gift far beyond any purse in the settlement. How I wanted to be the kind of man Manumina represented to me.

It was easy to talk in the dark.

CHAPTER 8

THE NET IS CAST

Everyone helped with the harvest. Growing up on a farm as he had, only Rygee had years of practice with the long scythes to be able to work all day. He would take one group out in the morning and another group out in the afternoon. He got up even earlier to start the day's baking.

I took out the tree climbers and gleaned the stone fruit from the orchards and wild plums and wild grapes from an abandoned homestead east of Manumina. The fieldworkers came home with blisters, and we collected bee stings. Rygee would grumble we could come home with the honeycombs as well, since obviously the hive was nearby, but no one ever volunteered for that.

Oro with his West Islands bow and Arden with a crossbow and his dog—named Mother of all things—would go out with Rell to fill the stew pot. Tiju Tia showed Siba how they preserved the meat with different spices in the West Islands to survive the Wet. Siba taught everyone to cook at least a little, and how to care for a house and their clothes. They would need those skills once they set up their nests across Kerek. Rygee was happy with all the help, but then he was usually asleep before the plates were cleared away after the end of day meal.

Those of us from Manumina were all determined we weren't going to go through another Wet like the year before. The Wrens from Lowertown couldn't believe just a little work could mean they could eat as much as they wanted, whenever they wanted.

***

One day, Piffik had taken one of the younger Wrens as far as Aldi with him for a furniture delivery. Ross was quiet with a long stubborn streak, and it was thought this journey with Piffik could help him turn his tenacity and strong will—as Piffik called it versus muleheadedness as Rygee and everyone else called it—to work for the good of Manumina. There would be three nights of sleeping rough in the back country, and Ross would be in charge of anything Piffik thought would help turn the boy around.

While they were gone, the other Wrens dreamed up all the scenarios in which only one of them would come back. I hadn't realized how much the Wrens had grouped themselves together with those who made them feel safe. Ross was liked because they thought he would stand his ground if they were in trouble. He was not liked because the others felt he didn't listen to another choice. An ignorance, Falan said, which would put them all in danger once they were out in Kerek. I had liked Ross because he was careful when taking care of Lou's dairy goats and our chickens. When Arden had brought home a nest of baby rabbits his dog Mother had found, Ross had taken care of them until they were old enough and big enough to be butchered for meat pies. I liked Ross, but then my life would never depend on whether or not he would carry out a responsibility. As I picked fruit and scythed oats over the days while Piffik was away, I started listening more to what the others were saying about the ones who had traveled from Kerek City.

Falan and Josef were often together. They had both been a part of Tiju Tia's information network in Kerek City from before. I was so shocked when Falan said her father had owned the gambling hall where Josef had worked, I had nearly fallen out of the tree.

"Your father owned the Red Cup? You were probably one of the richest girls in the Sinner's District: you had parents, food, and a house. Why would you leave to come out here?"

Callis was in the tree next to me. "Zren, you are such a fool. Our parents couldn't keep us safe forever. Lowertown is still Lowertown. The Sinner's District is not any better."

Falan glared at me. "Zren, Josef will tell you he was bought for his beauty. He was bought to be a distraction for the games with the highest stakes. He was given a room at the top of our house. But he could barely leave our home because of how someone might think they had been promised more during a card game, or that he would be taken while he was walking on the streets and broken because someone had lost too much coin and wanted revenge on my father, or someone wanted to own his beauty for a while. My parents kept him as no better than a pet.

"I was raised to read and write and count coins and count cards so my brother and I could take over my parents' house of misery. My life was not my own and neither was Josef's."

"Kerek doesn't allow the ownership of another person," I said tentatively.

"Tell that to Josef. Tell that to all of the Lost Boys and Girls and pickpockets and fancies in the Sinner's District, or Dockside, or Lowertown, who are forced to turn over all the coins they made to another person in order to be unharmed for another day. Tell that to any woman who has been forced to marry as her family bid her because she has caught the eye of one who has the power to help or harm or has a house in an area another gang has claimed as their own. Tell that to any man who has lost everything they own and must borrow coin from the coinlenders to care for his family. There are many kinds of ownership. But here? I am here by choice. At any moment I could walk for a day east and come to

Vikland and no one could stop me. No one." She crawled down and took her full bag to the wagon for emptying.

I looked at Callis. "Are there others of you who had parents?" I could barely fathom that someone would walk away from a family.

"Linna," she said. "Oro. Me. Well, Oro was sold by the Orphan Master to a Kereki family who wanted to show everyone how kind they were to take in a child with a Viklander face and golden skin." She was quiet for a long time. "Nelo told us you were from Lowertown. But none of us remember you because you did not work for Ngahuru. No one saw you with any of the Viklander softfoots or the Matasi missionaries. But I am told you can read and write Conrosan and Wester, and you speak Conrosan as well as Keresh. So I wondered if that was what had happened to you.

"Rell told us not to get discouraged if we still cannot hit the target with the crossbow. There are many ways to save a friend. She said she saw you kill a man much bigger than you are with nothing more than a Sailor's Curse. A man who had been in the Kereki army for many, many years…" She trailed off.

"Callis, I didn't even know what I was—a Conrosan—until two years ago. People in Lowertown just called me 'Red,' and I believed them. I don't remember how I ended up there, or who took care of me. I remember being hungry a lot. And afraid. I was always afraid. Tiju Tia was the first person—well, her brother was—I can ever remember being kind to me."

She looked over her shoulder at me. "A lot of us felt that way, Zren. It didn't matter if we had parents or not. It should not surprise you that Linna and Falan and I had families. But where we lived, our families would not be able to protect us forever. Eventually we would need to marry, perhaps to someone our father owed coin to, perhaps to someone who watched us while we were unaware. All it would take to lose our life would be a day in which we were followed, a moment of forgetfulness as we walked past an open alley, a careless promise to meet a friend and the time gets too late."

She took a deep breath. "Even here in the frontier, it is safer than anywhere in Lowertown. It is like that game where there is a coin under one of three cups, and you take all your chances, but you can never win. Lowertown steals the coin from the game, Zren. And you can never win.

"If you wonder why any of us are here, it is not because we think Vikland has been wronged. Most of us had never even known a Viklander well enough to talk to them until we were introduced to Rell Huena. We are not here because we believe Tiju Tia is here for revenge, even though she says her King is above that. It is because anything Tiju Tia has promised us is better than what we left behind."

I was quiet for a long time. "I wish I could be as wise as Siba Namikk. I could tell you the right words so you would know how much better your life will be," I responded, "but I am only a manabout and a boy who didn't even have a name until Tiju Tia found me."

Callis grinned cheekily at me. "Every day I look at you, I tell myself 'if it could happen to Zren Janin, it could happen to me.' There's nothing more you need to say, Zren."

I gave her a silly grin and started pulling myself out of my cradle of tree branches to climb my way down.

CHAPTER 9

AND SO IT BEGINS

Linna and Arden and his dog, Mother, were the first to leave us. Piffik had taken Linna with him on his delivery, and she had found a position in Cloa at the general store as a shop clerk. The Patron had been impressed she had been able to write so neatly and do sums in her head. Since no woman in Kerek could live alone, it was decided Arden would go with her and pretend to be her younger brother. I had asked Rygee how that could be possible since they looked nothing alike. But he said they both had brown hair, and in his own family of four brothers, there was not even that in common. Rygee bought them a little house on the edge of town, and Arden found a job working in the stables.

When Falan had snidely remarked that Linna would be forced to share her house with a dog to track in dirt and mud, Linna had only given her a sweet smile and said she was glad she had Mother to protect her when Arden would be away on rescues. Arden had only looked at Falan and said nothing at all.

I wondered if he could teach me that look. Even Falan fell silent under that gaze.

Tiju Tia had wanted better for Arden, a manabout at least, as he was a hard worker and clever. But he said he wanted to continue his lessons with Linna until he could read and write Keresh well enough that he could look for something more. He reassured Tiju Tia it was a good spot for him to hear news, pass along information, and have enough freedom to help Viklanders find their way to the Earles garrison.

Callis and Ross moved to Huk. She had wanted to work in the infirmary there, and Piffik had taken Siba and Callis there to inquire about an apprenticeship, but the healer asked too many questions and seemed far too interested in their lives. Callis regretfully turned away from the apprenticeship, knowing she would put the Wrens at risk because of the healer's nosiness.

It was decided Ross, who was now in charge of his own business of raising and selling rabbits, would have his older cousin, Callis, keep house for him while she worked as she could, in the toggery and tailoring. Callis reflected the many immigrants that called Kerek City home, and Ross was a West Islander. The Wrens shook their heads at Tiju Tia and said no one would believe them to be cousins. Ngahuru smiled and said people believed what they wanted to. They only had to say one or the other had been bought by the Orphan Master, which was true. Ngahuru told all of us she wanted Huk to be the center of the network.

Neither Ross nor Piffik ever mentioned a word of what had happened on that trip to Aldi, but Siba was convinced it was a Conrosan fairy tale where a changeling had been exchanged for the human child. Ross had come back with a rabbit hutch of three pregnant does, a responsibility his alone, and a quest to find every animal husbandry pamphlet or book in the settlement. We deferred to his opinions and knowledge on rabbits, and sometimes he learned to listen to others.

Tiju Tia had taken most of my traveling bag of coins from Miya and had left on a journey with Josef, Nelo, and Rygee, who had his own bag of coins along. Both Wrens had taken their traveling bags with them. Josef joked they would be back in a handful of days, lonely for the friendly noise and crowdedness of the guesthouse.

It was fifteen days before we saw the wagon again and this time, it held only Rygee and Tiju Tia. The two bags of coin had bought three abandoned settlements from the tax rolls. One north of Balza, where Josef was going to set up housekeeping, one south of Huk for hiding Viklanders, that would be Callis's responsibility to maintain, and one east of Earles within a day's or half day's walking distance of three of the great houses. Nelo would lay his head there.

It would be up to Dica, Tyra, and Kid to be taken into service at the great houses. Nelo would pose as a traveling manabout who visited his sisters on their half days and Kid as often as he was able. Nelo was further from the fighting, but it would be up to him to get Viklanders over the border, information to the Viklander garrisons, or to Manumina.

Falan was still at Manumina. Rygee and Tiju Tia refused to place her with Josef, and Falan refused each of the other assignments they had offered. It was a few tense days around Manumina until finally Piffik and Siba suggested the three of them look for the best position for her to be placed in Balza or nearby. She left with Tiju Tia on her first trip with the rag and bone wagon. I didn't know Falan as well as some of the others, but I didn't need to. The guilt she bore for how her family had treated Josef was a bundle as big as a peddler pack and just as visible to all of us. She wouldn't be content until she was close enough to Josef to keep him safe, or as safe as he would let her.

Oro went along to Balza with Falan and Tiju Tia as the Kereki male protector. I remembered what Koanga had said the first time I was to be Ngahuru's carry boy in Aldi. "The male can be a boy of ten, a man with no more wits than a bowl of porridge, or a grandfather who needs two canes to get about." I didn't know Oro well enough to joke with him on which one he was. I did think it was odd, however, that Tiju Tia would choose the only male who had a Viklander face. I wondered why she would want everyone to focus on him rather than her and Falan. But that was why she was the great Softfoot of the West Islands.

Piffik packed some of his finest small chests, carvings, and kitchen pieces, parts of a rope bed, and a basket of linens with him as he took Dica, Tyra, and Kid north towards the Cold Mountains. At Evensong, Regno, and Fortika—each of the great houses—he spun a story of his woodworking. Then he would casually mention his desire to see the children traveling with him well placed in a great house, "where they could learn a position and skills better than those they were born into."

Whether it was Piffik's ability to tell a tale and negotiate their wages, the children's talents or appearance, or the desperate need for help so close to the Cold Mountains, all three found a new place to call home. Although she was the youngest, Tyra was placed first. Her Matasi face found a home at Fortika, owned by a retired Matasi general. Dica was a new between maid at Regno, the farthest north but the largest estate with an owner frequently in Kerek City as a friend to the King. Kid would train as an under footman within Evensong.

Piffik stopped at Nelo's little cottage on the way back to Manumina and helped him set up the bed, gave him the basket of linens, and then together they built a rough table and two chairs. Piffik spent the night and then continued home.

The Wrens had flown the nest.

CHAPTER 10

LEARNING ON THE JOB

I shook my hands out. I was nervous even though I wasn't taking any of the risks. Tiju Tia had merely asked me to walk into the toggery in Huk and find Callis. I was to give her the clothes, ask her to mend them, and give her a coin purse with the instructions I would be back on Fourth night to pick them up. That was all. No one else in the store overhearing our conversation would know we were planning to ransom a Viklander soldier. No one, of course, unless I completely fell apart. I had a face that wouldn't let me lie, and it was a creative endeavor on everyone's part to help me phrase my words and stories so my face matched the words falling from my lips. I reached into the wagon and took out the neatly wrapped package of clothes. I walked inside the shop where Callis had been taken on just under two fortnights ago.

There were two women in the shop: one older with the old-fashioned twist of hair at the back of her neck and Callis behind the counter, a year or so younger than me. The Patron protecting his business, and their virtue, stood by the door with a thick cudgel in his hand. He was too old to catch a thief, but most of the Patrons counted on the Kereki culture of a man in charge of his hearth and home. As long as he was present, no one would give the women inside the store a difficult time. I walked up to Callis, and she looked blankly at me, as if she had never seen me before.

"I understand you are a tailor," I began.

"I can sew, but not as well as Koanga." Ah, good. The prisoner was here in Huk. If she would have mentioned another name, I would have known the soldier or the location had changed.

"I need these clothes mended, and here is coin to do your best work. May I come for them tomorrow?" meant, I have clothes for the prisoner and coin for the bribes. Are we still on for a rescue tomorrow?

For the first time, Callis looked nervous. "I must do this work on my own time, can you come in two days?"

The older woman drifted over, and I forced myself not to tense up. "It's true. My husband and I permit her to take in sewing because we like to see all of our shop girls to be hard-working. But she cannot drop her time in the toggery to take care of this." She looked at me closer. "Do I know you?"

"No. I'm Conrosan. We all look alike." I kept my face as bland as possible. This wasn't about me.

"Humph." She gave me a sharp look.

I turned back to Callis. "Two days is fine." I walked quickly out of the shop and back to the horse and cart. I leaned my head against the wood of the cart to hide my trembling. It was done. Callis would get the clothes and coin to Josef and Nelo who had arranged to bribe the Jailor for the Viklander. While the Justice and the others 'searched' on the Northern Track for the missing soldier, Nelo would take the soldier north to Evensong, a great house where Kid worked as a servant. He had arranged hiding places in the woods.

I would travel there in two days selling cheese and butter from my cart to the housekeepers and shops along the way. Kid and Nelo would slip the Viklander in the woods somewhere along my track on Evensong lands, and then it would be my responsibility to deliver the soldier to Manumina. If there were injuries, Rell and Siba would heal them. If not, Piffik and Oro would drive the soldier to the Vikland garrison at Ishes to be reunited with another patrol or regiment moving out.

It wasn't our first run; it wasn't even our first jail bribery. Tiju Tia always arranged them so my cart or hers or Piffik's would have the risk of being searched by the Justices before we picked up the soldier in the woods far north of the Track. If the stars were watching, she said, the same Justice might see us later, remember he had already searched the cart once, and let us pass without checking again. But every run I worried this time we would be caught.

I climbed up on the cart seat and shuddered out a deep sigh. I still had cheese and butter and salted curds to deliver. Lou had been busy, and we still needed coin to run Manumina.

A peddler in Kerek sleeps with his cart if he expects to have any goods to sell in the morning. I didn't want to go too far out in the woods and be an easy victim for hungry thieves, so I chose to camp by the safest place in town—the jail. I nodded to the Justice and the Jailor and offered them a packet of cheese curds. We chatted for a while and they let me know there were plenty of Kereki soldiers and Viklanders in the area, but the major battles were still north and west of Huk. Closer to Balza.

"Any casualties this way?" I asked nonchalantly. I knew Josef traveled as far west as Vingt, Falan worked in a general store as a shop girl in Balza, and Tiju Tia had left one of her Wrens, Jenny, whom I had never met, embedded in a Viklander hunt-and-hobble group working between Vingt and Balza. But I couldn't do anything for any one of them now.

"A grain train was stolen and horses taken near Balza." The Justice looked at me. "You're smart not to stable in the livery yard here. The Kereki army comes through often and takes every horse except the oldest or most unsuitable plow horses."

"Huh. I'll keep that in mind." I felt my panic bubble up. I knew Manumina kept a spare horse in each of the stables at Balza, Huk, and Cloa. We had one of our Wrens working in the Cloa stable, the boy with the dog, but I wasn't sure how much anyone would be able to stand against the army if they chose to take our horses. I took a deep breath; that was not the problem I needed to deal with right now or even at all. I reached for my old copper cup.

"Is there water nearby? Or do you want me to walk to the well in the village green?"

"Nah. I'll get you some." The Jailor pushed himself up and walked over to the brick building with their offices and their prisoners. The Justice and I just squeaked our curds and looked out into the late afternoon.

"You headed east or west?" The Justice asked, finally.

"I got a delivery on a track north of here for some great house who can't be bothered to send a servant here to Huk to meet me. Then I was going to Balza. Since you say there is trouble that way, maybe I'll just head south and around, or maybe just south to Aldi. Our cheese at Manumina is good. Just not worth dying for."

The Jailor came out with my copper cup filled with water and a West Islands steel flask. "Here, you can have this. We got a Viklander in there waiting for the hanging judge and she isn't going to need it anymore."

I nearly dropped the flask. "You hang them?"

"No," the Justice replied. "The men get delivered to the Kereki garrisons. The women are sold to the highest bidder. But the Kereki army says the hanging judges are the only ones who can do it—I guess they didn't like losing their profits. All we get to do is collect the braid for the bounty. They don't take kindly to us poaching their profit." He shrugged. "There are other ways to earn coin from a Viklander."

I took a long drink to steady my nerves. "What's the bounty for the braid? Worth giving up my cheese trade?"

The Justice and Jailor roared in laughter. "A little guy like you? Those Viklanders would knock you on the head and leave you face down in the dirt." The Justice sobered. "Their braid is worth a horse. They probably have some strange superstition about them, I dunno. But I've heard they fight hard to protect them." The men were quiet then, just eating their cheese curds. I felt like we were all waiting for something.

The Justice stood up and dusted himself off. "Well, we have to be going. Thanks for sharing your food with us. Sleep with one eye open. Food is scarce around here, not much makes it through from the port and Kerek City." He gave me a long look. "I am only one man."

I nodded my thanks and watched them walk off. I stood up, stretched, and walked slowly around the jail on the way back to my cart. The jail had no windows and no way in or out, except for the way the Justice and Jailor had disappeared inside. I understood now why Josef had sent us the news it would have to be a bribe rather than a forced barter. Better to have a Jailor and Justice so open to bribes, "more than one way to make coin from a Viklander," than to have someone worse. I rearranged the cheese cart to my satisfaction and laid down in the midst of it. It wasn't comfortable, but since I couldn't get a message to the Viklander waiting in the jail, I knew I would have a more comfortable night than she would.

***

I was awake at first light. As I put the mare back in the traces, I grumbled to myself. Whenever I had to get up early, Piffik was nowhere around to see it.

With the extra day added to my timetable, I thought I should check on Falan in Balza. If the war was close, she would have news. If the war was too close, she could leave with me. I made good time, and as I passed the place where we had camped our first night on Miya's thirteenth crossing, I wondered what would have happened if I had not hunted Mouser and killed Bitterboots. Would Rygee and Nebs have reported for duty at the Earles garrison? Would Mouser have hunted and hurt any of us? Would Nebs and Song be still alive because Bitterboots would have been Mouser's commander? I puzzled these out until I could feel pain beginning in my head. I decided driving a cheese cart gave me way too much time to think.

***

Falan was alone in the shop except for the Patron at the door. Falan looked startled to see me, but she recovered quickly.

"Ah, Padro Morto, I have your medicinals you ordered from me the last time you were here. Let me get them for you." I started to open my mouth to protest. I knew she knew who I was, but she gave me such an exasperated look, I clamped my lips together without saying anything. She ducked in the back, and I stood in the middle of the store away from everything so the bully with the big stick at the door wouldn't have an excuse to snap my wrist with his cudgel.

Falan returned with a small wooden box and muslin packets of seeds. "I am sorry for the delay," she said. "Deliveries from Kerek City and the port are very erratic. I also understand you ordered these clothes." She put a stack of Kereki pants and billowing shirts next to the box on the counter. "You should know if you do not pay for them today, I will need to sell the clothes to others because you have taken so long to pick them up." She gave me a harsh look.

"No, no, I'll pay for them," I said hastily. She named a price. It took every coin in my purse and a wheel of aged cheese before the Patron at the door was satisfied. I knew Siba would not have ordered foolishly, but I worried about traveling without any coin at all for the next three days.

"Thank you, sir. Have you any other business then?" She placed her palms flat on the counter—the signal she couldn't receive any messages or supplies. She was being watched too closely.

"The road to Vingt. Should I travel it or should I choose my life over the sale of my cheese?"

Falan looked at the shop owner for him to reply, turned, and began unpacking another box.

He answered from the door, "The Kereki army has opened the road from here to Vingt. There are always bandits, of course, but you look like you could pass—neither Kereki nor Viklander. Or," he laughed coarsely, "both sides would slit your throat for food to eat and the pleasure of a horse to ride."

I nodded my head. "Thank you. You've answered my question." I took my packages and walked out the door without giving Falan another look. I decided I would take one of the small trails north to Evensong, the great house where Kid worked, and I would pick up my Viklander. I mounted the wagon and turned the horse towards Huk, away from the fighting.

I waited until I was far from Balza before I pulled off the road and looked at the goods Falan had given me. She had called me *Padro Morto*—'Father Death'—which was the name the Wrens had given Piffik since he drove the coffin wagon. If she had given me his delivery, it meant there was some urgency—maybe. Was it the medicines? Were the Kereki clothes for a critical drop for the Vikland soldiers? She had taken all my coin, but that was going to go in the Patron's pocket, not hers. So there had to be a note. I held the jars from the wooden box up to the light. All looked fine. No messages, no letters, no tiny maps of troop encampments.

The clothes were clean and whole. We were forever running short of Kereki pants, boots, and shirts for the Viklanders to change into as we spirited them away through Kerek to their border garrisons. We bought as many as we could on the rag and bone route, mended them and pushed them back to our Wrens who stashed them in hidden barns and hollow trees, and carried them in their packs as they completed their late night rescues.

At first, I had asked why. If the Viklander uniforms were so dark and blended in with the night, why not let them wear their own clothes? But Tiju Tia explained that if a casual glance into the woods caught a group of people wearing Kereki clothes, an assumption would be made it was a patrol, a militia on their way to someplace else, or a band of friends headed home from a night out. If the same casual glance caught a movement of dark clothes, a braid swinging freely, well then, an alarm would be sent up and a hunt would begin.

"We want people to believe what they think should be in front of them, Zren. And if a Wren is leading them or has provided them with a map so they confidently go where they need to? Well then, why give the Kerekis nightmares?" She had smiled at me then, but it hadn't been a friendly one. Sometimes this Tiju Tia seemed very different than the Ngahuru who had rescued me on the road to Aldi.

I searched the clothes for a hidden message as well. Finally, a small piece of well-worn paper fluttered to the ground when I shook out a shirt. Ah, here it was. And it was written in Keresh, of course. Once again, I wondered why Siba had taught me to read and write Conrosan first instead of Keresh. Of course, the Kerek-Vikland war and our part in it was not even a thought in anyone's head back then, but even so. I should have sat in the classes when Siba was teaching the Wrens their letters. But my pride had gotten in the way, and I had said I was too busy with all the things that needed to be done about Manumina.

I picked out the words I knew, 'Matasi softfoots,' something something, and the name 'Rani.' There were other words after that, but nothing I could sound out and make sense of. Ngahuru had wished all of our Wrens would have a second language so we could have coded these messages, but we had laughed at her when she had said so. Not even half the Wrens had known to read or write at all. They *were* written in code for all it mattered to us.

"If wishes were horses, we would all ride behind the King." She had sighed as Falan reminded her that reading was not a necessary survival skill in Kerek City. Falan had snapped a little at Ngahuru as she said it. I had wondered why, since she was probably one who could read and write well. But I had learned from the very first days, Falan wore her anger like a favorite dress and only Josef and Callis could coax a kind word out of her.

I could do nothing but bite back my frustration at the message I couldn't read and climb on the wagon. I tapped the reins to take me back to the main road. Tiju Tia could sort out her own messages. I only hoped someone was not dying or hurt because of my ignorance.

***

I reached Evensong well before dark. The cook was busy as I knew she would be. I said I would wait; her business was that dear to me. Kid came out and brought me a bun to eat while I waited.

"Both are there," he said in a low voice. "Nelo will bring her to the woods as soon as he can. He will step out when he knows the way is clear. Don't shoot." He smiled at me, and I grimaced. My lack of skill with the bows was well known at Manumina, even if the Wrens thought I did it on purpose to make them feel less foolish as they learned their own weapons.

I gave him a small packet of salted curds and he walked back to the house, passing by the cook on the way.

She fussed about my cart and needed to take a small sample of nearly everything. I gave her a pointed look after she asked to have a sliver of taste of Lou's best cheeses.

"Madam, you are clearly one of the best cooks in Kerek for you have sampled only the most expensive cheeses, but I need to know if you are going to buy any or only graze at the wagon?"

She huffed but bought all of the remaining butter and two of the largest wheels of cheese. Perhaps I shouldn't have been quite so glib with her. As she dropped her numerous coins in my hands, I could feel my stress disappear over having to travel penniless.

"Could I bed down in your stables tonight? It's too late for me to reach Huk before dark, and I was warned in Balza there has been fighting nearby."

She pinched her lips together. "That's not for me to say. You will have to ask the horsemaster and he will say 'no,' but there is a shed at the edge of the south field where they hang game to age. Our butcher went off to war, so no one uses it. Tell no one I told you."

I nodded my thanks and took one of the largest coins out of the ones in my hand. As I handed it back to her, I added, "Your master doesn't need to know of this either."

She smiled and walked back to the house with her carry bag of butter and a wheel of cheese under each arm.

I found the shed just as she described. It was a little too close to the main road to Huk for us to use as a usual hiding place. But for this night it would be fine. The sun was setting as I cared for the horse and set her hobbles near the freshest grass I could find. I squinted up in the sky—it looked clear—so I decided to sleep in the wagon rather than the shed. I wanted to hear the night sounds better. Then with a heartfelt sigh because I knew how early I was going to be getting up in the morning, I tucked myself off to bed.

CHAPTER 11

A MISSION AND A MERCY

The mare snorted, and I snapped awake instantly. The sides of the cart were too high for me to look over, so I strained my ears to sense what startled her. I felt the entire world holding its breath. I wondered if someone was sneaking up on me while I just lay back staring at the stars. I carefully reached for my daggers beside me and wiggled my feet. Why didn't I have the sense to sleep with my boots on? I was just easing myself over to my stomach when I heard the mare sidestep and softly nicker. I heard a soft voice shush the mare and the sound of the hobbles quietly unbuckling. I slid down out of the wagon on my belly and let myself fold waist high. Crouching, I crept to the east, knowing that the thief would be on the left side. The mare scented me and stepped left, knocking the thief on his buttocks. I stood up.

"Don't move. I have steel and a horse that fights better than you do." I waited a moment. "Who are you?"

No response. I could have been talking to a tree stump except for the barest shadow on the ground. Huh. If I could barely pick out the dark clothes…maybe it wasn't a bandit. Maybe it was someone who was more interested in a horse to get away, rather than in taking my valuables or my life at the point of a knife. I had an idea. "I am a Conrosan, neutral in the fight between Kerek and Vikland, so why would you steal my horse?"

"A Conrosan? From Manumina?" I picked up the faintest Vik accent in his Keresh.

I hesitated because I still wasn't sure who I was dealing with. "Yes."

"I have been there and met Salik Oqina of your Council of Wisdom."

Oh, stars! Why couldn't he just step out into the moonlight? "I am Zren."

"Zren Janin? Who stayed behind to guard Chul the firemaster while Miyamoto Suki escorted me home to Vikland?" I heard him scramble to his feet. "I am Rani. Do you remember me?"

We both stepped out into the scant moonlight and looked each other up and down. "It is you!" "You're a long way from home," we said together.

"Why are you here?" he questioned.

"I'm here to pick up a Viklander who spent the last few nights in the Huk jail waiting for the hanging judge. We paid a bribe and friends are bringing her to me."

He looked startled. "Do you know who it is? Softfoot or soldier?"

"I don't know. She was picked up from a skirmish between Huk and Balza. It is good she was captured and taken to Huk where Callis was able to get us a message. The Justice and Jailor there are not necessarily friendly to our cause, but they are brothers. If we grease their palms with coin, they are willing to sell the Viklanders to us and look the other way. Balza and Cloa Justices, on the other hand, are very unfriendly to you and yours. You should know this."

"We do." Rani nodded thoughtfully. "You should know Evensong entertains the Kereki army from captains to the colonels. They are an infestation too well-protected for us to root out. You could have picked a safer place to hide tonight. But, I for one am glad you did not." Rani smiled. "Where are you headed next?"

"Depends. If the soldier is in good health and the roads are clear, I will deliver her to Ishes where she can make her report and be reassigned. If she has been injured, or the roads are festering with Trouble, I'll cut back country and hide her at Manumina until she is well enough for someone to slip her over the border."

"Then my friend, I would like to beg assistance. I have maps and documents to get to Ishes as soon as possible. It is why I needed your horse. But if you could do this for me, I could stay behind to learn the strength and supplies of a Kereki regiment camped in the Cold Mountains near Regno. It is also a need which I must do as soon as possible."

"That is very unfriendly land to Vikland." I considered carefully. "We have two placed in great houses near there. Is it possible for them to get the information? They are Kereki born and would not raise suspicion as you would. But know this, both houses are very loyal to Kerek. It is why our information is so good coming from the north."

Rani offered slowly, "We have a contact at Fortika…"

"So do we." I smiled. "Our farthest north Wren is at Regno, near the Kereki encampment. We have a traveler, one who pretends to be their brother and a manabout who visits Regno and Fortika every seven days and then gives the information to others we have traveling on the Northern Track. Would that help?"

Rani looked astonished. "It would! So…if your traveler can get me the information on the encampment, I can travel with you as far as Ishes and explain these documents and maps to the commander."

I walked back to the cart and pulled out a pair of Kereki pants, a shirt, and a pair of worn leather boots.

"Change into these and we will be off. Your dark clothes hide you in the woods, but they also announce to everyone you are a Viklander. Drop your braid between your collar and your neck. I have no need to sleep in Trouble's arms tonight."

I made Rani drive the cart so I could sleep. I didn't feel badly, he would be sleeping during the daylight when he was hiding among the cheese casks. He found the woods I had described without difficulty and woke me. We were both on the wagon seat when Nelo stepped out between the trees and the road. His hood was down, and his white-blond hair almost glowed in the moonlight.

Rani questioned the soldier as she covered her Viklander uniform with some of the Kereki clothes I had just gotten from Falan. There was only the one pair of Kereki leather boots for the two of them, and Rani gallantly pulled them off. But they were too small for her feet, and Rani blessed his tiny toes as he put them back on. Nelo pulled off his worn boots and gave them to her. They fit, and he started lacing up her black military boots on his feet.

"What are you going to say when you are found with those boots?" Rani was curious.

"I will say, 'The braid was already cut, and the life was already departed, but perhaps I should get part of the bounty for the boots.'"

The Viklanders sucked in their breath.

"What?" Nelo retorted. "You think I get information to help you by praising Vikland to all of your many enemies?"

I quickly explained to Nelo that Rani needed to know the strength of the Kereki encampment near Regno. Also what supplies the encampment needed or could be intercepted. I asked him to make contact with Dica at Regno and Tyra at Fortika, so we could get the information to as many as possible. I also mentioned Vikland had contacts at Fortika, and Tyra needed to know who they were.

"Yes, there are two. We know them and use them already." Nelo stood up and stomped in his new boots. "There is a kitchen boy—a scrub boy—so he can be in and out of the house. His name is Therin. He is young, very young, but he knows how to care for horses and can memorize long descriptions and conversations to repeat back to us in the woods.

"The gamekeeper's daughter, Inezi, is deadly on a compound bow so don't surprise her." He looked at me and explained, "It is nothing like I have ever seen, Zren Janin, the bow has pulleys at the top and bottom and I have seen her drop a large animal at a far greater distance than the West Islands bows we carry. I would like our Viklander at Manumina to see it and to shoot it." He turned back to Rani and frowned.

"You need to know we leave messages in the woods for Inezi so she expects us: stacked rocks, broken branches, things she can read without words." He looked Rani up and down. "I won't take you with me to the encampment. You look and sound like a Viklander and I would be compromised. Tell me where you are, and I can get the information you need."

Rani looked at Nelo a long time. I remembered at Manumina how I thought he saw a lot more than most. I wondered what he thought when he saw Nelo and heard his bitter words about the Viklanders. Did he understand they were just words and we meant to help him?

I scratched my head. Everything was a day's walk for Nelo. This wasn't going to be easy for him.

"Hmmm. Four days from now at midday at the butcher shop in Sary? I buy rennet there and am known."

"I know it…and if I dance with Trouble?"

"Fall back to Linna or Arden at Cloa. You can give them the information there and hide where you must." I pulled out the purse with the coins from the cheese cart profits. I fished out two coins for myself and gave the rest to Nelo. "Buy boots." I smiled.

He nodded without smiling and slipped the purse in his pocket. "Do you have any food for me?"

"All I have left is salted cheese curds. I'm running thin this trip." I pointed my chin at his pocket. "You have all the dairy profits. What's left of them, anyway. Buy some food for yourself, when you have a chance."

"Of course, I should have known." He looked to the east where the sky was just beginning to lighten. "Daybreak soon, and I have a long way to go. Four days, Sary butcher shop." He slipped into the woods and tipped up the hood of his dark traveler's cloak to cover his white-blond hair. Just like that, he disappeared between the trees.

I turned to the Viklanders and saw Rani give the shadow of a half smile. He turned back to me as I started talking.

"It is close quarters until we get to the other side of Cloa. I can't risk either of you sitting on the bench beside me until we are far south of the Northern Track."

I handed the woman her steel flask the Jailor had given me last night. "I'm sorry, there was no way I could tell you it was me last night and you were going to be all right. I once spent the night in a Matasi jail without knowing my fate until the next day. I know the thoughts that poison your mind."

She took a long drink and offered it to Rani. "I survived." She shrugged and looked at the cheese cart. The cheese cart was designed to rescue only one. Piffik had built a shelf along the back that dropped down to look like a solid bench but created a hidden space underneath the wagon seat. When he had the Wrens test it out, they joked they didn't know which smell was worse: the casks of aged cheese piled around them or the smell of the person on the seat on top of them. But all agreed—for a Viklander choosing between life and death, the space could be managed for the better part of a day.

I explained to Rani and the soldier how I could fit from head to toe. That once they were inside, I would drop the shelf, latch them in, and then pile the empty casks and crates about them. We would stop only twice on the way to Cloa, at deserted settlements where I could drive the cart into the broken down barn away from spying eyes, and let them out to stretch their legs, drink, and relieve themselves.

As I looked at the two Viklanders, I realized they were both taller than I was. They would have to be nestled like flower petals and remain motionless for decons to even fit.

I began to apologize, but Rani stopped me. "We are both alive today. That was not something promised to either of us at sunset last night." He crawled in first and curved himself so that as the wagon lurched along, she would have his body to cushion her. The soldier crawled in, and I latched the shelf and stacked the crates and casks.

We were off, just as the sun peeked over the edge of the world.

***

At the last stop before we reached Cloa, in a barn so decayed I wondered how much longer we would be able to use it, Rani had given me his purse. It was thin, but he asked me to buy bread and fruit at a shop if possible for Yden. We pulled into Cloa after midday, and I walked into the shop where Linna worked. It was crowded with late day shoppers. I caught her eye, she barely nodded, and then I wandered about the shop wondering what food I could buy for the three of us. I was staring at the bakery goods with my hands in my pockets when I saw the flash of her yellow apron at my side.

"I need food for three for today and another night of driving until we reach Manumina," I whispered. "I have coin, very little coin," I emphasized.

She pinched her lips together and walked away.

Slowly, the crowd thinned, and she called, "Conrosan. I have your shopping ready." I winced at her callousness, but then quickly realized it was best for her to focus on what everyone else did. I walked to the counter to pick up the small wrapped bundle. "Here, sir. When you gave me your purse earlier, I did not realize how much was in it. You have some coins left and, of course, your purse." She smiled at the Patron by the door and pushed the package towards me. Then she turned to call the next person by name and reached for a carry bag of vegetables. I grabbed the coin purse and food and kept my head down as I walked past the owner of the cudgel at the door.

At the horse trough by the village well, I let the mare drink her fill. I took a quick look at the coin purse in my hand. It was Conrosan made. I recognized Siba's neat embroidery stitches and the bright patterns she favored. I wondered if it was Arden's or Linna's; if it was the coin we had seeded them or if they were dipping into their paypackets to help us.

I blew out a noisy breath, startling the mare. All I could do was tell Tiju Tia what had happened. They were her Wrens, and she could learn the truth better than I ever could. I had learned during the Academy of Treason, all of them could, and had, lied to my face without a flicker of guilt or emotion. After living at Manumina for two years, it was unnerving to be faced with my past.

I stopped at the stable to exchange the horse. I would be driving nearly non-stop from now on, and I needed to let this mare have a rest. I didn't see Arden working, but he could have been on an errand for the stable master or on Wren business. We had stabled the three outrider horses Tiju Tia had brought with her at Balza, Huk, and Cloa, and now the stable boy brought out our horse and took our plow horse away for food and rest.

"I heard in Huk," I began, "That the Kereki army comes through and takes your horses without coin or complaint. Do I need to worry about the Manumina horses? We are neutral in this war between you and Vikland," I reminded him.

A farrier came out from the back stall where he was shoeing a horse.

"Which are your horses?" he asked. I pointed to the one the stable boy had in his hand, and the one I was hitching to the cart. He huffed at me, "Those horses look as old you are, boy. A Kereki soldier could run faster than either one of those." He shook his head and walked back to the stall. Soon I heard the sounds of his work. *Well, that wasn't much of an answer.*

I decided to go off the Northern Track and take one of Piffik's back country trails to Manumina. It was mostly empty land with little water and open pastures. We would cross into Vikland south of Ishes. But more importantly, it would allow the Viklanders to ride freely in the wagon and not in the hidden compartment. A decon south of Cloa and I stopped to let out Rani and Yden. Both sagged against the cart as their cramped legs unsuccessfully tried to support them. I divided up the food and gave Rani back his purse.

He looked inside at the coins, at the food, and scowled at me. "What did you do? Steal? Don't we have enough to worry about?"

"One of our Wrens works in the store. I don't know how she did it. I know she didn't cheat the Patron, we need her there, but now we have food to take us to Manumina. It's too much to take you to Ishes on the Northern Track and force you both to travel in that small space. So we'll take no roads from here and you can ride in the open."

I untied my cloak and felt the damp air. I tried not to shiver in front of them. "Take my cloak and keep the hood up. From a distance, our clothes and cart will hide who we are. This far south no one will suspect Viklanders. But if we run into bandits, I will need you both to fight with me. We three cannot die today. If my Conrosan face is found with your bodies, it will go badly for Manumina."

I saw Yden eyeing the last bun and stone fruit—my bun and piece of fruit. "Go ahead, Yden. I didn't wait for the two of you, I ate my midday on the way." She took the bun and bit into it gratefully; Rani looked at me and burst out in a tired laugh. "What?" I scowled at him.

"You are possibly the worst liar I have ever met in my life. You need to spend time with Bima Ritwik. It is said he can lie to the Empress and live."

I snorted. I folded up the food bag and rearranged the crates so Yden and Rani could sit more comfortably. She climbed in the back, stretched out full length, and prepared to doze. I handed Rani my cloak and motioned for him to climb up on the seat beside me.

"Let me tell you what happens when I spend time with Bima Ritwik." I started with the story of how we had met in Salisport at the embasado after Ngahuru's escape from Kerek City. I told him how Bima and three others had tried to lose me without coin, without reading or speaking the Matasi language, without knowing the city, just decons before I was to sail with Miyamoto Suki to Kerek City. How I had made my way back to the Vikland embasado without hurt or harm. Bima had been frantically looking for me until he had nearly earned the Ambassador's displeasure. He ran up to the checkpoints just moments before we were going to leave for the ship.

Then Rani told about *his* first training with Bima in the capital city of Alenti. Bima had taken him to a private dealer of West Islands goods and had purchased several daggers. Bima had insisted on carrying the daggers of West Islands steel and Rani had given him all but one. They had been stopped by a Kereki patrol when they were caught out after curfew. Bima spoke Mata fluently, Rani said, but he hadn't. While Rani didn't understand everything that had passed between Bima and the soldiers, Rani had spent the night in a Matasi jail while Bima did not. He had been forced to forfeit the dagger as well.

I tried not to laugh, so I told Rani of how I had met Kern, another softfoot, and how she had traveled with us from Kerek City to Manumina, "and well, you know the rest, Rani, you were there when she was reunited with her soldier who was thought to be lost."

At sunset, we stopped to stretch our legs and eat the last of the food. I asked Rani if he had heard how I had solved the mystery of the Ambassador's lost children. He had heard Bima Ritwik's version, he said. I looked down my nose at him—difficult since he was taller—and archly said since Bima Ritwik and Truth did not always sit at the same table, I would tell him mine. And so, we entertained ourselves through that long night over the open scrubland and pastures to safety.

***

Although the constellations had been out pinwheeling across the night sky for decons, Tiju Tia and Piffik were sitting on the porch swing in front of my house when I trotted the horse up to Manumina. Piffik stepped down and went through the side door to open the gates. I drove through and stopped at the stables.

"You're a day late, but unharmed? No trouble then?" Piffik started unhitching the horse and led him to food and water. "I'll take care of the horse and cart. Rygee left a cold meal for you in the infirmary. If you need Siba or Rell for healing, they said to wake them up."

I looked at Yden, and she shook her head.

"Just food and baths and sleep, I think." I looked to Rani and he nodded.

Tiju Tia looked over both of them. "So which of you was the mission and which of you was a mercy?"

I turned to introduce them. "Tiju Tia, this is Yden. She was the soldier we bought out of the Huk jail. I met both brothers, the Jailor and the Justice. It is as Josef and Callis said, they are open to bribes in the future for Viklanders, but we must be there before the hanging judge comes and takes away their profit." I waved my hand at Rani. "This is Rani the Softfoot. He has maps and plans to get to Ishes."

"Tonight or tomorrow morning?" Piffik asked. Then he looked closer and smiled. "It is good to see you again. I see you are still traveling through Kerek, does Vikland have no pleasure for you?"

Rani gave a tired laugh. "Piffik Qanaq? Ah yes, I think I am testing how many times you can rescue me." He considered, "Perhaps we should go very early tomorrow morning. I do not want to be shot at in the dark by an overeager sentinel."

I continued, "The Wrens call Piffik, Padro Morto—Father Death—because he drives a wagon full of coffins when he is rescuing Viklanders. Your softfoots should know this. If you hear our Wrens say Padro Morto is making a delivery, you will know you have a way to move maps and people without notice by the Kerekis."

Rani raised his brow but gave Piffik a deep Viklander bow. He turned to Tiju Tia.

"I have heard your name as well, but I was beginning to think you were a figment of our soldiers' imagination. I am beyond glad to meet you in person." He gave another deep Viklander bow.

"And Rell Huena and Siba Namikk are our healers…"

"Rell is still here?" Rani interjected.

I saw Piffik bristle, and I answered quickly, "She is the defense of Manumina and a healer who speaks Vik." I gave him a grin to soften my words. "She cannot return to Vikland until the war is over. We need your soldiers and softfoots, and your injured and damaged, to see a Viklander face at Manumina. She is too needed for our plans here. She is important to us."

Tiju Tia put her hand on my arm. "He understands, Zren." She looked at Yden. "Let me take you to the guesthouse. You need to rest. You are safe here." She walked off with the two Viklanders trailing her.

I patted Piffik on the shoulder. "Everything went well, but I am exhausted. I am going to take the food in the infirmary and try not to drown in my bath. If you need me to drive them to Ishes, wake me. Otherwise, I'll probably sleep until…"

"…daybreak." Piffik smiled. "I'll let you sleep until full daybreak."

I groaned and walked away.

CHAPTER 12

WHILE YOU WERE OUT

It was late morning when I drowsily came to consciousness. The sun was streaming in my window and the house was silent. I started to roll over and reach back for my dreams, when I remembered Rani and Yden from the night before. I threw back my covers and grabbed for a clean shirt on a hook by the door. I slipped on my baggy Kereki trousers and hopped toward the door as I pulled on linings and my boots. I passed by Rell's room as I raced down the stairs, but her door was open, and I could see her bed neatly made and the room empty.

I stepped outside on the front porch. It was cool and damp. The Wet was creeping in. The harvest was done, and the Wrens had made the difference. They had been as indefatigable as Rygee, working, training, and still cheerful. I looked over at Lou's goats, Ross's rabbits, and our chickens. Someone had fed them and cleaned their pens already this morning.

I walked around the stockade to the side door and slipped in. I could smell the huge tanks heating for the laundry, but not the smell of lavender, ash, and the sharp tang of lye, so it hadn't been started yet. I walked to the bakery to beg pastries from Rygee and found him surrounded by pans of rising bread dough, the smell of cooked ground oats and honey, and Siba, Rell, and Lou all with a fresh pastry in their hand.

"Here comes 'Two hands, two pastries.' Quick, everyone, grab another one before they're gone." Rell gave me a big smile. Lou swiftly reached for one. He hadn't quite learned when Rell was joking.

Siba smiled at me. "Good morning, Zren." She tipped her head to Lou reminding me to say nothing of last night in front of him. I wrinkled my nose at her. I was tired but not that tired to make such a mistake.

"I thought you would be bringing me my profits this morning from the dairy cart. Did you eat them all up again this past run?" Lou looked at me sourly.

"I didn't know you would be here," I explained. "I'll bring them over to the dairy building later." I tried to mollify him. "You should know, the cook at Evensong was generous in her praise for your cheese." I paused, not sure how to phrase the next question. "Hmmm, just how much should be in the coin purse for the sale of your butter and cheese anyway?"

Lou inhaled sharply. "Why do we even send you out on the cart if you can be swindled by anyone? Can you even count a handful of coins and know you haven't been cheated?"

Stung by his criticism, I retorted, "There were just a few salted cheese curds left. If you tell me what amount should have been in your purse, I will return your purse with that *exact* amount in it, and you will know I can count without having to take off my linings and boots."

He named his price and inwardly I groaned. I had some coins. I hadn't given everything to Tiju Tia, but perhaps I hadn't kept back quite enough. Rell would make up the difference, I knew, but I didn't want her entire bag of coins from Miya to be spent on everyone but her. I already thought she was paying for all of the supplies for the medicines she and Siba made for themselves and to sell in Sary.

Tiju Tia came in then and Lou pushed himself to his feet. "I better get started on the next batch to go out. I've half a mind to sell my own, in *addition* to taking care of my own goats *and* running the dairy." He stomped out and we all watched him walk across the green and out the side door to the dairy and the springhouses.

"Goodness, I miss all the fun, don't I?" Tiju Tia sat down in Lou's empty chair.

Rygee pushed the platter of pastries towards her. "Zren didn't have the coins for Lou from the cheese cart this morning."

Rell stood up. "I heard the amount, Zren. I'll get it and give it to him. Do you have a coin purse left or should I find one in Siba's workroom?"

"I gave most of the coin to Falan to buy the medicines and clothes she had waiting for us. The rest of the coins and the purse itself went to Nelo." With Lou out of the room, I quickly explained everything that had happened over the last few days. I told about Callis asking for an extra day to pick up the prisoner, my conversation with the Justice and Jailor and their not-so-subtle hint they would be available for more bribes.

I explained how I used the extra time Callis gave me to travel to Balza, see Falan, and get the clothes. "We ended up needing some of them already, because I met Rani on the grounds of Evensong." I talked about seeing Kid, and even though he was in the most dangerous place for a softfoot to work and still hide his purpose, he seemed to be doing well. Since I had both Rani and the redeemed soldier to clothe and feed, I explained how I had given Nelo the coin purse because I could give him neither Kereki boots nor food, and how the woods must have been owned by the Kereki militia since he was traveling freely.

"I didn't see Arden in Cloa when I swapped out the horses, but Linna gave us food and a small purse with coins." I turned to Tiju Tia. "I am concerned Linna may be using her paypackets to help us. I know you promised the Wrens their coin was their own."

I thought over what I had said and if I had forgotten anything. "Oh, the Justice in Huk said two things we should know. There is now a bounty for a braid of a Viklander. The Justice said the bounty was worth a horse. Nelo seemed to know of it and was not concerned. Also, the Kereki army is taking horses from the stables, without coin and without protest from the stable masters. I know we have three stabled along the Northern Track. But the farrier at Cloa didn't seem to think our plow horses were in danger, not because we are neutral in this war, but because our horses are so old. Piffik needs to know of this. Where is Piffik anyway?"

Tiju Tia glanced out the window before answering, "Piffik and Oro took Rani and the soldier to Ishes. They left long before first light. It's nearly a half-day's journey so they will arrive late enough in the morning a sentinel will see the Viklanders before they shoot. Piffik drove the coffin wagon, and Oro is beside him to guard him so the Viklanders can sleep on the way. We did not think he would be searched, so he let you sleep in. He said you could sleep until daybreak, but Rell did your animal chores for you. She is softhearted where you are concerned, I think." Tiju Tia gave me a sly smirk, but Siba choked back a laugh.

Tiju Tia continued, "Rani and I stayed up late talking. He had left the message for me with Falan. We were able to lay out maps so I can keep my Wrens aware of the unknown Matasi missionaries, but I will take the rag and bone wagon out soon.

We need to determine if they are truly missionaries, or if they are softfoots, and if so, for what country. We need more clothes, especially Kereki leather boots. With the Wet, the footprints in the mud can give away our Wrens and rescues as much as seeing the soldiers themselves. There are also Wrens you did not see this trip. I should find them and the others and let them know what Rani told us."

"We have another problem," Rygee said. "The Sary Justice and the Tax Collectors and guards came here the day before yesterday to collect this year's tithes and taxes. We did not see the Kerek King's standard in time so no one was hidden. But Rell and Siba were cleaning the infirmary and were able to conceal themselves in our rooms. I know the ones who took you were murdered or gone, but still it was good you were not here." Everyone nodded.

"They expressed concern they could not speak with Salik Oqina and the Council of Wisdom. They said they were dismayed to see names on the tax rolls but the handful of houses they searched looked neglected. They wondered aloud if the settlement had been abandoned and therefore could be seized by the King for his own purposes. They commented it would make a good garrison for Kerek so close to Vikland." He took a deep breath. "I thought we were doomed to arrest and imprisonment, and they would take Manumina for the King."

I swallowed hard. "What happened?"

"Piffik happened," Tiju Tia said. "Piffik could teach my brother Koanga how to spin a story out of fairy dust. He lamented of last year's Wet, a season so miserable from lack of food and supplies many of our people died of hunger and disease. He told of how our Council of Wisdom had even now gone to the King in Kerek City to appeal to his grace and goodness as a King for mercy and help. He wondered aloud if he could follow the Council with a fast horse and get them to turn back to Sary and meet with the Tax Collector—say within ten days' time. He appealed to Sary's Justice and asked for his wisdom. Perhaps a farm manager should be appointed to speak for Manumina in case such an event—where the council was not immediately available—would occur again. He assured them the Tax Collector and the Sary Justice were far too important to spend on such an insignificant backwater as Manumina, a Conrosan settlement neutral in the war between Kerek and Vikland."

I would have dropped my jaw to the floor if it hadn't been full of pastry.

Rygee laughed at my expression just as Rell came back in the room saying, "I paid Lou. He still thinks Zren is a half-wit, but he counted his coin and he's satisfied." She sat down, "What is so funny?"

Rygee explained, "Tiju Tia told Zren about Piffik and the Tax Collector."

Rell looked at me. "Siba and I were in hiding. We disappeared as soon as we saw the King's standard and the carriage on the green. I had my crossbow with me, but Piffik had said not to fire unless they were seized or we were in danger. Tiju Tia was dressed as a Kereki boy and hid in plain sight as she fed and watered their animals. Lou walked into the stockade from the dairy and then quickly backed out again. He is an army deserter after all. They saw his face, but only Piffik and Rygee talked to them. So what they *thought* they saw were three Kereki farmers and one Conrosan. Maybe because of this, maybe for some other reason, they granted Piffik his ten days. So, yesterday, while we were waiting for you to return with the soldier, we filled some of the coffins with bags of grain and fruit for the refugees. After smelling that all morning, Rani and the soldier will be very hungry when they are finally released out of their narrow boxes." She gave a low chuckle.

"After he drops Rani and the soldier at Ishes, he will continue on to the refugee camp in Vikland and bring back Salik Oqina and as many of the Council as will travel or can lie to the Sary Justice without a conscience. He is also going to ask the Council for permission to list Rygee Namikk as the Farm Manager on the papers in Sary. If Manumina looks like it is already run by Kerek, or at least a Kereki, perhaps the Tax Collectors won't seize it for the King."

We saw a shadow across the window moments before Lou stepped back into the bakery.

"I thought you said it was laundry day. I brought my clothes, and it's obvious the water in the tanks is hot, but it seems nobody's working today but me."

We all pushed back our chairs. "I'm baking," Rygee announced. "And I already pulled my clothes to be washed with Siba's. The rest of you can sort yourselves out."

"I have mending to do before I can take the rag and bone wagon out," Tiju Tia said and waved her hand with the sleeve shown shut. I knew she took her brown skinned hand out when there was no one around. But only I knew Tiju Tia had been kissed by the stars. She kept her West Islands body wrapped under Kereki clothes, appearing either as a boy with stained brown hair or as an old woman. Her lack of pigmentation leeched her face, hair, and right hand into a pale grey-white that could pass for Kereki—if one didn't look too closely. She could do many things for Manumina, but when Lou was about, laundry wasn't one of them.

"And I did Zren's chores for him this morning," Rell crowed triumphantly.

"That's why you were so quiet this morning and let me sleep in! I don't believe it!" I groaned as I fell back into my chair.

Siba smiled. "Come on, Zren. Get your laundry. Looks like you and I have an exciting day ahead of us pounding clothes and watching our fingers and faces wrinkle."

CHAPTER 13

ESCAPE AT EARLES

Piffik woke me early. Once again I beat the sun awake.

I groaned and flipped over on my stomach as I heard him say, "I leave in less than one decon. You can sleep until I whistle, and you can miss first meal of the day and Rygee's basket to go with us, or get up now and sleep in a coffin until we reach Regno. We have a rescue, and we need to go fast."

I rolled out of bed and reached for my clothes. I wasn't fully awake, but I knew Regno was a long day's ride just to get there.

"How do you know this?"

"Arden. He heard the news in Cloa and rode all night to tell us. He's at Rygee's now, eating, but he is forced to ride back immediately. Linna has messages out to Nelo and Josef to meet us there, but I won't know if either of them will get the news in time." He paused. "Bring all the throwing knives and steel you have. This will be a forced barter if necessary."

He left me speechless as he went down a landing and knocked on Rell's door. I heard her sleepy voice answer before he closed himself inside for privacy. Piffik practiced non-violence as much as he was able. It was a tenet of the Conrosans' beliefs at Manumina. For him to suggest I revert to my past life in Kerek City and bring more weapons than those for just self-defense, meant…well, I wasn't sure what it meant.

But I pulled my boot daggers and rolled up two sleeves of five throwing knives each. I thought I was probably meant to give these to the ones we were rescuing, but I hoped to get some of them back. They had been in Ngahuru's shipment from Raumati and were fine well-balanced steel knives. I grabbed one of the West Islands bows I had in my room and a quiver full of arrows. I wasn't any better on short bows than on the Viklander crossbows, but if we were stopped by Kereki soldiers anywhere along the way, Piffik had a much better chance of talking us out of a dance with Trouble if I wasn't waving the enemy's crossbow about.

I tied a double set of Kereki ties about my calves and ankles and tossed two handfuls of fist-sized rocks in my travel bag for riatas. Once I had safely tucked my favorite Sailor's Curse into my front leather pocket, I felt wide awake and ready to go. I walked down the stairs past Rell's open door. Her room was empty. She must have gone out with Piffik.

Oro had just finished harnessing the horses to the coffin wagon, and Arden was leading another one out of the stable.

"This one looks closest to the one I rode," Arden said. Together, he and Piffik moved the saddle and trappings of his spent horse to the other one.

Rell and Siba came out of the infirmary together, Rell yawning and carrying a silver flask. She waited until Arden was finished and she had his full attention.

"This is something we use in Vikland to keep us awake on long watches. Take just a few swallows each decon. It will make your heart race. If you start sweating or feel lightheaded, you have taken too much, and you must skip the next dose. There is much more than you need for today. I thought it might come in handy for you and the others in the future. Only store it in a West Islands flask—copper and iron will ruin it." She paused. "You should know if you drink it all at once, you will feel like your heart is exploding, and you will die."

He raised his eyebrows but only said, "Thank you." He nodded at Piffik holding the bridle. "I need to go. Linna knows I am gone, but I do not know how she will hide my absence from the stable master. I cannot let her risk her position for me. We need Cloa too much." He swung himself into the saddle and winced.

Siba handed up a bag to him. "Food, clothes, coin. Tiju Tia or Padro Morto may need to skip your stop this time on their travels if they hear of Trouble dancing with the Wrens. We do not want to draw any more attention to you."

He nodded again, and I walked to the gates to open them for him. As he trotted past, I asked him to trade cloaks with me. I opened mine so he could see.

"There are daggers in the inside pockets," I said. "In case you dance with Trouble." He swirled his mossy green cloak off and reached for my dark brown one.

"In case," he repeated. He clucked to the horse, and then they were gone, swallowed by the dark.

Rell had another small packet of medicines for Piffik and me. "We don't know how injured your rescued soldiers will be." She nodded at the packet. "Arden thinks there may be as many as ten. We only have pressed wafers for nine. Give one to each of the injured and they will rest less painfully as you lurch along in the wagon. I understand why you won't take me with you to tend to them, but I ask that you are careful."

She gave me a small smile. "Whatever you need to do, Zren. Bring him back to me alive." She gave Piffik a bigger smile. "Oh, and Piffik? Do the thinking for both of you, please. Zren will try to win the war all by himself."

We climbed into the wagon and Rygee came out with a big food basket, several filled waterskins, and another traveling bag.

"All the Kereki clothes I could find, a few pairs of boots. I hope it is enough for them." I nodded and hid the bag in the coffin closest to us. Piffik snapped the reins and we plodded through the open gates.

We passed through Sary without seeing anyone. Once we had safely reached the other side of the Northern Track, I reached into the food basket and untucked the cloth that held our first meal. Rygee had wrapped hot vegetables in a flat cooked egg and had tucked that in stonebread we could eat with our hands. The food was still warm, and I moaned in gratitude.

Piffik chuckled at me. "Why did you ever let him move out of your house, and into Siba's bed, if food was so important to you?"

I licked my fingers. "Because she makes him happy." I shrugged. "And I thought she would poison me if I made trouble." I cut a side eye and caught his surprised expression. "I am joking, Piffik." I leaned back and folded my hands over my contented stomach. "So tell me what Arden heard that would put him on the back of a horse for a night and a day and require us to get up before the West Islands constellations have tucked themselves away for the morning."

Piffik snorted but I could see him arranging the information in his head. "Vikland and Kerek have been fighting over the Earles garrison for three seasons. It's a key holding in the north, and frankly, Vikland tricked Kerek out of it before the war. The Viklanders told everyone who lived around it—and the garrison itself—they had bought it from the corrupt King and were now responsible for controlling the outlaws on the Northern Track. Since the bandits mainly preyed on foreigners, and since the garrison had not seen a paychest in almost two years, the Kereki soldiers were not opposed to abandoning the fort for Vikland gold."

"I know this. It's how Rygee came to Manumina. He was supposed to report for duty at Earles, but Miya and Mouser talked him into deserting." I nodded.

"Hmmm. Lucky for Siba," he mused. "Anyway, the Kereki militia had given up on retaking the fort for themselves and tried to burn the Viklanders out."

"No!" I sat up straight.

"Yes." Piffik told me the Viklanders had planned for something like this. They had dug a tunnel which had ended in a nearby woods. It became a war of numbers. Kerekis getting picked off by the Viklander bowmasters as they attempted to pile brush and wood against the outside walls of the fort. The rest of the Viklanders escaping through the tunnels and into the woods, occasionally to be stumbled upon by Kerekis gathering more brush and wood.

When the Kerekis finally set fire to the fort, the remaining bowmasters fled through the tunnel and into the woods as well. The Kerekis waited in vain for the Viklanders to flee the gates of the fort covered in flames, and then when that didn't happen, they searched the remains for toasted bodies. As they searched the burned out fort, they found the tunnel and it became a hunt to find the Viklanders. Every haystack, every barn, every shepherd's hut was being fired to drive out any Viklanders in hiding.

"They are being hunted like wild animals, Zren."

Piffik continued, "The Wrens are looking for them. Arden said this morning, Callis told Tiju Tia of the firing when she stopped in Huk for her delivery. Tiju Tia has abandoned her route to help search for them. Arden heard from a Viklander softfoot the soldiers are told to flee north to the Cold Mountains and the south barns at Regno or the gamekeeper's hut at Fortika to hide until we can pick them up and get them to safety. Josef told Arden there are friends of Vikland searching for them in caves in the mountains, and places to hide in the steep valleys, but it is only a matter of time. We have to get there and find the Viklanders before the Kerekis do."

There was little more to say after that. We passed the burned out shell of Earles just past midday. Piffik stopped to water the horses and let them crop while we ate bread and cheese. We walked through the ruins, wrinkling our noses at the stink of burnt clothes, lamp oil, scorched leather traveling bags, and wood ash. Piffik poked about in the ashes, and I rifled through our food bag and found a tiny packet of fingersweets Rygee had tucked away for us. I wondered what my chances would be of getting caught by Piffik if I ate the entire packet before he knew of its existence, when he came hurrying over to the wagon.

"Horses," he hissed.

I looked up just as four riders broke through the brush to the left of us. Kereki men, but not soldiers. They were startled to see us, too, and pulled on the reins of their horses.

The oldest one called out to us, "What are you doing here?"

"Making a delivery." Piffik waved his hand at the ruined fort and at the stack of coffins on the wagon. "I had no idea they were ordering for themselves." He gave a heartfelt sigh. "I suppose there is no chance of getting paid now."

One of the men, shorter and rougher looking than the others, spat on the ground. "Friend of the Viklanders, are you?"

"I sell coffins to anyone who has the right coin. Don't know if that makes us friends though. I prefer business associates." Piffik kept up a steady stream of conversation as he reached back into the wagon for his cloak. I did the same and then realized I had given mine to Arden. This one didn't have my daggers hiding in the extra leather pockets in the lining. I leaned back on the wagon seat and put my feet on the buckboard to give myself better access to my boot knives.

The men on horseback came closer, and I could see them tensing for a fight. I wondered why. We had done nothing to show we wouldn't be content to just nod and pass by. But both of us sensed it, and Piffik was not going to be stopped from getting to Regno. He swirled his cloak at their horses to startle them. I pulled my knives and threw both of them at the two closest riders. Then Piffik grabbed the horsewhip from our wagon and snapped it in front of the horse of the old man. The horse reared and the man fell to the ground. I jumped forward off the wagon just as the fourth horseman turned and wheeled away. I grabbed the bow and nocked an arrow, but I didn't aim, and it went wide. I was surprised to see the horse wheel about and the rider slump to the side and fall off, foot still trapped in the stirrup.

I watched as Nelo stepped away from the fourth rider, and quickly slit the throat of the old man curled on the ground with his hands over his face. He captured the reins of the horses, now standing still, and brought them to us.

I tried to smile but felt so sick I could only mutter weakly, "I sure am glad to see you."

I leaned down and pulled my knife from the belly of the first man. I felt my stomach roil and quickly looked away to pretend I hadn't killed anyone. Piffik leaned over and emptied his stomach on his boots.

"It's fear," I told Piffik. "It happens to everyone their first time." I thought about Goblin and Brick and how easily Ngahuru had killed them to protect us. How I had tried to do the same with Festus from the Sion Inn and had been so sickened by my actions, I would have been killed by Rusty if Ngahuru had not saved me then as well. "Truthfully, Piffik, it happens a lot more than the first time." I looked weakly at Nelo who gave me a steady look back. *It's been a very long time since his first Kereki metal poisoning*, I thought to myself.

"I got Linna's message. I am on my way to Regno now." Nelo looked at the dead men. "We should strip them of their clothes and weapons. We always need Kereki clothes and boots for maskovestos."

I bent down as Nelo did and soon we were stripping the bodies, searching pockets, feeling down seams for hidden coin and knives. It felt like scavenging bodies in Kerek City all over again.

"I remember you in Lowertown," Nelo said suddenly. "Not too many Conrosans named Red. You were older, so I stayed out of your way. But I remember you."

I stopped what I was doing and gave him a close look. Nelo's face was hard with a rough scar high on his cheekbone, just below his left eye. A rock, or something equally blunt, but not a knife, I could tell. He wore his white-blond hair long enough to tie back in a tail that fell just below his shoulders. His eyebrows and lashes were so light, it gave his face a naked appearance in contrast to his harsh green eyes. He was not as tall as Piffik or as broad in the shoulders. But there was nothing soft, or boyish, in his face. I remembered he had said he thought he was seventeen.

I would have crossed the street or abandoned the alley if I had seen him approaching me in Kerek City. I couldn't believe he had stayed out of *my* way.

I went back to stripping the bodies. "What was your territory?" I asked.

"Embasado street north to the Linen Market. I had a nest on the second floor of a warehouse. I ran Lost Boys and Girls. I would dress them up in pretty clothes and send them out into the street crying for a missing parent. You would be surprised how many people would offer them a coin or a bite of food and call it charity without doing anything to help them. I took throwaway children and used them as bait for gentlemen and sailors not happy with who was waiting for them at home. If you killed them before they touched the children," he grunted as he pulled off a stubborn boot, "they couldn't complain." He paused for a long time. "I lost my first friend to Mouser." He looked away from me. "I sold her clothes to buy a Sailor's Curse."

I stilled my hands and dropped my eyes. Nelo had laid himself bare. I wished I had Siba's wisdom right now, she would have known what to say to splint him back together into a man worth keeping. I wondered if she knew all the Wrens' stories; if I was only going to be the first one to need Siba and Piffik to drag me to the other side of a damaged past.

I was quiet too long. Nelo stood up quickly and dusted off his hands.

"You got an open coffin we can throw these boots and clothes into? I know someone who can clean them up for a few coins. She won't talk." He flashed me a feral grin. "She's part of Bima Ritwik's network, but he hasn't a clue what a treasure he has in her. Inezi says he complains because she can't read or write, and flirt with soldiers. But she can track a Kereki bounty hunter over rough ground, is strong enough to carry an unconscious soldier for a handful of furloughs, and read a trail left by Viklander boots as well as Arden's dog does. And best of all? Her father is ashamed because she looks like her Matasi mother. She won't be missed at home."

I knew he was talking of the gamekeeper's daughter. I grinned back at him.

"By all means, let's make her feel useful."

We stripped three of the Kereki horses of their trappings and saddles and put them on a lead line. While we had been going over the bodies, Piffik had been rubbing wood oil and stain into the fourth saddle to change its color and age it. Using a wood chisel, he gouged off the metal decorations and scratched the leather further. We swapped out the dull grey Kereki saddle blanket for the brightly colored Conrosan blanket Rygee had used to line the basket for the food and resaddled the horse for Nelo. At last, we were ready to go. Nelo mounted easily.

I chuckled. "That's not a skill any of us learned in Lowertown."

"Manumina was good to me." He reached for the lead lines of the three Kereki horses. "I'll take these to Fortika so we can change horses there after picking up the injured Viklanders. I hope these are broken to wagon hauling. Josef will try to meet you before Regno. If he doesn't step out on the road, go four furloughs beyond the main house. There will be a narrow path on your right. It should be wide enough for the wagon, but just. Half a decon or so beyond, there will be a shepherd's hut on the left. Wait there until Dica comes out." He thought for a moment. "Hail the house and introduce yourself first. Dica's an overly cautious one." He tipped his head to us and took off east weaving the horses between the widely spaced trees.

Piffik finally spoke, "Who would put a fort in the middle of a wooded area? These trees should have either been cleared out or the fort built with clear sightlines in every direction."

I stood up, turned, and looked about me. "This wasn't built here to fight Viklanders, Piffik, this was built here to protect the neighboring settlers from bandits. No gang of outlaws would ever be so foolish as to attack this if easier pickings were available. That's one of the first lessons you learn in Lowertown." I shrugged. "Besides, if you are a soldier who hasn't seen a paypacket in who knows how long, how inclined would you be to build a proper fort?"

"I'm inclined to keep my life," he responded drily.

"Ah, Piffik, that is why Rell sends me along—to keep you whole and sweet." I climbed back on the wagon.

Piffik looked about him. "You have all your knives and daggers? We need the Justice to be puzzled enough to shrug and walk away." He climbed up on the wagon seat beside me.

I looked at the four nearly naked dead men on the ground. Horses gone, weapons gone, most of their clothes gone. The only thing the Justice would wonder was why the thieves didn't take the three remaining saddles.

"All of mine and a few more besides. Thank you for that."

He clucked to the horses and we were on our way.

CHAPTER 14

RESCUE AT REGNO

The Trouble that had danced with us at Earles delayed us, and Piffik was worried it would be too dark to see the track beyond Regno. Although it made more sense for Nelo to wait with our fresh horses at Fortika, we would miss his fighting skills if we were carrying so many injured Viklanders and ran into Kereki soldiers. I was worried we hadn't yet encountered Josef.

Just past Regno, a thickset woman stepped out of the rhododendron grove. Her dark skirts were dusty and her grey shawl over her head and shoulders was tattered and worn. As we drew near, she pushed back the shawl from her head. Soft-looking, young, and prettily baby-faced, it was Josef. He had stained his lips and cheeks with berry juice and had brushed something reddish into his blond hair.

As Piffik pulled up, Josef batted his eyes and begged for a ride.

"Think of me as a she and protect me in the middle." Josef waved me off the wagon seat. "Convince yourself, Zren, and then when we run into Kerekis, they won't think I know how to fight until it's too late, and I have saved your life." Josef laughed at my scowl.

I slipped off the wagon bench, so she could give us all the news she had gathered. According to Josef, Dica's master had taken his family and most of his staff to Kerek City to meet with the King to talk about holding the North against the Viklanders. With only a handful of staff left behind, and those more interested in their own pursuits than the actions of a between maid, it was easier for the Wrens to find places in the border spaces for the Viklanders to be fed and hidden. Dica could tend to the injured Viklanders the Wrens had been ferrying to Regno.

Still talking, Josef pointed out the track we needed to turn on. Nelo had been right, it was just barely big enough for the wagon. I found myself dodging branches as I tried to listen to the rest of Josef's story.

Most of the Viklanders needed food, medicine for burns, and Kereki clothes to pass undetected through the next few days until they could reach Vikland.

"Especially the soft leather Kereki boots. I'm wearing so many layers right now," Josef laughed, "I think a Sailor's Curse couldn't even reach my ribs." She looked at me. "Not that I think you should try it."

She went on to describe how the fall of Earles had been a real blow to the Viklanders; now they had no real place in the center of Kerek to fall back to. There were regiments and patrols scattered across the north, but the main Kerek army was still west of Balza. The Viklander military was trying to defend too large an area, and the local Kerek landowner militias were better supplied. Skirmishes and battles could change a safe location into dangerous territory without warning.

"What do you need?" asked Piffik. "Not for tonight, but to supply your hiding places."

"Food that won't rot, coin, boots, medicine." Josef considered her words carefully, "You should know some of the Wrens are stealing to push more food to the Viklanders. Some of the Wrens have had close calls as well. Ross needs many more rabbits to sell. He has had to sacrifice them for the Viklanders rather than breeding more for the tables of the rich in Huk. And, Callis is being watched closely because her store Patron thought she was buying too much food for just her and Ross." Josef threw up her hands in a feminine gesture. "Who has so much time they can pry into another one's life?"

Piffik chuffed, "You should have lived in Manumina for the last twenty years." He nodded back to the wagon box. "If you are hungry, we have food."

I reached back for the bag and saw Josef bite her lower lip.

"I should save it for the Viklanders, I don't know how much Dica was able to feed them."

I put the bag slowly on my lap. I was ready to eat my third meal of the day, and Josef was worried about the Viklanders.

"You need to eat something, Josef," Piffik said gently. "We need you to be strong enough to fight if necessary." I reached into the bag and pulled out one of Rygee's buns thickly spread with butter and jam. I saw Josef's eyes grow wide, and I immediately regretted eating three of them at midday. I pushed it into her hands.

She had already taken three big bites when she said, "Why aren't you two eating? Am I taking your food?"

"No, no," Piffik reassured her. "We had just finished eating before we met up with you on the track. It is why we were so late in reaching you."

Josef looked closely at Piffik. "You could lie to your own grandmother. But truly, I am too hungry to care tonight. Thank you."

I offered her another one, this one with cheese. Josef looked at it briefly and said gently, "The Viklanders will need it. Don't worry, Zren. I am strong enough to fight."

Nelo still hadn't found us by the time we reached the shepherd's hut. Piffik pulled up the horses.

He hailed the house and continued, "We are Conrosans, neutral in the war between Kerek and Vikland. We seek water for our horses and a place to bed down for the night."

We waited a moment and there was no response.

"Let me down," Josef said. I slid off the wagon seat and Josef jumped lightly to the ground. As she walked to the cottage, she started talking, "I think I can do one of two things here. I can either strike a lucifer and put it under my chin to show you my pretty face which you haven't gazed upon for days and days, or I can tell the story of the first time I saw you wearing that ridiculous frilly pink dress with a sticky bun in your hand pretending to be lost and collecting coins from market goers."

I heard a rustle from behind the wagon and a thin girl dressed only in Kereki pants and a tunic stepped out on the track behind us.

"It would almost be worth it to hear you talk to an empty house half the night, but I am too busy and have no time for such fun." Josef whirled around and Dica stepped forward. "Good, I can see you're wearing the extra clothes I asked you to bring." She gestured at herself. "I've already given away my last shirt."

She looked at Piffik. "Padro Morto, I am beyond glad to see you. I have seven to go with you. We sent the others—the healthiest ones—on to Vikland the day before yesterday. Inezi is their guide to the border. She took the last of my supplies of medicine and food and Kereki boots for their journey. Do you have food or medicine? Some of these soldiers are hurt and all are hungry." She turned to walk back into the darkness. Only then, did I notice she was barefoot. "You'll have to leave the wagon here," she called back over her shoulder. "We are hidden a little way off the track."

I slung the bag of food over my shoulder and opened the coffin where we had thrown in the boots and clothing from Earles. Piffik and Josef grabbed the other clothes from Manumina, and we followed Dica into the thicket. The branches closed over my head and poked sharply at me as I trailed closely behind the others. Suddenly we broke into a small opening where the bushes had been cut down and shoved against the roots of the others to form an impenetrable dome of greenery. Three of the Viklanders were sitting splayed, backs against the green barrier. The other four were laid out on the ground. All were tired, dirty, battered, with bruises and burns over their faces, arms, and clothes. The enclosed area reeked of stale smoke, old blood, and unwashed bodies.

Dica introduced us quickly in Keresh and in Vik as "Padro Morto and his friends," who had answered her call for help. I threw down the boots I had and handed out food and water.

Josef started undressing immediately. No one stared or barely seemed to notice as she removed her skirts and shawl, two pairs of Kereki pants, three billowy blouses, and a pair of leather boots.

"You're going to need to change your clothes," Josef said in Keresh to the soldiers. "We need to disguise you."

"I thought this one," a soldier pointed to Dica, "said we had to ride in a death wagon."

Piffik sighed. "Actually, my friends, it is going to be worse than that. Because there are so many of you, we are going to have to put you in real coffins, not just the bottom row which has false sides. We will need to put a burlap bag over your heads to hide your braids and faces and bags over your hands to hide your skin. I will stop as often as I dare, and we will stay off the main road, but it is a full day to ride to our destination."

Some of the Viklanders went pale. I wondered which of them would be unable to handle the close quarters for so long.

"Why?" croaked one of the women.

"Because we *will* be stopped," Piffik said gently. "All wagons are searched. When we are stopped by the Kereki patrol and I am forced to open a coffin, all they will see is bagged heads and hands and Kereki dress. If there was another way, I would do so…"

"But you are all going home alive," Dica said sharply. "Put your Vik uniforms in a pile for me." She reached for a pair of Kereki pants and ruthlessly undressed one of the unconscious soldiers on the floor.

I grabbed a soft grey shirt and reached for another of the Viklanders curled away from me. I gently rolled the soldier back and saw Lomes. The last time I had seen them, the Softfoot had taken me out in Salisport and tried to abandon me in a place where I knew no one and could not read or speak the language. I wondered how long Lomes had been softfooting in Kerek.

"Hey there," I said softly, "Aren't you a long way from home?" Lomes' eyes fluttered open, and I smiled. "Remember me?"

"Of all the people to come to my rescue, is a person to whom I have done an ill-favor." They gave me a tired, lopsided smile.

"Shush, I remember no such thing." I eased off the black shirt and slipped the loose-fitting blouse over their head. "You'll need to tuck in your braid like so," I dropped the braid between the collar and the neck and then handed over a pair of pants. "Can you do these yourself?" They unlaced their boots and started to change.

"Were you fighting?" I was curious.

"Softfooting. I had news of our western patrols to get to our troops, but they were boxed in from the south. The Kereki army split our forces, and I took this splintered group and fled north. We have a helper at a nearby estate and I thought if we could just get there…"

"Fortika. Yes, I know. We work with her as well; Inezi, the gamekeeper's daughter."

Lomes gave me a long slow blink. "Are we compromised? Is she no longer safe?"

"No, just allies. She has taken an earlier group to Vikland. It is good Dica found you."

"Everyone ready?" Dica hissed. "You need to go."

Josef tied on her skirt again and wrapped the grey shawl about her head hiding her hair and most of her face. Dica had picked up all the Viklander boots and clothes and shoved them in a heap.

"Inezi will deal with these later when she returns," she assured Piffik.

"We don't get our clothes back?"

Dica gave the soldier an angry look. "Just how convincing would your maskovesto be if you pranced along with a traveling bag full of Viklander uniforms?" One of the other soldiers quickly said something in Vik to the first one. It didn't sound kind.

Piffik cleared his throat and the entire group looked at him. "Our healers gave me medicinals to make you sleep on the way." He handed out the wafers and passed a steel flask of water. "I will take the four most able-bodied first. You will be in the wagon the longest." Four soldiers quickly stood and followed him out of the enclosure and down the prickly path.

Lomes looked down at the two in the dirt beside them. "I worry for these two."

"We have healers at Manumina. If they can stay with us until then, they will have the best of care."

Josef came back alone. She hitched her skirt up, picked up the smaller of the two Viklanders laying on the ground, and turned to walk out. Lomes and I supported the other one between us, his arms pulled around our shoulders. Dica followed, using an old broom to sweep away all our tracks.

We put the two most injured in the outside coffins and Lomes in the middle. Without another word to us, Dica walked quickly back to the main house. Surprised at Dica's roughness, I looked at Josef who just smiled back. The three of us, Piffik, Josef, and I, climbed up on the wagon seat. We would change horses at Fortika and hopefully, pick up Nelo then.

Nelo's distinctive scar, white-blond hair, and habit of wearing Viklander boots made him easily recognizable. Word of him had traveled through earlier lost Viklanders; he could be trusted for help. Taking him along with us would reassure the others once we reached Manumina.

I had never traveled so far, but according to Piffik, Regno to Fortika was a short half-day's walk. Dica, our softfoot and between maid at Regno, and Tyra, our under kitchen maid tucked in at Fortika, would spend their off days ferrying clothes, coin, and occasionally messages back and forth and in the hiding places on the massive estates. Nelo, claiming to be their brother and an itinerant manabout, visited them both and took the information and messages to Piffik or Tiju Tia or Linna, nearby Viklander softfoots, or Inezi at Fortika.

There were enough outbuildings on both Regno and Fortika, a single Viklander could be hidden until Nelo or Inezi could guide them over the far north border to Vikland or down to Ishes, the easternmost Viklander garrison on Kerek soil. Dica and Tyra learned quickly how valuable their efforts were in hiding clothes, food, small coins, and maps of the area and of Vikland. More than once the girls had gone to the farthest outbuildings and found the maps and Kereki clothes gone and a pile of Viklander uniforms left behind.

I looked up at the stars and searched for the constellation the Soldier. Ngahuru had pointed him out to me all those years ago on the road to Matasi. I found him and silently wished for him to keep us out of the eyesight of any Kereki patrols.

We pulled into the Fortika woods in the middle of the night. Nelo was there with four horses and a small boy from Fortika. I had forgotten his name if I ever knew it, but I knew he was one of Bima's helpers. I wondered if I should get Lomes out of the coffin to speak with the boy, but when I asked Piffik he shook his head.

"It's not safe to stop here long. Lomes would have told us at Regno if there was something that needed to be passed along." Piffik and I eased off the bench. I started unhooking our horses from the traces when suddenly Piffik told Nelo, "These aren't the ones from this afternoon."

"No." Nelo looked frustrated. "We had to go back to the original plan, the ones from earlier are not wagon broke, they are only riders. Therin swapped these out from his master's stables. We should be safe enough. Josef and I will switch these out as quickly as we can." He slipped lead lines over our tired plow horses and gave them to Therin. Without a word, the boy moved off into the darkness to take our horses to an abandoned building to eat and sleep. He would care for them so no one at Fortika would know.

For us, the night was only beginning. Nelo and I mounted the outrider horses, and Josef fluffed out her skirts as Piffik climbed back onto the wagon.

"How do I look?" she asked.

"Like Trouble," Nelo huffed, "but to a Kereki patrol, you'll pass for grieving family." He looked at the night sky. "Let's go. We need to be over the Northern Track before dawn." Nelo moved off to the outrider position on the right, I took the left, and we began our journey to Manumina.

CHAPTER 15

REVENGE OR REWARD

We were two decons past dawn when we finally reached the Northern Track. Piffik didn't want to risk riding through Sary, and we had wandered through some small, fenced pastures trying to find a place where we could cross without detection. It didn't do us any good though, we had just turned left on the Northern Track to meet the road to Manumina when I saw three horses galloping up fast behind us.

Nelo had wheeled about and already had his short bow up when Piffik called out, "It's the Justice. Don't shoot." It took me a few moments longer before I recognized him also. I did not know the two men riding with him.

Piffik pulled up the horses. "Morning, sir."

"Morning." The Justice nodded sharply. "Looks like you're just headed home. Funny time of the day to be heading home to Manumina." He looked at Nelo and me on horseback and then squinted hard at Josef on the wagon bench next to Piffik. She dropped her eyes to the floorboards of the wagon.

Piffik said nothing, but Nelo nonchalantly nudged his horse to circle wide about the Kerekis. I stayed where I was to act as the *titiro mai ki ahau*. Nelo and I both knew he was better on the bow than I was.

"I'm looking for some horses," the Justice finally said. "Four of them, top-bred saddle horses. They were supposed to be delivered to Evensong, one of those fortresses north by the Cold Mountains. The Justice near Earles found three of the saddles and four dead men who were supposed to deliver them, but no horses. Now Mr. Qanaq, I know you drive all over north Kerek, and I was wondering if you might have seen these fine horses."

Piffik slowly shook his head. "Earles, you say? Too far west for me, that's north of Cloa." He lifted his hands. "We're east of Sary."

"I know where we are," the Justice spit out.

"Yes, sir." Piffik dropped his eyes, as meek as I had ever seen him. Josef sat still as death beside him, eyes cast down, hands hidden underneath her skirts. I knew without seeing she had a dagger in each hand.

The Justice looked at Nelo and me. "Since when does a death wagon need outriders?"

Piffik squinted at the Justice. "We heard there were Viklanders about and didn't want to wake up with a crossbow in our face—or not wake up at all."

One of the other men grunted, "Who you haulin'?"

"This one's family," Piffik jerked a thumb at Josef. "She comes crying two nights past, her ma and brother are dead, and can I come. I find my brother," he nodded at me, "and my friend and ask them to travel along in case Trouble wants to come dance with us." He casts a hard look at Josef. "We get to her house and find her whole family is dead—disease dead."

No one spoke. I watched as the silent rider moved up close to the wagon. I held my breath wishing him just to back away. *Please, no. There is nothing there you want to see.* Instead, he reached out to touch the top coffin.

"No!" I blurted out. He gave me a funny look and deliberately pushed the lid aside. Piffik whirled about on the seat and slammed the lid back in place.

"You fool!" Piffik snapped at him, and I stilled. Piffik wasn't acting any more. He *was* furious. "I *said*, disease dead. I *said* two days ago there were two dead and now I got a wagon full. You want me to come bury you tomorrow? What was filling up your ears you couldn't hear what I was saying?"

The Justice had his horse step back. "What'd you see, Penn?"

The rider, Penn, was petulant. "Like he said, a Kereki man, prob'ly the brother."

The Justice wasn't ready to concede just yet. "If it was disease, he shoulda had his hands and face bagged and boots on. Did you see that, Penn?"

Penn cast an angry look at Piffik, who just raised his eyebrows.

"Yes, sir," Penn answered reluctantly.

"Go on home, now," Piffik advised Penn. "Wash up good and take a good drink or two of spirits to wash out any disease you may have breathed in."

Penn looked frightened. Both the other rider and the Justice forced their horses to take a few more steps back. The Justice looked at Piffik.

"Anyone tries to sell you some horses in the next few days, let me know. I hear those are some truly fine horses I'm trying to find."

"Not much use for those at Manumina. We like plow horses that don't mind what they're pulling. But I'll let you know if I hear or see anything." Piffik settled in and slowly picked up the reins again.

We had just started pulling away when the other rider shouted out after us, "What're ya goin' to do with the woman?"

Nelo wheeled about and snarled, "I'm taking her to the kitchens at Manumina. If she can cook, she can stay. If she can't, I'll drop her on your doorstep." He turned to join us again, and we all trotted up the horses until we could turn right on the track toward home and safety.

***

Tiju Tia and Lou were out tending to the animals when we reached Manumina. She was dressed as a Kereki boy today since she had been doing my manabout chores. I saw Tiju Tia put her good hand on Lou's arm and say something, and then she came alone to greet us.

Josef jumped down from the wagon seat and together they went into the side door to open the gates so the wagon could drive through. Piffik didn't stop until he reached the infirmary and called Siba's name. She came out and said Rell was helping Rygee in the bakery. Tiju Tia hurried over to get her.

I helped Piffik open and move the coffins as he and I lifted the woozy Viklanders out and handed them down. Josef and Nelo removed the bags from their hands and heads. Rell came up and welcomed them and then spoke for a bit in Vik. Lomes gave her a sharp look, but the rest of them merely nodded, and we all paraded into the infirmary.

All of the Viklanders had heard the heated exchange earlier between the Kerekis at Sary and Piffik. Once again, I marveled to myself at how Piffik could seem to take any action and with a few well-turned words turn it into something completely different. I wondered how he could think so much faster and smarter than the rest of us.

We let the Viklanders talk it out and share their versions with each other. I noticed Nelo and Josef pretending to be nonplussed by the whole event, Nelo by acting cold and aloof and Josef by smiling and flirting with everyone. I knew we needed to convince them we had been in control the entire time.

Truthfully? It had frightened me badly.

"Food first," Rygee entered the room talking. "Food, baths, sleep."

I went to find Rell to ask what I should do for the wounded. She and Siba had already talked with each of the Viklanders to find out who were most in need of care, and she sent me back to the kitchen for buckets of warm water, clean rags, and soft soap.

Siba lit the incense which would make everyone in the room drowsy. We removed the bloody shirts from the ambush at Earles some of them had been forced to wear. I told Rell—in Keresh—what had happened at the burned out garrison and how Nelo had stolen the horses meant for Evensong, but luckily for us, they had never been broken to hauling, and so we hadn't been caught with them at Sary.

Lomes was lying on a bed listening to me tell the story. There was blood seeping out of their leg I hadn't noticed before. Siba left to make the sleeping draughts for the ones with the worst burns.

Rell watched her leave the room, and then turned on me. "Zren, I understand Vik you know. I heard the soldiers talk. It was much more dangerous than you said." She stared hard at me. "Which coffin did they open?"

I looked at her in surprise. "I don't know. Piffik was so fast, the rider just saw the clothes, maybe the bagged hands. The rider's name was Penn. He told the Justice it was a Kereki."

"But sooner or later, the Justice is going to wonder why we are bringing diseased dead to Manumina rather than just firing the cabin and taking the remaining girl. We also don't have a Kereki girl to impersonate Josef until the end of time either."

"Rell, it worked, all right? It worked."

She huffed and then sent me to see if Tiju Tia had two clean shirts she could have. I didn't think Tiju Tia would have any large enough, so I ran home and grabbed my last two shirts. I thought Nelo should have told the Kerekis we would have Josef do the laundry. That's where we needed the help.

Lomes was awake when I returned, and I asked if they needed something to eat before sleeping.

"I slept all night, Zren. It's the four of you who should be falling into your beds."

I nodded. "I'll be there just as soon as I know all of you will be fine." I waved my arm at the wounded and burned Viklanders resting and sleeping on the beds. Siba came out of the back room with a tray full of cups. I knew it was the sleeping potions that would cause the soldiers to sleep very deeply.

"They are going to be fine, Zren." Siba smiled. "The four of you need to get some rest."

I pointed to an empty bed. "Can I sleep here? I love the dreams your incense give me."

Siba shook her head, but she was smiling as she waved her hand at the empty bed. I smiled at Lomes.

"Truly, Lomes, drink the potion if Siba gives it to you. It will give you incredible dreams."

CHAPTER 16

WORKING TOGETHER

Tiju Tia and Lomes spent the day in the infirmary planning. I could hear their voices as I drifted in and out of sleep. Lomes was surprised to hear how extensive our network was—east to Balza, north to Regno. Connections to the garrison at Ishes and over the Vikland border both north and south of the Northern Track.

Lomes shared the rumors Matasi was finally going to act. Years ago, the Triune had promised the Vikland Empress to support her when the Viklanders attacked Kerek to hold them to their treaties. It hadn't happened. And now? Unfortunately, Lomes, along with the rest of the Viklander softfoots, thought it was still only rumors.

"Every time the Kerek King needs more coin for the war, the King confiscates more of the South Kerek farms and orchards 'for the war effort.' Then he only has to crook a finger and the Matasi landowners push up wheelbarrows full of coin to buy them, knowing the coin buys more soldiers to fight us—their supposed allies."

Lomes sighed and confided how the Viklander army was in a constant state of regrouping. Soldiers were moving from unit to unit wherever they could connect with others.

"We know what you do for us," Lomes said. "Our newest softfoots make one, maybe two missions before they disappear, and we fear they are captured. Kern can barely train them fast enough." It was quiet for a long time. I risked peeking over at them.

Lomes continued, "This war is very different than the old battles we study in our academies. During our three years of military service, we practice defenses and offenses, and refight battles over different terrain. But none of it was like this. In Kerek, militia and country soldiers do not come into open ground to fight. Instead, they skulk about, hiding where it is impossible to use our crossbows. There is no proper exchange of prisoners, no respect for rank. They take our men and hang them, take our women soldiers and sell them. Our battles are not lines of soldiers who can display their prowess, but desperate skirmishes and ambushes whittled down to single soldiers where even the short bong and jeong bong cannot prevail."

Tiju Tia was sitting in the shadows in a stiff-backed chair beside the bed, now dressed in one of her shapeless dresses with a grey shawl over her shoulders washing out her face even more. Lomes was still lying down with their bandaged leg propped up on the bedclothes.

"Tiju Tia, we are used to picking locks or studying languages to break coded messages and hiding in gathering places and overhearing careless conversations.

"The Wrens of Manumina, our soldiers tell us, change gender as easily as clothes, hide in plain sight as shopgirls, stable boys, and servants, and ruthlessly lie, steal, and kill to defend themselves and us. We hesitate and we are lost," Lomes said sadly.

"You were taught to fight a different type of war," Tiju Tia said quietly. "The Wrens and I were taught by the great softfoot Ngahuru when she was posted in Kerek City all those years ago." I jerked at hearing the lie and immediately shut my eyes. If either of them looked over, I wanted them to think I was dreaming.

"She built her network of information gatherers, people trackers, and street runners from those the city had thrown away and would never miss. Who better to lift a sensitive document than a pickpocket? What better distraction than a beautiful face to cause a castle official to gamble more than is wise, and thus be open to a bribe or blackmail? Who can follow a castle servant, a messenger, or any person of interest better than a child who has been taught never to lose a drunken mark, or they will be a victim themselves? Your softfoots have a few seasons of training in the embasado, the palace, or the Juisiti academies. The Wrens have spent most of their lives learning softfooting skills just trying to live to the next day."

"So you grew up in Lowertown?" Lomes asked uncertainly.

"You and I, Lomes, would never have survived Lowertown." Tiju Tia shook her head sadly. "The Wrens have their own stories to tell, but some of them are silent because they want that life to be behind them, others because the stories of what they were forced to do to live will never be believed."

"So why do it? Why help Vikland? The Wrens are Kereki, you are Kereki. The Conrosans here at Manumina have lost so much at the hands of the Kereki army. Is it revenge? Punishment for the Wrens' childhood in Lowertown? The poverty here at Manumina? What has Vikland done for you to help us at such a cost of your lives?" Lomes stopped, and then continued slowly, "Or is it only, we are the least of your enemies?"

Tiju Tia looked thoughtful. "I cannot tell other's stories. Perhaps the Wrens may tell you why they joined the fight, perhaps they may not." She paused. "Viklanders pride themselves on being honorable. On defending the defenseless and fighting for what is just. You carry it to such lengths your hair is never cut unless you commit an act of dishonesty or act dishonorably. A

Viklander without a braid is to be shunned. Isn't that the way of it within your borders?"

A small smile played about Tiju Tia's lips. "So if two handfuls of children save a Viklander life or two or ten, make the difference in the outcome of a battle with plans pilfered from the other side, or provide weapons, or a horse, or a safe place to hide until a soldier or softfoot can be rejoined with others, what would that be worth to your Empress? A future home in Vikland? An education? An apprenticeship? A dream of safety and home? Freedom from fear and hunger? Your Empress knows what we are able to do for her. I know what the Wrens deserve after this war is over. I think we can come to an agreement."

Lomes curled their lip. "You're a mercenary then. Selling your children's lives to the highest bidder for the greatest reward."

Tiju Tia laughed out loud. "Ah, Viklanders! So you believe no one else ever has pure and noble motives? That I could only be a seller of children?" She sobered. "Take this message to your Empress, or anyone else who needs to hear it. Because of a great favor I did the softfoot Ngahuru, the King of the West Islands has granted me a boon—an unclaimed gift. If the Vikland Empress does not wish to honor the debt she owes the Wrens of Manumina, then I will take them to the West Islands King and explain why I have so many children who need to be rewarded with a place to call home."

Lomes was silent for a long, long time.

I could hear the smile in Tiju Tia's voice. "You are wise to remain silent when you have so much to think about. But I suggest, if you are able to walk a bit on that leg, we should go out and see what the others have done with my steel sewing needles this afternoon. Zren is starting to wiggle over there, and I think he will suddenly wake and find he needs to inspect the infirmary's plumbing. I do not wish to be in his way when that happens."

I groaned in embarrassment, but I think it was hidden under the sounds of Lomes' grunts as they pulled themselves up and out of bed. I peeked under half-open eyes as they made their way out into the late afternoon sunshine. As soon as Tiju Tia had pulled the door shut behind her, I jumped up and hurried to the chain commode in the other room.

When I walked outside, everything had changed. With Piffik, Josef, Nelo, and I sleeping the day away to make up for our day and night without, Rygee and the healers had found tasks for the four healthy Viklanders. They had slept enough with the wafers they had been given, they had said. With baths, hot meals, and fresh ointments and bandages on their wounds, burns, and bruises, they declared themselves ready for work and asked for a task to help us in return.

Tiju Tia had rummaged through the rag and bone cart, Siba had contributed a number of damaged shirts and pants from the infirmary, and Tiju Tia had passed out her precious West Islands steel sewing needles before going to sit with Lomes.

The Viklanders had spent the afternoon relaxing in the safety of the stockade, mending the escape clothes for those who would come after them. Oro and Rygee did laundry. As soon as the Viklanders had finished mending the first batch of clothes, Oro handed them the freshly laundered, but torn and slashed pants, shirts, and tunics, to be mended as well.

"This is the most valuable work you could do for us," Siba had said. "You are helping the next soldier pass undetected through Kerek to rejoin another unit or travel through the countryside to report and be reassigned."

I stood outside and stretched as I listened to Tiju Tia and Lomes explain the new plans for the soldiers. After their few decons of rest and work, Oro would take the four healthy Viklanders over the Vikland border to a shepherd's cottage the Conrosans used to hide from the Tax Collector. Oro would spend the night with them there and then take them up through Vikland to the nearest garrison for them to report in and post out. The plan was to have the Viklanders meet and introduce Oro to the commanding officers in Vikland. They would share where Tiju Tia and Padro Morto ran their routes and show maps of new hiding places for Viklanders now that Earles had been burnt to the ground. If it was close to six days as Oro returned, he should divert to Ishes and pick up Josef.

As they loaded the wagon, Rygee had brought out two big baskets of food and told the soldiers he would be insulted if Oro came back with any food left over. They grinned widely and promised to do their best.

CHAPTER 17

THE MAKING OF MEN

By the time Lou had come back from working in the springhouses all day with his cheeses, Oro had already left with the four Viklanders. Tiju Tia, Piffik, Nelo, Lomes, and Josef came to Rell's and my house after dinner. Siba would stay with the two remaining wounded, and Rygee would distract Lou by talking about farm business until the cheesemaker made a night of it.

"Here is what I am thinking to return the horses and get you back home," Tiju Tia began. She offered several options and Piffik suggested others. They asked Nelo's and Josef's opinions on alternative settlements and dates and solicited their thoughts on almost every step. When it seemed like we had a way through all of the actions that needed to take place, Piffik started the process all over again. He wanted every step to have a back-up plan with different places and different people who had different strengths.

Listening, I learned Nelo liked less interactions because he thought attacking first and fast was his best option. He was also very protective of his information sources at the great houses. He didn't want Tyra, Dica, Kid, or Bima's Therin and Inezi taking unnecessary risks. He would rather absorb them himself.

Josef on the other hand, counted on his soft looks and his feminine clothes stashed in buildings, trees, and other places to switch from male to female and back again almost under the Kereki soldiers' noses. He knew horses, and boltholes, and costumes. He told the others he had found like-minded friends who didn't ask questions. He had safe places to hide, he said, no larger than a coffin.

Josef would only use violence when his plans went sideways, and he couldn't flee or hide or charm his way out of a dance with Trouble. Even though neither would admit it, the way Nelo and Josef talked about each other as they worked through the plans showed they respected each other's strengths. I listened and watched, not just to understand Josef and Nelo better, but also to try to learn how Tiju Tia and Piffik were teaching them to lead themselves.

At last, the four of them had a plan, and I listened for my part.

Nelo and Tiju Tia would return the two horses borrowed from Fortika yesterday by using the rag and bone wagon. To look more harmless, and because they thought crimpers would not take a single male protector, Josef would dress as a woman, and Nelo would be driving his mother and his sister. Near Fortika, Josef would switch to male clothing, and he and Inezi would go to the abandoned barn, where Therin would be caring for the four stolen horses captured from the Kerekis at Earles and our two plowhorses. Tiju Tia and Therin would take the plowhorses and continue to Fortika; Inezi and Josef would take the stolen ones and ride for the Vikland border far north of Ishes. As nice as the horses were, they weren't worth the trouble they would be if they were recognized in Kerek. Once in Vikland, Josef and Inezi, if she could accompany him, would head south to the main road, sell the horses, and find a ride to the Ishes garrison where Oro would be waiting to pick them up in six days.

Nelo and Tiju Tia would have the plowhorses Therin had been caring for and continue on to Regno. There they would pick up the Viklander clothes and boots from Dica and mix them with the other clothes for sale in the rag and bone wagon. They would deliver a freshly mended and laundered batch of Kereki shirts, tunics, pants, and soft leather boots. At Evensong, they would meet with Kid on his half day and hopefully have a long talk about everything Kid knew and learned from the Kereki army officers who dined regularly there with the owner and his family. Nelo would then ride with Tiju Tia south to Cloa and somewhere close to there, Nelo would disappear into the woods back into his own territory.

I would ride with Lou on the cheese wagon from Manumina along the Northern Track and meet Tiju Tia in Cloa. I would take the *titiro mai ki ahau's* place on the wagon as Tiju Tia swung back east to return to Manumina. Anyone who caught a glimpse of her more than once would only see her and a male dressed in Kereki clothes.

"Take the bright blue traveler's cloak, it's the most eye-catching," Josef suggested. "People will remember the cloak but not the person wearing it. All the male protectors traveling with you will be remembered as a lump of blue."

Piffik, Rygee, and Siba would take the orchard prunings, scrap wood, broken furniture, and anything else they could find to burn and build a large fire south of Manumina. If anyone suddenly did question why they had taken disease ridden bodies, they would point them to the ashes and claim a funeral pyre.

Rell would continue to help the wounded Viklanders heal. Then Lomes and the remaining Viklanders would be delivered back to Ishes with the Viklander clothes Tiju Tia and I would bring back to Manumina when our route was done.

Lomes leaned back in gratitude.

"This," they said. "This is the part we were missing. We are immediately known for strangers. Even though your Wrens wear the faces of other countries, they are not Viklanders. Bima and Rani and Kern have built a collection of hideouts filled with clothing, coin, maps, and message drops for the new softfoots, but we have nothing to link us all together. Our new softfoots must travel from their territory without a way to blend in, ask questions of which properties are abandoned, where the battles have been fought, or even hire a horse. If you have a map, I will show you where our drops are, and we can work together."

***

Rell offered to take Lomes back to the guesthouse "to talk about Vikland" she said. Lomes gave her an odd look but followed her out the door. Piffik went back to our kitchen and made some of Rell's coffee. When he came back to the table, he had the tiny cups of coffee, but I also saw he had pulled some fingersweets I had been hiding behind Rell's coffee beans. He saw my shocked expression.

"Zren, if I made Rell's coffee for all of us, she might say I presume upon our friendship too much. If I add your fingersweets and tell her you offered us coffee and sweets for the long night ahead, then she will be pleased you have learned such fine manners. What am I to do?"

I squinted at him. "Rell never gets upset at anything you do. She only gets upset at what you do not do. On the other hand, she claims I can be even more annoying than all of her little brothers together, and I can also be sweeter than a spoonful of honey. I only hope when she does not have any coffee to drink, that it is the day she thinks I am sweet and you are not."

Josef smirked at Nelo. "So this is what Arden must put up with living in the same house as Linna. No wonder he and Mother spend so much time in the woods looking for Viklanders."

Tiju Tia looked sharply at him. "Is there a problem with some of the Wrens? Must I make some new arrangements?"

Nelo and Josef looked at each other and then at her. Nelo sighed.

"There are no problems, Tiju Tia, but there are words that need to be said. Linna says Arden is in danger of losing his position at the stables in Cloa. We have all used Linna and Arden as our stronghold when you and Padro Morto are not on your routes. Arden is our best tracker and a better thief. He is in the center of all of us. He always comes when we ask for help. Linna reads the documents we steal and tells us where we must take them and what we must say before we hand them over so we are not harmed. She hears things in the store because the Justice comes in every day to talk with his friend the Patron. She is pretty and sweet and gathers news as easily as she smiles. She tells Arden and then he must get the news to us. When he does not find us quickly enough, he takes care of it himself."

"I see," said Tiju Tia. "So we need to get the two of them some help. Tell me about Callis and Ross at Huk. It was meant to be the center of all of you. The two there were only meant to have occasional work so they could move freely. It is the friendliest of the Northern Track cities to us."

Nelo nodded. "It is friendly because the Justice and Jailor and others in the town are open to bribes. They know if they tell the Patron in the store Callis works at, someone will approach them to bribe them for the Viklanders' freedom. We believe they still think their contact is the Patron."

"Does Callis help Ross? Could she tend his rabbits and he take over for Arden?"

"No," Josef said promptly. "Do not make that mistake, Tiju Tia. Ross is the *titiro mai ki ahau*. Callis will dress in men's clothes and help us with our nighttime work. She also likes the healing she learned from Siba. She has taken injured Viklanders to the house south of the Track and mends them if they are not so badly wounded. Ross could be more than he is, he is strong enough and smart. But he does not listen to others, and I do not trust him with my life as I trust Callis. She is more than competent, but without another to help her, she is already doing more than one person could or should."

"This is good to know," murmured Tiju Tia. She turned to Nelo. "Dica and Tyra were yours before they were mine. Tell us about the northern estates. What do you need to say?"

"Just what I said earlier. Dica stands alone at her house, but she hears much and sends it along to Tyra on her half days. Tyra fits in well with Bima's network. She hears the news in the house, tells it to Therin who gets the news out to Inezi that a Viklander has been captured, or a battle has been fought, or Trouble is coming to dance. The gamekeeper's daughter is disregarded at Fortika. They call her misbred because her mother is not Kereki. Her father is ashamed of her and ignores her when he is with others. Because she is so disregarded, she can travel as she pleases. She takes Viklanders over the border or meets with a softfoot she calls Kern and turns over papers and maps. I meet with both of them often and move information and people." He paused and looked at me when I startled at Kern's name.

When I said nothing more, Nelo continued, "Kid is critical to us at Evensong. He is like having a traitor in the general's tent, there are so many Kereki army officers entertained there. He writes down what he hears and sees and hides it in places where I know to look. I try to get to Evensong often because I can take his written words and bring them to the Viklander softfoots or Inezi. He says he has less risk than he did in Kerek City, but it is not a position I would choose. He has a braver heart than I do."

Tiju Tia narrowed her eyes. "Do I need to know what are in these written words?"

Nelo looked surprised. "I don't know what they say. Kid has told me they are a code he has from Rani and Kern. Even if I could read Keresh, he says I would not know these words and therefore I cannot be in danger. He told me…" Nelo stopped abruptly.

I waited for Nelo to say more, but when he didn't, the room fell awkwardly silent.

Finally, Tiju Tia said, "He has always had a strong stomach for danger, that one." She drummed her fingertips on the table as the others sipped their coffee. "If I lost Balza and Falan," she began.

Josef choked and put his coffee cup down suddenly. I noted his fingers were white as they gripped the table. Tiju Tia gave him a long look.

"I can see I should have said that differently," she said drily.

"I meant to say, 'If I closed the stop at Balza and moved Falan to Cloa,' could I free up Arden to be another traveling manabout—someone without a position to wander where we needed him?"

Nelo cocked his head. "Linna wouldn't be safe in Cloa. Their house is too close to the streets of the village, and she is too pretty to be living alone, or even if she and Falan lived together. Linna and Arden work well together. They are both very clever, and sometimes when I think there is no hope for a rescue, they create a plan no one else could see. You made the right decision to put Arden and his dog in Cloa together with Linna. It is up to Josef and me and the others to determine how we can use him without losing him."

CHAPTER 18

ZREN JANIN AND THE BRIARS OF BETRAYAL

I climbed into the rag and bone wagon and marveled at my good fortune. The sun was a solid hand's width above the horizon. I had not gotten up before everyone else, in the middle of the night, or been forced to run off to a rescue without first meal. In fact, on the wagon seat next to me was a basket of bread and cheese, jams, honey, cold meat pies, and West Islands steel flasks of cold spring water. As little as three years ago, I had never traveled anywhere but on my own two feet. And while I would never willingly choose to ride a horse if there were alternatives, I quite liked sitting on a wide wagon seat between a sturdy team of horses and arriving at my destination with my feet as fresh as when I climbed out of bed that morning.

Tiju Tia and I were traveling together this time. She and Oro had some difficulties on the last run, or specifically Oro did. It seemed some people in one of the smaller remote settlements had taken offense to his Viklander looks and tried to make trouble. Cooler heads prevailed and Tiju Tia and Oro had been permitted to leave without harm. Now Tiju Tia had decided I would accompany her on the routes, and Oro would take over more of the manabout duties at Manumina.

Oro was definitely not pleased and protested he was being punished for nothing he could do or change. It was true he could do nothing about the grandparent who had given him his Viklander straight black hair and his pale golden skin. But what else could be done?

Piffik expressed his pleasure at having him help in the woodworking shop during the Wet. But Oro was still sulky. I tried hard not to take offense at how he viewed my work at Manumina.

I leaned back on the wagon seat and waited for Tiju Tia. The wind had already freshened, warning us we probably would be caught in a sudden downpour or two, but I was truly looking forward to the next eight days.

Tiju Tia came out of the guesthouse wearing another of her traveling disguises: a shapeless, sand-colored dress which washed out her face and hair, worn soft leather Kereki boots, and a patched and faded traveler's cloak in a color so nondescript the Wrens called it "dirt."

We would be hauling supplies this trip. There would be few stops to buy and sell clothing along the way. It had been fifteen days since the rescue at Regno, and Lomes had given us maps to the Viklander drops. Since then, Josef and Nelo, and then Arden and Josef, had been searching them out, fortifying them, and leaving the messages and clues Rell had written in Vik for Viklanders needing help. Tiju Tia and I were to get more Kereki clothes to them, and food and coin to the Wrens for their own use as well as the rescues. Maps, news of recent activity and where, and coins—the Wrens needed it all.

Tiju Tia pulled herself up beside me. The left sleeve of her shirt had been sewn shut and I watched as she quickly adapted to using only her right hand. The casual observer would focus only on her missing hand, forgetting what we looked like. Well, unless we looked like Oro.

"You're certainly cheerful this morning," she noted as she reached for the reins.

"I am," I agreed. "You understand the importance of the proper start to the day. None of this traveling in the middle of the night." I smiled at her. "Or before first meal." I released the brake on the wagon, and we were on our way.

In the years before I had even heard of Manumina, Piffik and his father had been the main contacts with the Kereki settlements and towns. With his father, Piffik had sold handmade goods to the stores and people, purchased what the Conrosans could not grow, make, or butcher themselves, and served as the face of a community who kept themselves apart. Piffik's father had been known as Mr. Qanaq and Piffik had been called "Boy" until the day came when Piffik rode the cart alone. No one asked after his father or expressed their sorrow at his passing. They looked up, saw one person on the cart, and addressed him as Mr. Qanaq.

Once Piffik's father had died, other Conrosans would occasionally make the trip to Sary, Ahni, or Ishes, but anything farther fell solely into Piffik's travels. To that end, he had made a number of half-tracks and shortcuts across the flat scrubland. I had seen the maps when he had shown Chul all those years ago. They had saved my life then, and they saved the Wrens now.

Piffik drew his maps for the Wrens from memory and told us which neighbors had granted permission to cross their lands, and which settlements were so neglected or abandoned, they could be crossed without concern. He told us where he had spent nights sleeping rough and where he had seen evidence of bandits or outlaws. We knew when he was traveling alone he carried no weapons, his belief in non-violence was so strong. However, he said, he had learned to be a little more flexible when there were Viklanders or Wrens in his care. He told us in all the years he traveled, he had never been hurt nor harmed, although he had lied for his life on more occasions than he had fingers and toes. He said this so the Wrens understood the skills learned in Kerek City were also important now. He made the Wrens feel as if the years they had done what they must to survive were of value. They should not be ashamed of their past.

So while Tiju Tia and I would check on the Wrens, Piffik and Oro would head south to Ahni, and Roy, and Hall, to deliver furniture, buy wood from the sawmill, and hopefully pick up some commissions. I smiled in my contentment and put my boots up on the buckboard.

Tiju Tia raised an eyebrow.

"Life is good." I thought a little more. "Everything I am and that I have, is because you and your brother stopped to do a kindness on the road to Aldi. It was only a moment's decision for you, but it meant everything to me."

"We seldom know the reach of our actions. But I have told you before, it was Koanga who insisted we stop and help you. I would have been content to continue my journey home. I had already lived in Kerek for three years and thought you were a trap that meant us harm. So you must blame my brother for your life and not me." She cut her eyes at me and smiled.

"I used to believe that." I kept my eyes on the surrounding scrubland. Kereki bandits found far richer pickings by following and ambushing army wagons, but if they were bored or desperate, we would make an easy—although poor—target. Tiju Tia kept a short bow at her feet, but I was still helpless at anything beyond hand-to-hand fighting.

I had taught Rell to fight with a dagger and a Sailor's Curse, and in return, she tried to teach me the Viklander crossbow while she was teaching the other Wrens. When I missed the target all three times, Rell had given me a long look. Then she had marched me up to the target and had me shoot a quarrel at a distance no longer than a coffin. I was embarrassed, but I hit it dead center. Then she backed me up the width of a house, and I hit the target again. Then we walked back to the original starting point, and I missed the target completely; going so far to the right, I missed the surrounding bales used for protection.

"Huh," she had said. She had looked at the target a long time, and then said, "Well, you don't teach a bird of prey to swim." And that was my last crossbow lesson.

"Silver for your wisdom? You've been quiet over there for a while, and it's too early to be thinking about midday and the sweets Rygee may have packed for us."

I thought about what I wanted to say. "When you were training the Wrens at Manumina, you talked so much about *titiro mai ki ahau* and *titiro atu*—'look at me' and 'look away.' Things to do to keep our enemies focused on what we want them to be focused on and not what we are doing. You praised Josef and

Arden for understanding that instinctively. That even as children, Josef used his beauty as a 'look at me,' and Arden used his dog as a 'look away.'"

"Were you learning as well as listening?" I could hear the smile in Ngahuru's voice.

"I think," I said slowly, "I think when you and Koanga found me on the road to Aldi, you used Koanga to keep my attention so I would not learn who you were and how you were hunted by three nations. As I became infatuated with your brother, because I had never known kindness before, you were content to have my heart smashed because you knew my feelings would be non-returned. Then, when you learned I was not one of your many pursuers trying to capture you for King or coin, you decided to use me as a 'look at me.' Few people on the Coast Road, or even in Matasi, would have ever seen a Conrosan. In fact, I didn't even know I was a Conrosan. So by dangling me like a bright and shiny charm, again, no one would look too closely at you."

I sat back triumphant. Ngahuru said nothing and finally, I asked, "Well, is this not true?"

"Of course, it's true." She smiled gently. "Well, except for getting your heart 'smashed.' I needed to get all three of us out of Kerek City and to a safe port. I am sorry you felt I would willingly sacrifice you, but I was not sorry your feelings for

Koanga meant you would protect us until we reached Salisport. At the time, I felt I had enough to worry about. I didn't need to worry about whether you would turn on us in our sleep. We were too exhausted to set watches."

She smiled mischievously. "It is also true, this is my plan now. People will spend so much time admiring you from top to toe, I'll hand off the supplies to the Wrens in plain sight."

She patted me gently on my knee. "Don't look so sad, Zren. I enjoy your company, I must, because of all the fingersweets Rygee packed for us, I'll only see but one or two." She laughed at her own joke, and I only pretended to scowl at her.

We were headed to the very western edge of Tiju Tia's network. Ven Wila, one of the Viklander soldiers who had accompanied Ngahuru home to the West Islands from Salisport, was running a "hunt and hobble" group of soldiers, softfoots, and other assorted Viklanders with special talents. One of Ngahuru's favorite Wrens, Jenny, was part of this group as well, but she had never traveled to Manumina, and I had never met her.

The purpose of all the "hunt and hobble" patrols was to be a line from the Cold Mountains and over the Northern Track which supplies, weapons, and Kereki softfoots did not cross. The group's strength was to hit their mark and hide, merging into the countryside only to turn up days and distance away from the smoldering ruins. Their endurance and cunning were renowned and talked about by other Viklanders. It also made them nearly impossible to resupply from their own army. Instead, Jenny was in rare contact with Falan in Balza or pulled emergency supplies from Josef's house when he was out softfooting on his own and she was in the area.

For this trip, we would first meet with Falan in Balza. As a shopgirl, we would hope she would have news for us, and we might have a message from Jenny. But between now and then, were two nights of sleeping rough, meals over a fire, and decons of time to pass.

"Tell me a story," I prompted.

"I should make you tell me a story, one of the Constellation tales in its original Wester. But then I would feel compelled to correct your pronunciation and your words, and the story would lose its joy for both you and me." She gave a long pause. "Alright then, I shall tell this one in Conrosan. It is a Conrosan fairy tale, and I can never have too much practice in a language not my own." She handed over the reins, leaned back, and dropped her voice into a storyteller's cadence.

"In the days of long ago, the border between Conrosa and the fae was not so well guarded as it is now. Sprites and goblins, monsters without names, and mists without faces would dance in the land of the humans to cause trouble and strife.

Now in those times, there was a hero born. No one in Conrosa knew his parents, or his age, or his place of birth. Some said he was a changeling left by the fae who took a liking to the humans and decided to be their champion…

As Ngahuru told the story of Zren Janin and the Briars of Betrayal, I let my mind drift. She was a good storyteller in her own right, but all of the Conrosan fairy tales had a message and a caution. I wasn't sure what briars were, but I certainly understood the "thorns of broken trust are sharp indeed."

I thought of the Wrens and how they often put their lives in each other's hands. How the Conrosans of Manumina trusted those of us left behind to keep a home they could come back to. How the Viklanders had been told there were Kerekis willing to help them and to trust the maps left behind for them. How Piffik and Siba, two friends from childhood, had worked together to tame a half-wild child—me, and heal a completely broken warrior—Rell. How Rygee had been afraid he would be murdered every day of Miya's thirteenth trek across the Northern Track, and now he was the farm manager of Manumina. How I had trusted Ngahuru to help us just on the strength of a letter I had written.

"…And so Zren Janin reminded the foolish little boy, to 'Remember the good in people and keep the confidences entrusted to us,'" she finished with a flourish.

"Mmmmm. That's a nice one too," I said neutrally. I hadn't realized I had drifted off to my thoughts that long.

"I chose that one specifically for you today."

I sat up a little straighter. "Why?"

She waved her left hand, the one with the sleeve shown shut in the air. "Remember when I first arrived, and you saw my sleeve rather than my hand and glove, and I said there was a story behind it, and it wasn't what it seemed?"

I tried to think back. "Yes?" I offered tentatively.

Tiju Tia carefully looked away from me, and I worried.

"The Wrens and I encountered Ven Wila after their group had hunted a camp of thieves. They had eliminated them but had injured among them. Ven Wila thought I was an old woman with a wagon full of children fleeing the city and had thought to offer a night's protection in exchange for help."

"I remember this," I said. "You told me Solkka Ulani was a part of her group as well."

"But even though I introduced myself as Tiju Tia, he looked closely at my face, and his eyes dropped to my left hand where I was wearing my black glove. He gave me a large grin." She shot me a look. "'Tiju Tia of Kerek City,' he had repeated slowly, 'I do remember you,' he said. 'You were introduced to me by your friend Zren Janin, who has since become my friend as well. You and your children are welcome at our fire.'"

She was silent for so long, I tried to think of what she was trying to tell me. "I did not know you were so well acquainted with Solkka Ulani," she finally spoke.

"He and Bima came to Manumina. You heard this story," I protested. "It is how Chul Swyler the firemaster took Piffik's sister, Aajan, to Juisiti to be educated in the academies because the Qanaqs could never have afforded her to go."

She sighed. "And in return you betrayed my secret?"

"What? No! I would never tell anyone you have skin of two different colors. You said it was important no one outside of the West Islands knows."

"And yet, Solkka Ulani knows. I am sure of it."

"Solkka knows only Ngahuru and Tiju Tia is the same person. He said he saw you twitch an imaginary glove over your hand in Salisport at the Ambassador's reception and that made him curious. He remembered a street runner in Kerek City who always wore a glove—supposedly to keep the messages he carried clean and unmarked from grime and sweat. Then in the West

Islands, he saw you in disguise as a Kereki youth with a glove on your left hand, and it all snapped together for him. He told me when he was here and begged me not to tell anyone. That Matasi and Kerek, and even Vikland, would hold your life in balance for your secrets."

"Solkka Ulani wouldn't say that," she scoffed. "Some would consider it treason against Vikland for him to know and say nothing. You broke my trust, Zren. It has been hard for me to understand because I cannot fathom why you would do such a thing."

She lifted up her hand, and carefully unbuttoned the sleeve to uncover her hand, rich with dark brown color, pink-palmed, whole and complete. Then she held up her other hand, the one leached of color, grey-white. I had seen her swim naked in a pond once and knew the pale skin ran from her face to her right hip in a diagonal line, blotted with color above, and dips like old candle wax below.

This was part of the secret that made Ngahuru the great Softfoot. She could change the color of her skin. She said she claimed no gender and therefore could wear anyone she chose. Her tongue had no accent whether she was dressed as a Kereki or a West Islander. She was built close to the ground as most West Islanders were and could pass for a Kereki youth at the edge of childhood, an old woman, or a wealthy West Islands matron. I had seen all of these maskovestos and others.

"You thought I would share such a thing? Tell your story that did not belong to me? Why?" I felt so hurt she would even consider such a thing about me.

"And that's what I have been trying to figure out. You don't feel guilt or don't show it, so I am at a loss, Zren, I am truly at a loss." She looked sad.

I took a deep breath and pulled together my thoughts. "Ngahuru, in all the time you have known me, you know my face will not let me lie. Then let me tell you this. It was Solkka Ulani who told me you were able to change who you were, but he did not know how. He told me you were a treasure of the West Islands, and I should never reveal your secret and he would not reveal the secret either. At the time, I thought he meant he would keep your secret in exchange for my body, but he said no." I gave her a small smile. "I like Solkka, Ngahuru, I like him a lot. But, you should know I would not trade your secrets for him to like me in return."

I stopped the wagon and looked into her face. She searched me so long, I felt she was looking into my very heart.

Finally, she merely said, "We should have had this conversation when I first arrived." She reached for the reins, and I handed them over.

We continued on to Balza.

CHAPTER 19

TIJU TIA SHOWS MERCY

"Do Viklanders have stories? How come I have never heard any?" I mused aloud.

"They do. They're called the Wisdom of the Warrior. The Viklanders write down their stories and study them. They tell of historical and mythical battles, strategies, conquests, and rebellions. The stories teach a code of ethics and give cautionary tales of those who seek too much power or seek wars for the lust of battle."

I wrinkled up my nose. "That sounds…dull."

Tiju Tia laughed. "Compared to Zren Janin and the Briars of Betrayal? Yes, I suppose it does." She pointed at a little valley just below the rise we were traveling. "But we've whittled the day away and I can see the cottage we will be staying in for the night."

I looked ahead. To call the dilapidated building 'a cottage' was optimistic at best.

"Will that stay upright for the entire night?" I asked. "I would hate to cough and find myself surrounded by rafters."

"It will hold." Tiju Tia smiled. "Please ensure we will be the only inhabitants, and I will cover you. Remember, 'cio claro' if it is clear. Anything else, and I shoot the first one out the door, even if it is you." She bent down and grabbed her short bow and quiver.

I jumped down from the wagon seat and pulled a dagger from my waist sheath. There were two more in my boots and a Sailor's Curse in my felted tunic pocket. Ngahuru watched me as I silently touched them all, but she didn't say anything. I think she knew touching my weapons made me feel safe. I started down the hill.

I walked around the back of the building first. There were no windows facing north. I looked for footprints, water markings, and tie-outs for horses. Nothing. I circled east and picked up recent hoof prints. One horse—headed to the house. I backed up quickly and signaled Tiju Tia. She turned the team sideways and stepped down to hide behind the wagon.

"Hail the house!" she called. "We are neutral in the war between Kerek and Vikland. We seek water for our horses and a fire against the night." She continued to stand protected by the wagon, while I jogged around to the west window and peeked in.

The horse was unsaddled and stood in the middle of the one room. There were two young men, both in the uniform of the Kereki army. One was obviously injured, laying on the floor, white-faced and breathing hard. The second boy didn't look up at Tiju Tia's call but continued leaning over the injured soldier.

I circled to the front of the house and signaled her to know she had two in the house, one injured, one horse, no visible weapons.

She nodded and continued talking, "One of us is Conrosan, and I have some small healing skills. May we help you?"

I stepped into the open doorway just as the younger one pushed to his feet.

"Can you help?" he asked anxiously, "It's my brother."

I waved over Tiju Tia.

Once she arrived, I introduced her as Tiju Tia had taught me. "This is my mother who took me in when I was small. Should I stand out here, or may I come in to protect everyone in the house?" Tiju Tia pushed past me with a small leather bag of medicinals. She had read the situation exactly right. The two didn't care who we were as long as we could help.

She examined the boy on the floor and then stood aside so I could see the damage as well. It was a quarrel. A Vikland bolt must have been shot at fairly close range to be driven in so deeply to the shoulder.

"When did this happen?" Tiju Tia asked sharply.

"Yesterday morning at dawn. Just northwest of Huk. Our patrol had been tracking a small group of Viklanders separated from their main regiment. They had stopped to rest for a few decons, so we were going to take them at dawn. Our captain said half of them were girls, so we didn't need to send a messenger asking for more soldiers."

"Hmmm." Tiju Tia muttered under her breath, "And that was his fatal mistake."

"Their watch saw us and before we were even in the clearing they were armed and ready. When Dony went down, I just grabbed the nearest horse and threw him on. I wasn't going to wait around for the bodies to be counted."

"Where were you headed? You know you're south of the Northern Track now." Tiju Tia pulled out a narrow steel knife no longer than my hand. She cut deep around the quarrel and the injured boy twitched. "Red, hold him down." I smiled at my old name, dropped to my knees beside her, and braced the soldier on the floor. Tiju Tia looked up, "Where were you headed?" she asked again gently, "Home?"

The boy nodded miserably. "I thought if I could get him home, Mama could take care of him. He never wanted to join the army in the first place. When I said I was going to run away and join up, Papa said he would make my brother go along, and did I really want to do that to Dony? I didn't think he was serious." He looked down at his feet. "I was wrong."

There was a flash of white bone, and Tiju Tia grabbed the quarrel, slimy with blood, and pulled it out. She looked up at me just as the upright brother fainted mid-sentence.

"Kill them both?" I asked reaching for my Sailor's Curse.

"That seems a little harsh," Tiju Tia said, "especially since I just went to all that trouble to save this one." She gestured at Dony, now unconscious from the pain. "Walk with me." She pushed herself to her feet and we stepped outside. She started walking to the wagon and I followed.

"Think on this, Zren." She tipped her canteen over her bloody hands and wiped them on an old apron in the cart. "They know us as Red and his mother. We happen by with horses, I heal the injured boy, we share some food, and in exchange we get Kereki battle numbers, locations, and I am guessing some Viklanders still separated from their unit. These two just want to go home. They don't care and they won't tell. Hardly worth a murder or two, is it?"

"We're staying here? With them?" I was incredulous.

"Well, no. I didn't say we were going to be foolish about it. They are still deserters, and both the Kereki army and Viklander patrols will not look on them fondly. Now let's take out just enough food to make us look generous." She poked about in the food bag and then sifted through the old clothes for rags to be used as bandages, two pairs of pants and two Kereki shirts and felted tunics. She reached in one of the hidden compartments for Rygee's apple jack.

"We're sharing that?" I was dismayed. We all loved Rygee's apple jack, especially me.

"It's worse than that, Red. We won't be drinking it. But I don't have any other spirits to wash out the wound." She loaded up my arms with the clothes, took the food and drink herself, and we walked back to the cottage.

The younger boy was awake and rubbing the side of his head. "For a moment, I thought you two had hit me on the side of the head and robbed us."

"No." Tiju Tia smiled. "Just went to get some supplies. I thought maybe you two hadn't eaten for a while." She passed over buns stuffed with cheese and jam. Then she smeared honey on the wound and soaked one of the rags with apple jack and bandaged Dony's shoulder. "I'm sorry I don't have any raw spirits, but have your mama change the bandage as soon as you get home, and he should recover. You'll be doing his chores for a while."

"As long as I bring him home alive," he said fervently.

"This is a delicate matter, but if you are not planning to rejoin your regiment, it might be best not to be wearing your uniforms. My boy, Red, picked out some clothes that might fit, and I thought I might take your uniforms in exchange for payment."

The boy looked relieved. "Thank you. I'll make that exchange and gladly."

Tiju Tia handed over another bun. "So where were you coming from? Since it's just me and my boy, you can understand how we wouldn't want to be running into soldiers—of any kind." She didn't make eye contact as she gave Dony some apple jack to drink. When he sputtered awake, she substituted a waterskin. He drank while she continued to ask questions.

"Huh-uh. And how many people were in your patrol? How far away is your main force?" As Tiju Tia walked the younger soldier through all the information she wanted, she got the injured brother sitting up and focusing. She handed him a bun as well and soon both of them were eating greedily. Tiju Tia pulled two apples out of her pocket. "Do you have a knife to cut these?" she asked the brothers. "Or should I have my Red do it?"

Dony gestured to his boot and his brother pulled out an old iron knife.

"I'm afraid I lost mine in the battle. I remember I had one to cut the tie out line on the horse."

"Oh, is that a Viklander horse?" Tiju Tia peered at it closely. "I haven't seen one of those before." I snorted, and Tiju Tia raised an eyebrow at me. She handed me Dony's knife, and I handed her the cut apples. She passed out the cut slices of apple chattering easily about the Viklander horse while I slipped Dony's knife into my boot.

Finally, she must have decided she had enough information. She discreetly cleared her throat.

"If you boys can change your clothes, then my boy and I will be on our way. We need to find shelter before dark." She pushed herself to her feet. "We'll just stand outside and wait." She gathered up the remaining food and pretended not to notice how their hungry eyes tracked her movements.

"Wait," Dony said. "I have a little coin. Could we buy some more food?"

Tiju Tia pretended to consider. "Actually, I'll trade you the rest of this food for that Viklander travel roll behind your saddle."

Dony's brother walked over and unbuckled it from the saddle.

There were two more buckles around it and he reached to undo those as well, Tiju Tia quickly murmured, "Oh, that's fine, I'll just take it like so."

She left the food in the carry bag on the floor but picked up the waterskin. "We'll just be outside. Just come out with the other clothes." As we stepped out into the sunset, I looked at Tiju Tia and there was a small smile playing about her lips. I knew she was happy with the day, even if it meant we would be sleeping rough. The younger boy came to the door with the uniforms.

"We're keeping our boots," he said gruffly. "They were ours and not given to us by the army."

"I noticed," said Tiju Tia. "The army did not do well by you. I wish you a safe journey home." She nodded to me to take the clothes from his hands, and together we walked to the wagon. Our patient horses shifted a bit, and then we both climbed up on the wagon seat. Tiju Tia picked up the reins. We slowly and silently clopped west on a nearly invisible track.

We took the first opportunity after a decon's ride to find fresh water and protected shelter. Not bothering with a fire or a watch, we tied out the horses, and rolled ourselves in our traveler's cloaks to sleep.

It wasn't until the next morning Tiju Tia was willing to tell all her secrets. My curiosity was getting to be more than I could bear, but every time I started to ask, I held my tongue. So I unbuckled the hobbles and put our two mares back in their traces. As we rolled up our cloaks and I rooted in the food basket for first meal, Tiju Tia quietly hummed under her breath.

"So, Zren." We climbed up on the wagon seat, and I lightly slapped the reins while she fished out a bun with cheese. "Tell me what you learned yesterday."

Finally! I told her the younger brother was so talkative with worry even the Wrens would have shushed him. I thought the supply trip was going to be turned into a rescue mission although the Viklanders could be anywhere and was this how she did rescues? Just drive around until Viklanders stumbled into the roadway? When she was in this disguise as Tiju Tia and not in her West Islands paints as Ngahuru, how did they know she was a friend anyway? What was the point of the uniforms? Wouldn't it look like we had murdered and kept the Kereki uniforms if a Justice would search our peddler cart of used clothing? And most importantly, why was she so giddy about a Viklander blanket she would trade away food—enough for two days of travel?

"I recognized a Viklander mapcase behind the saddle. I would have left them food anyway. They were nothing more than children, Zren, but once I saw that, I knew we could do a barter. I was worried he knew what it was, and I would have to give up a steel flask or even do a forced barter—thanks for taking away Dony's knife by the way—but I think the little one was so scared and he fled so quickly, he never had the time to assess his belongings or surroundings."

I craned my head over my shoulder to look at the buckled saddle roll.

"It just looks like an extra blanket."

"That's the point, Zren." She smiled. "It's many layers that have a seam down the middle and folds in half like a book. Now within the 'book' are several pockets or pages to store maps or important dispatches."

"And the first rainstorm of the Wet comes early and…" I interrupted.

"And then we have another gift of the West Islands to the world—bee paper."

I squinted at her. "You're making this up."

She laughed. "When the beekeepers have removed all the honey, they sell the honeycombs to the bookbinders and mapmakers. They, in turn, boil the honeycombs and skim off the impurities. Then when only the beeswax is left, it is melted again and poured into large shallow pans. Maps are then sunk into the hot wax and coated on all sides. Then they are allowed to cool and dry over other pans. Once they are cooled, they can be rained on, drenched in a water crossing, or suffer the waves on a West Islands boat and still the map will hold fast. West Islanders have freely shared this with Matasi and Kereki sea captains, Viklander diplomats and soldiers who must cross the Silver Mountains, and now Conrosan manabouts."

"Huh." I rocked back on the seat. "Can I see these maps?"

"I would like to turn them over untouched to a Viklander patrol captain or even a softfoot so they know their work is not compromised, but that will depend on what we find northwest of Cloa. Usually there is something on the buckles or just inside the mapcase to tell the receiver if the case has been tampered with. But if you wish, I could teach you how to do it when we are back at Manumina. I know there are ground bees where we can get the wax honeycombs if Siba and Rell don't have any."

I was content with that. I watched the broad backs of the team in front of me for a while. I wondered how young the two brothers truly were that we had met last night and how long they had been in the army. I thought about Rygee and Nebs and if they would have been fighting the Viklanders if Miya hadn't convinced them to desert. I wondered about Kerek City and the others I had known in Lowertown. Had the army come through and conscripted any of the people I had known? What if the Wrens met someone they had known from before? It wasn't so unusual. Brick and Goblin had found me, although it hadn't ended well for them. They had died by Kereki metal poisoning, which was a fancy way of saying 'self-defense' in a country where what you owned was what you could defend. Ngahuru had killed them both.

And that was so depressing, I changed my thoughts.

"What stories are you going to tell me today?"

Tiju Tia snorted. "Well, not Conrosan fairy tales. Any more folktales about Zren Janin and you are liable to float right off this wagon seat. Mmmmm. No more tales of the West Islands, I want you to hear them from Koanga in person. You are still planning to visit the West Islands some day?"

"I am. I would like to see your brother again and offer him my friendship—now that I know what that is." I let the chagrin show on my face.

She smiled gently. "You're a treasure, Zren. Just when I think I have seen all the bright and shiny you can offer, you smile like that."

I didn't know what that meant and I didn't get to ask, because Tiju Tia decided to tell me stories of the Viklanders—the Wisdom of the Warriors—she called it.

They weren't dull at all. There were warriors who defended entire villages in single combat, and warriors who challenged villains that turned into monsters as they fought. There were stories of how the jeong bong became a revered weapon almost always fought in pairs, and how the tahn bong grew from a weapon of rebellion among the peasants to the weapon used to demonstrate beautiful fighting and grace before Empresses.

But my favorite story that entire day was how Vikland archers won the battle from monsters in the sky. The winged monsters only thought they had to win against jeong bongs. Their strategy was to dive from the sky and kill every other warrior rendering the jeong bongs nearly useless.

"Instead," Tiju Tia continued in a dramatic voice, "as the monsters raced screeching to earth, with their wings pulled back and their talons outstretched, a woman cried out, 'Weapons up! Crossbows fire at will!' Before the winged monsters could fathom what the crossbows were, much less what they could do, the quarrels flew straight and true and saved the sons and daughters of Vikland!"

"Wow!" I exclaimed. "That was a good one!"

She gave me a big grin. "I like that one too," she nodded in agreement.

"So why do Viklanders use crossbows and bolts and West Islanders use short bows with a quiver full of arrows?" I nudged my foot against Tiju Tia's short bow resting at her feet.

"Crossbows are easier to use. Once the bow is cocked, it doesn't take any extra energy. Vikland's border has always had trouble with Kereki raiders. And if you are an eleven-year-old child with a Kereki raider running at you with a pike and an iron knife, any advantage you have will help you live to fight another day." Tiju Tia gave me a long look. "There are many places in the known world where children are not allowed to be children."

I nodded sadly. I had lived, and barely escaped, from one of them.

"Short bows like we use in the West Islands are lighter and easier to carry distances for hunting small game. Some sailors tie a fine fiber to the shaft of the arrow and use it to spear fish. But truthfully, we don't have enemies in the West Islands. An invading army could not sail as fast as our small boats. Our inventions from the Smith with metals and foundries can defeat the poorer weapons of other countries. We share our knowledge freely. That is why the murder of our Ambassador in the streets of Kerek City years ago was such an atrocity. This King must be held accountable," she ended sharply.

I could say nothing to that, and so we rode on silently through the scrublands of Kerek.

CHAPTER 20

WELL HELLO, OLD FRIEND

We came over a small rise and ahead of us was a tidy homestead. The house had deep scorch marks up to the roof on the east side. *A runaway cooking fire,* I thought. The barn still looked to be in good shape, and there was a fenced in paddock with green grass and a working bubbler—water shooting up between rocks. Artesian wells were not common this far from the coast in Kerek, and I wondered why settlers would abandon a home with such a reliable water source. There were no gardens or fields for a family to survive on. I looked at Tiju Tia and asked her.

"This place is one of ours, Zren. Rygee bought it with some of the coin from Miya. We may have to keep an eye out for trespassers, but everything you see here is ours. We'll sleep here tonight." We started down the rise, and I thought I saw movement at the barn.

"Barn!" I shouted and rolled off the wagon seat to hide behind the wheel just as I saw a man step out from the shadows of the barn door.

"Tiju Tia, cio claro!" he called. "It's Josef."

I stepped away from the wagon wheel and began to walk down the rise. Tiju Tia picked up the reins and drove the wagon beside me. Now I could see Josef's blond hair tied back in a tail. He was dressed in male Kereki pants with double Kereki ties about his calves and ankles. His farmer's shirt didn't billow at all but fit too snugly across his chest. He wasn't wearing an overtunic and had on Viklander boots. As one of the tallest Wrens, Josef, more than most, ended up giving the shirt off his back for the more muscular Viklanders. If he was here, I would guess there were rescued Viklanders in the house.

"This is unexpected," Tiju Tia muttered to me. "I thought he was meeting Kid near Evensong, or possibly even softfooting by the burnout at Earles."

"Is it a trap? Is he in trouble?" I pulled myself back up on the wagon seat.

"No, we have words for that. The all clear meant I can safely travel." She choked back a laugh. "He was just trying to prevent us from shooting him. He obviously doesn't know of your lack of skill with the bows."

I looked down my nose at her, but she had already slapped up the reins to hurry us down to the barn.

Josef held the barn door open, and we drove straight in. There was another wagon there and three horses munching away contentedly in their stalls. The barn itself looked clean and tidy as if the farmer had just stepped away for the day.

Josef talked as he unhitched the horses from the rag and bone cart. "Sure am glad to see you. Falan is in the house with four Viklanders. One is seriously injured, one is a softfoot who needs to get to Vikland as quickly as possible, and two are soldiers that want to rejoin any unit in the area or go back to Ishes and get reassigned out. Their strength is crossbows, and they kept their weapons. Falan has been collecting her Viklanders for the past three days, and we were hoping they could safely wait and recover until I could move them on. I sent Ross with word to Arden to help us, but Arden is being watched too closely by the stable owner—something about a missing horse we had to borrow for a rescue. We didn't get it returned before its true owner came looking for it."

"Are these?" Tiju Tia waved her hand at the horses in the stalls.

"All hired out. I had to use our coin. Ross and Callis brought them over from Huk. Callis thought it best for us to stay away from Balza. It's much too hot with skirmishes and stolen horses.

Falan said we needed to let the fuss die down in Cloa around Arden a bit."

"Good—what about Falan's position at the toggery? Won't she be missed?"

"We waited for her half day and came last night. She drove the wagon and I served as her outrider. She'll go back tonight." He explained their original plan had been for her to race back to Balza on the outrider horse, and he would take the wagon on to Manumina. It would put Falan at terrible risk if she met anyone, but they didn't see any other options.

"Your horses are rested?" Tiju Tia asked.

"Yes. Fed, watered, and rested. As are the soldiers inside."

"Well, let's go meet them." Tiju Tia led the way out of the barn and into the house.

Falan was standing in the kitchen over a table sorting out meager bandages with two of the soldiers. I could see another one lying down on a rope bed through an open door to the bedroom. The fourth person stood by the window looking out, but said nothing as he turned and watched us as we walked in.

"Bima?" I felt my jaw drop.

"Good evening, Zren. And I presume, you must be Tiju Tia. I heard your name called by the young man outside." He paused. "So you have come to our rescue." He didn't sound altogether pleased about it.

"We will merely help you along your way. The only one who needs rescuing is that injured soldier. You three are merely traveling along with us to keep each other company." Tiju Tia was nonchalant.

Bima gave a great sigh. "Even your manners are far better than mine. I apologize for my rudeness Tiju Tia. I am—all of us are—very grateful and appreciative for your assistance."

"It is always easier to give help and encouragement than to receive it. But we dance together, Bima, just out of the arms of Trouble. The Wrens of Manumina know if they are hunted to seek out you and yours just as you spread the word we have safe places to hide, and we will aid you however we can." She hesitated for a moment. "Your wounded soldier?"

"It's serious, but he will survive. We are traveling with a healer." Bima waved his hand at the table and one of the women looked up. "They want to get reunited with a unit as quickly as possible, but Falan couldn't make contact with the next stop so we all ended up here."

Tiju Tia tipped her head to the side. "Perhaps we should take a walk—you and I—there is something I traded for yesterday which might interest you." She opened the door again and ushered Bima out.

A moment later, Josef came in from the barn, crooked his finger at me, and I joined him outside. We walked up the same rise Tiju Tia and I had driven down earlier.

"So how is Manumina?" he began conversationally.

"Fine. I am fine. Tiju Tia is fine. Everything is fine." I squinted at him. "What do you truly want to know?"

He gave me a mischievous grin. "I want to know if you are traveling with Tiju Tia as a punishment or as a reward. I want to know what happened to Oro who is as tall and lanky as a sapling and could never be mistaken for you. I want to know when someone will be coming through with coin for me to buy food, and boots, and a pretty dress. I want to know if there are enough Kereki clothes for us on the rag and bone wagon for me to keep my own boots on occasion."

My jaw dropped. "You thought of all that just now?"

Josef's laugh was deep and unforced. He sat down in the grass and patted the ground beside him.

"Zren, I spend all my days listening and softfooting. This is the first chance I have had in—I don't know how long—just to do nothing except talk about nonsense and news." He leaned back and put his hands behind his head. "So talk until I fall asleep, Zren."

So I did. I told him how Tiju Tia and Oro had run into problems with some hot-headed youths who had taken exception to the grandparent who gave Oro his fine Viklander face. How my beautiful Conrosan face is now supposed to so dazzle Tiju Tia's customers she can make her deliveries under everyone's nose.

"I hope those are Tiju Tia's words because then I will recognize them as the sarcasm they are meant to be. Otherwise, my feelings will be hurt she didn't ask me."

I thought he was serious. "You are very beautiful, Josef, and no one will ever say I am handsome, but you are here and I was there…"

"I'm joking, Zren, I'm joking." He waved his hand in the air. "But go on. Tell me what good things are on the rag and bone wagon for my costumes."

"Mmmmm. Kereki army uniforms?"

"No! Truly?"

"Yes, we got them yesterday, but what would you do with them?"

Josef explained having uniforms would allow the Wrens to make daylight shifts of Viklanders from safe hiding locations to eastward connections. No one in the small towns and settlements would challenge them.

"You do it yourself, Zren. You drop your eyes when a Kereki patrol passes you in a town or on the Northern Track. No one makes eye contact with the unknown soldiers and prisoners. While everyone is trying not to be noticed, we could just ride right through. This is wonderful news! What else are you hiding for us? Boots? A shirt that fits better than this one?"

I told him he could pillage through the cart after Tiju Tia was finished with Bima. I told him about the two boys we found in the abandoned cottage a day's drive east of here. I looked around at the settlement.

"Who takes care of this place?"

"We all do. It's only a day's walk from Balza and Huk. It's our bolthole in case we have trouble, or just need to hide a Viklander and we know the Kereki army will be passing through town. Callis uses it the most. There are weapons here, and some foodstuffs, but only the kind Rygee can preserve. No one is here long enough to tend a garden."

"Are there other places like this?" I wondered aloud.

"Yes." Josef then told me of the ones the Wrens used north between the Northern Track and the Cold Mountains. Most were barns, sheds, empty cottages from absent landowners. The worry there, of course, was anyone could use them. But there were other holdings like this one, he said, where Rygee or Piffik had bought the place and the Wrens maintained it well enough it was left alone.

"I live in one, as does Nelo. We must sleep rough many nights to be everywhere Tiju Tia needs us to be. Zren, I never thought I would have a place to sleep of my own through the night without care. It is this size—a front room, a bedroom, a hearth, no running water as you have at Manumina, but it is mine. Linna's is a little larger; it has a sleeping loft. You know Arden and Linna share a house as brother and sister just on the edge of Cloa? She continued to teach him his Keresh letters and now he and I can pass messages onward without involving the girls in their shops to read them first and tell us where we must take them."

He paused for a long moment. "Oro likes to talk with Linna when he comes with Tiju Tia to make deliveries. I thought that might be why you replaced him. That Tiju Tia was worried for Linna's maskovesto."

He grinned at me. "I have learned it is not so easy to be a brother, Zren. If Arden bristles too much when Oro appears, some Kerekis may think it is their right to 'help' Arden discourage Oro's visits. If Arden doesn't object enough, people may be suspicious the pair of them have Viklander sympathies. If they spend more time than they need to watching Arden's activities, that could put us all in danger if either of them are followed or questioned harshly by the Justice. The Cloa Justice is not our friend and cannot be bribed."

I thought of the letter Oro had given me before I left Manumina. "Tell no one of this, Zren. No one. But make sure Linna gets it even if you have to give it to her in the shop." At the time I had thought it was coin owed, or instructions, or to be truthful, I hadn't thought of it at all.

We had all been taught to pass along messages from Tiju Tia, Padro Morto, or the Wrens without question. I wondered if I should say something to Josef, but then I remembered Tiju Tia's story about Zren Janin and the Briars of Betrayal. I kept my silence.

"So Falan has to go back tonight." I changed the conversation.

"Yes. She must be in the shop tomorrow morning. She slept a little earlier, but tomorrow will not be an easy day. However," he trailed off, "Falan is formidable."

"You say that like you are afraid of her," I teased.

He gave me a small smile. "Do you know my story, Zren? No?" He paused. "I grew up in Kerek City. When I was very young, before I can remember, I was either sold to or found by Falan's father. He took me home and taught me songs and tricks to amuse those who came to gamble. I was to distract them from their losses. One time, a gambler said I was prettier than Falan, and her father had the idea to put my hair in curls and dress me like a little girl. They locked me nearly naked in my room to sleep every day, and every night I was dressed up and brought out to perform. The gamblers thought it was amusing to see me dressed as a girl one night and a boy another night. I had songs to sing and bits of clever talk to say. I was as young as Tyra the first time someone offered to buy my body. Falan stood up to her father and said I was too unripe. The price would be much better if he waited more years. Make a competition of it. He could build the anticipation, involve more bidders.

"That's when she started to take me out on the streets of the city. While her family was asleep after staying up all night, she would unlock me out of my room, dress me in her brother's clothes, and take me out into the city to memorize a way to escape. It is how Ngahuru found us. She needed softfoots in the gambling dens to see who was losing too much money and who would be open to bribes. In exchange, she promised Falan she would take us in at the West Islands embasado whenever Falan decided it was too unsafe for me to remain at the Red Cup."

He cleared his throat. "And that's how it began. I would tease and coo and gather secrets, then tell them to Falan as we looked for Ngahuru in the streets the next morning. If we didn't see her before I had to be locked back in my room, Falan would travel out again after midday with one of her father's men and pass the messages with a coin or a sweet to Dica. Did you know Dica used to be one of Nelo's Lost Girls?" A pause. "And then, Nelo would get the message to Ngahuru."

He blew out a noisy breath. "I know what it is to kill in self-defense—forced barter, death by misadventure. It is all Kereki metal poisoning. But I prefer to listen as scouts and patrols go by and capture the information I need and move it forward. Bodies are messy and raise questions I might not want to answer. But Falan… Falan prefers the short bow Tiju Tia gave her and is not so concerned with those questions."

"How do you know this?" I asked.

"I have known her all my remembered life. And she has a gambler's tell. She always strips the boots of her victims when she retrieves her arrows and searches the bodies for messages and maps. It makes the Kerekis nervous when they come across the bodies. As if the army scouts have so little value they are merely murdered for their boots." He grimaced and I wondered if he regretted telling me.

I considered his words and his mood. "Huh." I tried to keep a straight face. "Is that why you wear Viklander boots? So she would have to take the time to unlace them rather than just slide them off?"

I saw the shadow and I rolled away just as he let his arm flop to the ground where I was laying. "Funny, Zren, very funny."

I grinned at him. "Happy to be your amusement for the day." I pushed myself to my hands and knees and caught the movement of Bima and Tiju Tia walking across the yard.

"Look, they're headed back into the house. You want to raid the clothes now or wait?"

"She's carrying the food bag," Josef noted, "Let's go in the house first. I'm hungry."

While everyone ate the last of Rygee's already made food, Tiju Tia laid out the new plans. She would take the rested horses, the rag and bone cart, and Falan back to Balza with Josef as outrider. After leaving Falan, Josef would join her on her route as her *titiro mai ki ahau* and Kereki male protector. I would stay behind with the Viklanders and the other wagon. After an overnight rest for the horses, I would take everyone back to Manumina where we would pick up riding horses. Someone would take them over the border to Vikland where Bima would get everyone sorted out.

"Any questions?" Tiju Tia only waited a moment. "Good. Viklanders, we will need to find you other clothes. Your uniforms stick out like crows against the clouds. Zren will take the half-tracks so you should not encounter anyone else. No one will expect to see Viklanders so far south, but keep the hoods of your cloaks up and your weapons at the ready.

"We encountered deserters last night. You can hide your uniforms in the wagon if there is a place. You will need them once you cross your border into Vikland." She turned to walk out and saw Josef grab another meat pie and an extra piece of fruit. "You better come along as well. You need a new shirt at least." He winked at me and followed behind the others.

I wandered back into the bedroom where the soldier lay sleeping. He had a bandage about his head and the swollen wad of cloth covering his ear was dotted heavily with blood.

I backed out quickly and asked Falan, "What happened?"

"A long knife, I'm told. He deflected it away from his face and it took most of his ear. Lots of blood. That's why their healer gave him so much of their sleeping herbs. If we can—you can—get him to Manumina, the healer said he can be healed. It will take a while, but it is better than the alternative he was facing." She gave me a feral grin.

"Does he speak Keresh or only Vik?" I explained, "Will he know we are helping him, or will he think he was captured and I must watch my back?"

"I don't know. He's been like this since we picked him up two days ago."

"Well, Bima can talk Vik to him on the way and Rell can explain at Manumina." I looked back to her. "You are still safe in Balza?"

"Safer than Kerek City. I'll live, Zren."

"I'm trying to show off my good manners, Falan, don't be mean to me." I pouted to show her I was teasing.

She rolled her eyes. "I'm tired, Zren. I'm tired, and now I have to crawl back on a lurching wagon, drive all evening and half the night, and appear at my workplace tomorrow morning as if there is no place in Kerek I would rather be."

I said nothing.

"Oh, Zren. Fight with me. Snap and snarl like Nelo, or bite off some sarcastic remark like Josef does to help me sharpen my claws. Living at Manumina has taken all of Lowertown out of you."

That stung. "And living at Balza has done nothing to change you," I bit out. I paused. I didn't want to fight with her. "Why do you take the Kereki soldiers' boots after you kill them?"

"We always need boots for Viklanders." She sounded truthful but didn't meet my eyes.

I considered. "That is one reason, but that is not the reason you take the boots."

She gave me a long look. "Fine. I take the boots and put them over my own if they fit. If they don't, I wear theirs and put mine in a cloth bag around my neck. Anyone that comes across the bodies sees a trail of the dead men's footprints stomping about in multiple directions and it's harder for them to pick up my trail of tiny feet that come to the bodies but never leave."

My jaw dropped. "That's brilliant!"

"Yes, well, I learned it from Arden's dog. Arden gives it a pair of Viklander boots to sniff and then track. They use a funny oil on their boots to make them shine and his dog tracks the smell. It is why he can find so many lost Viklanders. So I wondered, if I tucked my skirts or my pant legs into the boots I stole, would Arden's dog be able to find me?

"We tried it and Arden said Mother found it very difficult. We think I could have gotten away if she hadn't seen me and recognized me. The Justices don't use dogs yet, but we don't want to wait until they do and then have a path lead straight to our doors."

"Does Tiju Tia know this?" I questioned.

"I'm sure she already knows. And since Arden's dog is smarter than the entire Kereki army, I am sure I am not detected as I move about the woods." She looked up as a shadow moved across the window.

"Are you ready to spend the next six decons with this pretty face?" Josef called out cheerfully. "I've hitched the fresh horses to Tiju Tia's cart and made a bed in the back for you of rose petals and Conrosan fairy dust." Josef gave me a sideways smile.

"Pretty is as pretty does, Josef. If you didn't share your smiles with half the countryside, I might consider it less of a burden to travel with you." She gathered up her cloak from the hook by the door and passed out into the early evening twilight without even a backward glance.

CHAPTER 21

BIMA AND TRUTH SIT AT THE SAME TABLE

After a flurry of goodbyes, nearly all from Josef, the Viklanders and I retreated to the house. The healer went back to check on the sleeping soldier, and Bima took up his vigil at the window.

"There's no main track near here," I offered. "We are between the Heartland Trail and the Huntsman's Trail, and you know the Northern Track is nearly a day's walk from here."

He grunted but said nothing. I stared at him, and now I could see the lines in his face. He tipped his head a little and the setting sun sparked off a flash of grey in his hair—just a few silver strands slipping through the black braid. I remembered when I first met him, I thought he and Miya were mid-thirties. But I hadn't known how to tell ages then. Now he looked so tired and discouraged, I wasn't sure how old he could be. I thought of Ngahuru and how she could make herself appear to be any age and wondered if Bima could do the same. I was going to walk away and leave him to his solitary watch when suddenly he spoke.

"Do you know, Zren, it's been three years since I have seen my family? I wonder if my youngest daughter would recognize me if I passed her on the street tomorrow. She seemed so young when I left."

I nearly squeaked in surprise. "You're married?"

He turned to me then and gave me a half smile. "I am. I have a wife I adore and two daughters. My heart nearly bursts when I think of them; I love them so much."

I tried all the bits and pieces of what I knew of Bima and nothing came together as a devoted family man.

"But," I scrunched up my face, "Didn't Miya and Solkka mock you for…" I fumbled for what I wanted to say.

"Tumbling out of other people's beds?" he sneered.

"Well," I cast about for a way to soften my response. "Well, yes."

He hesitated as if he was trying to come to a decision. "Zren, the academies at Juisiti are difficult. If you have good tutors and schools in your home district, if your parents take you to the festivals and the Empress's celebrations often, so you are not overwhelmed by the city and its pleasures when you arrive, then it is just one more step in your progression from child to adult. My parents were wealthy enough my sister and I did not lack, but we were indulged. If we did not appear for our classes, it was the tutor's fault. If we did not master the material, it was the tutor's fault. If we did not care for the tutor, it was the tutor's fault. By the time my sister and I traveled to the academies we were hopelessly behind and couldn't stay. I entered my military service early, my sister traveled to the West Islands and avoided even that responsibility."

He looked out the window again. "I met my future wife at my first posting in Matasi. I was a guard at the Alenti embasado. She was a few years older than I was and worked as a translator. I was barely eighteen when we married, which was legitimate, if not necessarily wise. As long as I was posted in Matasi, she and I would live together. Whenever I had to travel elsewhere, she, and then she and the babies, would move back to her parents' home in Alenti. Because her family was wealthy and her father could care for my family when I was away, we thought it best to stay in Matasi. My plan was to serve Vikland in Alenti. Now because of the war, I can't get to Matasi. Without me accompanying her, she and my daughters cannot move to Vikland. My parents have never met her in the sixteen years we have been married.

"My fellow softfoots and soldiers jape with me because they think I was married at the end of a Matasi farmer's pitchfork and forced to convert to the religion of the Lost God. None of those are true." He sighed. "But it doesn't matter, in the last few days, I have begun to despair I will ever see any of them again."

I sputtered, "But Josef had the extra horse, why didn't you take it and go? You would be at the Matasi border in six days. The three of them could have ridden in the cart together."

"Desert my post? Walk away from my responsibilities? It's love or duty, Zren. Today, duty wins. I pray to the Lost God he has seen this and gives me an easier choice tomorrow. I don't know that I could survive another battle like today." He was quiet for a long time, and I was too shocked to interrupt the silence. Finally, he nodded at the door. "I'll arrange the watches with the other two. Sleep tonight, Zren. You'll be driving all day tomorrow while we are tucked up tight in the wagon hiding our Viklander faces." He opened the door and slipped out while I stood there speechless.

CHAPTER 22

A TRICKSTER TALE

It was a quiet ride towards Manumina. The soldiers took turns riding with me on the wagon seat, crossbows unnocked, a quarrel in the hand, and barely hidden under their traveler's cloaks. Both spoke Keresh with thick accents and were content to ride along silently.

I wasn't sure if he regretted speaking so frankly with me, had a premonition of danger, or if he was still struggling with his soul, but Bima sat quietly in back with the injured soldier, hood up on his cloak, his face hidden. By the time we reached the rolling hills near the abandoned cottage, my nerves were screaming for someone to say something.

I set the brake on the wagon and wrapped the reins about. "I'll check to see if the cottage is empty. I need you to cover me. If I say, cio claro it means—"

"All clear," Bima said quietly. "It's Mata for 'all clear' or 'all is well.'" He smiled. "We'll all look out for you." He scrambled over the end of the wagon and crouched down next to me. All four of us slithered to the edge of the rise.

I heard the voices before I saw them. There were four soldiers and four fine horses. Two of the men were using crude shovels to pat down the soil on two freshly dug mounds the length of a man's body. There was already a wooden X at the top end of each grave. Another decon and we would have missed them entirely.

Bima whispered to the soldiers, "Officers first, diggers second." They nodded and nocked their quarrels. I had just turned to ask him what he was doing as the whoosh, whoosh of the crossbows responded to his quiet command of 'fire.' The officers dropped and died before the diggers could comprehend what had happened. As they straightened in surprise, two more quarrels struck true. The diggers collapsed in the dirt.

At the smell of death one of the horses nickered. No one came out of the building, so I pulled my waist dagger and crawled backward away from the edge. Once I reached the wagon, I walked in a large arc so I could come around the cottage from the north where I knew there were no windows. I could hear the stomp of another horse inside, and I felt a sick thud in my stomach as I guessed what I would find—the Viklander horse from the night before. Whether by accident or by design, the deserters had been discovered by other members of the Kereki army. The officer in charge had obviously served as Justice and executioner, and the bodies buried. I looked in the west window. There was no joy in finding out I was correct.

I pushed my dagger back in its sheath.

"Cio claro!" I called, and the three climbed down from the hill. The soldiers dug out their bolts and Bima searched the bodies and horses for dispatches, maps, letters, or anything else of value to a softfoot. I took a deep breath and walked inside the house. The Viklander horse was still standing, piss and dung beneath and behind it. The boys must not have wanted to risk taking it outside for any reason. I leaned my head against its flank and tried to think what to do. We couldn't stay here, but to push through to Manumina would mean six decons of night travel on a half-track.

Bima stuck his head in the door and silently took in the horse.

"Viklander." He snapped his eyes to me. "Viklanders are not buried, they must be burned on a pyre. We'll need to fire the house with them in it."

"No, Bima, they were Kereki. They were the two Kereki deserters Tiju Tia and I met last night. It's how you got your mapcase. They had fled a skirmish on this horse and had no idea what they had. They were just boys. Tiju Tia said they wouldn't tell—they had more to lose than we did."

Bima looked at me critically. "Tiju Tia didn't say they were alive when you left them."

"It doesn't matter." I sighed. "They're dead now."

"We can't stay here. Others may be looking for those four out there," Bima reasoned.

"I know, we'll push on. We'll get there closer to dawn but there is no help for it. Any campfires we see between here and Manumina will be bandits. I'll need to have you all ride as outriders."

"Certainly," Bima said. "We'll take all the horses." It wasn't a question. He put the Viklander horse on a leading line. "She'll have to walk behind the wagon. Viklander patrol horses aren't broken to hauling wagons. It will be too obvious if one of us rides her. Too bad, she's probably the most rested among all of them." I reached for the saddle and trappings on the floor and followed him out the door.

The soldiers took the news we would be continuing on very well. I'm sure they had drawn the same conclusion we did. I did notice, however, they both had released a soft sigh when Bima told them the horse had been stolen. Even so, they uncovered the graves enough to see the faces of the two Kereki boys.

Bima shot me a quick glance. "As you said, deserters, and not Viklanders." But he didn't apologize.

I felt the sinking sun on my back as we loaded up and headed southeast. I tried to make sense of everything that had just happened. I had thought once we saw the Kereki soldiers at the cottage, we would just wait for them to leave. The horses had already been saddled, they were patting the dirt on the completed mounds. There were already tied pieces of wood in an X shape at the top of the graves. Another decon of silence and the place would have been ours for the night.

But Bima had had other ideas. The Viklanders shot to kill as soon as the scene had unfolded beneath them. I understood now how violent my death dance with Bitterboots had seemed to the Viklanders on Miya's thirteenth crossing all those seasons ago. To me, it was hurt them before they hurt you. To the Viklanders back then, it had been an act of random violence. My hunting Mouser had made as much sense to me then as killing those four soldiers made to the Viklanders now. Scavenging the bodies, stealing the horses—all were survival skills in this war of attrition. Falan was right. I had left Lowertown far behind.

I don't know when I fell asleep, but when the wagon lurched and I felt the wheel sink into the soft sand by the track, I snapped awake. It was dark. When did that happen? The horses snorted in surprise, and I heard hoof beats coming close.

"What's wrong?" Bima asked.

"I went off the track. The wagon is stuck. Call your soldiers, we'll have to muscle it out."

Bima made a low bird call, and the two riders soon came into view. All three slid off their mounts and we soon had it back on firmer ground. Bima checked on the horses and came back.

"The team is spent. We'll need to stop for a bit and move the horses around. Hopefully, a couple of the Kereki army horses are broken in for hauling."

I checked the sky for time and direction. Five decons until dawn and still heading southeast. Good. I hadn't gotten us lost.

"What are you looking for?" one of the soldiers asked.

I stood just behind her, took her hand, and pointed it to the brightest star. "The West Islanders tell direction by the constellation 'The Smith at the Forge.' The brightest star is the flame in the forge. That star always points north. From there, you go straight east," I pulled her hand along, "to there. See those three stars straight up and down close together? That's the constellation, 'The Soldier.' He always guards the West Islanders from Trouble from the east." I patted her on the shoulder. "That would be Kerek, never Vikland. And if you look down between the Soldier and the horizon you can find four stars in the shape of a square, like a sail, with a long arrow of stars below it. That's the Seafarer constellation and it appears to move across the sky so you can tell the time, just as you use the sun during the day. Right now the Seafarer has not even reached halfway, so we still have four or so decons before dawn."

She turned and gave me a fixed stare. "And you can do all this without an astrolabe?"

I shrugged. "I don't know what an astrolabe is, but yes, it's how we find our way about at night since there are so few settlements to guide our way."

She gave Bima a pointed look. "This would have been helpful to us before we were dumped in Kerek, don't you think?"

Bima snorted. "A great many things would be helpful."

I rummaged around in the back of the cart and found the cloth bag Tiju Tia had given me before she left. There wasn't much; we were headed back to Manumina after all. The bread was stale. It had been three days since Rygee had baked it, but there was stonefruit and grapes and lukewarm water to wash it down. I pointed to the soldier sleeping in the back of the cart.

"How long since he's eaten? Do you need to make him swallow something?"

The healer shook her head. "He's better to sleep and then wake at your home. Falan said there is a Viklander healer there?"

"Yes. Rell." I started to say more but Bima interrupted me and spoke quickly in Vik. I didn't understand it, but the healer wrinkled her nose and turned away. I cocked an eyebrow at Bima, but he pretended not to notice. He walked away from the wagon, and soon the others followed. It felt good to stand, to walk, to step away from the wagon, and use the darkness to cover the body's needs.

It took more than one try, but we found two geldings that seemed to know what we were about when we backed them into the traces. We ran lead lines on the three mares. That left only two for outriders—the two which trailed the wagon earlier. It couldn't be helped: someone would need to ride the Viklander mare. Bima said he would ride with me on the wagon and before long we were back on the track heading to Manumina.

I thought Bima may have offered to ride with me to keep me awake or to allow himself to doze off. For a long while this could have been true, as he was silent, and I was content with my thoughts. Drifts of clouds were moving in, blocking the stars. I thought we would be seeing a miserable drizzle within the decon or two.

"How many West Islands tales do you know, Zren?" Bima spoke out of the darkness.

"Not many. Koanga, Ngahuru's little brother, told them on the walk down the Coast Road to Salisport, but I didn't realize they were more than just stories to pass the time. When all this is over, I want to travel to the West Islands and hear the stories again in their storytelling way." I thought for a moment. "Why doesn't Kerek have any stories like that?"

Bima sounded surprised. "They do, Zren. They're Trickster tales. Sometimes the Trickster is Death, or Despair, or Greed, but it is still someone thinking an ordinary bargain is being made, and it turns out not to be so."

"Do you know any? Because truly, I have lived in Kerek all my life and I have never heard one."

"Yes, well," Bima responded drily, "I think you were too busy living them in Kerek City." He leaned against the wagon back. "Mmmmm. This one is called How Death Saved Her Brother from the End He Deserved." He paused and pitched his voice a little lower.

"Now listen closely my children, for Death is a Trickster who changes her appearance as often as the weather changes in the between time of the Dry and the Wet. Sometimes she appears as a mother who promises peace and rest from a life of burden. Sometimes she appears as a mischievous child coaxing children to disobey—just this once— because the river is not so fast or so deep, the cliff is not so crumbly or so steep, and the fire is not so hot or painful as said by those who say 'no.' But one of Death's favorite disguises is when she appears as a woman,

not so young as to be inexperienced, but not so old as to lessen the joy of the danger.

Now Death had several older brothers—Disease, Despair, and Desolation, but she had only one younger brother—Destruction— that she doted on with all her heart. He made such glorious messes; it sometimes took her days to sort out the souls afterwards. But as with all of those we love, we can be blind to their faults as well as to their virtues, and so it was with Death. She loved all of her brothers and waved away any criticism as mere annoyance.

Children, you may think someone like Death would have few friends, but you would be wrong. There are always those who like to dance with Trouble and if the danger is high, the taste is so much sweeter.

One day, Death and her friends were daring a storm by the sea. They spent the day chasing each other in and out of high crashing waves, racing down the narrow cliff paths, and standing with arms outstretched calling to the lightning for a kiss. They built great bonfires of driftwood and brambles on the shore, eating and drinking as the storm grew wilder.

Suddenly, one of Death's friends called out, "The cliff—the village cliff!" Everyone turned to look. There at the very edge of the cliff stood Death's little brother, Destruction. He had altered the flow of the river to course through the streets of the village. The storm had turned the falling river into a torrential waterfall and as they watched, the entire cliff crumbled, sinking the village beneath the waves of the sea. Even Destruction disappeared under the water.

Oh, my children, only Death's sisters, Hunger and Hope, were as immortal as she was. Her brothers, alas, were not. Death and her friends stood still in the storm, silent.

One of Death's friends, Grant, came to his senses. "My brother was in that village. He could not have survived that fall. Please! He is dearer to me than all the world. Please restore him to me!"

Death looked him up and down. "A life for a life. I also lost my brother in that collapse. I will restore your brother, and you must agree to let me restore mine."

Her friends grumbled at this. Destruction had been an affliction since he was old enough to toddle after them. More than one of Death's friends thought with Destruction gone, Death's unintended consequences would not be so, well, destructive. A great argument arose, some begged Grant to let his brother be the sacrifice to rid the world of Destruction. Others said it was a fair exchange because she wasn't asking any of them to die instead.

While everyone was arguing Death stood silently and watched the waves. Soon others could see one tiny head bobbing in the water. The shore was not so far, if one was a swimmer... Death raised her hand for silence.

"You must choose, Grant. Do I restore your brother…and mine, or do I let them sink beneath the waves forever?"

Grant looked wildly at the crowd, now sullen but expectant. His shoulders slumped, he turned to Death.

"It shall be as you say—a brother for a brother, let them both live."

Death flashed a grin and looked to the sea where everyone could now see two tiny heads bobbing in the water. Only as the swimmers grew closer, could they see Grant's brother was towing Destruction into shore.

"Ah, I should insist my brother learn to swim!" Death smirked.

And that my children, was how Death was once again able to save her brother, Destruction, from the end that was his due."

I laughed. "That is such a Kereki story. Grant's brother was never in danger."

Bima smiled. "It is, isn't it? All Trickster tales trade away something a person already has for the Trickster's bargain."

I stiffened as I remembered where I had heard those words before. Chul had told Buku Pramana, the Spice Islander Zadah and Piffik had found alive in a barren pasture with a knife in his back, that his Viklander softfoot had made a Trickster's bargain with him to free his men and his ship. I had always wondered, who had been the softfoot who so willingly sacrificed a Spice Islander's life merely for maps and routes of the Kereki Tax Collectors?

"Do Spice Islanders have stories?" I asked carefully.

Bima looked at me. "I'm sure they do. Everyone has stories, Zren. Why do you ask?"

"Do you know any Spice Islanders?" I asked slowly. "Have you ever worked with any?"

I could feel Bima's scrutiny, and I wondered what he saw in my face. He paused a long time, and then sighed.

"Zren, I do not have a gift for languages. I never learned Wester—either the dialect used in the Spice Island or in the West Islands."

I noted how he didn't answer my question. I remembered how the Spice Islander said the softfoot spoke Mata—which I knew Bima spoke very well if his wife and daughters still lived in Matasi. I wondered what would happen if I told Bima I thought he was the softfoot who had nearly bargained away the Spice Islander's life. I wondered what he would do if he learned the Spice Islander was still alive. Would he be delighted with the captain's resilience? Would he be proud the Spice Islander had survived all of Vikland's trickery like a Vik softfoot in training?

I didn't think so. I realized it was important the Viklanders think the Spice Islander had died from his metal poisoning on the plains of Kerek. The best gift for Buku Pramana was not to discover his softfoot and almost-murderer, but to let him slip away unnoticed and free.

I cleared my throat. "Tiju Tia told me some of the Viklander Wisdom sagas—lots of monsters and warriors and battles. So how else are you going to entertain me?"

"I could tell you more Wisdom of the Warrior sagas. I know I heard enough of them growing up. But if you would like, I could tell you parables of the Lost God. Have you heard many of those?"

"Only one, back in Matasi. The one that sounded like a Traveler tale from the West Islands." I wiggled myself into a more comfortable spot on the wagon and gave him a big grin. "I'm listening."

CHAPTER 23

STORIES FROM MATASI

Bima thought for a moment. "This one is called The Gifts of the Father," he began.

"In the writings of the Lost God, there is this parable. In the highlands of Matasi, there was a farmer. He rose early to plant, to tend, and to harvest his grains, his orchards, and his gardens. He felt the sun on his back, the breeze on his brow, and stretched out his hand when the rains of the Wet began. He knew the earth and the earth knew him."

Bima continued his story telling of the farmer's pride in his lands and in his daughter and two sons. He told of the oldest son learning to take his place beside his father. I suddenly thought of the Wren, Falan. What did her father think when she had left his home rather than take her place at his side running the Red Cup?

"The second child listened to his father's wisdom, but his heart yearned for the sea. He would watch the breeze through the grain and

imagine the sound of the endless waves. He would look at the trees in the orchard and imagine masts and sails standing tall against the flat horizon. He would weed and harvest the gardens and imagine the foods of a hundred different countries.

His father knew how the second son felt. At every opportunity, he reminded his son of how hard he worked so his children could carry on his legacy. He talked of the power of ownership, and the son reminded him of the costs when the Wet came early and the year's work was washed away. The father refused to listen whenever the son spoke of his dreams of the seas.

Finally, the son told the father he was leaving and asked for his blessing. The father refused, saying his son would soon return. The young man walked away to a life on the seas."

I thought of Zadah and how a man who had never seen a ship could be willing to walk across three countries to sail on the seas on the strength of his dream. I understood that the parable Bima was telling me said as much as the Constellation tales, or the stories of Zren Janin. I wondered how the storyteller decided what was the right story to tell at the right time.

"Now the third child saw how hard her oldest brother worked to know the earth and to have the earth reward him. She saw the struggle between what her second brother wanted and what her father expected and the high cost of following a dream. So she chose

another course. She stayed at home and enjoyed the life her family's work provided. She was witty and charming, and her parents took delight in her company as they enjoyed the farm together, riding horses, picnics, and all the power and privileges of owning land.

The seasons passed. The father wanted to gift his children all he had, so he could see the joy on their faces and listen to them marvel at his generosity. He showed them the map of his lands and gave them each a third of his holdings. He sat back in his chair, waiting for the astonishment and the joy and gratitude from each child.

Instead, he received shocked silence.

The second son spoke first, "Twenty years ago, I asked for your blessing as I followed my heart to the sea. You refused. Now I come back to show you my joy and happiness at doing what I love, and you still try to force me to your will. Why do you hate me so much?"

The youngest daughter cried out bitterly, "You told me owning the land was power. To delight in ownership by taking advantage of all the gifts and enjoying the pleasures it provided. Now you want to burden me with all of this? To dirty my hands, darken my skin from the sun, collapse into my bed exhausted from labor? Why do you hate me so much?"

The oldest son spoke in a very small voice, "How did I displease you? All these years I have cared for all your lands and now you give me only a third. Neither my brother nor my sister has helped, and yet you leave me only a third for my own. Why do you hate me so much?"

And the father was so ashamed by the ungratefulness of his children, he kept it all and lived extravagantly to the end of his days."

Bima leaned back on the wagon seat.

"That's it? That's the parable?" I sputtered. "But that is not even a proper story!"

"Of course, it is!" Bima smiled. "It's a parable. It has many different meanings. Here, let me show you. So tell me, what do you think the father should have done?"

"Give it to the oldest son. He did all the work and provided for the family."

"So only children who do what their fathers tell them shall inherit?" Bima questioned.

I thought of Rygee then. He had been raised to take his place among his father's lands. He had learned at his father's knees, managed by his father's side, and when Rygee refused to marry at his father's command, he had been discarded and forced to find his own way. Should he be no longer part of his family for no reason other than his desire to make his own decisions just as the second son in the parable did?

"Well, no, the second son followed his own heart," I offered uncertainly.

"The world would never move forward if we did not seek new horizons," Bima agreed pleasantly. "And remember, the second son only wanted his father's blessing, not to do his father's will."

I thought about it for a while. "The youngest just needs coin to support herself, the second son wants a blessing, and the oldest wants the farm as a reward for a lifetime of labor. The father gave the wrong gift to each child." I looked at Bima. "Is that the correct answer?"

"So why should the children expect any gift at all? If everything belonged to the father, why can't he give it as he wishes?" He paused. "Or, we can say the father didn't know his children at all, and only wished to be thought of as a generous man instead of giving his children what they needed."

"So, a parable is a story with twists and turns and no happy ending at all?"

He laughed. "Parables are to make you think. There is no one right answer, just as there is no one right gift. If we think on the parables, we can learn many ways to do something, and hopefully somewhere along the way do a few right things."

"Huh!" I was quiet for a long time. Finally, "You better tell me another one."

"Ah, but if I tell you another parable what will you do with it? Tuck it up tight and keep it a secret? I don't think so. I think you will share the story with others so they will look at you as a man of knowledge. That's important to you isn't it, Zren? So. As a man of knowledge, show me again how to tell time by the stars." He smiled. "And then I will tell you another."

I pulled gently on the reins and the horses stopped. I took his arm and pointed out the Soldier, the Seafarer, and the Smith at the Forge. I taught him directions by the stars and where in the sky the Seafarer would be at certain times of the night. I told him how I had found my way back to Manumina from Earles by keeping the sun on one side of my face in the morning and on the other side after midday. He nodded as I picked up the reins. My heart sank as I realized I had probably told him I had lied to Kern. I hadn't known my way home at all.

But I didn't want to talk about it, so I quickly asked him again, "Tell me another parable."

Bima continued looking into the night and then turned back to me. "This one, this one is a parable of allegiance," he said quietly.

"In the writings of the Lost God, there is this parable. There was a Matasi farmer who had many fields. Because he had no daughters or sons to stand beside him and care for the land, he had three stewards to help him oversee his vast holdings.

In his youth, the man had been a follower of the Lost God. He understood what it meant to follow the seasons as he worked with his hands, to treat his workers as he would like to be treated, to share in the bounty and the want. But time passes for all of us, and as more desirable land came into his hands, he struggled with his wants and the Lost God's will.

I am sad to say, my children, that as the seasons passed, he became known as a farmer who reaped where he did not sow, and when his granaries were full, instead of sharing with those in need, he built more granaries outside his windows so he could gaze upon his wealth.

Now the farmer decided to go on a far journey and see the beauty and marvels beyond Matasi. So he gathered his three stewards, laid out a map of all his holdings, and explained what he wanted done while he traveled the known world.

To the first one he said, "You have been with me the longest. Together we have grown my holdings from a single farm to the vast estates I have today. I entrust you with half my holdings to manage them as I would manage them. Secure the rents, plant, harvest, and ensure each tenant pays his due." The woman nodded, pleased she had received so much.

To the next one he said, "You are the newest of my stewards, but you have proven yourself worthy. I give you half of the half remaining, to manage and increase my holdings."

To the third one he said, "You know what lands remain. They are neither my most fruitful nor barren. But they are yours to manage until I return." And with that the farmer rolled up his maps and left for the city of Vesaport and the seas beyond.

Now the seasons passed. The stewards began to believe the farmer would never return. The first steward bought and sold as she had been taught, driving a hard bargain, rejoicing when the rains of the Wet drowned her neighbors' fields and left hers fertile and green. As she took the earnings and bought more land, she thought to herself, 'Surely, the farmer will make me an heir for I have doubled what he has entrusted to me!'

The newest steward looked to the efforts of the oldest one and thought to himself, she has doubled the wealth of the farmer at the cost of her neighbors. She has bought and sold but saved nothing for herself. How shall she live when he returns, and she is too old to be his steward?

So, the newest steward made a different plan. He took the coin from the harvest and bought land over the next hills. He planted the farmer's seeds sparingly and sent the rest to his new lands. He set day workers to harvest the farmer's lands and spent his own days tending his own farm for he thought, 'I am the newest of the stewards and not so dear to his affections or so shrewd in my dealings. When the farmer returns, he shall count my earnings as his and I shall be nothing but a steward again. Better I should use the earnings made as a result of my labor to buy myself *a farm and live there when he returns. I shall work fairly for him, but he shall receive only what he has given me and nothing more. He is taking his ease, and yet, I am ensuring his wealth remains.'*

Now, the third steward had received the remaining one half of one half. She had stood by the farmer when he had demanded rent from a tenant whose fields had washed away in the Wet. She had sold holdings and turned out the remaining family when the able-bodied sickened and died, leaving the crop to rot in the field. She had bargained hard to take a farm to add to the farmer's many holdings, knowing it was the sole livelihood of a family she bargained against.

Now in relief and gratitude, the steward thought she had enough coin and land to live as her heart demanded. When someone fell ill on her farmer's lands, she sent others and paid their wages to till or harvest for the ones who could not work. When floods washed out fields, she joined in as they rebuilt the terraces and borders and replanted the seeds. When a fire burned a granary in a village under her care, she sent grain from another so none would starve. She noted her holdings decreased, but her tenants and neighbors blessed her.

After many years, the farmer returned. He had lived well in his years in the West Islands and was ready to rest and live richly on his Matasi farmlands. As his carriage pulled up to the grand house, the servants fluttered in excitement! The master had returned! A feast was prepared. The master invited the three stewards to attend him and to bring their account books.

The steward who had been with the farmer the longest showed her account book first.

"Sir, you entrusted me with double the lands of the other stewards, and I have doubled it again. I drove hard bargains, was the first to market to get the best prices, and replaced any tenants who did not increase your yield from year to year. You are now the wealthiest farmer west of Alenti!"

The farmer beamed in happiness.

The newest steward asked to go next.

"You gave me lands not as rich or as many as your first steward. I did what I could with what you gave me. I have planted and harvested, invested and redeemed. While you have taken your ease for years, you now return exactly as rich as when you left with no effort at all on your part. This I have done for you." The farmer narrowed his eyes at him but said nothing.

The third steward approached.

"You are a man who has made your wealth on the misfortune of others. You reap the harvest of others and call yourself clever. You buy when others are forced to sell because of calamity and call it shrewd. You scatter the crumbs from your table and call it charity. I have taken what you have given me, and I have shared your bounty with the poor, I have given shelter to the homeless, and fed the hungry. I *have helped the sick and the lame, the widows and orphans. All this is not without cost. Of the half of the half you gave me there is one coin left."*

She reached in her pocket and laid it on the table in front of him. "With this coin, you are still richer than when you came into the world."

And thus ends the parable of the farmer and the three stewards."

"What! You can't end the story there," I protested.

Bima laughed a long time. "I just did, Zren."

I grumped. "Well give me some time to figure it out then. Wait, first tell me if any of the stewards did the right thing."

"That is not the correct question, Zren. The question to ask yourself, is 'whom do you serve?' If you serve your master and your master cares for you, then the first steward did the right thing. She could dedicate everything to the master because she felt although he was a selfish man and unkind, he would be kind to her. She trusted that she was privileged in his affections and would be cared for in her old age.

"The second steward saw the master was a harsh man and felt he would not be treated well. So he followed the letter of the law but not the spirit. He took care of himself first because he trusted himself more than he trusted the master. He returned to the master exactly what was given—no more, no less.

"The third steward trusted in the value of others. She worked together for good because she believed all people were worthwhile and trustworthy. She disrespected her master so much she gave him only one coin to show how little he had when he came into the world."

It suddenly made sense to me and I jumped in, "So the first one served her master, the second one served himself, and the last one served others." I paused. "And they all did the right thing… or the wrong thing, depending on whom they served."

"Yes," Bima smiled at me but it didn't seem kind. "This is the parable I tell myself whenever I look on you."

I stilled. Then I remembered it was so dark, he could not see my face.

"I was told of one of yours, a woman, my injured Viklander thought. The two of them had stumbled across a pair of drunken Kereki men during a night-time escape. My man was without a weapon and too damaged to fight. Your Wren was grabbed, her dress was torn. She slashed them open with a knife my softfoot didn't even see and left them dead on the ground. Then she took off the bloodied dress and apron of a Kereki housewife and rummaged in a traveling bag. She changed her hair and her clothes to a tied-back tail and men's trousers and tunic and wiped the stain from her lips and face. As they went on their way, the only comment the Wren made about the attack, was 'Another pretty dress ruined.'"

"Josef," I laughed in relief. "It had to have been Josef. We have a terrible time keeping him in dresses."

Bima gave me another odd smile. "The soldiers who come back to Vikland must report in before they are reassigned back out. Many of those soldiers, and my best softfoots, Lomes and Rani and Kern, tell us of a group of street children, none older than you, from Kerek City. Most of them are illiterate and cannot read the maps and battle plans we give them to pass on. They ask if we know our Conrosan folk heroes. They call themselves 'friends of Zren Janin' when they offer to help us. They move injured soldiers and softfoots. Our soldiers say they have been found by your Wrens from the northern estates to our western front and all along the Northern Track. These friends of yours, these Wrens as they call themselves, give us food, and Kereki clothes so we can pass through the countryside, and take us in cheese carts, rag and bone carts, and coffin wagons. We hear names like Padro Morto—a Mata name for Father Death, Tiju Tia, but most of all, a Conrosan folk hero—Zren Janin.

"Even tonight, you showed us how to find our way and to tell time without an astrolabe or sunshine. You know how helpful that would be to all our soldiers and softfoots? It is knowledge from the West Islands you have adapted to the Kereki scrublands."

He leaned back on the wagon seat. "Whom do you serve, Zren Janin? When Solkka Ulani and I came to Manumina and asked the Council of Wisdom for help, they refused. But there were five of you who said you stood with us. The Kereki farmer and his wife the healer, you, Rell, and Piffik Qanaq. None of you, I think, are smart enough to run a softfooting network this extensive, so well run. So then I wonder, who have I underestimated? Lomes says it is Tiju Tia, Rani says it is Piffik, Kern says when I think of you, I must always expect the unexpected.

"When I ask Miya if it could be Rell Huena, he shrugs and says he doesn't know, she was younger than all of us in the academies and new to the Diplo when the war began. I thought I knew her as a bowmaster with unusually keen eyesight and endurance. Now I am not so sure.

"You asked for Solkka's and my help to keep your people safe when we came to Manumina before the war. I do not think you learned so much from us in one night. Not in strategy, not in softfooting. But I see Ngahuru's hand all over this, Zren. You spent ten days with Ngahuru from Kerek City until she sailed out of Salisport. Even if she taught you the entire way, you would not have learned enough or had enough coin to bring out all your friends from Kerek City to do this. Or taught them what they needed to know. And if it is the Kereki farmer-soldier, then I wonder when Vikland will be betrayed."

I said nothing. I thought of Tiju Tia and her Wrens. She had found them when she was a diplomat and softfoot in Kerek City to be her street runners and information gatherers. They had years of training to survive Lowertown, Dockside, and the Sinner's District. When she gathered them up and brought them to Manumina, none of them had known how to travel in the woods, live in a house and tend to it, ride a horse, or work for wages. Again, she trained them. It was their will to learn, and Ngahuru putting all the needed teachers in place, which made her network strong. In all the time they had been softfooting and rescuing, we had not lost one Wren.

"You know we stand with you. What more do you need?" I pretended to be unconcerned.

"I want to be sure the right gift is given," he said cryptically. "I need to know whom you serve, Zren."

I thought about all of my different answers. If Bima learned Tiju Tia and Ngahuru were one and the same, would he force her from her disguise to embarrass the King of the West Islands and his claim of neutrality? How powerful were Ngahuru and Bima? How could they hurt each other? What would it serve? Whom would it serve? I shuddered as I realized Bima had told me his parables not for entertainment, but because he wanted information from me.

Bima had met Ngahuru, the great Softfoot of the West Islands, well-spoken and multilingual, regal and with skin and hair the color of the deepest almonds, in Salisport, Matasi years ago. He had spent time with Tiju Tia yesterday with her nimbus of white hair, nondescript clothes, and slumped posture, and did not make the connection. I could not, after all she had done for me, give up her secrets so casually. I still did not know who had been willing to throw away Buku Pramana's life just for the secrets he had known.

I did not know why Miyamoto Suki would say to me that he and Bima Ritwik would never be friends, or why Koanga said he did not like Bima all those years ago in Salisport. I did not understand why this mattered so much to Bima Ritwik. But I knew my answer mattered very much indeed.

I needed a *titiro mai ki ahau* to deflect attention and calm the Viklanders. Bima was right; too many people knew I wasn't smart enough to keep this running. To say it was Rygee would only make them anxious a Kereki could turn back and support his own country again. It also had to be a lie I could maintain, and that might be the hardest or the easiest part of all. There was only one person I knew who would understand Bima Ritwik well enough to protect us at Manumina. I spoke carefully, and every word that fell from my lips was true.

"I called for help, Bima, and help came. I consider the Wrens my friends. They were offered no coin to make them come, only a chance to escape their previous life. Your soldiers and softfoots may marvel at their skills, but you should know this is true; every one of them has a better future now than the past they left behind in Kerek City."

I looked him full in the face so he would know I was telling the truth. "Rell Huena taught the Wrens how to shoot and hunt and use the bongs, although many of them also use the skills they learned in Lowertown. She is more than a bowmaster at Manumina. She is important to me, to us. You should know, Bima Ritwik, Rell Huena tells me to do something every single day."

CHAPTER 24

PIFFIK'S PUZZLE

I woke to sunlight streaming in over the bedclothes, so I knew it was very late morning or even midday. I lay sideways on the bed as I had fallen last night, my boots and pants off, my face smashed into my pillow. I pulled my feet in under the covers and stretched out. *Ahhhh!*

We had reached the gates of Manumina closer to dawn than I had wanted, but the horses had been so tired we had let them plod at the pace they could maintain. I had knocked at Rell's door, and she had unbarred the gates and led us into the infirmary. Bima gave her a long look but had said nothing. As he helped me carry in the wounded soldier, Rygee came down the stairs, dressed only in a pair of trousers. He took one look, turned, and ran up the stairs. It seemed but moments later, both he and Siba came down fully dressed and wide awake.

While Siba, Rell, and the Viklander healer were discussing what to do with everyone, I went out to put the horses away.

Rygee came out and took the leading lines from my hand.

"Go to bed, Zren, you are barely on your feet. I'll take care of the horses. Siba will put everyone to bed in the infirmary. Sleep now and we will talk about everything that happened to you later."

I nodded and turned away.

"Zren, is Tiju Tia all right?"

"Yes," I replied hoarsely. "She's doing the route with Josef."

"All right then, good night."

As I lay there, I realized I had not said a word to Bima once we had arrived at Manumina. He had kept me awake with his stories through the long night, even after the outriders had tied their horses to the wagon and crawled in to sleep next to the injured soldier. We had done what we needed to get everyone here, now our reserves were gone.

I thought I should get up and look for the Viklanders. Find Rygee and tell him what happened. Beg food. Find Rell to learn how the injured soldier was doing. Instead, I closed my eyes and let myself drift back to sleep.

A while later, I heard a noise outside my room. I rolled over thinking I needed to get up when I heard a light rap at the door.

"Zren, it's me, Rell. Can I come in?"

I grunted as I pulled the covers over me, and she pushed open the door. She smiled.

"I remember those nights when no watch had to be set. How are you feeling?" She crossed the room and sat at the edge of my bed.

"Good. Are the others awake?"

"Awake and gone." She nodded at my surprised look. "They said they had slept on the way and you had kept them safe. They wanted to get to Ishes. Rygee and Siba took them this morning. The two soldiers will be reassigned at Ishes, and Bima will get the injured soldier to the healing academy at Juisiti."

She smiled and teased, "Did you forget to feed them? Together the four of them ate more than a dozen eggs with vegetables, drank the meat broth Rygee was making for stew, and finished off yesterday's baking," she paused, "including your favorite kolaches."

I groaned and pulled the pillow over my head. "I'll starve," I whimpered.

"I'll cook." She laughed at my appalled look. "Don't worry, Rygee set some back for us. He and Siba are going to cross over into Vikland and check on the cottage the Conrosans use to hide from the Tax Collector. They won't be back for two days. Piffik and Oro are in Ahni picking up wood at the sawmill and will be back this afternoon. Bima told me all five of the horses are now ours. He said you knew some of them are only riders and not wagon broke?"

I nodded.

"I recognized a Viklander saddle along with four Kereki saddles. Since you were going to be with Tiju Tia on a supply run for eight days and now here you are sleeping the day away in Manumina only four days later, I thought you might have some interesting stories to tell. So why don't you get up? I will scrape some food together, and you can tell me all about it."

Before we even stepped down from our porch to cross the gardens and reach the gates of the stockade, we could see the wood wagon in the distance. Rell's and my house faced west, the only occupied house outside the stockade facing the breakaway, now that the rest of the Conrosans had made their way to Vikland. We watched as the wagon came closer, and finally I could see Oro, tall and lanky, sitting next to Piffik, broad-shouldered, and with his distinctive Conrosan cap. I looked at Rell and she just smiled.

"Wonderful! They're back!"

***

I helped Piffik unload the wagon full of new lumber he would use to make his furniture. This was not the usual wood for his coffins, so I asked if he had some new commissions.

"I do, Zren." He smiled broadly.

He had said nothing when Rell and I had opened the big gate for the wagon, and Rell had announced she and I were the only ones at Manumina.

It was Oro who had groaned and in mock despair cried, "The two worst cooks in Manumina and I am so hungry I could eat my boot!" At least I thought it was mock despair. For while Piffik and I unloaded the wagon, Oro and Rell went to turn out something the four of us could eat.

Once the wagon was unloaded at the woodshop, I grabbed the halter to take the horses over to the stables. Piffik helped me with unhitching the other team and then wandered over to the new horses munching contentedly in their stalls. Now that I could see them all together, even I could tell how much better and more spirited the Viklander mare was. The four Kereki army horses were also finer than anything ever owned by the Conrosans. These were no common horses conscripted by the Kereki army from the hire stables along the Northern Track.

I watched Piffik as he examined the horses. He looked at our plow horses, broad-backed, tired geldings and mares—

nondescript work horses. He looked at the Viklander mare with her long lines, lush coat, and deep colors. He stared at the Kereki army horses and then walked over and looked at the tack someone—Rygee? Rell?—had carefully cleaned and hung nearby while I had fallen into my bed and slept the morning away.

He scratched his head for a moment. Cupped his hands over his elbows and then pulled them apart and put them on his hips. Finally, he turned to me.

"Let me see if I am at least starting with all the pieces. You and Tiju Tia left four days ago with a team of Conrosan horses and the rag and bone wagon. The horses are here," he waved his hand, "as are you. Tiju Tia is still with the rag and bone route?"

"Yes." I nodded. "We ran into…"

He raised his hand for silence. "Our other team of horses and Rygee and Siba are gone. However, they are plow horses and not riders. But we are not missing a wagon. And we have five new horses which have the distinct look and training of army horses, and the tack and saddles of both sides—Kerek and Vikland." He was quiet for a moment. "You and Rell are both here and unharmed." He raised an eyebrow. "No Viklander hiding in the infirmary after singlehandedly eliminating four Kereki soldiers on our village green?"

I shook my head and let a faint smile show.

"Siba hasn't taken up horse thievery, has she?" A smile played about his lips as well.

I snorted.

"You did it, Zren. You have completely puzzled me. I cannot string any set of scenarios together that will lead to what I am seeing right in front of my eyes." He clapped his hand on my shoulder. "Let's go find the others and some food. We can hear of your adventures."

***

As Rell filled my water cup, she began, "So tell me, Zren Janin, how is it you leave with Tiju Tia for eight days of resupplying Wrens and come home four days later with five extra horses, four Viklanders, a new wagon, and no Tiju Tia?"

I started with the deserters. How Tiju Tia had gained information and a Viklander saddle roll with a mapcase by trading food and removing a bolt from the older boy's shoulder. I saw Rell's jaw tighten, and I winced, thinking I should have started my story in another spot. But she didn't interrupt even when I said we left them the cabin and slept rough that night. At least I knew better than to mention they had been riding the fine Viklander horse.

I made everyone laugh as I described Josef and his clothes which didn't fit, and how he made saving Viklanders seem no more complicated than stealing stonefruit from an untended pushcart. I described Arden's wonder dog, Mother, and how Falan said it found hiding Viklanders by the scent of the oil they used to shine their boots. How Falan stole the boots from the Kereki soldiers after they died to confuse anyone who might try to track her. Falan used only a West Islands bow and arrows and would stomp around their ambush sites in boots many sizes too big, leaving tiny footprints that only came to the site of the murders but never left.

"Very clever." Rell nodded in approval. "She sounds even fiercer than when she was here training."

I thought of Josef's story and what his life might have been if Falan had not intervened as a child not much older than he was. How Tiju Tia had said Balza was too close to the fighting to risk a Wren, and Falan had packed her traveling bag and found her own position and a place to live in a widow's house. How she had snapped and snarled at me, not because she was angry with me, but because she felt her Lowertown upbringing is what kept her sharp and safe.

"She is," I explained. "She has to be. If Tiju Tia and I would not have come, she would have had to ride a horse alone back to Balza during the night so she could be at work the next day. She would have been at risk from Viklander patrols who needed to keep their location a secret, bandits who wanted her horse, and Kereki soldiers and men for merely being a woman traveling alone at night. Instead, she rode on the rag and bone cart with Josef and Tiju Tia, and I brought the Viklanders here on their wagon."

"Mmmmm. Well, that explains the extra wagon, but five horses?" Piffik mused.

"Ah, when we got back to the cottage where we had met the deserters, there were four men on a Kereki patrol. I do not know whether they were tracking the deserters or whether it was just Trouble looking for a dance with strangers, but the four were just burying their dead when we came over the rise. The Viklander soldiers and Bima assumed they were burying Viklanders and before I could explain, the archers had killed all four of them." I fell silent and Rell looked at me for a long time.

She gave a deep sigh. "I hear what you are not saying, Zren. In the sagas, the armies line up, the warriors challenge each other, and there are brave deeds done by heroes. Is that not so?" she said gently.

I nodded. "But I have had time to think on it, Rell. Now I understand why you all were so appalled when Bitterboots got in the way of my Sailor's Curse when I was hunting Mouser. You thought the threats on Miya's thirteenth crossing were all on the Northern Track, and I thought Trouble was traveling with us as well. The Viklanders who have survived this war so far think everything is a threat until they understand otherwise."

Rell nodded. "It is a war of attrition. And the Viklanders are scrambling to hang on until the Matasi navy sails into the Kerek City harbor with their own army and pinches Kerek in the middle." She gave me a half smile and continued, "Rygee and Siba took the Viklanders to Ishes at first light. He told me to get you up to care for the horses, but I had taught you on the Northern Track. Since there were no injured for me to attend to, I cared for the horses this morning, Zren, while you were sleeping. The Viklander mare is beautiful. So now we have five horses and more saddles than riders. It has been so long since I have been out riding horse," she finished wistfully.

I looked at her shocked. "You can't leave Manumina."

"I know," she said sadly. "I promised the Council of Wisdom not to put Manumina in danger by flaunting my appearance in the nearby towns."

"No, that's not... I meant you haven't been able to leave this settlement for two years since we were found by the Conrosans. I've never thought about it. You're trapped inside here."

"Well, now you're making me feel bad. And I went out with Aajan once. And then again when I taught the Wrens to hunt with the short bows and crossbows."

Oro cleared his throat. "So you didn't go to Cloa?"

I turned to him then, shocked and remorseful. "Oh, Oro, I completely forgot to give your letter to Tiju Tia or Josef to give to—"

"No, that's all right," he interrupted quickly. "I'll talk to Arden soon enough." I saw the plea in his eyes to say nothing more. "You can just give me the letter back."

I looked at the others. Piffik had a faraway look in his eyes that said he was plotting something. Rell was just looking at Piffik. Neither of them paying any attention to Oro or me. I slid the letter out of my pocket and slipped it under the table to Oro.

Piffik looked up at me. "If I show you what must be done, could you and Oro start on the wood tomorrow? I'll need it sanded and measured."

"Sure." I glanced at Oro. "We can do that."

"Good, good." He turned to Rell. "You have told me your family is less than a half day from the Rishka estate where the Empress has settled the Conrosans. Does your family own horses they would be willing to sell or trade for Kereki army horses?"

"Certainly." She raised an eyebrow. "But why go to all the trouble?"

"We have five horses in our stable we cannot keep. The Conrosans of Manumina have declared themselves neutral in the war between Kerek and Vikland. If we show up in Sary riding Kereki army horses, the Kerekis are going to think we murdered for the horses, and the Viklanders will think our friends gave them to us. And before you say anything, Zren, that's the way it works. People always assume the worst and write their own stories of what they think happened. So we will take these horses to Vikland and trade them for good solid plow horses everyone will sniff at and no one will care to own."

He looked at his feet in embarrassment, then looked at Rell. "The Viklander mare is far too spirited for any of the three of us to ride. I can ride one of the army geldings—they seem mild enough—and we can string the others. But I must ask you to ride the mare, to cross over with me to Vikland and negotiate for us with your family to trade or sell as you see fit. I'll go to the refugee camp and talk to the Council of Wisdom and wait for you there. We can talk more as we ride, but is this agreeable to you?" He paused. "If you wish, Zren and Oro can be our outriders on our plow horses and turn back once we safely reach the border of Vikland."

She gave him a sly smile. "You have work for them here, and Siba and Rygee will be coming home tomorrow. They cannot come home to an empty Manumina." She patted his hand. "I will bring my crossbow and protect you from all harm."

His eyes flashed with warmth. "Well, then I better get those commissions started."

CHAPTER 25

RELL LEAVES MANUMINA

Rell worked late into the night making lists of medicines and supplies she would purchase in Vikland. She also kept me awake as she rummaged around in her room below mine, trying to find clothes to pack. Like Siba, once the Conrosans had left for Vikland, she had shifted to wearing only Kereki trousers and blouses and occasionally the tunics. She could never pass for anything but a Viklander, but Tiju Tia had said, Rell Huena only needed a moment of uncertainty from those who would do her or Manumina harm before she would have the upper hand.

Finally, the sounds of the house quieted, and I rolled over ready to sleep. There was a knock at my bedroom door.

"Zren, it's Rell." She pushed open the door a crack. "Do you still have your Vikland pants and shirts you bought or wore in Salisport? I've found one shirt that fits, and I have already tried all the clothes in the infirmary which haven't been ruined."

"Rell, it's the middle of the night!" I smashed my face into the pillow.

"Please, Zren, it's important! I haven't seen my family in five years, and I don't want to show up like a throwaway Viklander crawling home in failure."

"Wow!" I sat up and pulled on a nightshirt over my head. "When you say it that way…" I put my feet on the bare floor and padded to the door. "Come in then."

I pulled open the door and then walked over to the row of hooks where I hung my clothes. I crouched down and pulled out the wooden chest Piffik had made me to hold my belongings when I first came to Manumina. I pulled out two pairs of the close-fitting pants and the dark shirts.

"This is all I have, but it is still nice. I never wore it except at the embasado in Salisport and Kerek City."

"Thanks, Zren, you're the only one my size."

"Rell, I'm the only one at Manumina who has Vik clothes—except for all the stuff you cut up in the infirmary."

She laughed. "Oh, Zren. I always appreciate how you serve your cup of kindness with a dash of spark and snap."

"Grumpf." I threw myself back in bed. "Don't forget to take that candle with you when you go," I called out after her.

***

Piffik got me up with the sun. Why should I have been surprised? We walked out to the stables and talked through each of the horse's traits as I knew them from our night's journey: which were only broke to saddle and which had worked as a team hitched to the wagon. He made several admiring comments about the Viklander mare now that Oro and I had brushed her to a glossy shine.

"I wish Rell could keep this one, but with no place to ride, it would be both cruel to the horse and to Rell."

"You could leave it at the refugee camp for Aajan. Your sister could ride a spirited horse like this," I offered.

"Aajan has the horse Miya gifted her. And she should still be in Juisiti studying. This one belongs in Vikland with one who rides daily…and well." He heaved a sigh. "Besides, Zren, we need the coin. Selling five like this and buying two lesser work horses will help us get through the Wet. Rell already uses her coin from Miya to buy medicines for Manumina and our work with the Viklanders. And you and Oro work very hard for receiving nothing more than a roof over your head and food in your belly.

"But that has to be the way of it for now. We need coin for next Dry to hire farmhands for the fields and the orchards. The Wrens helped us this past season, but we won't be able to count on them again." He blew out a hard breath. "This won't be an easy meeting with the Council of Wisdom. Perhaps the rains will be so much this year, I won't need to see them again until the next Dry."

I tried to look on the positive side. "At least this trip to Vikland, you will get to meet Rell's family."

He looked at me in horror. "I will not! I speak Vik like a peasant, dress like a peddler, and have nothing to my name but a strong back and poverty. They need to think her friends are a better class than we are. You think her family would let me near their estate? Zren, I have met Miya, and Kern, and Bima, and Solkka. I know they are all sons and daughters of noblemen or princesses, or whatever they have for fancy folk. Rell's family would probably mistake me for the new stable boy."

I tried to keep a straight face, I truly did. "Of course not, Piffik. You know little to nothing of Vikland horses, you are afraid to ride one as spirited as this one, and you are far too old to be a stable boy." I grinned. "It doesn't matter. Without you and Rell to keep me awake at both ends of the night, I plan to lie abed each day until it's time to eat."

He snorted. "Rygee and Siba will be home today or tomorrow, maybe he can get some work out of you." He smiled and started pulling bridles and bits from the wall pegs.

Maybe it was what I said, or maybe not, but while Piffik was content to let me saddle the Viklander mare, he took the reins to walk her out of the stables and on to the village green. We let the horses graze there while I went to find Rell and tell her Piffik was ready.

I hardly recognized her. The night before we all had decided she should dress as a Conrosan wife as they crossed Kerek lands. Up close, she would fool no one in Kerek. But a faraway shepherd or a distant patrol on horseback would only see a settler couple, one wearing heavy skirts, the other the distinctive Conrosan cap, bringing a string of horses home or to market. Once they were at the refugee camp at Rishka, she would change into her Viklander clothes, take the horses, and leave Piffik behind to meet with the Council of Wisdom.

This morning, she had brushed out her long black braid and twisted up her hair as a married Conrosan woman of Manumina would do. She was wearing a blouse with the big sleeves to the elbow and a dark brown skirt that flared over her boots of soft Kereki leather. Her over apron was a faded pink. Rell had always been small for a Viklander, my size in fact, and I wondered if the clothes were Aajan's. I stared and her look turned nervous.

"Say something, Zren. Tell me if Piffik and I are stopped by Kereki soldiers, Piffik will be able to convince them I am

Conrosan in everything but the color of my skin. Tell me they will believe we are neutral in the war, and they will let him pass unharmed. Tell me…"

"Rell," I interrupted, "You look like you could be Piffik's wife. You will pass and you will be able to keep him safe. He would not do this if he thought you were in any danger. You are too precious to him—to all of us—to lose you on a pony ride."

"A pony ride!" she laughed. "I have wanted to ride a horse like her for ages, Zren. I just hope Piffik can keep up."

"Piffik will scold you not to ruin the horse just so you can feel the wind." I sobered. "You have your crossbow?"

"Yes."

"And knives?" I continued.

She lifted her skirt and showed me a sheath strapped just above her knee, and carefully slid another out of a boot sheath I had given her last night.

"Good. Rell, if you can, would you buy another crossbow? I still have a little coin, but it is in Tiju Tia's room. I'll pay you when you get back. I know you and Rygee are the only ones strong enough to shoot your bow, but maybe a smaller one would work for Piffik and me."

She smiled. "Don't you remember your last lesson?" My face flooded with shame. She went on gently, "Zren, I don't believe your failure to shoot a crossbow across the village green to a target is a weakness of your skill. I believe it is a weakness of your eyes. And Piffik would rather think his way out of trouble than fight. But you are right, we gave away everything we had to the Wrens. We need more weapons here at Manumina. Oro and Tiju Tia have their short bows, but if they are traveling…well, I will see what I can find."

She picked up her travel bag, her crossbow, a separate pocketful of bolts, and her dark red traveler's cloak. I recognized it as the one she had received from Nebs years ago on Miya's thirteenth crossing. We walked out of her room together.

We slipped in the side door of the stockade. Piffik turned to greet us and stopped hard.

"It's her maskovesto," I said proudly. "You said last night she should dress like a Conrosan to hide in plain sight. Isn't she perfect?"

Piffik was silently staring so long, Rell started to fidget.

Finally, he said, "Yes, she is." Then he frowned. "But I am not sure how all of that dress will fit on the horse."

Rell rolled her eyes and handed me her crossbow and travel bag. She tied on her pocket full of bolts over her apron and swirled her red cloak about her. She slid her foot in the stirrup and in one graceful motion, pulled herself up and on the horse.

"I'll need the stirrups shortened," she groused. Piffik jumped to assist her. She smoothed out her dress and cloak over the rump of the horse, and then reached out to me for her traveling bag and her crossbow. Once she had them sorted out, I gave her the lead lines of the other horses.

I was wrong. She didn't look like a housewife. Sitting so tall and straight, she looked like a warrior hiding in a dress.

Piffik mounted. Not as easily or as gracefully as Rell, and I handed up his travel bag and a small food bag.

"Now remember," he started, "tell Rygee we'll be at the Conrosan refugee camp by tonight. I don't know how long it will take to arrange the sale of the horses. We are dependent upon the grace and kindness of Rell's family for that, but we will return home with enough coin for farmhands for the plantings next Dry."

He paused. "Zren, please. I can't be late on those commissions. Please have the wood prepared so I can work quickly on my return." He gave me a sad smile, and then urged his horse forward. I ran ahead to open one of the large gates for them to slip through. Then I ran up the inside stairs to the lookout to watch them turn northeast on the quickest path to Vikland. The track was nothing more than faint lines in the dirt.

There was no formal crossing there, but it was one of the places we slipped soldiers over the border to find their way north and home. Even so, with the number and quality of the horses, I was glad Piffik had Rell and her crossbow.

Watching her on the fine Viklander mare, with the trailing lines of the others, I wondered what it must have been like to grow up with such wealth to be able to go riding every day. To ride fine horses and not plow horses, to look someone in the eye and negotiate from knowledge. Well, maybe that would be someone else. I had never been to Vikland as close as it was and had no idea how those things worked.

But I did know how Piffik's woodshop worked. He built fine furniture and his work was in demand as far as he would travel. To save coin he bought his wood unfinished, and then planed and sanded it before the first cut. My adventure had drastically changed his plans. The horses had to be sold before they were seen by anyone else, and neither Oro nor I could ride well enough to sit a horse for a day's ride to the refugee camp. I had put Piffik in this predicament of too little time and he was too honest of a merchant to let the deadlines slip by. I sighed as I thought of my bed one last time, and then walked through the beginnings of a misty drizzle to the woodshop to get started.

***

The rains increased, and by midday, I was ready to stop for food and to find out why Oro hadn't joined me. He had heard Piffik's instructions as much as I had. I walked to Lou's springhouse to see if he was there. Lou was checking on the weather and debating whether or not to take the cheese cart out to Sary. He fed me smoked meat and cold cheese while he complained of the rains. Finally, he decided to make a batch of curds and hoped the weather would improve by the next day. I escaped from his request for help by reminding him I was supposed to be looking for Oro.

I found buns and figs and fingersweets in the bakery, but no Oro. I helped myself to a small cup of apple jack and wandered about the stockade with the hood of my cloak up to avoid the worst of the raindrops while I searched for Oro's hiding place. He wasn't at home at the guesthouse, the infirmary, the round church, or any other of the public buildings. I couldn't imagine him walking through the empty houses even if there wasn't anyone living there.

I walked through the livestock pens, checking on the animals, then into the stable to see if the remaining two horses had been fed and watered, and realized one of the horses was gone. It was one of our most even-tempered geldings, so broad you could take a nap on his back, but as slow as a sunbeam during the Wet. Had Oro gone to Sary for supplies? To the Vikland cottage to intercept Rygee and Siba? To Ishes for dispatches?

I thought over the previous day and remembered the look on his face when I had said I had forgotten about his letter to Linna. Oh, stars, if he had taken a horse and ridden to Cloa, Tiju Tia was going to…well, I wasn't sure what she would do, but it would almost be as bad as what would happen if he came across Kereki idiots who for their sport, decided he was more Viklander than Kereki. Oro was tall, as tall as Bima or some of the other Viklanders I had met, but as narrow as a sapling. Any more than one opponent and I couldn't imagine him winning without a great deal of pain involved.

I counted the days back since Tiju Tia and I had left Manumina. This was day five. Tiju Tia and Josef should be meeting Kid or Nelo somewhere around Evensong and dropping off supplies for Dica and Tyra. So it was possible Tiju Tia's and Oro's paths would cross in Cloa the next day. Or she was already through and would be coming back to Manumina through Sary. But while I could think through different scenarios, in reality there was nothing I could do. I knew Arden was at Cloa with Linna, and if Oro was in trouble, the Wrens would work together to rescue one of their own.

CHAPTER 26

ORO DISAPPEARS

Rygee and Siba came back at dusk. Both wore that rosy happy glow I had seen on their faces almost continuously after he had first moved into her house. Ah, good, so they got the Viklanders off to Ishes and found the shepherd's cottage in good shape and now resupplied.

"It's about time you got back here. I've been near starving for two days." I grinned as cheekily as I could.

"It's good to see you too, Zren, and your manners haven't improved enough for me to feed you." Siba grabbed her skirts in her left hand and reached out for me to lift her down.

I set her down gently. "I'm a growing boy responsible for all of Manumina while you are out frolicking with a well-rested husband. You can't just leave out a cup of oats and a handful of carrots and expect me to be content."

"Where is everyone?" Rygee unhitched the horses and walked them over to their stalls to be rubbed down, watered, and fed.

I leaned over the short wall. "Tiju Tia is still out—probably with Josef posing as her male protector. I expect her back in three, maybe four, days. She should be around Evensong about now. Piffik and Rell took the string of army horses to Vikland. Rell is going to take them to her family and have her father help her sell them. Piffik is going to meet with the Council of Wisdom at the refugee camp to talk about either having some Conrosans come back next Dry to help us or buying out the conscription contracts for us to have farmhands next spring."

"Rell?" Siba was incredulous. "Rell went to Vikland? Left Manumina?"

I tried to keep the smile from my face. "What else could she do? Piffik told her she was the only one experienced enough to ride the Viklander mare—the horse had too much spirit for the rest of us. He asked her to handle the negotiations because he speaks Vik like a peasant, and this was too important to all of us to let his pride get in the way. She was the only one with the connections in Vikland, the skill in riding, and the Vik language to save Manumina during the upcoming Wet." I smirked at Siba. "When Piffik put it that way, of course Rell went."

I turned to Rygee. "He said you will have coin for your farmhands for planting. He said, you can start the requests with the Justice at Sary to get workers out of the men eligible for those conscripted this Wet. He didn't know how long the process would take, Manumina has never bought out the contracts of soldiers before."

"We did it at the farms where I grew up. I can wait until he gets back. We can go together, and I can show him how it is done. You want those who want to take the job as farmhands, not just those who do not want to be soldiers," Rygee explained.

Siba shook her head. "I don't know why Piffik doesn't just go out to the fields and convince them to plant themselves. His tongue is clever enough."

I agreed. "If he would have grown up in Lowertown, he could have been the best trickster on the docks. No one's coin would have been safe from him."

Rygee burst out laughing and didn't stop. Even Siba was smiling broadly.

"Zren, Piffik wouldn't last a moment in Kerek City."

"I know." I sighed. "It's a waste of his gift. Rell wore a maskovesto. She wore her hair like you do when you leave Manumina, Siba, and a Conrosan dress with an apron. She carried her crossbow and knives under her red cloak so she can keep Piffik and his gifted tongue safe."

"Good, that's good." Rygee nodded. "What have you been doing while everyone has gone adventuring?"

"Sleeping late and eating all the food," I answered promptly. I looked at Rygee as he finished the last of the horse chores. "Isn't there something you could make right now to keep me from fainting away from hunger?"

Rygee waved at the wagon bed. "The garrison commander gave us some foodstuffs 'for our trouble' in bringing them the Viklanders. Carry this into the bakery if you please, and I will have something ready by the time you are done." He reached in, grabbed a bag of flour the size of a four-year-old child, casually lifted it to his shoulders, and walked out of the barn. I looked at Siba, my eyes round.

She patted my shoulder. "Marry a baker, Zren, you'll never regret it."

✳✳✳

Later, over a bowl of vegetables and noodles, I told Rygee and Siba it appeared Oro had taken a horse and left Manumina. If Piffik or Tiju Tia had given him instructions to do so, I didn't know what they were. I tried to keep the hurt out of my voice, but I wasn't sure I was successful.

299

Rygee leaned back in his chair. "Oro is our age, give or take a year or three, there is nothing saying he has to stay here. He's free to travel about. It's disappointing since Piffik specifically asked you to help him in the woodshop, but again, Oro has free will."

"Rygee, you could ride into any town or settlement in Kerek, and no one would give you anything more than the casual glance they give any stranger. It's why you do all the buying and selling and talking for Manumina. Me? They'll look me up and down a bit, trying to figure out what I am, but my small size lets everyone dismiss me as harmless. Oro, on the other hand, has the height and just enough Vik in his face to dance with Trouble in a country at war with Vikland. Oro wandering about Kerek is far different than you going out for a ride," I reasoned.

"Maybe. But I am not going to hover over a grown man like a hen and her chicks with a hawk in the sky. He'll come home with his plans accomplished or with his lesson learned." Rygee considered. "I can't do anything about Oro, but if you will help me in the fields tomorrow from sunup to midday as we clean the sluices for the rains, then I will help you in the woodshop and every day thereafter until Piffik returns."

I smiled gratefully. "I would like that. Not the getting up at sunrise part, but all the rest of it."

***

Piffik and Rell came back on the fourth day, huddled on a wagon seat, behind a team of chunky plow horses, drenched from the never-ending drizzle. Which was good, because for all of Rygee's many talents—baker, cook, farmer—he had no patience or talent for woodworking.

On the morning of the fourth day, when he asked me what to do, I handed him the sanding block and replied, "Same as yesterday."

He gave me a long, long look, and said, "Truly?" Then he gave me a huge put upon sigh and reached for the sanding block.

We spent the morning talking about anything I could think of. But every time I veered towards Oro and what he could be up to, Rygee would cut me off and say, "He's old enough to know his own mind. Let it go, Zren."

At midday, Rygee said he needed to leave to make food for the three of us.

I looked at him. "Siba can't do it? You're sort of busy, aren't you?"

He grinned at me. "That is exactly something Piffik would say."

"What's something I would say?" Piffik's broad shoulders filled the doorway.

"Thank the Lost God, I am beyond glad to see you," Rygee said fervently.

Piffik walked in and touched the boards we had been working on. He walked over to the finished pile and lovingly stroked the boards.

"These are beautiful, Zren and Rygee, these are beautiful." He turned to look at us. "But to have the Farm Master of Manumina working in the woodshop is a story I would like to hear. Where is Oro?"

"Gone. Four days past with no word," I said abruptly. "If Rygee would not have taken over the woodshop, we would never have had your boards finished in time. As we are, we didn't get any of your measurements marked."

"I can work with that, Zren. Rell is looking for Siba to show her the new medicinals. Let me dry off the horses and put them away, and we can tell you what happened."

Rygee dusted off his hands and brushed the sawdust out of his hair. "Let me make midday. Stories are always better with food and drink."

***

Siba and Rygee spoke first. I had already heard their story in bits and pieces as Rygee and I had worked in the woodshop.

But we all agreed stories are best told from beginning to end, and therefore this one should begin the morning I had arrived back in Manumina with a wagon full of Viklanders and horses enough for my own hire stable.

Rygee and Siba had taken the Viklanders up the half-track to the garrison at Ishes. Usually, the track was heavily patrolled by Viklander soldiers and the way was free of bandits. In all the years since the war had started, no one had encountered Kerekis.

"Until now." Siba sighed.

"Until now," Rygee agreed. "We were not yet halfway when we saw three soldiers on horseback trotting towards us across the field. I dropped my hood even though it was still drizzling so they would see I was Kereki born and bred. I was glad we had taken the high-sided wagon. Siba told all the Viklanders to lay flat on their stomachs with their hands underneath their bodies and their hoods up as if they were sleeping. Bima had said the archers could take them, but I didn't want bodies I had to explain or stop to bury.

"When the soldiers got close enough, I hailed them. They asked what we were about with the sun still resting on the horizon. I said I had been to Manumina to visit my wife's family, and I had purchased the services of the four manabouts sleeping in the wagon behind me. I wanted to build a bigger barn and to have them help with the livestock. We had gotten an early start because our own lands were near Fortika. I told them I always wanted to pass Ishes early while the Viklander sentries were still sleeping. We all laughed at that. They said they were looking for deserters. Too many soldiers were sneaking off during the Wet and trying to spend the rainy season tucked up by a warm fire."

Rygee looked at us about the table. "I thought they were going to search the wagon to see if these 'manabouts' were their deserters. Instead, my clever wife saved me." He looked at Siba to continue.

Siba smiled at us. "I had packed two food bags, a smaller one for the Viklanders for their midday and a larger one for us to last us until we reached Manumina again. I reached at my feet and pulled the smaller bag. 'You have a long day ahead of you and the weather is not cooperating,' I said. 'I am a baker of some small skill, please let us give you our midday so your task is not so tedious.' I handed the bag to Rygee, and he handed it to one of the soldiers who stepped close to the wagon. 'The weaving of the fabric is a Conrosan design. We do like our bright colors.' I then quickly dropped my eyes to the floorboards like a proper Kereki wife."

Rygee picked up the story again, "They wished us a good day and rode off. I don't think those Viklanders moved for another decon." He paused. "When we were close enough to see the fort, we had Bima and the two archers trade places with us on the wagon seat. We sat with the injured soldier. I knew if we were fired upon by the garrison, Siba would be able to replace me with a better husband. But, we were driving the best horses left in our stable, and Piffik would be hard pressed to forgive me." Rygee gave Siba a cheeky grin.

"The commander had lots of questions for Siba and Bima, so I helped the garrison healer with the soldier with the missing ear. The two archers followed another soldier to change clothes and eat. Someone else brought their Kereki clothes back to us. Siba thought she may have recognized one of them in a Viklander uniform later in the ramparts, but we didn't see them to speak to them again. Bima told the commander about the Kereki patrol we had encountered. He said our narrow escape was only because we had given away our food supplies. The commander offered to escort us home to Manumina, but I knew they were interested in going over Bima's mapcase and dispatches. So we accepted a gift of flour, boiled and dried cane, and a small bag of coffee beans. We said our goodbyes and headed to the Vikland border."

"And the shepherd's cottage?" Piffik asked.

"We resupplied it with the food we had in the larger bag that would not spoil, and what we had sealed in Siba's apothecary jars. The commander said he would have additional Kereki trousers and boots for us the next time you pick up dispatches.

"He also recommended I not travel there without a Conrosan, or to do what we did today, and have the Vik soldiers drive the last furlough or two. They have had two attempts where a Kereki drives up a wagon dressed as a laborer and claims to have injured in the wagon bed. When the Viklanders approached the wagon to help with the injured, Kereki soldiers burst out of the back with knives. Their archers on the ramparts saved the day, but the commander believes the Kerekis are now focusing attention on retaking the garrison," Rygee said.

Piffik pursed his lips. "Mmmmm. Good to know. Although I hope they recognize us even when we don't have soldiers with us. And we could certainly use the clothes, we always need more for the soldiers moving through."

"Why only trousers and shoes? We need shirts too," I questioned.

The table was silent. Then Rell said, "Viklanders are very good shots."

"Oh," I said in a small voice.

"Rell, don't tease him," Siba admonished. "They make bandages out of them, Zren. We do here as well." She looked at Piffik. "You had an adventure of your own? And you met with the Council? Do you have news?"

"I do." Piffik nodded. "But first the horses." He looked at Rell. "If you would begin?"

She smiled and looked about the table. "The horses were strong and well-bred so we were able to make it to the refugee camp at Rishka in one day, although we arrived well after dark. We frightened Piffik's mother badly. I was still dressed in the Conrosan clothes, and she thought we were coming to tell her we were married." She gave Piffik a pointed look. "But after everyone apologized, we were able to stay the night in her small room.

"The next morning, I changed back into my Viklander clothes, left Piffik behind, and took the string of horses to my home in Axefield. Truly, I do not know if my littlest brothers were happier to see me or the horses!

"My parents and I visited well. They hear such terrible stories of Kerek and the war, but I explained I am safe here at Manumina and working as a healer. My brothers tell me most in the Diplo have been recalled back to soldiers or choose to go to battle.

"The horses," Rell smiled broadly, "The horses were a delight to my father. He is convinced Viklanders will pay good coin for the Kereki army horses if for no other reason than to say how much better the Vik horses are. And the Vikland mare! She rides like the wind and as smooth as a cloud in the southern sky. Truly, I do not know how Bima could bear to give her up!"

I snapped my eyes to Piffik, and he gave the tiniest shake of his head. "But I can see how she is so beautiful she would hinder in his softfooting." Rell sighed.

"My father bought her as well as the Kereki horses. My brother Dylis will ride her against the day I can claim her as my own." She reached in her waist pocket, pulled out a purse as large as Piffik's hand, and plunked it on the table. She named the price her father paid, and I was reeling. Even Rygee who had grown up on prosperous farms looked stunned. I slid my eyes to Piffik and he just looked…sad. Suddenly I realized he meant what he said before they had left. He wanted Rell's parents to believe she had better friends than those of us at Manumina.

"Your father is generous." Rygee smiled. "You have made the difference, Rell. We can plant next year as if all the Conrosans will return from Vikland. You have made sure the rainy season will not be a season of want for those of us who remain behind, and you have smoothed the way for the Wrens as we aid Vikland. I am beyond glad your family chose to help us."

"It was a fair price for the horses," she insisted. "My mother and I also went to Juisiti. My parents thought it would be best for me to go and explain why I did not serve in the battlefields and accept the consequences no matter what they might be. But someone had smoothed my way with First Soldier Joon. I am not listed as a deserter or invalided out. I am on the rolls as a healer and translator assigned to Manumina, an infirmary waystation for Vikland. I do not know who would have done this for me. But I left the palace without a stain on the Huena name. I know you may not know what that means, but I have younger brothers coming up in the military and in the academies. My brother Dylis is already through his service. But if he ever decided to leave my father's business, it is important to him as well that the Huena name is carried with honor. Anyone who abandons their duty brings dishonor to the entire family.

"My mother took me to the shops near the Academy of Healing. I replenished our medicines and purchased what we cannot grow or make here. I did not know what others needed, but now I know I can return easily. I would be willing to go again if it was necessary."

Piffik hid a smile as he looked at his hands. Did he know? It had to have been Miyamoto Suki. In any case, we finally had proof our Rell was returned to us and no longer broken. We could all hear the pride in her voice as she said the Huena name was not dishonored.

Rygee cleared his throat. "And Piffik? While Rell was saving Manumina, how went your visit with the Council of Wisdom?"

Piffik sighed. "They are doing as well as can be expected. The Empress has provided them with a place to live and for twenty people it would be grand. But they are nearly two hundred and space is tight. People live in every building on the Rishka estate. Every building. They have food and have built gardens to grow more. It is sufficient for their needs, if not their wants." He blew out a breath.

"They will not thrive there. I gave them all the coin I had from my last sales before Rell came back from Axefield. They also had more horses than they could feed or use, so we took a team and wagon back with us and saved more coin in this manner. They agreed that buying the contracts of conscripted soldiers was not against our pacifist beliefs—I did not tell them I would do it anyway—and they will talk to those manabouts to see if they will return to us when the Dry begins to help us with the planting." He pinched his lips together. "I think they are needed there to hire out to Vikland and feed those at Rishka. But there are many rainy nights between this day and that day, and we shall see if they will consider my ideas."

"Well then," Rygee passed the apple jack around again, "I think we need to celebrate our successful venture into horse thievery. We're obviously very good at it." Piffik winced but lifted his glass with the rest of us. We were warm and dry against the afternoon rains and for a while we just sipped and smiled and enjoyed the feeling of being together again.

At last, Piffik put down his empty glass. "Rygee, do we owe you time in the fields for the time you spent in the workshop?"

"I'll check the fields this afternoon and the orchards this evening. The animals will need to be fed, but I can do that so Zren can stay in the woodshop with you. There is no hurry to go to the Justice in Sary to buy out the army conscriptions. You and I should first walk the settlement and see how many and what skills we need."

"Rell and I can do this," Siba waved at the table, "and then we will be in the infirmary for the rest of the day, going through her packages from Juisiti."

Chairs scraped back from the table, and I followed Piffik out to the woodworking shop. He carefully opened his order book, and for the next decon, selected, measured, and marked each piece of wood. I knew from past experience he liked absolute silence for this part, and I let myself sink into my own thoughts while I sanded the last few boards.

At last, Piffik was finished, and the boards were lined up in the order he wanted them. He came around to the last board I was sanding.

"Thank you for your patience, Zren. Now what couldn't you say in front of the others that you wish to say now?"

"The Vikland mare wasn't Bima's. He had no horse when Falan picked him up."

"It is the story he told her when they were getting ready to leave that morning. I think he wanted her to think so, rather than wonder who wouldn't return to Vikland."

"Oh," I tried to add this kindness of Bima's to the other pieces I had learned, and those I thought I knew from before. I still hadn't decided if Bima was a friend or not. I remembered how he had jumped in to explain—in Vik so I wouldn't understand—who Rell was to one of the soldiers. She had wrinkled her nose and turned away. But then he had told Rell the Vikland mare was his. I decided I needed to think about it more before I said anything else.

"Oro is gone." I waited for a response. Receiving none, I tried again. "Oro is gone, and no one seems to care. When I tried to talk to Rygee about it, he just said Oro is old enough to know his own mind and changed the conversation."

"But you feel differently? Did Oro not leave under his own will? Wait. Tell me from the beginning in your own way." He leaned back against one of the heavy worktables, resting his hands flat on the surface behind him.

"So." I ordered my thoughts in my head. "The last I saw Oro was the night before you and Rell left for Vikland. You were making plans and told us to prepare the wood since you were going to lose so much time traveling. The next morning, I saw you off. I thought about going back to bed since it was so early, but the drizzle had already started so I went to the workshop instead." I smiled at him. "It was closer and dry. At midday, Oro still hadn't joined me, so I went looking for food and him. I went looking in all the public spaces and the livestock pens and then the stables, and that's when I noticed one of the horses was gone. When Rygee came home that night, I told him, but he just said Oro is our age and free to come and go. But it has been days, Piffik, days and nobody seems to care!"

Piffik dropped his eyes to the floor, saying nothing. I threw the sanding block on the table in frustration.

"You don't care either!"

His head snapped up. "I do care, Zren! And I feel the shame of it. But even though I drove him away, I don't know how to bring him back. I can say I'm sorry, but he must appear in front of me before he can hear the words. What else would you have me do, Zren?"

I was confused and my face must have shown it.

"How is this your fault?" I asked.

He blew out a breath. "In Manumina, we hold all things in common. But to avoid chaos, each trade must have a master, journeymen, and apprentices. When I was planning to leave for

Vikland, I was distracted by all that must be accomplished, so I gave you orders as if you were ten-year-old apprentices: when the others say, 'do,' they must do, and when the others say 'go,' they must go.

"Bless the Wester stars, Zren, you never take offense when you are asked to do something. I fear Oro is not so…willing. When I told him—and you—to have all the wood sanded and measured, I thought he packed his bags and left for Vikland. Am I wrong in thinking this?" He looked at me closely.

"Oh." I was silent for a moment. "I thought he went to Cloa to see…Arden and Linna. I worried he would have a misadventure traveling alone."

"I see." He crossed his arms in front of him. "Did you tell Rygee this?"

"No," I answered quietly, "I only told him Oro was gone."

"Ah. Rygee thinks like Rygee. He travels easily wherever he chooses and speaks his mind without deference because he is Kereki in the land of his birth. He grew up by his father's side expecting to run a farm of his own someday and was well-trained to be a leader of men. He has many skills and a wife of wisdom and talents of her own. To him, Oro is making his way in the world just as Rygee plans to soon."

He paused. "This is not my story to tell, but you should know Rygee has no desire to live at Manumina after the war. He plans to go confront his father and his brothers for the wrong that was done to him and reclaim his place by his father's side."

"Rygee is leaving us?" I whispered hoarsely.

"He will, and Siba is happy to go with him and see more of the world." He added slowly, "and now I finally understand what is your true sorrow." He paused. "You are concerned if you left us as Oro did, no one would seem to care, and we would go about our day with only a wave." He flapped his hand in the air. "Zren is a man about the world; he knows his own mind!" He added the last words in a thick Conrosan accent, and I laughed in spite of myself.

"Zren, you would be missed. I would miss you immensely. I would not hold you to Manumina as a prisoner, but I would feel the hole in my heart." He gave me a half smile, and I knew his words were true. He continued, "Are you sure Oro is in Cloa?"

I tilted my head considering. "I would not say beyond a doubt, but I cannot think of any other place."

He nodded. "I'll talk to Rygee tomorrow. Thank you for talking to me about this. I blamed myself for driving him away. I could not see through anyone else's eyes on this, and I did not want to confess to my shame."

CHAPTER 27

ORO RETURNS

Three days later, we had a rare day during the Wet—overcast with a bite to the breeze, but blessedly drip free. Rell and Siba scrambled to do the laundry. Lou bundled up his cheeses and his butter and insisted he was going to run his dairy route himself because I ate up too many profits. Rygee and I helped him load up and then watched him drive out and south to Ahni.

Piffik must have gotten up before first light—of course—to work in the woodshop. Rygee said Piffik had pilfered some pastries he had planned to take to Sary to sell.

"Either that, or you got up in the middle of the night to eat them, which actually isn't that far gone of an idea." He grinned at me. "But I know how much you love your pillow."

I helped Rygee hitch up his horses as well. As long as the skies were holding back the day's rains, he thought he would drive to Sary with a load of baked goods.

"If it's not pouring rain after you finish the animal chores, Zren, if you would go out to the orchard and see if you can find any fruit we missed during the harvest, I'll bake a pie or two for tonight when I return."

It was close to midday, and I was out in the orchard when I saw a cart and a single horse turn down the breakaway from the Huntsman's Trail to Manumina. It was still a ways down the track, but I thought it could be the rag and bone cart—one small enough to be driven by one strong horse if a team wasn't available. I went down to go in the side door to tell Rell and Siba I thought Tiju Tia had returned, and to open the gates for the cart to drive through.

The women gratefully stopped their work and waited with me to greet the travelers. There were two of them as expected, Tiju Tia bundled in her much mended and dirt-colored cloak, the hood thrown back to show her white hair twisted in short tight curls. I had expected Josef to be sitting next to her, but instead Oro towered over her small frame. He had a bad bruise on his jaw, a black eye, his shirt was torn from shoulder to hem, and a white bandage encircled his arm where his sleeve should have been.

I cut my eyes to the healers standing next to me.

"Looks like I have to finish the laundry, doesn't it?"

"He's sitting upright," Siba said thoughtfully. "It could be Tiju Tia already mended him."

"I thought Tiju Tia did the damage," Rell said under her breath.

We all choked back a laugh; they were close enough to hear us.

"Hello!" I cried out.

"Hello the house! Hello to all of you!" Tiju Tia called back. She drove past us, and I followed to unhitch and care for the horses, while Rell and Siba pulled the gates shut. In the stables, I lifted her down from the wagon.

"What needs to be done?" I asked.

"I was going to ask you the same question."

"Siba and Rell are doing the laundry now that we finally have a day without rain. But I was going to take over so they could look at Oro." I turned to him. "How many of them were there this time?"

He grimaced. "Two." He didn't say anything more although I stood there clearly waiting for more of the story.

Tiju Tia jumped in, "We saw you picking fruit. Do we need to be in the orchard today?"

"I was only looking for late strays not ripe at the harvest. If there is enough, Rygee was going to bake pies for us tonight. Piffik is building some commissions but said he didn't need my help. Lou is out on the cheese rounds and won't be back for twelve days. Rygee has gone to Sary to sell baked goods to the stores and talk to the Justice. He and Piffik will buy out the conscription papers of farm boys this season so we have help for the planting next Dry. Rygee said they would do that where he grew up. Once he knows when the names will be drawn, he and Piffik will go back to Sary, and he will teach him how buying the contracts are done. Piffik said both men have to sign the papers—Rygee as a farm manager and Piffik as a voice of the council. Does that make sense to you? I'm not sure I told you right."

Tiju Tia snorted. "Zren, before I came to Manumina, you could have told me yams grew out of trees and I would have believed you. I'm the daughter of a tailor, remember? We are all very fortunate Rygee chose to make Manumina his home."

I thought with a sick twist of my stomach how Rygee was planning to leave someday and take Siba with him. I started to tell Tiju Tia, but then I remembered Piffik had told me it wasn't his story to tell. It wasn't mine either, I realized. But there was other news.

"Piffik and Rell sold the horses."

Tiju Tia stopped sorting out the clothes at the back of the cart and looked at me and then at the stalls with our Manumina cart and plow horses contentedly resting.

"It must have been an interesting time while I was away." She put her hand on Oro's arm. "See Rell. She may have something for the pain." He nodded stiffly to her and went out.

I put the last of the tack away. "What happened to the two horses you started out with? This is the gelding Oro rode when he left Manumina."

"Callis had hired them in Huk and brought them to Josef. When we met up with Oro north of Cloa, Josef said the gelding was strong enough to pull the rag and bone wagon alone. He took the hired horses to bring back to Callis at Huk as he traveled to his home. Thank the seas and stars, Oro took this one. I didn't realize some of the horses could pull the cart as a single." Tiju Tia leaned over the short wall to stroke the big gelding's neck.

"Actually, they all could. The rag and bone cart and the cheese cart are both much lighter than the iron plows they have to drag through the dirt in the planting season." I paused. "Is Oro going to be all right?"

Tiju Tia gave a heartfelt sigh. "He will. His pride is hurt most of all. But it is not my story to tell. I am not sure if he has decided to make it a funny adventure he will share with all of us, or if this has wounded him deeply." She gathered the clothes she had bargained for and we walked together out into the yard. "Zren, if you don't mind, why don't you let me help Siba with the laundry and you go back into the orchard? I really don't care to be climbing about in trees if I can only do it one-handed. You said Lou is gone, and inside the gates, I feel much easier about showing both hands."

"Truly?" I was astonished. "Of course, absolutely! There is only a small chance of being stung by bees while picking fruit. When I do the laundry, there is a very great chance of being scalded by boiling water!" I touched her lightly on the shoulder. "It is so very good to have you back." I grinned at her. "Stories are going to be good tonight!"

***

When Siba cooked, it was all good Conrosan comfort food: sweet potatoes and other root vegetables, ramps, wild greens, and savory spices. She didn't use meat, like Koanga she didn't eat flesh, but tonight she had a side plate of cheese, figs, and some salty olives Rell had brought from Juisiti. Rygee had tasted olives before, they were common in South Kerek and in Matasi, he said. Siba must have sampled them in the kitchen, so we all watched Piffik to see his first reaction. Rell had told him to eat the fig, the cheese, and the olive in that order. I knew he would make the same mistake I did when I had tasted them for the first time in Ribelo. They were not sweet like figs. His face puckered up and we all laughed.

"Do you eat those? Truly? Or was this just to mock me?" he demanded.

Rell reached over to his plate, took two of the olives, and popped them casually in her mouth. "They are delicious, Piffik! How can you think otherwise?"

He reached forward and cautiously tasted another. "Hmm, they are unusual. But good… if you don't have expectations."

"Like our travels these past days," Tiju Tia started. "Zren, why don't you begin the story first? I assume everyone knows how we met Falan, Josef, and the Viklanders at the southern settlement, but once I left with the Wrens and the hired horses, I have no further knowledge of anyone's adventures."

I explained how we had left the next morning with the Viklanders dressed in Kereki clothes and had reached the same abandoned cottage for the first night's stop.

"But it wasn't abandoned, Tiju Tia, there was a Kereki army patrol—four of them—patting down the graves of the deserters from the night before. The two Viklander soldiers shot them before the patrol even knew we were there. I could not explain in time."

"The deserters were both so young, the age of my Wrens. I had hoped they had made it home and left the war behind." Tiju Tia sounded sad.

I went on to tell her how Bima thought the soldiers were burying Viklanders. They had uncovered the faces of the dead to be sure, and I had asked Bima to read the Keresh word carved in the X at the foot of the grave. Once they had read 'Deserter,' they were convinced. We took the four Kereki army horses and the Viklander mare still in the cottage and pushed through all night to Manumina.

"Bima rode up in front to keep me awake. Oh, Tiju Tia, you never told me there were Kereki Trickster Tales! They're horrible!"

She chuckled, and I went on to tell everyone we had continued to swap out the horses through the long night to keep moving forward, but by the time we reached Manumina, all the horses were spent.

"When I woke up the next morning, the Viklanders were gone with Rygee and Siba and the old plow horses." I looked at Rygee and Siba to continue.

"You sure it was still morning when you woke up, Zren?" Siba said drily. She looked at Rygee, he nodded at her, and she began.

"My talents are in healing. I am not meant to be wandering about the countryside with Viklanders in my wagon bed. I have no softfooting skills, and I cannot tell a falsehood. Even so, my husband tells me Zren has been awake all night and he wants to let him sleep. Would I like to go on an overnight adventure, first to visit the garrison at Ishes and then to resupply the shepherd's cottage in Vikland? I, the foolish woman that I am, say yes, because I have been beguiled by my husband's charm since the first time he invited me to eat a meal he cooked with his own hands.

"We are not even halfway to Ishes when our luck is stolen by Conrosan fairies. Three Kereki soldiers stop us and ask us our business. The Viklanders hiding in the wagon are lying on their stomachs hiding their hands and their faces beneath the hoods of the cloaks we have provided them. Yet I cannot imagine how any of them are as frightened as I am. I keep my eyes on my hands in my lap and listen in astonishment as the man who has promised never to lie to me has no trouble telling falsehoods with a very smooth tongue and innocent face. He tells the soldiers, he has been visiting his wife's family at Manumina, he has farmhands sleeping in the back of the wagon, and he lives near Fortika—which everyone knows is a Kereki stronghold near the Cold Mountains. And with just three lies he has told the Kereki soldiers we are not who we seem to be.

"After my husband spins his tale and gives away the Viklanders' midday meal, we are permitted to go on, and my husband jokes with me as if this is something he does often. Just within view of the garrison at Ishes, Rygee asks Bima and the soldiers to exchange places with us. He has never been to Ishes, he says, without Piffik. He worries Viklanders think all Kerekis look alike…and look like the enemy."

She sighed. "Bima and I tell the commander of our narrow escape, the wounded soldier is whisked to the infirmary, and the two soldiers disappear into Vikland clothes never to be seen again. The commander gives us food, we head directly for the Vikland border and down south to the shepherd's cottage, and finally, my husband gives me the lovely adventure he has promised."

It took us a moment. Siba has told her tale so demurely, with so much wide-eyed wonder at first we don't hear the words she says. Then Rell whooped, Ngahuru snorted, Rygee and Piffik blushed. I just sit there with my mouth open. Siba laughed at all of us.

Rygee leaned over and very gently kissed her on the top of her head.

"I love that you surprise me. I love that you are brave. I love you."

CHAPTER 28

ARRELLA HUENA OF AXEFIELD

Tiju Tia cleared her throat. "So now I know how we gained and lost four Viklanders. Tell me Piffik, how we became horse thieves." She smiled, but Piffik grimaced.

Rell jumped in to tell the tale, "Well, we all know Zren is such a delicate flower, he cannot sit a spirited horse for a day. The horses were far too recognizable to stay here at Manumina, and most of them were trained for riding only. So Piffik asked me to ride the Viklander mare and travel with him to take the Kereki army horses to sell them for coin over the border. My family was happy to see me and thrilled to buy the horses—all five of them. My brother Dylis delivered me back to the refugee camp at Rishka, and Piffik and I took a wagon and a team of horses from there to here.

"You should know, my mother and I went to Juisiti. My family thought I needed to report to the Diplo service, and if I had been declared as a deserter, to plead my case and accept the consequences. My younger brothers would be entering their military service in the next two years, and my family did not want a cloud of shame or doubt over our name.

"But in the offices of First Soldier Joon, I was shown the rolls of the sons and daughters of Vikland, and I am listed 'in active service as a healer and a translator at Manumina, an infirmary way station for Vikland in the war against Kerek.' Piffik and I talked about this on the way here, and we have decided not to address the issue with the Council of Wisdom. They are still dependent on the mercy of the Empress for their place to call home in Vikland, and he did not want the elders' morals to get in the way of the children's meals."

Rell laughed. "It is one thing for me to show up unannounced with five horses. I am not sure what my father would say if I showed up in Axefield with two hundred Conrosans and begged to keep them as well."

"Why is your home called Axefield? That is a Keresh name," I asked.

"True. It is Keresh. It is an old story and one that is actually told in one of our Warrior books of Wisdom. Would you like to hear it?" Rell looked about the table. We all nodded, and she leaned back in her chair and began.

"Not so long ago, and not so far away there was Vikland, a vast land of forest and fields, mountains and meadows. It was a land

worthy of the warriors who walked upon it, and in return, those who ruled ensured the warriors and their families were worthy of the land.

Now Vikland, for all of its many riches, is a land with mountains on three sides. The Cold Mountains are to the north with the Northern Sea kissing the other side, the smaller Silver Mountains rise to the south with the country of Matasi and their terraced farms guarding the southern face, and the Sun Mountains to the east. The Sun Mountains are so tall and forbidding no one has seen what lies beyond. On the west, my friend, oh, on the west lies the tiny country of Kerek, a land so small you can walk across it north to south in eight days and from west to east in ten days.

Now the land of Kerek did not love its people as Vikland loved its warriors. There were no endlessly thick forests, and only South Kerek could grow orchards and lush fields with much hard work and anxious looks at the rainless skies. But the Kingdom of Kerek owned access to the sea, and while the land was a miser in her favors, the sea opened her arms and embraced the ships of trade, the fishing boats, and the pleasure craft of the wealthiest of Kerek City, the seat of the Kings of Kerek.

For all the years past, Kerek needed the riches of Vikland, and Vikland needed a port to sail its goods around the world. The Empresses of Vikland and the Kings of Kerek wrote out lengthy trade agreements, signed them, and it was so.

Ah, my friends. Greed is the devil who steals men's souls. The Kerek border settlements looked at the wealth of the Vikland villages and wondered how they could gather that unto themselves. For Kerek was crowded with too many people in a small country, and small holdings lay alongside of each other like quarrelsome siblings. A border misremembered, a fence in disrepair, a neighbor's flock gone missing and found in another's vegetable patch, too many sons, and not enough land. And then eyes would look east to Vikland with its wide spaces, well-tended farms, and tidy prosperous villages.

Greed roared.

The first border raids were successful because the Viklanders could not believe friends and neighbors for generations could eat at their table, drink from their wells, and murder them where they stood. Entire villages were fired into ashes. Before the smoke had cleared, Kereki settlers were exchanging pikes for pitchforks, driving a stake in the ground, and saying, "Mine!"

Now every Viklander knows the stories from the books, The Wisdom of the Warriors. And from the bravery of those in the past, and the cleverness of those who looked beyond the obvious, the Viklanders knew they could defeat the devil called Greed who had whispered poison into their neighbors' ears.

They looked to the longbow their hunters used in the far eastern reaches of Vikland and thought how could a child use this? Or a man or woman advanced in years who had the strength to draw, but not to hold? And the crossbow was born. They looked to the slingshots the children used to bring down small game for the stewpot and thought, how could we use this to stop their armies? And kettles to be lit with flame and fire were mounted on wheels to fling into the approaching raiders. They looked to the men and women who could draw and hold the longbow to hunt large animals to feed a village or defend their holdings and they taught them to shoot arrows tipped with fire as well as cold metal.

All this the warriors did to defend those under their protection and stand for justice for their land and their lives.

Now the village of Ssaum lay a full two days walk from the border of Kerek and Vikland. During the Dry, their youth would travel to the eastern edge of Vikland to work in the forests in the high hills under the watchful eye of the Sun Mountains. But once the Wet had drenched the roads, and the rain and fog clouded their vision, the men and women would gather their paypackets, their axes, and their belongings, and find their soggy way home. When they arrived, there would be rejoicing and food to celebrate the return of so many to spend the Wet among their families.

One day, Kereki raiders decided to push in farther to Vikland. They had captured or burned many of the border towns. Whether the soil was enriched by fire, by blood, or by greed, the Kerekis declared it better than their own. The raiders decided to strike during the little

Dry, the few days in the middle of the Wet when the clouds take a rest from the daily showers. They would not be expected then, and it would be dry enough to see and fire the buildings and murder those who fled their homes and barns.

They chose Ssaum.

Just at dawn, the raiders crawled and slipped into place. Suddenly the geese in the village began to squawk and honk, waking up not only the poor goose girl, but all the people in the village. The raiders first charged the geese thinking to silence them, but the villagers saw them and gave a battle cry. All of the Viklander youth, women, and men, grabbed their work axes and ran out into battle. The bowmasters grabbed quarrels and bolts and called the children to line the windows, crossbows ready to help their older brothers and sisters.

Before the sun had cleared the horizon, the battle was over. The raiders had never encountered the strength of those who wielded the axe. Their knives could not reach. Their wooden shafts of pikes and spears shattered like kindling before them. And those who did not hide behind a Viklander? The quarrels and bolts flew true from the children's crossbows.

These raiders were not warriors who deserved the funeral pyres at dusk. Instead the victors loaded the bodies on to the wagons the Kerekis had brought with them to hold the spoils of war. The horses were pointed to Kerek and driven off to show what happened to those who tried to take what wasn't theirs. Then the Viklanders decided to go further, in case the Kerekis thought to try again. They renamed the village Axefield, a Keresh word, so even the ignorant and foolish among the border raiders would know this village homed warriors of renown.

"This is my family's home," Rell finished simply. "This is why it has a Keresh name even though it is far from the border of Kerek. I am Arrella Huena of Axefield, Vikland."

Tiju Tia smiled. "It is a home worthy of you. And so is Manumina. You have fought your way across Kerek with Rygee and Zren, you fought your way back from a very dark place. And I will continue to stand beside you here at Manumina, way station of Vikland or not."

The room was quiet until Piffik cleared his throat. "So tell us Tiju Tia, how you could travel out on a simple resupply run with Zren and then begin a chain of events that led us all to the adventures of the last few days?"

"Life is never simple, no?" She told us how she had driven Falan and Josef back to Balza. The tense conversation Tiju Tia had carried with Falan's landlady, who was not at all pleased her charge had been out all night. She and Josef had rested for the day at one of the northern hideaways and then spent the evening resupplying Josef's caches with Kereki clothes and disguises, storing food that would not spoil, and burying tiny purses of coins.

Josef was known to the Viklander encampment fighting in the area. They had left the rag and bone wagon at Josef's homestead and walked to the encampment. Josef wore a bright blue cloak and whistled a tune as he and Tiju Tia approached the sentries. They stopped for news of fighting in the area, dispatches to be carried by Tiju Tia to Ishes and onward, and word of missing or separated patrols to be on the lookout. They had slipped unmolested, if not unchallenged, through a large swath of Josef's territory and then swung down and picked up the rag and bone wagon as Josef traded his bright blue cloak for a drab grey one to resupply Callis and Ross at Huk.

They had set up their rag and bone wagon near Huk's village green. Tiju Tia now dressed as a Kereki boy called Will, with stained brown hair and grey clothes to wash out a faded face and right hand even further.

Ross had visited early in the afternoon. He had looked up and down at Josef, at the almost new long dark green skirt, pale green blouse, and black lace up Viklander boots peeping out.

"I suppose if you are wearing those ugly boots, then there is no chance of me getting a new pair." He showed off his feet dressed in leather scraps and rags. "They took my coin as well. And all I was doing was walking from a settlement a half day's walk from here—Therla—do you know it? Northeast of here."

"I do," Josef had replied. "There must have been more than two of them or you would be bruised from the fight you gave to keep your belongings."

"Yes. There were three. They headed east fast—too fast for me to catch them." Ross shrugged. "I have friends east of here."

"Most of the Kereki army is east of here," said an older woman pawing through the clothes. "If your thieves are any bigger than you, they'll be pressed into service." She blew out a noisy breath and looked at Josef. "Don't you have any traveler's cloaks? I need one for my son, he's almost as tall as you…" She paused and looked closely at Josef. "And looking for a wife. You're very tall for a woman."

"I am. It's why I am not married," Josef lied glibly. "I have such a pretty face, but I refuse to marry any man I would look down on."

Tiju Tia looked about the table. "I thought I would choke on my laughter. Here is Josef trying to gather information on the three Viklanders Ross has just moved east on horses and supplied with clothes, maps, and coins, and some old busybody wants to bring him home for her son as easily as I would buy a meat pie for my midday."

She continued, "We were able to replace Ross's boots and send another pair with him. Ross left satisfied knowing we would replenish his supplies in the woods."

Then she sighed. "Callis came after work late in the day, but she had news. Two Kereki army patrols were traveling from Huk to Evensong for meetings with the landowners with large holdings in the north to discuss arming another local militia. There were also soldiers acting as crimpers sweeping through looking for unemployed manabouts and layabouts. Callis had looked down her nose at Josef and said, 'I am not worried about you, but you should pass the word to Nelo and Arden, they're the sort of men to be grabbed for soldiers.'

"Josef had replied he could see how Callis would assume he was far too clever to be taken, but he would take the other Wrens under his wing and make sure they stayed safe as well." Tiju Tia chuckled. "I do not fear for that one. He has a mind as quick and clever as yours, Piffik."

From Huk to Regno, they changed their maskovesto again. Josef aged his face to be an old woman on the rag and bone wagon, traveling with Will, a Kereki boy too disfigured to be taken by the crimpers, yet old enough to ensure his mother was not traveling alone.

They stopped at Nelo's home and as they were unloading his supplies, he had appeared out of the woods carrying two rabbits for his meal. He spitted them over the hearth and while they waited for the food, Tiju Tia passed along Callis' news of the impressment gangs and to be on the lookout for Ross's Viklanders fleeing east on horses. Nelo had an idea to which barns Ross may have sent them.

As it was on the way to Cloa, he would stop to see if they had passed through, and then continue on and warn Arden at the Cloa stables. Dressed as they were, Tiju Tia and Josef would continue on to Regno and leave supplies for Dica and Tyra at a shepherd's hut on Regno lands. They slept that night at Nelo's—only the second night without a watch since Tiju Tia had left Manumina.

At Regno, Dica had not been available to see them, so they traveled on to Fortika. Tyra had been a wealth of information. Tiju Tia had been able to pass the Viklanders' dispatches on to Inezi, the gamekeeper's daughter at Fortika, who would get them to another softfoot.

Inezi warned them Evensong was fortifying itself to be a garrison of the north and to avoid traveling there in the future. There was a footman there who was friendly with the cook and with Tyra and fed her information. Neither Inezi nor Tyra knew if he was part of their sedition, or if he was just boasting of all he knew.

Inezi told them of a curing shed on a neighboring farm where they could spend the night. She didn't trust any of the buildings on Regno or Fortika and certainly not Evensong. There were many Kereki army patrols in the area. Josef took the watch so Tiju Tia could drive the next day. The plan was to work their way down through Sary and avoid Cloa altogether. Nelo would need to supply Linna and Arden this time.

Tiju Tia paused and looked at Oro. When he didn't say anything, she continued, "A day and a half later, Nelo stepped out of the woods a decon north of Sary to intercept us. I was driving and Josef was sleeping, so it would have taken me a moment to pull my short bow. He dropped his hood in time for me to recognize him. Nelo had a package for me he said, one picked up from Linna in Cloa. I woke up Josef and the two of them went back in the woods to collect it. I was expecting one of the Viklanders Ross had told us about in Huk. Perhaps one had been injured or separated from the others. But instead, Josef comes out of the woods leading our old gelding and beside him, Oro, as battered and bruised as you see him now." She glanced at Oro, who dropped his eyes to the floor.

"The four of us talked out new plans. Oro said no one else was in danger, but he refused to say more. Nelo would add nothing except Arden said it wasn't his story to tell and Linna had not been hurt. Josef decided the gelding could carry the cart alone, and he would take the hired horses back to Huk. Josef said he would let Ross know his Viklanders had made it as far as the barns Ross had marked on the map, and they were still on three horses. They would probably make it back to Vikland as they were now less than a day and a half from the border.

"Since Oro would go back with me, Josef loaded another saddle bag of clothes, food, and coin for Linna at Cloa. He changed out of his dress into Kereki male clothes and exchanged his grey traveler's cloak for a pale fawn-colored one from our cart. Nelo transferred the saddle from the gelding Oro rode to one of the hired horses and fashioned a short lead line for the other. Josef mounted and rode out. Nelo packed a small amount of food for himself in an extra shirt from the cart and faded back into the woods on foot. Oro and I climbed up on the wagon seat, and we rode unchallenged the rest of the way. Now here we are."

As one, we all swiveled our heads to Oro to find out what happened next. He looked at the floor and mumbled. The silence grew longer and then uncomfortable. Suddenly he pushed himself to his feet and stomped out.

"Was it because he looks Vik or because our Wrens are compromised?" Piffik asked softly. "We need to know that much at least to best protect him and the others."

"It is neither," Tiju Tia blew out a noisy breath. "I had hoped he would make light of it and tell the tale himself, but I don't know much more from him, except he says he was not hunted, and the Wrens are not in danger." She paused for a long moment and then added, "I treated his arm for a dog bite."

Siba leaned back with a thoughtful look at Tiju Tia.

"He needs time and space. As long as no one else is in danger, I think we can give him that. How good Nelo was able to intercept you north of Sary." She paused. "Do you think the older Wrens are safe from the crimpers?"

Tiju Tia stared at the ceiling as if she could read the answer there. "Arden is protected by his position in Cloa. As long as the stable master speaks for him, I do not worry. Kid has the ability to hide in plain sight, as does Josef, although for different reasons. I am worried for Nelo. He has no visible employment and neither Dica nor Tyra has enough influence in their great houses to save him. Provided the soldiers are but one or two, I think the boys would be underestimated enough they could escape or fight their way free—more than that, and all my Wrens would be at risk."

For myself, I could only piece together that Oro had ridden to Cloa, presumably to give Linna the letter, somehow he had been bitten by Arden's dog—how or why I hadn't a clue—and Nelo had picked Oro up and taken him along after he had gone to warn Arden of the crimpers. I decided Tiju Tia had been the Softfoot of the West Islands too long to be able to tell the truth so well without telling the truth at all.

Our little group broke up soon afterwards. Siba and Rell went to the round church building where Piffik had built huge wooden drying racks to hold all our clean laundry and the clean and mended items for the rag and bone wagon. I asked to wash the dishes thinking Tiju Tia would join me, and I could ask her more questions then. Rygee said he would take on the animal chores, and Piffik was going to disappear into his workshop to work on his commissions.

Tiju Tia never joined me. As I was drying and hanging up the last of the pots and pans, Rygee came in and washed up in the bucket beside me. I watched as he lathered up the soft homemade soap and pushed it up his white Kereki arms. I wondered what it would be like to be able to walk into any place in Kerek, get a quick once over, and then be ignored to go about business without a second concern. I wondered how much of Rygee's confidence came from his knowledge of farming and animals or of Kerek embracing him as one of theirs.

"Are my fingers going to fall off, or did I miss a spot?" Rygee plunged his arms in the deep pail and rinsed them off.

I realized I was staring and looked up. "Do you have to worry about the crimpers?"

"Mmmmm. I didn't think of that. I don't think so. I am listed in Sary's tax rolls as Manumina's Farm Manager and husband of Siba Namikk, a woman of Conrosan birth, so I should be exempt. But I am a deserter, Zren, and could be hung for not reporting for duty." He grimaced. "They would have to find me first."

"Truly?" I was astonished.

"Truly. It's one of the reasons I took Siba's family name as my own when Piffik and I went to register me as the farm manager in Sary. Well that, and I am not feeling very charitable towards my father, even after all these years."

"What about the Wrens?"

"I don't know, Zren. I hope they have enough warning to either go to ground or make it here to Manumina. I gather Piffik is in his workshop right now trying to decide if the four oldest males should be replaced with Conrosans—you, Siba and Piffik—which would have my very strong objections, or whether he and Tiju Tia can come to some sort of an agreement."

"Piffik and I could go—not Siba," I offered.

"Zren, your face won't let you lie, and Piffik's conscience won't let him kill. I cannot think of two worse people to overthrow a kingdom within Kerek—yet here you both are." He clapped me on the back. "It's late and I'm for my bed. G'night, Zren." We walked out into the night, and he walked across the green to the healer's house above the infirmary. I slipped out the side door of the stockade to the house I shared with Rell.

CHAPTER 29

THE CRIMPERS

The days rolled by—wet, but calm. Oro's bruises faded, his arm healed with a small round bite-sized scar. Piffik finished his commissions on time by burning lanterns at both ends of the day. Tiju Tia and Rygee bred more of the rabbits and marked others for meat to be delivered to Ross in the next resupply run. Lou returned from his cheese route and gleefully dropped the coin purse of profits on our midday meal. He announced I would never again be allowed to drive the cart and sell his goods. Piffik had pursed his lips at Lou's news but said nothing. I knew Piffik was not upset about Lou driving the cart and being gone more from Manumina, but the Wrens needed me to drive the third cart to help them between Tiju Tia's rag and bone run and Piffik's deliveries. I wasn't worried. I knew Piffik or Tiju Tia would come up with a new plan for me.

We were all exhausted. In a normal time, the Wet was when work slowed down. Animals were cared for, but they rested for the Dry planting season. There were no gardens to tend, food to preserve, fields to weed and scythe. But we were too few trying to run the settlement. Laundry wasn't just for the six of us, it was all of Tiju Tia's rag and bone bargains, Viklander uniforms to be mended and washed and taken to Ishes or the shepherd's hut in Vikland, Kereki clothes to push out to the Wrens. Siba spent all of her time sewing when she wasn't washing clothes, decocting potions, and fixing up Viklanders. Rell had taken on the manabout chores with the animals so that Piffik, Oro, and I could earn more coin for Manumina by working in the woodshop every day some of us weren't making a delivery. Rygee spent more time on horseback away from the settlement learning news from the Justices, buying supplies, and selling Manumina's medicinals, baked goods, and the occasional chickens or rabbits. Oro and I were everyone's second pair of hands in the settlement and the unseen and unnamed second bodies on the carts and wagons to Mr. Qanaq, Mr. Namikk, and Tiju Tia.

I collapsed into my bed one night after a day of getting Lou off after first meal for another dairy run of eight days, a morning of helping Rell with animal chores, an afternoon of folding laundry for Tiju Tia's cart, and an evening of loading coffins for Oro to take the next day to Ishes.

I dreamt the horse was running at me at full gallop. I was lying on the ground too tired to get out of the way of danger. I knew in moments I would be trampled. I tried to force my limbs to move and suddenly, I was awake. I gasped in relief it had only been a dream, when I realized I did hear hoof beats galloping closer.

I rolled out of bed, grabbed my pants, and crouched low to get to my window. One horse, one rider, veering off the main track and heading down the breakaway for Manumina. One of ours most likely, or a Viklander on a stolen horse. I grabbed a shirt and raced down the stairs, stopping at the landing only long enough to pound on Rell's bedroom door and call out "Rider," before hurrying down. I unbarred the door and stepped silently outside to the darkness of my front porch. I heard Rell slide open her window, and the clunk of her crossbow against the windowsill. She would recognize the rider long before I would.

The rider didn't rush for the gates but knew to pick their way along the west wall where Rell and I lived outside the stockade. One of ours then.

I called out first in Conrosan, and then "Cio Claro!"

"Bless the stars! I'm Kid. I need Tiju Tia right away!" He angled his horse and threw back his hood so I could see his face. "Quickly!" he added hoarsely.

"Let's get you inside and take care of that horse before Piffik sees it." I stepped off the porch and opened the side door into the blockade. He dismounted and gently led the horse inside. I pointed him to the guest house where Tiju Tia and Oro still lived. "I'll take care of your horse, you go wake her and tell her your news. Her house should be unbarred."

He nodded his thanks and stumbled across the green. I looked at him as he mounted the steps to the house. I had been so worried about the horse I had forgotten to ask if he was hurt. I turned and led the bay into the stables.

Rell found me a short time later. I had dried and brushed the horse, put out food and water, and was wiping down the tack and saddle.

"We need you inside, Zren, to make our plans. Nelo has been taken by the Kereki army. He was pressed by the crimpers near Fortika. Kid heard it at Evensong from Inezi, one of Bima's softfoots." She stepped into the next stall and looked at the horse. "Kid said he exchanged horses on the way, so there is more than one stolen horse between here and the far north holdings."

"Nelo?" I followed her out of the barn. "I never thought he would be taken. He is far too clever."

"I didn't hear the entire story," Rell shrugged. "Only 'Nelo was grabbed by the crimpers three nights ago south of Fortika,' and then I was asked to go to the stable and bring you in."

The rosy glow of dawn was just lightening the sky as we walked across the grass.

"Kid rode all night?" I asked.

"He did." Rell nodded. "When Inezi rode over to tell him, she brought Kid her master's fastest horse. She told him of a settlement where he could steal another and leave that one in its place. She'll get it later today and hopefully slip it back into the stables undetected. It will be up to us to get this one back where it belongs."

Rell opened the door to the guesthouse, and everyone was there sitting around the table. Kid looked exhausted; everyone else just looked sleepy. Piffik came out of the kitchen with a tray of tiny cups of Vikland coffee. I wrinkled my nose at the smell, but everyone just ignored me as they eagerly reached for the hot cups. Tiju Tia waved at me to sit down.

"Here's what we know to be true," she began immediately. "Nelo was on his walk to Dica at Regno to bring her supplies and pick up messages on her half day. When he didn't arrive as planned, she ran to find Tyra or Therin at Fortika. They said they knew crimpers had been in the area, but not anything more of why Nelo could be delayed. Dica had to hurry back to Regno. That night Inezi came and told her she had been going to meet Nelo in the woods to check the outbuildings for supplies and messages. From a distance, she had seen Nelo coming down the road, but before she could reach him, she saw four men on horseback overtake him on the track. She slipped into the woods to hide because she didn't know who, or what, they were. She watched as one of them had thrown a riata at Nelo while he was running away. Nelo fell to the ground and didn't move. They were tying him up when he started fighting, so Inezi knows Nelo is still alive, but not if he is hurt. Dica said she did not ride a horse well enough to ride all the way to Manumina from Regno. She asked Inezi if she could get a fast horse to Kid at Evensong." Tiju Tia looked at Kid. "Do I have the right of it?"

"Yes," Kid answered. "At Evensong, I heard they are not taking the forced soldiers to the nearest garrison, but to Pagta Hall on the Heartland Trail between Aldi and Ahni. Far enough away it will keep the impressed men from having their Patrons or Farm Managers demanding they be released as unfairly taken. If Nelo is forced to walk from where he was captured, he won't reach Pagta Hall until tonight. That is the one chance we have. Otherwise, he will be sworn in and then his escape will be desertion—and a hanging, if he is caught."

Siba paled and flicked her eyes to Rygee before she focused on Kid again.

"Has anyone here been to Pagta? What do we know of it?" Tiju Tia said briskly.

Piffik cleared his throat. "It's a crossroads town: stables, inns, taverns, market day travelers. Lots of strangers, pushcarts, and back of wagon sellers. No one will take much notice of us once we are there."

"And the Justice? Is he fair? Must he be bribed? Will he listen if we say Nelo is ours?" Tiju Tia questioned.

Piffik lifted his shoulders to his ears and dropped them. "I've only tipped my cap to him. There was no need for any other interaction."

"So he has seen you? Will he remember you?" Tiju Tia sounded sharp.

"Yes. I've delivered furniture there before. I'm sure he's heard of Manumina."

"Rygee, you have the papers from the Sary Justice saying you have bought out the conscriptions for the Dry. Do the papers have a physical description of the Kereki farmhands?"

"No. Only names, ages, the settlements they are from, the dates we expect them to work, and the forms we must sign if they do not show and must report to the army." Rygee checked off his fingers.

"Good." Tiju Tia leaned back in satisfaction. "Very good. Then we tell the truth, but tell it so slanted even Zren's face will match his words." She paused for a moment gathering her thoughts. "Piffik and Rygee will go to Pagta."

"No!" Siba said forcefully. Rygee leaned over and put his arm around her shoulder.

"Hear me to the end. Then we will talk over the objections. Piffik must go because he has been there before and he is known by his charming Conrosan face, if not by name. Rygee must go as the Farm Manager looking for his missing farmhand with the papers from the Sary Justice. We will find some that can be used for Nelo. The papers will claim Nelo works for Manumina—which is true. He was visiting Dica at Regno on her half day—which is true. We were aware of his actions and when he did not return, we grew alarmed—which is also true. Hearing there had been crimpers in the area, we immediately headed to Pagta Hall to ensure our farmhands were not mixed in among them. It will be up to you two to convince the authorities Nelo must return to Manumina."

Tiju Tia looked at me. "Zren and Siba, you must leave immediately and take Kid back to Evensong. His master is not favorable to Vikland, and we can't risk harm or discovery. I am sorry, Kid, you are going to have to sleep in the wagon; there is no time for you to rest here.

"I will dress as a Kereki boy and return the stolen horse. Kid, you must draw me a map with the settlement marked so I will be able to find it. I must wait a day for the horse to rest. Zren and Siba, Kid will draw you a map of where to meet me after you return him to Evensong. You will be traveling nearly continuously, that is why there must be two of you.

"Oro and Rell, all the responsibilities of Manumina will fall on your shoulders. Some of us will return in two days, more for Piffik, Rygee, and Nelo."

"I should return the stolen horse," Oro said. "It is too dangerous for you, Tiju Tia."

"I will be in disguise," she replied. "Farmwork is not suitable for those missing a hand. Neither is the Kereki army. The crimpers will not take me."

"Maybe Oro could travel with Zren. Siba could remain at Manumina," Rygee suggested. "I understand why there must be two people to take turns driving the wagon, and I agree two Conrosans would draw less attention than two males because there are crimpers in the area, but because there are roving bands of men in the area, I am unhappy with Siba traveling."

"I could take her place," Rell said slowly.

"No!" The entire table of people responded.

"Then take my crossbow at least."

"Yes, I will, and thank you, Rell," Siba said gravely.

There was more discussion about the table, but in the end the plan stood as Tiju Tia first laid it out. Rygee and Siba went to go make food for us and talk together. Piffik went to see to the horses which could make such a long journey to Evensong with so little rest. Rell walked with me to our home for me to pack my weapons and her to gather her crossbow.

Rell was quiet almost the entire walk there, then, "Zren, do you still have those little knives you used to kill Bitterboots?"

"A Sailor's Curse. I do, yes."

"And Kereki ties you could use to make riatas?"

"I do, yes."

"Good. Zren, do whatever you need to do to bring Siba back. She saved my life. I can only do this for her, but I know you will keep her safe." She stopped and waited until I looked at her. "You have a Viklander heart, Zren. It is why I call you my little brother. Well that, and you can be so annoying sometimes." She surprised me with a hard hug.

"I will keep her safe." I gave her a half grin.

I ran up the stairs, dressed in fresh clothes, added my knife sheaths and knives, grabbed Kereki ties and a traveler's cloak, and headed back to the guesthouse for first meal. Rell was already there showing Siba how her crossbow worked.

"Without practice, you won't be good at any distance, but if you are overrun, you can't miss the length of a wagon bed."

I handed two daggers to Kid. "These are…"

"…West Islands steel. I know," he finished. "I also have my Sailor's Curse."

Rygee brought out bowls of steaming vegetables and stonebread.

"It's the quickest I could make with what was in the cold room." We all grabbed our bowls and used our stonebread to eat. "Rell, I didn't have time to start the baking, but there is some fruit that must be baked, canned, or stewed today. I'm sorry. It cannot wait until I return." She nodded in response.

"Zren, can I talk to you a moment?" I grabbed my bowl and followed Rygee into the kitchen. "Zren," he blew out a breath, "I remember how you killed Bitterboots. Whatever you have to do to keep Siba safe—do it. Kid will be asleep; I know it will be up to you."

"You stay safe as well. Bringing home Nelo is the more difficult task. Kid and I will keep Siba safe on the way to

Evensong, Tiju Tia and I will keep her safe on the way home," I assured him as I continued to spoon in my food.

"Zren, you need to go," Piffik called from the other room. "Your horse and cart are ready. Don't abuse the horses by making them wait half the day for you."

I tipped up my bowl to get at the last of the juices and pushed the empty dish into Rygee's hands.

"Siba is very precious to all of us." I looked him in the eye. "Rygee, I will protect her with my life. Truly, I will not come home without her."

CHAPTER 30

THINGS THAT GO BUMP IN THE NIGHT

It was a long day. Kid slept, or tried to sleep, for most of it. Siba looked about everywhere, reminding me she had never been north of the Northern Track before. Every time we passed a small settlement, she would wonder aloud about the family who lived there and what their lives would be about. We talked about the academies of Vikland, and she told me she had wanted to study at the Academy of Healing as her aunt had. But there had been no coin for such learning, and in any case, she had never learned Vik at Manumina.

"Who would have taught you? Who taught your aunt?" I asked.

"Over the years, Manumina has had people like you—lost or on their way to someplace else. Some of them come to us because they are broken, or cannot live in Kerek, and some seek us out because of our beliefs to hold all things in common and to act in peace for all people."

"Why don't they stay?"

"Manumina is small: few people, tiny places to live, little coin, and nowhere to hide. At first, they are charmed. Then they are impatient with us for not changing. Then, they leave."

"I heard," I began slowly, "you and Rygee will leave."

She was silent for a long time. "Yes. Rygee wants to return to his family farm as a man to be reckoned with. He says he likes his body to be as busy as his brain, and so he runs Manumina's farming, and bakery, and feeds all of us. But it is not enough for him."

I looked at her a long time. When I couldn't figure out the answer for myself, I just asked, "How do you feel about that?"

"I am excited to see more than just Manumina. I am interested to learn how other people live. But I am afraid once Rygee steps into a bigger world, I will not be enough for him."

I nearly dropped the reins. "That is not true!"

She gave me a side eye. "You know this because of your vast experience in the world?"

"I know this because…" I started again, "You know the story of Bitterboots and Miya's thirteenth crossing?"

She nodded. "Rygee told me when we were still walking out. I said I could not believe you had grown up in Kerek City. We heard such wicked tales of the King's stronghold and port, you see." She saw me bristle and laughed gently. "Oh, Zren, woe to anyone who judges the size of your heart and your courage by the size of your footprint.

"Rygee told me the story of Bitterboots as he knew it. He said he had never seen a man murdered before. Each day after, you acted no differently, as if you killed a man without remorse every day of your life." She looked off into the woods. "You frightened him badly. Nebs too." She was quiet for a long time. "I wonder what kind of man Nebs would have become? If his family ever wonders what became of him?"

I thought about it. "He didn't choose the army. He was conscripted," I said slowly. "I don't even know if Nebs was his birth name or his family name or if it was where he came from. Miya thought the Kerekis were sent along to spy on us, so he didn't want us mingling much."

She snorted. "You were guards who did not need to be paid for protecting the Kereki army payroll."

"True." I gave her a wry grin. "But I killed Bitterboots because I thought Mouser was a threat to me and mine. I hunted Mouser because I thought he was the kind of man who looked for weakness. He would stab us in the back, single someone away from the others, and hurt or kill us one by one. But Bitterboots wasn't innocent. He got in the way of my Sailor's Curse because he thought he was grabbing a woman who could not fight back." I snorted. "If he only would have known, between me and Rell, he got the weaker of the two of us." I nodded to the crossbow at Siba's feet. "Rell saved my life with that crossbow. I expect you to do the same."

We arrived at the edge of Evensong long after dark. Siba wanted to see a great house, so she walked with Kid the last furloughs to see the brick fortress from the edge of the clearing. I stayed behind with the horses and made up a handful of riatas outside of her sight. Without Kid to fight with us, our chances dropped considerably if we encountered army patrols, crimpers, or bandits. And I knew the truth of what I said earlier, if Siba was harmed or killed, I wouldn't be welcomed back at Manumina.

I had just arranged the last of the riatas so they would sit in the wagon within easy reach without rolling around, when Siba returned, her eyes round.

"I never knew one family could live in a house so big. Kid says there are fourteen other servants who work there in addition to him."

I smiled. "Aren't you glad you only have the seven of us to care for at Manumina?"

She smiled back. "Piffik has been to the Rishka estate in Vikland where the Conrosan refugees have been settled. He said they all live in the house, the stables, the summer kitchen, and all the servants' quarters. I did not understand what he was talking about until now." She pulled herself up into the wagon, and we moved off into the night.

We had traveled about a decon when I realized my mistake.

"Siba, one of us was supposed to be sleeping at the same time as Kid. Now we are both tired. If you talk to keep me awake, then I will not hear anything moving about in the shrubbery." I groaned. "Why does far north Kerek have all the trees for the entire country anyway?"

Siba looked about uneasily. "I am not afraid of the night and the things that belong in it."

"Good. Because I am afraid enough for both of us." I smiled in the darkness.

She snapped her eyes back to me. "You are not funny, Zren Janin."

I said nothing in reply, and we continued on. Soon I couldn't deny the uneasy itching and cold chills up my neck and arms. We were being stalked. Not just followed—stalked. I slowed the horses to a crawl to see if I could hear a hoof beat, footfalls, or a wild animal.

"Zren, what…"

"Shh! Listen!" I stopped the wagon and slowly reached for a riata and my boot knife. I whispered to Siba, "Now would be a very good time to notch a bolt in that thing." I used my knife to point to Rell's crossbow.

Siba reached down and picked up the crossbow. She loaded it slowly and carefully and let it rest in her lap. She silently looked about the shrubbery. We waited. I heard old wood snap behind me. I whirled around and saw a flash of black fur about knee height.

"Animal," I breathed, relaxing. "Too small to go after the horses."

"Cio claro!" A hoarse whisper drifted in from the woods on my left.

"Cio claro," I responded. "I am Zren." I let the ribbons of the riata slide through my fingers and drop on to the wagon floor as Arden and his dog stepped out from the woods.

"I hope you knew it was me. I've been trailing you for the last half decon or so."

I slipped my knife back into my boot sheath and sat down hard on the wagon seat.

"Of course I did, your dog gave you away. I hope you realize it's going to get you killed some day," I retorted. I hadn't known he was stalking me for that long. If we had been hunted by bandits with short bows, Siba and I both would have been dead by now.

"Yes. Well, her name is Mother, and she has saved my life four times, which is four more times than you have. So I am inclined to keep her at my side—against your better judgement, Zren," Arden snapped at me.

I wisely changed the subject. "Where are you headed?"

"Anywhere I can get a ride from you." I could hear the smile in his voice again.

I motioned to the back. Arden lifted the dog gently into the wagon bed and came around to climb up on Siba's side, protecting her between us.

"Smart man." I nodded and picked up the reins. "She'll keep you alive longer than I will." I was still stinging over my inability to detect him until the last moment.

He grinned at Siba and his plain face looked much younger.

"You are Siba, the healer of Manumina. How charmed you must be by our Zren to be wandering about on a moonlit buggy ride so far from the comfort of your bed."

She chuckled wearily. "I am here because Tiju Tia needed two Conrosans to return Kid to Evensong and escape the crimpers." She looked at Arden. "Did you hear? They took Nelo."

He nodded sadly. "It is why I am here. Callis risked a message with a stranger who was traveling to Cloa. It could only say 'Nelo was taken.' I came to his holding to see if he had been grabbed as a softfoot, and I needed to get the Wrens to fly to safety, or if the Kereki army just wanted his pretty face behind a pike. It looked like it had been many days since he had been able to sleep in his own bed, so I thought I should see Kid at Evensong for more wisdom. His nobleman frequently entertains the Kereki command and Kid's news is always valuable.

"But no," he shook his head, "my poor dog and I walked all this way only to learn he was not there. His mother lay dying, and he had fled to be by her side and beg her forgiveness," he finished dramatically. Then, more cynically, "He knows that will only work once, right?"

"I don't know what Kid knows or doesn't know, but he fled to Manumina on a stolen horse and another one from Kaumpft's to warn us. Piffik and Rygee are in Pagta now to try to win Nelo's release. They will claim he is a manabout whose services were already purchased from the army many days ago."

"Mmmmm. That may work, but if they question Nelo, he will know nothing about the duties of a manabout. He is as

Lowertown born as you and I, Zren. You have had two years to learn your knowledge. Nelo and I? A handful of days, maybe… and frankly, I was more interested in learning how to hunt with the bows from the Viklander."

"I know, but we didn't have a lot of choices. Tiju Tia is meeting us at the Kaumpft settlement to return the second stolen horse. Hopefully, Inezi has already retrieved her master's horse and slipped it back into the Fortika stables."

"Kid rode horses from Fortika's stables? He has more courage than I do." Arden looked off into the woods. "Kaumpft settlement"—he pronounced it 'Koomf'—"is not for or against Vikland, Zren. They are just four families trying to work together to survive on their holdings." Siba started and stared at Arden, but he was still peering into the woods and missed her look of astonishment. "If you have enough coin to share with them, they will overlook the use of their horses. Inezi should have told Kid so. They are one of hers," he finished and turned back to us.

"She may have," I admitted. "And Kid may have told Tiju Tia. I was only to deliver Kid, drive all night, and pick up Tiju Tia all without getting crimped by the army or killed by bandits." I was getting irritable from lack of sleep.

Arden looked at us thoughtfully. "I drive a wagon about as well as I ride a horse, so why don't the two of you crawl in the back and sleep. I will drive to the Kaumpft settlement."

I gratefully pulled back on the reins, set the brake on the wagon, handed them over to Arden, and climbed over the seat back into the wagon bed without saying another word. I didn't care if it was Siba or the dog nestled against my back, I was asleep as soon as Arden clucked the horses forward.

CHAPTER 31

WHAT HAPPENED THAT NIGHT

I woke with the dog snoring in my face. I hastily rolled over and tried to gulp down some fresh air. I was awake, if not rested, so I pulled myself up.

"Want company?" I whispered to Arden.

"Always."

I pulled myself back over the wagon seat and dropped lightly beside him. "Where are we?" I peered into the darkness around us.

"A little more than a decon, less than two from Kaumpft's. I was thinking I would have to wake you soon. I am not sure where Tiju Tia is going to step out and make herself known. But if she is deadly on her short bow, and if she is expecting two Conrosans on her wagon and sees one Kereki thief instead, she is liable to shoot first and apologize to my dead body later." He smiled at me. "Your curls look like they are going to fly off your head in one hundred different directions."

I scowled and finger combed them down. "I need to ask you something."

"Need and want are two different things," he answered lightly. "Ask me your question."

"Your dog bit Oro, didn't it?"

He stiffened beside me. "Is that what Oro told everyone?"

"No. He has told everyone the Wrens are not in danger."

"They're not," Arden said flatly. "At least, not from Mother."

"Can you tell me what happened? Or at least tell Tiju Tia? Someone needs to know, Arden. Piffik was ready to pull in all the Wrens if they were in danger."

Arden gave me a long look. "Even in darkness, your face gives you away. How did you live in Lowertown without the ability to lie to save yourself from a beating?"

"I ran faster than anyone trying to catch me," I admitted ruefully.

"We did what we had to do," Arden said cryptically. He handed me the reins, leaned back on the wagon seat and stretched out his legs. "All right. You know Linna and I share a house on the edge of Cloa? We say we are brother and sister even though the only look we have in common is our brown hair.

But I accompany her to and from work as I am able, and I have started to walk out with the daughter of the man who owns the stable to lend truth to our maskovesto."

I gave him a disbelieving look. "She is such a sacrifice to be seen with? This wealthy daughter?"

He smiled. "No. She is the middle daughter of the stablemaster. She has a kind face and a good heart. Linna suggested it could smooth my way when I started having trouble moving Viklanders and being present at the stables at the same time. However, he may soon decide his daughter's affections may be better served by a more ambitious man than I am." He paused. "I hope so, anyway, I have learned she is far too sweet to have her feelings treated badly."

I waited a moment. "And this is how Oro came to be bitten by your dog?"

Arden looked down his nose at me. "You are worse than Mother with a fresh bone. No. Oro liked to talk to Linna whenever he and Tiju Tia came to Cloa. Someone, or many someones, decided Linna was too kind to a stranger who looked as he did, and said something within Tiju Tia's hearing which made her think the Wrens could be compromised by appearances."

He gave me a withering look. "So now, I am sleeping in my bed in my house when someone tries to force the window in my room and slip inside. I know it is not Viklanders because we are too close to the heart of the village. I know it is not Wrens because they would use the door and our signal. So, I think it is someone with the intent of doing Linna harm."

He grinned wickedly in the dark. "Now, most households in Kerek have the parents or the daughters sleep on the main floor close to the kitchen hearth and leave the sons and the brothers to fend for themselves in the cold loft. But Linna decided it would be better to have Mother and me between her and anyone who tried to come through our door. In the loft, she is too high to be reached by anyone from the outside and too well protected from the inside."

He shrugged. "Or so Oro learned, when the fool thought to enter the house through the bedroom window. I had fisted him twice while he was still coming through, and Mother had grabbed his arm at my command and bitten him. He roared Linna's name, and she recognized his voice. She begged me to stop. I stepped away and lit a lantern to see what I had done."

I couldn't help it. I laughed. I could imagine Oro trying to fold his long length through the window and I laughed harder. I could picture him stuck as Mother came bounding through the room and latched on his arm.

"It is not amusing, Zren. If I would have had my knives nearer, he would have been dead before I knew who he was." I heard the sorrow in his voice.

I stopped laughing.

We were quiet, and then I gave a sigh and added, "I know. I have killed a man in the dark only to learn it was not the man I hunted. It is something you never forget, and no one lets you forget."

We said nothing for a long while.

Finally, Arden spoke, "Zren, my dog only responded to my command to attack. She would not have bitten Oro otherwise. I do not want it said she is uncontrolled or vicious. She is not a common pup from the dog fights. I thieved her from a litter in a wealthy man's house when I was just a boy and learning my trade. She is a Dunker, a scent hound. It is true, I stole her without realizing all her talents. But as she and I have grown together, I have learned she is loyal, smart, and a great help in finding lost Viklanders."

I hastily assured him, "No one blames Mother. Everyone knows your dog is smarter than you are. No one is blaming anyone."

He laughed a long rolling sort of laugh. "Ah Zren, you should softfoot with us. We could always use your kind of comfort." He gently pulled the horses to a stop. "You should wake Siba now. She should be on the wagon seat as you pull into Tiju Tia's line of sight. I'll rest in the wagon while you tell her I am with you. You should know, I have considered your words and you have the right of it. I will tell Tiju Tia the truth of what happened with Oro. But then I must leave quickly to get to Cloa before daybreak. Thank you for the ride. My feet thank you," he turned back to the snoring dog, "my dog thanks you."

Arden changed places with Siba, and I threw down my traveler's cloak for him to tuck under his head. Siba sleepily asked where we were.

I answered, "Less than a decon from Kaumpfts, I think."

I turned to ask Arden if I was right, but he was already asleep. Siba looked over the edge at him as well.

"Asleep, he looks so young."

I paused while I put some pieces together in my head. "Siba, somehow you knew back at Manumina, Oro had been injured by Arden and Mother. You said to heal, he needed time and space. But if it was just an accident—Arden didn't know who he hit and Mother bit—why would Tiju Tia need to keep them apart? What am I not understanding?"

Siba took a long breath. "Arden was defending his hearth and home and all those entrusted to him. As you defended those you traveled with on the Northern Track. Oro does not mean harm to anyone; he only wanted to spend time with Linna. Yet they collided, because all three of them are just starting to know their own hearts. It is difficult, but the three of them must figure their feelings out on their own." She paused and then added, "I am glad I am not in Cloa."

I gave her a long look. "I don't understand anything you just said. No wonder Tiju Tia doesn't want you leaving the safety of Manumina."

She scrunched up her nose. "My role is to make sure you all live to fight another day. Whether I am inside or outside of Manumina, I can accomplish that."

We plodded along and I could feel the horses dragging with the effort of the never-ending travel. It was longer than a decon by my reckoning, and I was just going to wake Arden and ask if we were supposed to take a breakaway from the main road, when I looked to the right and saw a tidy settlement of four houses, a few outbuildings, and Tiju Tia stepping out from beside the stables, still tying on a skirt about her waist.

I pulled lightly on the reins, and we came to a gentle stop. I silently pointed to the wagon bed. Tiju Tia walked over and peeked inside. I jumped off the wagon, lifted Siba down, and we walked away to the front of the horses so we could speak without waking Arden.

"We got Kid safely to Evensong. We picked Arden up about a decon south of there, no more than that. He had a message from Callis only saying Nelo had been taken, but not by whom or why. He rushed to Nelo's holding to see if the Wrens were in danger, and we needed to pull everyone back to Manumina. Finding nothing to tell him what to do, he ran to Evensong to see if Kid had more information. But we had Kid with us, so he gathered no news. We left Kid at Evensong and gave Arden a ride. Actually," I admitted, "he drove while we both slept."

"I see. He's going to be hard pressed to make it back to Cloa before he begins his workday." She pinched her lips together and glanced at the horses. She stepped closer and took another look. "These horses are done for. We can't go back to Manumina tonight."

I could see Siba hesitate, and then, "Arden said these families are neutral in the war and need coin. Perhaps they would allow us to rest our horses here, sleep in their stable, and hire a horse to Arden so he could ride to Cloa."

I sucked in a breath. "That would take a lot of coin."

Tiju Tia considered. "It would mean not setting a watch. But I don't know these people to ask such a favor in the night between dusk and dawn."

"I think Arden does." Without another word to us, Siba walked back to the wagon bed and spoke softly over the side. I heard Arden's sleepy voice answer and she spoke a little more. Then she reached inside her apron pocket, untied a coin purse, and handed it over the side to Arden. He sat up, smiled sleepily, and pushed himself out of the back of the wagon. He came around to the front and threw his arm around Tiju Tia.

"Thank you! You will let me hire a horse to Cloa? May the Lost God bless you! May your Wester stars bless you! My feet bless you!"

"You still have to negotiate for your horse," Tiju Tia said drily. "Don't keep us waiting, I have a dusty stable waiting for me."

He walked away to the house. Tiju Tia and I both turned to Siba.

"You lied to him?" Tiju Tia questioned sharply. "We don't lie to the Wrens."

"No. I said there was enough coin in the purse to hire a horse for him to ride to Cloa, buy us a peaceful night without a watch, and food and rest for our horses, but I didn't speak Mata well enough to ask. I needed him to negotiate for me. All of this is true."

I leaned back and studied her. "How do you know they are from Matasi? For that matter, how do you know Arden speaks Mata? I didn't know. Tiju Tia, did you know?"

"I did not." She looked at Siba closely.

Siba just gave us a grin and before I could ask her again, footsteps approached.

A Matasian man, years older than Piffik, carried a night lantern with three sides pulled down.

He held it up to our faces and in heavily accented Keresh said, "Conrosan?"

"Yes," Siba answered. "From Manumina. I was a child when you were there."

I shot Siba a quick look.

He nodded and walked to the front of the horses. He shook his head and said something in Mata. By the chagrined look on Arden's face, I suspected he was listening to how badly we treated our horses. The two went back and forth a bit and then they shook hands. A bargain had been struck. Arden reached in the coin purse and pulled out the coins he needed without looking. Lowertown boy indeed.

The farmer pointed to the nearest barn and started back to the house. Arden turned and looked to us.

"Your horses can be cared for here. Follow me." He walked towards the barn. As we unhitched the horses, Arden told us the rest, "He is waking up his wife now. The women must sleep inside the house. Don't argue, it is their way. Zren, you'll sleep out here to keep an eye on the animals. He doesn't trust us with his horses, but he said he was going to Cloa within the next two days. He's getting the list of wants from his wife and then he'll take me in his wagon and do his shopping after. I can sleep or talk as I wish, he says. My dog is also welcome."

Tiju Tia was skeptical. "That's very generous for the small coin passed between you."

"He and his family follow the religion of the Lost God. Their faith says they must treat everyone as if the Lost God himself was asking for help and mercy." He smiled slyly at Tiju Tia. "Be nice now. Nelo would love to have this as a safe house when he is restored to us." He gave Siba a softer smile. "Thank you for such a gift. Manumina's kindness to them when you were a child means a generous heart to us now."

The farmer returned with a travel bag and his wife. Her hands were full of blankets which she gave to me and pointed me to the hayloft without speaking. She took Tiju Tia and Siba with her and headed back to the house. I heard Tiju Tia say greetings to her in Mata, and the woman's relief in answering.

I scrambled up the ladder one handed and then listened to Arden and the farmer as they hitched a small wagon to two horses. They chatted easily back and forth, and I realized Arden knew much more than just a few words of Mata. He lifted his dog into the back, walked the team out of the barn, and closed and barred the doors. I looked out the window and could just make out the two men as they bowed their heads and folded their hands together. Soft murmuring reminded me of my walk across Matasi with Ngahuru and Koanga and the prayers said at the guesthouses every morning for safe travels.

Huh, just huh. I crawled back to my blankets and fell into a dreamless sleep.

CHAPTER 32

SIBA'S SECRETS

I waited until we could no longer see the Kaumpft's tidy wood and stuffed bramble fences before I started questioning Siba.

"You said you had never been north of the Northern Track! How did you know they were Matasi? How did you know they would help us? How did you know Arden spoke Mata? Even Tiju Tia didn't know, and she has known Arden for years. Years, Siba. Have you even been to Cloa? Have you even met Arden before today?" My fear that I had missed something very important made my questioning ever more wild.

"Shh, Zren, shh. I have met all the Wrens. I met them when they first came in the settler wagon. I've fed them and taught them and listened to them," she spoke in a calm voice.

"You've met the Kaumpfts before," Tiju Tia stated. "Yet you said nothing in Manumina. Neither did Piffik. This would have been good for me to know."

"I have. Years ago. When they first came from Matasi on the way to homestead where they live now. Their travels from Matasi to their new home took longer than expected, and it was already the Wet when they reached Manumina. They had heard it was a Matasi settlement and had thought to shelter there as they had elderly parents with them. The trails and tracks were such a muddy mess that year they could hardly move forward from day to day.

"When they found Conrosans there instead of Matasians, the Council of Wisdom offered them a place of sanctuary over the Wet. They traveled to their new home the following Dry. Truly, I did not know where the Kaumpfts had settled when they left us. I had been just a girl. I had almost forgotten them until Arden said the name. He pronounced it as they did when they were at Manumina—'koomf.' You and Kid and Zren said it differently—'kawmt' and talked as if it were a place, a settlement, and so I did not know it was one and the same. I cannot speak for Piffik, but I believe it is also true for him. We did not see the letters on paper and so we relied on what we heard. What we heard from you and what we remembered were not the same."

I grunted. "So you knew them as people and Tiju Tia and Kid thought it was a place. But how did you know Arden spoke Mata?" I thought back to when I had first met him at Manumina. "He's a Spice Islander, isn't he? All Spice Islanders speak Wester and Mata."

Tiju Tia shook her head. "No, Zren, I have known Arden since he was a child. He was a thief. I caught him stealing from another. Just another Kereki street child who had no fear of heights. Small enough to crawl in windows in almost any house in the Flower District for me."

I looked at Siba. She had a strange expression on her face, and I could tell something was wrong. I wondered what Tiju Tia had said that would make Siba look so unhappy. I knew Siba knew all of the Wrens had pasts like mine. Well, most of them anyway.

But then she smiled at me and teased, "That's not my story to tell. But I can tell you, Zren Janin, people who wake up early learn the most interesting things."

"Oh," I groaned. I didn't say another word. I didn't want to give her the satisfaction of criticizing my sleeping choices. Siba didn't understand, could never understand, the joy of sleeping deeply without fear of robbery or death before morning. I could not explain the luxury of knowing you could awake whenever you chose, unhurt and unafraid.

It wasn't long before Tiju Tia asked to rest in the back of the cart. She told me to stop in Sary and pick up rennet for Lou, leavenings for Rygee, and more muslin for Rell and her dried medicinals. Just like that, she had put the adventure behind us.

CHAPTER 33

CRUELTY AND KINDNESS

It was four days before Rygee and Piffik returned from Pagta. It had looked like the skies were clearing for a bit, so Rell and I had hurried to our house to gather our laundry.

As soon as we stepped outside the side door, she whooped as she noticed the wagon down the track, and then cried out, "There are three of them!"

I squinted as hard as I could, but I could only see the wagon.

"Are you sure it's not Lou?" I asked. She just gave me one of her looks as she raced back inside calling for the others. Together we opened the large gates for them to drive through.

Most of the others in Manumina had gathered in the green by the time the wagon pulled all the way in. Piffik stopped in front of us. Nelo was on the outside and stepped down very stiffly. Tiju Tia stepped forward and grabbed him in a hug. He stood there shocked for a moment and then awkwardly brought up his arms. She stepped away quickly.

"I'm so sorry. It's just so…I was just so afraid I had lost you."

Nelo gave her a sad smile and looked up just as Siba came out of the cookhouse kitchen and ran into Rygee's arms. We all discreetly dropped our eyes to the ground, but I could hear her whispering brokenly, "You came back, you came back, you came back." Rygee patted her on the back and then just held her hard.

"How bad was it? Did they listen to reason? Or did it take coin?" Rell asked Piffik.

He looked her in the face, and I thought I saw something broken. I wasn't sure, but Rell must have seen it too because she stepped into his arms and hugged him tightly. I watched him relax into her.

I looked at Oro. "I guess we get to take care of the horses, then." He huffed at me.

Piffik pulled back. "It's a story to tell, but it's been a long trip and we could use food, a bath, and sleep. Rell, you should also look at Nelo if you please."

Rell shot a look to Nelo.

"You should have said you were hurt!" She and Tiju Tia took him away with Nelo protesting he wasn't going to die, and he would rather eat something first.

"Siba, could you make food for us to be ready, say in a decon? Rygee and I will clean up and then we can gather and eat and talk before we fall asleep where we stand," Piffik asked.

"Zren, please unload the wagon." He stepped closer to me and whispered, "Tell no one what you see and bury what you find, except throw the boots in Tiju Tia's rag and bone cart." I tried to hide my surprise and then ducked my head as Piffik asked Oro to close the gates—and let Zren put the horses away.

***

Tiju Tia came into the stable a little while later.

"Zren, the food is ready. Can you hear me? I said…" She turned the corner and saw me in the far stall with my shovel. "What are you doing?"

"Just thought I would clean up a little here while I was waiting for the food to be ready." I looked up at her but dropped my gaze almost immediately.

"Oh, Zren, don't lie to me. If you can't tell me something,

just say so. Otherwise, I feel I am not a good enough friend to be trusted with the truth."

I carefully hung the shovel on its peg.

"I'm sorry, Tiju Tia—Ngahuru—you are my friend, but I cannot tell you. I'm sorry, I can't."

"That's all right, then. Come on, let's go hear what the others have to say."

I washed up at the kitchen sink and joined the others. The food smelled delicious. All three travelers were clean after washing off the stink of the journey, but they looked exhausted and discouraged. Nelo had left his long white-blond hair unbanded and drying across his shoulders. It made his scar less noticeable somehow, and less menacing.

Siba brought out the platters and I watched as Nelo shoveled the food in. Every now and then I watched Piffik pick at his plate. Everyone else ate their meal as if the plate would run away if it was not watched closely enough.

Instead of fingersweets, Rell brought out cooked fruit and sauce in the tiny cups we used for Vikland coffee.

"I was telling Siba this is a dessert we have in Vikland. Since we had all the spices, I thought I would make it for you." She placed a cup in front of each of us.

"You made this?" I was about to make a remark about Rell's infamous cooking skills when Piffik caught my eye and made a tiny shake of his head. I looked closer at him. I was wrong. He wasn't broken like Rell had been after the Battle at the Bridge. But the look in his eye was as if he had misplaced some part of himself and it made him sad. He looked…lost.

I swallowed my remarks and responded instead, "Thanks, Rell. I mean it." I looked her in the face so she could read the truth of it.

Her scowl turned into a tentative smile. "I think you might like it."

I did. The fruit was warm which surprised me, but it had a spicy, sweet sauce that just made me want to lick the cup.

"This is wonderful." I looked up. "Is there more?"

Rell flashed a grin at me. "You pick it, I'll cook it."

Rygee pushed his empty cup forward. "It's time to tell you what happened." He nodded at Nelo. "You start."

Nelo leaned back into his chair and crossed his arms gingerly across his chest. "I was walking to Regno. Inezi was going to meet me. We were going to check a few buildings together to see if they needed new supplies before I met with Dica and gave her the rest of the clothes and maps. I had softfooted the day before at Evensong. There had been a fancy meal there with some of the Kereki military commanders. I worked as an extra hand in the stable for all of the horses coming in. I wanted to learn from the soldiers sent to guard, and not to eat, and then Kid and I could add our news together and move it through the Wrens and softfoots.

"I was already on Fortika land when I heard horses behind me. I slipped into the woods to let them pass by. I realized too late they were not army officers from Evensong and that they were hunting me. I turned and ran. I felt a riata hit my back, and then…" He shrugged stiffly.

"When I woke up, they were tying my arms and legs together. While they were doing that, a wagon with army horses pulled up and they threw me in the back. There was already another Kereki there, but I didn't recognize him from any of the great houses. They did the same for two more men as we traveled to Pagta. We were held in the jail at Pagta Hall while the garrison commander was sent for. That is when Piffik and Rygee came." He added in a softer voice, "I did not know anyone knew where I was." He turned away to hide his face from us.

Rygee picked up the story quickly, "Piffik and I had worked on our plan on the way. We found the Justice immediately and said we thought one of our manabouts had been taken while he was on his way to visit his sister at the great houses of the north. We had given him permission to travel so far during the Wet because we knew there would not be time once the planting began. We demanded to see the men. He demanded to see our papers.

"Piffik was known to the Justice by face, and so he said, only Piffik would be allowed to see the men. Piffik just had time to say, 'There you are, Gardie Sanor!' before the soldiers pulled him out and dragged him elsewhere. Now they had the three of us in separate rooms with no way for us to know what the others were saying." He paused. "They questioned us."

Piffik continued the story, "For me, they wanted to know if we were neutral in the war between Vikland and Kerek because we were cowards. Was I not grateful to Kerek? They had allowed us on their shores, given us land, permitted us to marry their sons and daughters, and traded with us, no? I had replied that our grandparents' ship had been wrecked on the Salt Reefs, the only place we had been allowed to settle was an abandoned Matasi stockade, and trade meant mischarged more often than not."

He sighed. "When they asked, 'Why do you not fight for Kerek?' I said we practiced non-violence. They wondered if carving me up into pieces could inspire me to violence, or perhaps carving up my wife." He paused a long time. "I said I didn't have a wife, but Rygee…"

"For me, they took my papers. They wanted to know why someone named Ry Namikk would have a Conrosan name, a Conrosan wife, a Conrosan home, but look so Kereki. Was I hiding with the Conrosans because I had murdered someone? Stolen horses or someone's wife? Or was I running from the law for some other reason? Now what could that reason be?"

I stilled. Until this moment, I truly had not understood Rygee had risked his life to save Nelo. I had forgotten the conversation earlier when I had watched Rygee wash his white arms and had asked if he was in danger of the crimpers. Now I remembered he had said they would have to find him first. I realized, if the army had known they had a deserter in their grasp, he would have been hung without delay as an example. I had thought Nelo's capture had been an inconvenient trip to Pagta, not a dance with Trouble in which Rygee might not come back to us.

Rygee was still talking. "My papers said I was the Farm Manager at Manumina and had been for a year—were the Conrosans such lazy fools they hired Kerekis to run their farms? Or was there another reason? Did they think themselves above such work?" Rygee bit off his comments and turned abruptly to Nelo. "For Nelo…"

Nelo's face grew dark. "After they jerked Piffik out of our holding area, I heard a punch thrown, and it was quiet outside the door as I heard someone dragged away. Then the captain of the guard came in and called out, 'Who is Gardie Sanor?' I said, 'I am.' The soldiers came in with cudgels and dragged me out. My legs were still tied. They continued to drag me down the hall and into another room with three men—not soldiers. One of them said, since I wouldn't be marching off to war, they didn't need to be so careful of my pretty face." Nelo didn't say anything more, and I remembered the stiff and careful way he had climbed off the wagon.

No one moved in our room as we all absorbed what each of the men had said…and not said.

Finally, Rygee finished, "After spending the day with them and paying a small fine, they let the three of us go. With our papers, with Nelo, and with all of our belongings. It is finished, Nelo is home." His eyes met Siba's and held. "My wife, my heart. Please tell me what you saw on the road to Evensong."

She smiled at him and began gently, "I saw my first great house at Evensong. I saw a dog so smart she has saved her master's life four times. I saw friends I never thought to see again, and I learned I knew a secret Tiju Tia didn't know."

Nelo picked up his head at this. "Now this is exactly the kind of story I want to hear."

She smiled at all of us. "Kid stretched out in the wagon bed and slept, but as you all know, Zren could weave a story out of feathers and fairy dust. He and I traveled awake from the

Northern Track to Evensong. Each time we saw the distant fences and the buildings of a homestead, we would imagine the family who lived there. We talked about their plans for the future and what they imagined when they looked at the stars. When night fell, we reached Evensong, but neither of us had remembered to rock ourselves gently asleep on the wagon bed."

She cocked her head to the side. "Piffik, I know you have talked to me of the Rishka estate where the Conrosans have been settled in Vikland. But just as a blind child doesn't understand the difference between the colors red and blue, so I didn't understand how so many families could live in one building. Kid took me to the edge of the clearing to see the great house with candles and lanterns shining in countless windows. Then he slipped back to his home and his duties, and I turned back to Zren and the wagon.

"Now Zren had told me Rell had saved his life with her crossbow, and he expected no less from me if we should encounter bandits or crimpers or army patrols of either side. It is true, she had shared with me her weapon of renown, but not the knowledge to clear a battlefield.

"However, just as in all the Conrosan fairy tales, where Zren Janin has his magical weapons, his wit, or his friends to save him, we too had a hero join us. Just south of Evensong, a young man with beautiful brown eyes and the longest lashes I have ever seen, and his brave and loyal dog, Mother, stepped out on the road and asked to join us on our journey."

Nelo snorted and grabbed his ribs, and Siba pretended to frown at him. "Arden had received a note from Callis that Nelo had been taken. So he had hurried to Nelo's holding to see if the rest of the Wrens needed to fly to safety under Tiju Tia's wings.

"Finding nothing to tell him why Nelo was a guest of the Kerek King, he had run to Evensong to find out if Kid had news. Only to find out Kid was gone, and horses had been stolen from nearby. Fine horses, the kind that get horse thieves hung.

"Arden, like most of Zren Janin's friends, has a little bit of magic. While we slept, he drove us to a place I never thought to visit, with friends I never thought to see again. Piffik, it was the Kaumpfts! Do you remember the Matasians who stayed with us over the Wet all those years ago? The parents have passed on, but all three boys, their wives, and the daughter who trained with my aunt have families now. All are alive and well. Arden was able to charm us a bed for the night, food for the horses, and a ride to Cloa for him to make it to his post in the stables before daybreak."

Siba smiled at us. "We have returned to Manumina, Tiju Tia, Zren Janin and I, with Rell's crossbow to protect us, Rygee's purse to feed us, and an adventure of our own to tell."

I could feel the gentleness of a sigh within the room.

Rygee smiled. "My heart, I am glad to hear it went so well, although I am not so fond to hear of Arden's beauty and how you noted it so keenly."

Siba looked at him round-eyed. "The big beautiful brown eyes and the longest lashes I have ever seen? But my love, I was talking of the dog!"

We erupted in laughter and even Piffik smiled. Siba had read our somber mood exactly right and crafted her tale to soothe us before we crawled into our beds.

CHAPTER 34

ONE LOWERTOWN BOY TO ANOTHER

Nelo stayed at Manumina for a few days to mend. He and Piffik would work long decons in the woodshop.

If I came in to help, Nelo would fall silent, as if he had been talking, and Piffik would gently say, "Thank you for offering to help us today, but I think Nelo and I have the right of it," whether I had said anything or not. Piffik had said nothing to me about the night I had buried his secret in the horse stable. But I thought all of the riders on the wagon that day would know of it, and I just needed to learn who would tell me what I wanted to know. I knew Piffik was planning on making a delivery soon, and so I waited.

Tiju Tia took out the rag and bone wagon on a delivery to all the Wrens, but she took Oro instead of me without giving me an explanation. Siba and Rygee went to resupply the shepherd's cottage in Vikland. Rell told me not to say anything foolish before they left, and I was so afraid of what anyone would consider foolish, I hardly said anything at all.

I was so desperate for someone to talk to that I helped Rell wash and mend Kereki clothes and Viklander uniforms for what seemed to be enough for a regiment of our own. Then I spent two days with Lou in his springhouses making butter and cheese.

Finally, one day, I walked Piffik and his horses out of the stockade and watched him travel down the breakaway until he turned his delivery wagon northwest to Sary. I closed the stockade gates and then walked straight into the woodworking shop.

Nelo was staining a coffin for a rich man in Ahni. He was lost in his thoughts. I watched him run the rags over and over, turning the wood and his hands into the deepest almond color of Ngahuru's legs and feet. I thought I might ask to hear the story of the secret of what was buried in the horse stall the night the three of them had returned.

I stood in front of him and waited for him to finish the side. He looked up at me, raised an eyebrow, but said nothing until he wiped his hands with a dry rag.

"So am I the first, middle, or last person you are asking to find out what happened?"

"The first," I promptly replied.

"I suppose I should be honored. Or do you think I tell the best stories?"

"I think you will tell me the truth and not make it pretty so it doesn't offend anyone," I answered truthfully. "I know both Piffik and Rygee forgot some details in their retellings."

He gave me a half smile. "One Lowertown boy to another?"

"Something like that." I waited.

He lowered himself gently to an unfinished chair and I took one nearby. I could see him remembering and then he started and discarded a beginning or two.

At last, he sighed and began, "Rygee told everyone how we had all been released with our papers and our belongings. What he didn't say is that 'small fine' took everything in his purse. Zren, I am sure the Orphan Master in Kerek City has sold entire families of children for less.

"We left Pagta immediately because we had no coin to stay anywhere or buy any food to eat. Piffik sat in the middle driving the wagon, Rygee was on the right with a crossbow at his feet. They had offered to have me rest in the wagon bed, but I didn't want to be lying on my back defenseless, so I was on the left with Oro's short bow resting in my lap. It wasn't needed, but it felt good not to feel powerless. I know you understand."

I nodded but said nothing.

"We stayed off the Heartland Trail. Piffik knew a half-track which would shorten our way a bit, he said. Two decons into our journey, we came over a small rise to see bandits at the end of a skirmish with a Kereki army patrol. Our wagon was still unseen and Piffik quickly stopped so we could jump off the wagon, hide, and arm ourselves. We didn't hurry to help because the bandits would just prey on us after they had killed the soldiers, and we weren't feeling charitable towards the Kereki army at the moment.

"We watched quietly, hoping to remain unnoticed, until all were dead except for the last two bandits who were pulling out a Kereki army pay chest. That was the first I realized we had interrupted a robbery of the paymaster wagon. I wasn't thinking, Zren, or maybe I was, or maybe I will always be a Lowertown boy and no better. I called 'left,' Rygee called 'right, and fire at will' and we killed the last two bandits."

Nelo paused. "Piffik was…Piffik said he was appalled. In his mind, it wasn't self-defense at all, and he said, 'We were no better than the thieves we had just murdered.'

"Rygee disagreed and said the bandits would have knifed us just for being there if they had seen us. He said, in his mind, it was getting rid of future trouble. They would just prey on someone else. And who was to say if that someone else in the future could be Piffik?

"As for me? I was still angry at my beating and didn't care." Nelo shrugged. "We went down to the paymaster wagon and took the army chest. Piffik released their horses from the cart and their harnesses, and I showed Rygee how to search the seams and hidden pockets of clothes for anything of value. We took the saddles and bridles and bits off from the bandits' horses as well, but all of the horses were marked. So, we left them to wander on their own to find water and a place to bed for the night. We knew someone would find them."

Nelo smiled crookedly. "I pulled all the boots. You should tell Falan; she'll be happy." He sobered slowly, "Piffik wrestled with his conscience all the way home. Rygee told him to think of it as a Conrosan fairy tale where the mythical Zren Janin leaves a chest of gold for a village unfairly treated by men of ill-intent. That the beating and the robbery of our coin in the name of the Kereki army was no different than one we would have received from bandits. That putting a uniform on it didn't make it right. Then he told Piffik the coin would keep the Wrens alive. Rygee said he never wanted to be in a situation where a Wren was harmed for lack of coin. I think it helped, but Piffik struggled the entire journey, and it was a hard fight."

Nelo let out a sigh. "Don't get me wrong. Rygee is strong and smart and his sense of justice is Kereki-born, so there is more than a cupful of revenge stirred in. But Piffik? I was beyond glad when they allowed Piffik in for that one moment at Pagta. When

I saw him and he called out 'Gardie Sanor,' he looked right at me, and I knew I would be safe. He is something else entirely. How is it there are men like him in the world?" Nelo tipped his head back to look at the ceiling.

I said nothing so my heart could listen to what my ears had heard. I wasn't so sure I agreed with Nelo. I didn't think Piffik had finished wrestling with his conscience. I just wished he would quit fighting as soon as he realized he and his conscience were on the same side.

Nelo inhaled deeply and reached for the staining rag. I remembered something else.

"Did you know Arden speaks Mata?"

He snorted. "Zren, you have met Arden. He can barely read and write Keresh. And that is only because Linna is still teaching him his letters since they moved to Cloa." He turned back to his work. I knew he was lying to me, but I wasn't sure why.

"No, Nelo. I know this to be true. I was there. He spoke to the Matasians at…" I tried to pronounce it as Siba had— "Koomf's. I heard him. He speaks it well, not just bits of words."

Nelo turned back to me and sighed. "Yes. I know. He speaks with the Matasian missionaries when they go through Cloa on the Northern Track. Inezi says Bima Ritwik has a softfoot who uses a missionary wagon as a maskovesto. Arden is part of this in Cloa, knowing who they are, and where they are traveling. They have canvas tops on their wagons and can carry the wounded east for us when we know Padro Morto won't be coming for days. Tiju Tia has been spending more time away from the Northern Track, and you no longer drive the cheese cart. We needed more help, a lot more help, and Arden arranged this for all of us. The missionaries can travel directly into Vikland or the garrisons where we would be stopped."

Something felt wrong about everything Nelo had just told me, but I wasn't sure what to ask next. I wondered why Falan and Josef, Callis, Nelo, and even Arden pretended he was not as smart as his dog, yet he and Linna were the center of the Wrens. I knew Nelo wouldn't offer the information on his own, and if I didn't ask the question just the right way, he would be able to slide around the truth again.

"Tiju Tia didn't know."

"Tiju Tia doesn't know everything." He paused. "Falan says Tiju Tia is spending more time in Kerek City. She barely stops to see us but has us deliver to each other." He gave me a hard look. "There are things Tiju Tia doesn't know, and some things Tiju Tia should not know."

I wondered why Nelo would care so much to hide something from Tiju Tia. I wondered what he was hiding and tried to think what else he was telling me.

"You're talking about Oro, aren't you?"

Nelo smiled at me and he almost looked…relieved. He explained that Linna was a Wren and all the Wrens knew to take joy when they could. But Oro was bought from the Orphan Master and raised by a Kereki merchant who liked to show off his charity. This meant Oro didn't always act the way the rest of the Wrens did.

Oro had promised to take Linna to a street fair coming to Cloa the next time he would be back with Tiju Tia. Linna had been pleased because she knew she wouldn't be able to go alone, but she didn't know if Arden would be in Cloa or not. Sometimes a promise was made and then a Wren found himself holding the hand of a dying Viklander six furloughs away. Or Tiju Tia needed a trip made to a great house in the opposite direction.

It was possible, Nelo said, all could have happened as planned, but then Tiju Tia had taken me as her *titiro mai ki ahau* along instead of Oro. And then with Falan's Viklanders, Josef and I had traded places, and Oro's letter to Linna had been brought back to Manumina. Oro felt without reading the letter, Linna hadn't known why he had not come. There was no harm to Linna. She didn't take offense. She had just walked through the fair with Josef and Arden. But Oro, Oro felt differently and thought he had to explain why he had not been able to come when he had asked her to the fair. It nearly cost him his life. Nelo paused and looked at me soberly.

I squinted at Nelo. "You think Mother would have killed him?"

"Not the dog, you idiot. Don't let those 'beautiful brown eyes and longest lashes I've ever seen'"—he mimicked Siba—"fool you. If there is only one Wren in all of Kerek I could have with me in an uneven fight, I would want it to be Arden."

He paused. "Or maybe your Viklander with the crossbow. Rygee says she stands at one end of the stockade and shoots to the other end and can hit the center of the target every time." He sounded skeptical and hopeful at the same time.

"Rell Huena?" I nodded in agreement. "She is our first and best defense. If you come flying in on a horse to Manumina in the middle of the night, call out your name, or my name. Rell keeps her crossbow ready beneath her windowsill, and when you hear her window open, your heart is already on its last heartbeat."

He laughed and his entire face softened. "You have a strange way of comfort, Zren, but I like it." He pushed himself to his feet. "But I have to work on this coffin. I promised Piffik I would have this staining finished before he returned from Sary, and after he saved my life, I am disinclined to disappoint him."

CHAPTER 35

MORE TO THE STORY

Nelo only stayed a few more days after that. After Tiju Tia's return, she fussed about the large territories her Wrens were forced to cover, and the confines of the Wren's positions in the shops and stables and great houses which made the softfooting possible, but limited their movement.

She argued with us on whether or not she would need to pull back from the farthest reaches, talk to Lomes or Bima or Rani and turn over more territory to the Viklanders, even though they "stood out like crows against the clouds," or reassign Wrens to new locations to shift with the battles. It was a side of her I had never known before. She snapped and growled, or she spent long decons over her maps and ignored the rest of us.

Rygee felt he had to call the farmhands in. He believed, in spite of everything which had happened that day in Pagta, we had been fortunate with redeeming Nelo. He was also concerned if the crimpers were so active, our contracts would not be honored.

He told Piffik they could use the 'new coin' to pay them for the extra time. There were a lot of things around Manumina needing repair; we were too few to take care of everything. They would start the farmhands on mending the stockade and repairing buildings until the fields were dry enough to work.

Together Tiju Tia and I went to Huk to push clothes and coins and maps to Callis and Ross. We brought Ross eight additional rabbits, and he proudly showed us his collection of "breeders and feeders" as he called them. He also told us about Josef's visit the day before, and the plans to be moved forward to Linna in the next town of Cloa.

"Give those to Linna, Tiju Tia, and she will give them to Arden to deliver," he said confidently.

"When does Arden sleep? He seems always to be about traveling or in the stables working," Tiju Tia asked nonchalantly. Ross looked guilty, and immediately my curiosity was up. Tiju Tia said nothing more, just gave him a thoughtful look. Ross thanked us for the rabbits, and we said our goodbyes.

We reached Cloa at dark. Linna and Arden were both home to our knock and invited us in. I had heard Josef describe his house, and I had seen the one Falan's Viklanders had hidden in. Neither of them prepared me for what I saw now. There was a small meal table and three chairs, with pottery for two already set on a pale blue cloth. The kitchen was clean and bright with the smell of soup and fresh bread. In one corner, there were two comfortable chairs and a small table between them with flowers in a glass jar and two battered books. Real books.

Beyond that, the bedroom door was open, and I could see a narrow bed with a thick blanket neatly covering it. A tattered blanket lay on the floor—Mother's, I presumed. Mother herself was standing in the bedroom door, alert but silent, her eyes on Arden for his command in response to our presence. Arden dropped his hand to his side, palm down and she went quietly to rest on her blanket on the bedroom floor.

Back in the kitchen and over the meal table, Arden had hung two lanterns on hooks from the ceiling. Instead of small circles of light for them to cook and eat by, now the entire room was bright as daylight. By the door were three wooden hooks on the wall, holding traveler's cloaks for Arden and Linna, and a hook with two travel bags of different sizes hanging by their straps.

Tiju Tia beamed. "This is beautiful, Linna and Arden. Well done. Well done."

Arden still stood by the closed door. He smiled.

"Our Linna had a proper home with parents in Kerek City. It didn't seem right that she should want for comfort, while she lived a life of adventure on the frontier."

Linna smiled. "Arden likes to talk. It will be good for him to have a different audience. Can you join us for end of day meal?" She paused, uncertain. "Is there some urgency, or can Arden eat first?"

"We can stay." Tiju Tia nodded. "I have papers to go to a Viklander encampment not far from the old Earles garrison. Do you know of one?" They both nodded, and she continued talking as she unpacked the papers from a pocket within her cloak and handed them to Arden. "Ross tells me these papers came from Josef."

"I should go now, then." Arden pulled his long hair forward and began to braid it like a Viklander would wear. He tied off the end. "If they came from Josef, they have already been traveling three days."

"I think you should eat first, and we can talk over our food," Tiju Tia said. She unclasped her cloak and deliberately hung it over Arden's on the hook. I took mine off as well and hung it up on the next hook over.

Linna and Arden exchanged a look, and Linna nodded wordlessly. He climbed the ladder to Linna's loft and handed down a three-legged stool to me. Linna pulled another bowl and a cup and two spoons from a shelf.

"I am sorry, we sometimes have three for a meal, but this will be a first for four," Linna explained.

She set the cup as a bowl in front of the three-legged stool as I set it at the table, and the other bowl in front of the chair. While Arden climbed down from the ladder, and as Linna turned to the kitchen to bring the pot of soup, Tiju Tia promptly sat on the three-legged stool with the cup and spoon. I laughed at Arden and Linna's surprised looks.

"Come, sit down." Tiju Tia waved her hand. "Bring the soup and bread. Zren is far too hungry to wait while the two of you argue who should sit in the fourth setting. So I have stopped the argument, and now we don't have to hear Zren's stomach rumble for one more moment."

We sat and ate. The food was good, not like Rygee's, but still hot and filling. The biscuits were odd shaped with garden honey and fresh butter for them.

"You eat this well every night?" I asked Arden.

"Not on the nights I'm cooking." He nodded at the biscuits. "It's good you came tonight. The last time I tried to make biscuits even Mother couldn't eat them."

Linna smiled. "I learned to cook at home. Arden is learning now, and it takes time. Sometimes he can sleep while I am cooking. So I don't mind."

"That's what I want to talk to you about." Tiju Tia put down her spoon. "It's too much for you and Josef and Nelo. Josef and Nelo have a much larger territory to cover than you do, but they do not have to walk all night just to be ready to work at first light. It is also getting much too dangerous for Kid to stay at Evensong much longer. He says some of the Kereki officers are now billeted in the house. This is why his information is getting much better than just news and gossip. But he is no good to me swinging at the end of a rope because he stole papers from the wrong soldier, and you are no good to me with a knife in your back because you were too tired to be careful. I thought Nelo was too clever to be taken by the crimpers, and I was wrong. We were able to retrieve him, but it will take him a long time to mend from the beating he received."

Arden protested, "We are all careful, Tiju Tia. We have been gatherings secrets for you for years—since we were little children. Your name may change, your maskovestos may change, but we do not forget overnight what you have taught us."

"I am not saying so," Tiju Tia said gently. "What I am saying is I am concerned for you," she looked at Linna, "as a girl who gave up her parents' home in Kerek City to become a woman on the frontier." She nodded at Arden. "A boy who was a clever thief to a man who has many skills. And because of this, I am not going to say, 'do that, or go here.' I want you to talk with the others and come up with a better plan. I will listen and we can adjust our Wrens to match your wisdom."

Tiju Tia picked up her spoon again. "If you wish, you can consider this idea. Kid should leave Evensong. It is too dangerous, and there are so many there who tell secrets, Dica and Tyra hear the news within the day. If you wish to leave your position at the stable, Arden, you could leave and Kid could try to gain your place. If you would rather work at the stable and pick up news, then Kid could be the one who softfoots through the countryside."

"Kid would live here?" Linna asked quickly. "Where would Arden go? Would he live here too?"

"That is for you to decide. You have grown to be women and men before my eyes, I am not going to tell you where you lay your head."

Arden finished his soup. "I should go deliver the documents. You have given me something to talk about with the others. But you should know this Tiju Tia, Falan and Callis dress as men to help Josef move Viklanders eastward. They take many more risks than I do. When I cannot be here, Linna wears my clothes and takes Mother to do what needs to be done. We connect Viklanders with other wagons to take them to Ishes when Padro Morto is not nearby. There are far more soldiers we are not reaching. We are all spread thinly, and if you have received word I am not enough, please tell me now."

Tiju Tia hastened to reassure him, "You are always enough, Arden. All of you are more than enough. I am only concerned for all of you. The crimpers just reminded me of how important you all are to me, which is why I offer to shrink our territory and bring you all a little closer to Manumina if there is trouble."

He gave her a long look as if trying to decide if there were words he was not hearing.

"I will talk to the others, and we will have ideas for you the next time you come through." He paused. "I must go. But are you going to lay your heads here tonight or change your horse at the stable and take the half-track back to Manumina? I must ask, because I need to know whether Mother should stay and protect Linna and give the illusion that I am here, or should she go and protect me? You see, she is also spread too thinly."

He pushed himself away from the table and headed for the door. "I have not forgotten I still have your cloak, Zren Janin, the clever pockets for my blades saved my life—though not as many times as Mother has. I will return it to you tonight and have Callis add pockets like yours to my cloak."

He paused, and in a much gentler voice said, "Thank you for the soup, Linna. Bar the door behind me. I do not think I will be back before morning." He swirled my cloak—his old mossy green cloak—about him, tucked the documents inside the large pocket, and slipped outside the door.

Mother bolted upright and stood inside the bedroom door, tail wagging uncertainly. Linna looked at Mother and then at us and sighed.

"He's tired. So very tired. But Arden will listen to what you said and will talk it over with the others. Please do not take offense at what he says tonight."

She paused a long moment, and then she spoke with a firmness in her voice I had never associated with her quiet demeanor, "Tiju Tia. Arden must stay in Cloa. I do not know what you hear from the others who live at Manumina, or those who whisper secrets to you. Arden is a man who does what must be done. When he knows he will be gone for many days, I can wear his cloak and have Mother walk with me at dawn and dusk. His dog helps with the illusion that Arden is here with me even when he is many furloughs away helping the others. It's true, Callis, Falan, and I take risks, but the burden falls on Josef, Nelo, and Arden. You should know this."

She took a deep breath. "Kid may join us, I will consider that, but if Arden must leave, I do not know if I can stay in Cloa. What we do here, who we know who can help or harm us, and who knows to trust us, is too important to throw away because of someone's idle words."

She waited for her words to soak in before continuing, "But his offer of a bed is true. Please take your horse to the stable and spend the night with me. If you go to the stable and exchange your horse this late, too many will know it is just the two of you on the road all night."

CHAPTER 36

THE CALM BEFORE THE STORM

Tiju Tia was quiet as we drove to Manumina the next day. I had tried telling her a story or two, but she wasn't listening, and I soon gave up. I felt both Arden and Linna had told Tiju Tia something very important last night, but I wasn't sure what it was. It was more than I wanted to puzzle out, anyway. I knew if someone thought it was important, they would tell me what to think and do about it.

When we returned, I helped Piffik in the woodshop for a day while Oro went to Ishes to pick up dispatches and news. Piffik told me of his trip to Sary with Rygee to gather more farmhands than the ones they had originally requested. He explained how Rygee had said that was how they brought on extra help on the farms while he was growing up. Kerek had always had a conscription, although not as large as the one now.

"Can you believe it, Zren? Farmers needing help just go to the local Justice and look at the list of boys selected to report to duty to the army within the season. Rygee says if you were known for hard work and good sense, a farmer would pay the Justice a part of your wages, and you would be released from reporting to the garrison. You would receive the other part of your wages when you worked on the farm. Imagine, Zren. To be told you must go to war and then a farmer you know comes and says, 'Come plow my fields instead. Come harvest my grain and stay far from the battles.' What an incentive to carry a good name." He grinned slyly at me. "A name as strong as Zren Janin perhaps."

I laughed.

Piffik went on, "If you were not a good worker, would rather be soldiering, or there was not enough work to earn your coin, the farmer just needed to go back to the Justice. He would sign paperwork to release you. You would either need to report to the garrison, find another to buy out your contract, or disappear. Failure to report to the garrison is desertion."

Rygee came into the woodshop then to talk to Piffik and had heard the end of our conversation.

"Do I even want to know what you are discussing?"

Piffik smiled and said he was telling me yet another thing he had never known growing up in Manumina and how smart I was going to be with everyone teaching me something new every day.

Rygee just laughed. "Actually, I came here to talk to you both about the farmhands. I think we should put Zren in charge of them. We have eight seasonal contracts with the obligation to keep four of them. This means after the planting season, I must go back to Sary and get them exempted season by season. I will teach Zren to manage them and their work as my father and brothers taught me. I will pay them their wage at the end of the day, but Zren will manage their time and their work.

"We need hard workers who won't talk or be too curious about what is going on here, and ones who truly want to farm and not just avoid their call to arms, Zren. It's a good system. If they want to go soldiering, they only need to work badly. If they like being a manabout, they need to be one of the four best." He paused and gave me a stern look.

"They are also day laborers. Once they go home each day, the remaining chores are ours. It is an incentive for you not let them be slack in their efforts. It is also best for none of them to be about if Viklanders come under cover of darkness seeking our aid."

"But what if they don't listen to me?" I looked at Rygee's strong build and tried to imagine my slight frame standing next to him. I doubted I would listen to me either.

"I was much younger and smaller than you when my father first told grown men to do as I say. I learned to work as hard as they did—which no one will doubt of you, to make reasonable demands, and admit my mistakes. Also, I plan on meeting with you in the bakery every morning. As long as you can eat pastries and listen to what I tell you to schedule for the day's work at the same time, you will be the master of this very quickly." Rygee grinned. "They start in four days."

Piffik nodded in agreement. "Zren, you are the right man for this."

I ducked my head to hide my pleasure. I couldn't wait to tell Rell.

***

I found her on the porch swing in front of our house. I ran up the path waving my hand. Not that she would need any help recognizing me. I saw her make a quick swipe over her face, and I slowed to a walk wondering if this was the wrong time to tell her my news.

"Rell?" I stepped up on the porch hesitantly.

She cleared her throat. "Zren?"

"I was going to tell you some good news but if this is a bad time, I can come back…" I trailed off.

"No, good news should never wait. It's like fingersweets, best when fresh out of the oven." We both laughed at that.

I told her Piffik and Rygee thought I could learn to manage the new farmhands. She would no longer have to do the manabout chores and the laundry and the mending on top of her medicinal gardens and potion-making.

"Potion-making!" She laughed. "You make me sound like one of those evil fairies in your Conrosan stories cooking up misery and trouble. Lou will be happy anyway. I think he can turn himself into knots trying to avoid me when I am working outside in Kereki clothes." She smiled. "That is good news, Zren. You work hard for your knowledge and your skills, and you deserve all good things." She dropped her eyes, and I saw the letter on her lap.

"Are you writing a story?"

Her face crumpled a bit and then she took a deep breath. "No, there was a letter for me in the papers Oro just brought back from Ishes. Piffik will need to go back out tomorrow to let the Wrens know there is trouble coming and how to prepare. The war is going to get much worse, much faster."

"The Matasi navy?"

"No, but you're close. Chul Swyler has invented another new weapon."

I crossed over and sat next to her on the swing. I knew Chul as a firemaster who had sacrificed his ability to walk without aid and the use of his hands to save us at the Battle at the Bridge. He had been sold by the Kerek City Orphan Master to Viklander diplomats and survived two horrible massacres on the Northern Track—the first one when he was only eight. He was the smartest man I had ever met and many others thought that as well. He thought of Piffik Qanaq as one of his good friends and had made inventions here at Manumina to make life better. He loved happy endings.

"The war isn't going to end soon, is it?" I said sadly.

Rell shook her head and her eyes filled with tears.

We rocked on in silence.

ACKNOWLEDGEMENTS
(BUT I PREFER TO CALL THEM GRATITUDES)

All Softfoots and Wrens will tell you, a lie is best when it has part of the truth.

This book is fiction. You will not find a bibliography. However, I read many books of children who fought against occupiers and soldiers during times of war. I read stories of children grown up too quickly during the Seven Years War who carried guns nearly as long as they were. And I will never be the same after reading books about child soldiers in Africa, human trafficking around the world, and child brides and grooms in many cultures. As Ngahuru says, "There are many places in the known world where children are not allowed to be children."

I firmly believe helping someone else through difficulty is where our humanity starts. This book, my middle child, is both my favorite and my most painful. The Wrens are braver, wiser, and more resilient than I could ever be.

There are many people who help me tell these stories:

Thank you to the team at Paper Raven Books. I feel like our journey has been a matter of the right hand and the left hand working together from the start. Thank you for your patience, your insight, your enthusiasm as each book in the series, *The Tales of Zren Janin*, goes to print.

A Viklander mapcase full of thanks to my beta readers who took an entire Zoom call to talk about the scaffolding of the book. You insisted on a cast of characters, better chapter titles, MAPS, name changes, backstories of the Wrens, and the lovely, lovely name of the "Academy of Treason." You helped me redirect and focus on the story I wanted to tell.

A HUGE thank you to Gary Dunker who read books and stories about teenage Hudson Bay adventurers, women explorers, the Dust Bowl, women spies, civil war drummers and buglers, child soldiers, Rogers' Rangers, orphans, the Polish resistance, soldiers and flyboys, the Darien Gap, teenage wildfire fighters in Montana during WWI, Alaska homesteaders, and then handed them off to me as "you might like this." I did, Dad, I did. I liked them all.

Angela Lawson, Stephanie Dodge, Gary Dunker, and Florence Dunker—Editors, readers, and givers of good advice. I owe you an online box of red pens for all the knowledge you shared.

Bonnie Johnson—Thank you for all of the recommendations of WWII-era books! You must have been a librarian in a previous life. I am blessed to have you in my circle of friends.

Lawrence Sutin—Author of *Jack and Rochelle: a Holocaust story of Love and Resistance* and one of my many writing professors at Hamline University. As I read my way through your canon of books, I knew you were the right one to lead my independent study and guide my novel. I didn't realize it would take so many years for me to get everything out of my head and into print. Thank you for your encouragement and insight, and for your parents' courage for telling their story beyond your family memoir. May their memory be a blessing.

LR Swenson—An Alaskan pipeliner with a political science major specializing in the Cold War. Now there's a story more than one softfoot would be happy to know. Thank you for sharing books, stories, and even more books. The story of the two young girls riding their bicycles through the countryside damaging the Nazi supply trains haunts me still.

Janet Moen—Your stories of your uncle and his work as a priest during Central and South America's civil unrest in the 1980's collided with my interest in liberation theology and my Anabaptist social justice upbringing. The Matasi missionaries are the result. Thank you!

Dr. Rene Harder Horst and Marlene Harder Horst—Thank you for the conversations, the stories about your time in South America, and for your book, *The Stroessner Regime and Indigenous Resistance in Paraguay*. You both helped me frame the concept of otherness and build the series' nonrelenting lack of understanding between countries and people.

Lynne Chung—How can one person be so wise? Every time we interacted at Target I came away richer. You have given me inspiration in casual conversation, validation, and support. It was a sad day for me when you moved so far away. You are amazing!

As always, David and Bridget (and Sylvia!), Ryan and Briana, Jenny and Zach, Katie and Nelson, Almond, Brandon, Liz, Kaeden, Callie, Peyton, Philip, Lauren, Ryla, Rinoa, Gunther, Lark, Hayden, Max, Nordica, Penelope, Cory, Catherine, and Hallie. You are the faces of the next generation. The dreamers of dreams, the conscience of the country, the readers I write for.

And finally, and most importantly, Steven Dodge. You helped save the Wrens, kept Bima at the table when Truth came calling, and reminded me over and over Falan and Nelo would do whatever was necessary to keep safe those entrusted to their care. The fiercer the face, the softer the heart. Thank you! Thank you! Thank you! Thank you!

Turn the page for

War and Wrens bonus materials

including TWO bonus short stories:

How Nelo Got His Scar

and

Falan's Shadow

Also a preview of *Exile: A New Beginning*

Book 4 in *The Tales of Zren Janin*

Need to write a book report?

Try using some of these questions as idea starters!

1. Imagine you are Ngahuru receiving Zren Janin's letter. What do you think about his new home at Manumina? Are you surprised he can now read and write in Wester and Conrosan? What do you think about his confession about not understanding the difference between friendly and friendship? How would you share this news with Koanga? What does this mean to you?

2. If the Kereki army would not have stolen their livestock and tried to burn out the Conrosans, do you think Manumina would have been able to maintain their neutrality in the war? Why or why not?

3. From the beginning of the book until the end, Rygee Namikk continues to take on a greater and greater role to keep Manumina functioning and the Wrens provided

for. How does his role as a *titiro mai ki ahau* make Ngahuru's network possible?

4. During the Academy of Treason, Zren states the children lose their hunted looks, gain in weight and height, and learn new skills. He ends the chapter with "We were happy." Do you think the children share his same thoughts? Why or why not?

5. Many of the Wrens hide certain skills, or protect their secrets, not only from those at Manumina but also from each other. What examples can you think of where we learn a Wren is deliberately misleading Zren or the others?

6. Did your impression of the Wrens change from the time they arrived at Manumina until the end of the book? How so?

7. Bima and Zren have a very complicated relationship. He listens to Bima Ritwik tell the stories during the night's rescue (*How Death Saved her Brother*, *The Gifts of the Father*, and *The Three Stewards*). They discuss the meaning of the parables: finding the right gift as a reward and the concept of 'whom do you serve?' Although they have only interacted a few times, Bima understands Zren's need for security very well. Why do you think it is so important for Bima to know who is running the

Wrens? What do you think of Zren's response? What do you think Bima is going to do with Zren's information?

8. Storytelling continues to play an important part in *War and Wrens*. There are several instances where the same series of events are told and retold with different details for different audiences. In the retelling of the death of Bitterboots, Zren describes his childhood and Mouser differently each time. Why do you think this is? In the story of the crimpers, Nelo, Piffik, and Rygee all leave out details in the group telling, that Nelo shares with Zren later. Yet Zren feels even then that Nelo isn't saying everything. Why do you think it is so hard for people to share the truth? How do we build trust?

9. During the Academy of Treason, Callis was one of the most capable Wrens. She could read and write Keresh, she was a tailor, and she was the best Wren on the bongs. Yet, Josef and Nelo tell Tiju Tia and Piffik the center of the Wrens has moved from Callis and Ross (Huk) to Linna and Arden (Cloa). Why do you think the Wrens, Falan and Callis, took over Ross's responsibilities moving Viklanders and papers rather than tell Tiju Tia he was not working with the others to help the Viklanders? Why was location (friendly to Vikland) less important than the Wrens' abilities to work together?

10. How did you react to the news that Bima is married and has a family? Why do you think he has hidden this information from others in the past? Why tell Zren now? In Book 1, Miyamoto Suki had said, *"We are not friends, he and I, we will most likely never be friends, but he has many skills that help Vikland, and in that we are in agreement. You should know this, Bima Ritwik will never run away from duty. He will defend to the death those that need his protection."* Why do you think Bima chose his duty to Vikland over his desire to see his family again? How do you feel about Bima?

11. Falan says Ngahuru is in Kerek for revenge. She says the Wrens aren't on Vikland's side because they agree Vikland has been wronged, they just wanted to get out of Kerek City. Why do you think this motivation is important for Zren (and us) to know?

12. Why do you think Nelo tells Zren he remembers him from Kerek City? Why is Zren unable to respond to Nelo's sharing that he casually murdered men before they could hurt the children? What is Nelo truly telling Zren? Do you think Nelo can get over his first friend's death at Mouser's hand?

13. After Rygee and Piffik bring Nelo back from the Pagta jail, Nelo spends a lot of time with Piffik in the

woodshop. What do you think they are talking about? Think of a person in your life who stood by you when you went through a difficult time. How did this make an impact on your life?

14. When Siba and Zren return Kid to Evensong, they encounter Arden and his dog on the way to the Kaumpft homestead. Is the story Arden tells Zren what you expected? Why or why not? Why do you think Oro kept this a secret from the others at Manumina?

15. Zren learns the backstories of the Wrens as the book progresses. He realizes all of the Wrens have a different story from his own and from each other. How do you think the trauma each of them struggles with will impact their decisions in the future?

16. Who is your favorite Wren? Why? Do they have characteristics you have or you wish you had?

17. A critical component of the book series is something the author calls "otherness" defined as an unrelenting attitude towards others that says they do not deserve the same treatment or kindness for any reason: lack of wealth, skin color, tenets of belief, gender/sexuality, abilities, lack of opportunities/privilege, or even no reason at all. Remember how unsympathetic Dica

seemed at the rescue at Regno? Why do you think the Wrens feel they are not appreciated for the risks they are taking? Consider how the Viklanders think about honor. How would they perceive the Wrens who are helping them but committing treason against Kerek at the same time? Why is it taking so long to change perceptions?

18. Zren interacts with Viklanders he met earlier in *A Gift of the Stars* and *Manumina*: Rani, Lomes, and Bima Ritwik. He also hears from the Wrens that Kern is softfooting near Fortika and Solkka Ulani is fighting north of Balza. Does this make the war seem more or less real to you as the reader? What foreshadowing do you see?

19. Arden tells Zren his dog, Mother, is not a common pup from the dogfights. He says it is a "Dunker"—a scent hound. The Dunker is an actual dog breed especially bred for hunting by smell. How do Falan, Arden, and Linna convey to Zren and the others at Manumina how important Mother is to their work and their safety?

20. The last chapter is called the Calm before the Storm, and Rell and Zren talk about Chul's new invention. Because you as the reader know Chul Swyler from his earlier time at Manumina, does hearing about his new weapon seem less ominous? Or more? Why?

HOW NELO GOT HIS SCAR

(This story takes place four years before the events of War and Wrens)

Nelo hurried through the streets of the Sinner's District. It was decons before sundown, but Nelo was alone. At thirteen, he knew he was no match for anyone who decided he had something they wanted.

A few shopkeepers eyed him, and he tried to look innocent. It was too late in the day to try to thieve food now anyway. There were end of day shoppers on the streets, and Patrons with dangling cudgels, who stood in the doorway of their shops checking carry bags. He had enough coin in his pockets to buy some bread and fruit for the little ones, but he wouldn't buy it here. His coin would go further in Lowertown.

He heard running footsteps behind him and without even turning to look if he was the intended victim, he took off at a sprint. At the next corner, he turned left and ran down the alley. He popped out the other side and tucked himself behind a pushcart piled high with kindling and firewood. He grabbed a piece as long as his arm and tested its weight. It would have to do.

A moment later, another boy ran by him, a little older, with the olive skin and the dark, curly hair of Matasi. The boy smiled, spoke Mata, and tossed something in the air at him.

Reflexively, Nelo caught it in the hand not holding the wood. He realized it was a nearly empty coin purse just as a Kereki soldier came through the alley and saw him. The soldier reached for his knife. Nelo dropped the wood and took off running. He crossed into Dockside and prayed the soldier had enough sense not to follow. He turned down another street leading to Lowertown and his hideout, when he heard the soldier shouting something behind him. He turned just enough to see the soldier pull up and stop.

Bloof! He plowed into the first man without ever seeing him. It was like running into a wall. Nelo felt huge hands grip him and looked up to see another grab him by his hair. Nelo winced at the pain.

"Well, what have we here?" The first man squeezed his arm and Nelo imagined the bruise that would rise up later. The longshoremen had forearms the size of Nelo's thighs and a grip that could break bones. Nelo focused on the tattoos running down the men's arms and fervently hoped they tired of their game quickly.

The soldier pounded up and sighed. "Thanks. He stole my purse, the nasty brat."

Nelo protested, "It wasn't me! It was a Matasian. You're blind! You can't possibly have confused the two of us."

The one who had grabbed him by his hair gave another tug.

"It's attached. I've never seen a Matasian with hair and skin this white. Then I've never seen a Kereki with hair so light either. You sure this is the one?"

Would the men defend him from the soldier? Nelo allowed himself a glimmer of hope.

The soldier reached forward and snatched the thin purse out of Nelo's hand.

"I'm sure. Here's my purse." He looked inside. "My papers are here, but the coins are gone." He scowled at Nelo. "You didn't have time to spend them, where are they?"

The longshoremen gave nasty grins. "We'll hold him, and you can search his clothes. If you take one coin more than is in your purse, we will crush the bones in your thieving hands."

Nelo saw the understanding break in the soldier's face. The longshoremen wouldn't help the soldier recover his stolen coins.

They were going to rob them both. How much pain they would inflict depended merely on which one they started with and how soon they lost interest.

The soldier held up his hands and started backing away.

"I recovered the purse and my papers. You caught the thief. Any coins you find of mine on this boy, consider that a reward."

Nelo felt despair crash over him. He wondered if the little girls and boys waiting back in the warehouse for food would cry themselves to sleep from hunger, or would they ignore his warnings and venture out after dark? He wondered how long before they died of starvation or abuse. He wished for them an easy death. He wished himself an easy death.

***

Nelo came to himself when he felt hands pulling at him. His face felt sticky, and his arms and head ached. He remembered what had happened and was surprised to find himself alive. He groaned and heard a sharp hiss.

"Shhhh! If you can stand, I can get you off the street. But we have to hurry. It's late and no time to be dancing with Trouble in Dockside. Can you walk? I'm too small to carry you."

Nelo painfully opened an eye and saw a sun-dark boy younger than he was. Nelo slowly rolled to his side and pushed himself up. The boy moved under his arm to help him. Nelo could feel the thin bones of the boy's shoulder as he pulled him forward.

A few streets later and Nelo realized they were back in the Sinner's District. The lantern lights were already flickering in the twilight of the dens where pleasure came in a pipe, a bottle, or a bed of questionable beginnings. The boy said nothing, but only turned a few more streets and then slid down a space between buildings so narrow, the two had to shuffle sideways. The boy propped him against the building while he used a set of steel keys and opened four locks on a building that looked as if it would blow down in the next sea storm to hit Kerek City. Nelo couldn't make sense of what was in front of him. The locks and keys were West Islands steel, but the building looked worthless. The boy pushed open the door.

Once they crossed the threshold the boy locked the sturdy door against the evening. Then he lit a small lantern on the table merely by touch. Nelo blinked rapidly in surprise at the growing light. It was all a maskovesto, an illusion. He was standing in a room within a room. It was small, true, but as solid and well-built as an oak cask of the King's wine. It was clean. The three windows were smudged and darkened at the top and boarded at the bottom so no one looking in would think it anything but as decrepit as the outside appeared.

Nelo heard more locks opening and a door at the back of the room opened to reveal a woman dressed in a heavily stained skirt and blouse. She rushed forward and helped Nelo to a chair. He recoiled when he smelled the indigo dye on her blue arms and hands. She pretended not to notice and reached for a pitcher of water. As she pulled off the scarf covering her dark brown hair and dampened it, Nelo noticed the gold rings in her ears. *A Spice Islander,* he realized. She handed the cloth still dripping to Nelo and motioned to his face. He touched the cloth to the stickiness and grimaced as he smelled the fermentation used in the dyes. Then he pulled it away from his face and realized the stickiness was blood. His blood.

The woman and boy walked into the other room, and Nelo could hear their soft voices. He tried to focus on their words, but it wasn't Keresh. Mata maybe, Wester probably. It didn't matter, he didn't know either language. He felt ill from his hurting head and the smell of blood and dye.

The woman came out alone.

"You must stay here tonight. It's too late to try to get you to your home. The boy tells me you run little boys and girls as lost children but do not sell them. Your care for the little children is the reason he has broken our rule never to bring anyone here."

Nelo nodded slowly, wondering what she knew. He wondered how long she had been an indigo dyer. She didn't have the poisoned look many of them had from the fumes and vats.

"Is Tae one of yours? Aisha?" Her Keresh didn't have any accent.

Nelo hesitated. "Why do you ask?"

"Your hesitation is your answer." She nodded sharply as if coming to a decision. "I will care for you tonight. I do not have so fine a needle to sew your face. You will be marked, but you have your life. I assume you have taught the little ones to hide away. They will be safe enough for one night without you?"

Without waiting for an answer, she went on, "Tomorrow at first light the boy will take you as close to your home as you will allow. We will give you food for your children for one day. In exchange, you must never come here again. You must never acknowledge that you know the boy in any way if your paths shall pass again. You should know his life may depend on it. We do not know if or when he is watched by those who work for the Harbor Master. Do you agree to this bargain?"

Nelo nodded uncertainly. He wasn't sure why the boy had stopped to help him. He didn't know why the woman knew two of his Lost Girls. But he would worry about it tomorrow. Tomorrow when the pounding in his head subsided. Tomorrow when he could get back to the warehouse and feed the little children before he had to turn them out on the street to beg for coin and food, lost and alone and dependent on the kindness of strangers.

You will learn more of Nelo and Kid in Book 4 – *Exile: A New Beginning,* and Book 5 – *The Wrens Fly Away*

FALAN'S SHADOW

Josef followed Falan carefully through the pasture. She was wearing those oversized boots again and he placed his feet carefully in her steps for no other reason than she had told him to. He wore both a bulky Kereki skirt and a black traveler's cloak over the clothes he was wearing to give to the Viklanders. Falan carried the food basket allowing Josef to carry a dagger in each hand. Secretly, Josef thought he should have carried the food basket. He was sure Falan's knife skills were better than his own. But she had insisted on that as well, saying he needed the practice. She claimed he was so slow to defend himself, he would be dead and buried before he ever cleared the knife out of its sheath.

Falan turned and motioned him forward. He could see the curing barn ahead of him now. The night skies were obscured by cloud cover—a good night for moving Viklanders. Falan had said there were no injured, at least none so badly they wouldn't be able to keep up as he guided the soldiers to the Viklander camp north of Balza. Josef merely had to lead them back to his favorite sentry point and let them talk their way back into safety. He started humming one of the ditties the sentries had taught him. He felt Falan stiffen beside him. Of course, she would prefer to slither into the barn and risk getting bashed by one of their bongs. Josef liked to let them know he was coming.

Falan pushed open the door without entering.

"It's me," Falan said into the darkness, "I brought the one who will lead you. Light the lamp I gave you." She pushed Josef in ahead of her and closed the barn door. He held his breath as he waited for his eyes to adjust to the dark.

A lucifer flared and a lantern door muffled close. A weak circle of light steadily grew brighter until Josef could see the circle of Viklanders, bongs and crossbows up and ready to defend themselves.

"This is how this will work," Falan said as she ignored the weapons and handed out bread and cheese and fruit. "You need to wear a Kereki shirt over your clothes. Our friend here is your guide. He knows the way, don't second guess him. Don't lag behind. If he tells you to do something, do it without question. Carry your bongs like you don't know what they are, or how to use them. Like a cudgel, or over your shoulder like a club. Keep the crossbows under the cloaks. You need to look like just another Kereki vigilante group out hunting for lost Viklanders. Keep your hoods up if you are lucky enough to have a cloak. Drop your braid between your neck and your collar if you don't. If your Keresh has an accent, keep your mouth shut. You will be passing through heavily patrolled areas. You must look big enough and Keresh enough to look like a patrol of your own so no one will look too closely."

Josef was already peeling off the billowy shirts and pants he wore under his skirt handing them to the soldiers. The room was silent. Josef could see the weariness and worry etched into the soldiers' faces.

Falan looked critically at the soldiers.

"Don't be foolish out there. It was a lot of work for me to keep this one," Falan pointed at Josef, "alive in Kerek City. I would be more than angry if you lost or damaged him now." She looked at Josef and snapped, "Give me that skirt. I know you are hiding battle leathers under those baggy pants. You wear more protection on a night walk than these soldiers do fighting." She jerked her hood up and turned to go. "You know what to do. I'm going home." Everyone stilled as she slid through the door and into the night.

Josef turned and smiled broadly at them as they finished their food.

"Shall we go?" He looked carefully at the six soldiers in front of him. "Are any of you pretending not to be hurt? Because I would truly hate to be running across an open field just to learn one of you is bleeding from a knife wound and leaving a trail of blood a child could follow."

One of the soldiers laughed nervously, but all of them shook their heads. He wondered why Falan had told them he was wearing Viklander battle leathers under his clothes. Was that to protect him or warn them? He hoped the night would be quiet and the paths empty. He wondered what the Viklanders thought when they had met Falan, and she had brought them here. Did they go to sleep at night wondering if they would see morning? Josef wondered what it would be like for them not to know if he could be trusted, if Falan could be.

It would be like Lowertown, he decided. He smiled again at them. Lowertown was survivable and so was this. He reached for the lantern on the ground.

"If you have finished your food, we should go. It's not a difficult walk, but it will take some time."

The barn door made a muffled thud as it was slowly pushed open.

"What did you forget to tell us, Falan? Miss my pretty face already?" Josef turned to look at the sound.

It wasn't Falan in the doorway.

The boy was six, maybe seven years old. Kereki, with dirty blond hair. He wasn't dressed well against the rain just starting outside—a pair of ragged pants, a thin shirt, barefoot.

Josef felt his stomach clench. What was he supposed to do now?

"I won't say anything," the boy pleaded. "Let me hide here tonight and I won't say anything. I don't see anything here. It's just a warm dry barn to me, I don't see anyone here at all. I won't say anything." The boy's eyes were round with fear.

A Viklander pushed by Josef and went down on one knee before the boy. "I am a father. I have two children just a little older than you. If you tell anyone we were here or how many of us, I may never see my children again. Do you understand how important this secret is to me? I want to see my children again."

The boy nodded quickly.

"I won't say anything," the boy repeated.

The soldier asked, "Where is your father?"

"Dead."

The soldier winced. Someone behind Josef muttered darkly in Vik. Another soldier answered him in the same cold tone. Not for the first time, Josef wondered just how wise it was he didn't speak Vik.

"We need to go," a third voice, this time in Keresh. "We gain nothing by standing here."

Josef nodded.

"The boy lives." The one who knelt stood up and placed himself between the child and the rest of the soldiers. "I will be the last one out."

Josef blew out a sigh of relief. The decision was made, and it wasn't his. He led the others out into the night.

***

The clouds were rolling in but the square in Balza was just as busy as ever. It was the Wet. Of course there would be daily raindrops. It was market day and shoppers just clutched their cloaks a little tighter. Josef looked about the square and wondered how much longer he and Tiju Tia would need to stay. He would have asked her, but she was still haggling with a man over a shirt at her rag and bone cart. With all of the soldiers and crimpers in the area, Tiju Tia had thought it best to dress as a Kereki boy guarding and protecting his older sister. Josef rather doubted the Kereki army would take him for a soldier. He thought he was too young, but he was tall, and if Tiju Tia said to dress as a woman to avoid a dance with Trouble, Josef would dress as a woman. He didn't mind. It was far easier to wear his Viklander battle leathers over his chest, legs, and arms under a dress.

The man walked away with a bundle of clothes under his arm and Tiju Tia looked at Josef.

"You look like a girl that's never been to a town before. Your eyes aren't quiet," she said disapprovingly.

"It's such a lively place," Josef responded cheekily. He tipped his head to the toggery where Falan was just leaving. He gave a long slow look about the square to see if anyone appeared a little too interested in a traveling rag and bone cart and its customers.

A boy was standing just outside the stables. He was staring at Josef with wide frightened eyes. Josef puzzled over what he or Tiju Tia could have done to earn the fear in the young boy's face. Then he realized where he had seen the boy before. It was all those nights ago, in the barn north of Balza. The boy was better dressed now and clean, but Josef was sure he wasn't mistaken. It was the same boy.

Josef frowned. From there to here was quite the distance for a boy as young as that to travel alone. The boy backed up carefully and disappeared into the shadows of the stable.

Falan and Tiju Tia were still talking over the cart. They were sorting out clothes Falan could take now, and those that would need Callis's fine needlework to make them serviceable again. Falan was complaining about the lack of boots. Josef knew what she meant. With the daily rains, the heavy black Viklander boots left tracks anyone could follow. The Kereki boots had soft leather bottoms, and while they leaked badly and often slipped in the mud, they hardly left a track at all.

Josef leaned in close to the cart and whispered, "You need to go to Ishes, Tiju Tia. I am sure there is a mountain of Kereki clothes in a pile by the gates. The Viklanders are pulling them off as soon as the sentries pass them through."

Falan snorted. "It is more than just Ishes, I would think. Nelo should send his Lost Girls out to the edges of their estates. I am sure once the Viklanders see the border, they are shedding their maskovesto and waving their braids in the air." She stopped suddenly. "Josef, have you been stupid? There is a woman standing near the well staring at you. Don't look, you ninny, she'll know we are talking about her." Falan pushed the clothes hard at Josef and a shirt fluttered to the ground.

Josef bent down to pick it up and casually looked about. There wasn't anyone looking at him, but there was a woman standing on the green looking carefully at the stables. He followed her gaze and saw the boy quickly give a sharp nod and disappear back into the shadows.

He stared at the woman, memorizing her features. She was older than Falan, but not as old as Tiju Tia. Her dress and apron looked nicer than anything in the rag and bone cart. She was well-fed with soft features. Her hair was tucked up like a married woman, but he could see it was the same straw color as the boy's, maybe a little darker. She looked like a rich Kereki housewife, and he couldn't figure out her connection to him or to the boy.

"Josef?" Tiju Tia sounded concerned. "Do we have a problem?"

He dropped the shirt back into the cart and smiled at Tiju Tia and Falan.

"Of course not. She was merely admiring my pretty face. I'm quite used to it already. I can see why Falan was worried, it seldom happens to her, I think. Now can we go and get something to eat? I feel as if I have been standing here all day and my belly is within reach of my backbone."

***

Josef had been expecting the knock for days, ever since market day in Balza. Now that it was happening so early in the morning—just quiet taps and not the pounding he had expected—he wondered what he would find at the other side of the door. A patrol of Kereki soldiers? The Justice of Balza? A home militia from one of the neighboring settlements? He swallowed hard and pulled on his pants and shirt. He thought about lighting the lantern, but it wasn't dark enough anymore. It would just make it easier for them to grab it and burn him out.

He walked to the door, took a deep breath, and opened it.

The boy was there. But not just the boy. The woman from the Balza square stood behind him with a Viklander soldier draped heavily over her shoulder.

"Can you help?" the boy whispered. "The soldier cannot walk."

Josef pushed past him and pulled the soldier off the woman.

"Come in quickly."

They crowded in, and Josef put the soldier on a chair by the table. He pointed to the washbasin and his towel near the window, and the boy rushed to bring it over. The woman started washing the wound in the thigh, and Josef could see the broken off arrow, the injured flesh gaping around it. He felt his stomach heave and looked at the ceiling quickly.

"She can't stay here," Josef said, still looking at the ceiling. "I can help, but I was told never to let anyone stay here where they can be tracked or seen."

"We know. It was why we didn't know you were one of us. You are so very careful." The woman tore at the fabric to make it easier to wash around the wound.

Josef looked hard at the boy.

"You said you wouldn't tell. You said you saw nothing."

The woman looked up sharply at the boy.

"Have you two met before? I mean before you marked him in the square for us? I thought you said it was the woman you had followed in the woods."

The boy smirked at Josef. "I said nothing."

The soldier fainted then, and the next moments were focused on cutting and pulling out the arrow while the soldier was unable to feel it. Josef choked back his bile and went to boil water while the woman finished cleaning out the wound and wrapping it in bandages. Josef lifted the unconscious soldier and half dragged, half carried her to his bed.

"You'll have to undress her. I have clothes." He went to a wooden chest and started pulling out a Kereki dress and small clothes.

The woman came and kneeled beside him.

"She'll only need a shirt for now. We can't move her like this. Tomorrow night either the boy or I will come with a wagon to transport her. We will need you to dress as a man to act as my

Kereki protector and take us to the fort at Earles or to the Vik encampment. Do you have contacts in both places?"

Josef stared at her. "You must think I am a fool to believe you so willingly. How do I know you did not wound the soldier yourself in order to bring her here and test me? I could be merely a person who would help anyone who came to my door injured and in need of a safe place for a few decons. You know nothing about me, and yet you are so willing to spill your secrets. You wouldn't live a day in Kerek City."

The woman turned and glanced at the boy. "Tell your story."

The boy looked at Josef. "On the day my father died, he and my mother argued in whispers almost the whole morning. I did not know what it was about, but I knew he had been sneaking about at night. I heard my mother ask him, 'What would become of the children?' He had gotten angry but said we needed the coin. He promised my mother he would only go one more time. I followed him because my mother specifically told me not to leave the yard. I thought it was a game at first. I stayed far enough behind that he would not know I was there. Twice I lost him. I think he had gone off the road to check on some buildings or perhaps hiding places. It was towards evening, and I began to be uneasy. I did not think he was going to be gone so long, and I knew my mother would worry, or worse, know that I had followed him. I was just going to turn and go back when I heard horses. My father slipped off the track into the trees, and so I quickly did the same. It was a Kereki patrol. They saw my father and hailed him. They all talked pleasantly, from what I could hear anyway, and I thought it was going to be all right. They nodded to him and galloped on.

"We walked a little further and a while later, my father stopped and waited by the promise tree. Do you know this place?"

Josef gave the boy a measured look. "I know the place. There is a tree so large three men can stand about it and only touch finger to finger. There are no trees nearby."

The boy nodded. "That is the tree. A Vik softfoot came and my father gave some papers to him. They talked for a little while, and I heard my father tell him he would not softfoot again. The Viklander thanked him for his courage, gave him coin, and left. I thought he went east, but I do not know that for certain. My father started walking towards me, and I thought I would step out and walk back with him. I knew I would be punished for my willfulness, but I had disobeyed before, and I thought that was better than to try to follow him home in the dark."

He paused. "A Kereki man, one of the ones from before, came riding out from the north. I did not know they had not all gone away. He called my father a traitor and tried to run him down. They fought but the other man was on a horse. A quarrel came out of the night and killed the man on the horse. Then a second one came and killed my father."

The boy took a shuddering sigh. "I do not know who fired the Viklander crossbow. It could not have been the softfoot, I do not think. He was not wearing a crossbow when he met my father. It could have been the other Kerekis who shot their friend by mistake…or not. I do not remember any of them carrying a crossbow when we met them earlier. It could have been a Viklander separated from his unit and trying to find his way back in the dark. I do not know."

The boy looked at Josef. "I waited all night to be sure I would not be discovered as well. But I must have fallen asleep. When I woke in the morning, both men were off the track and their clothes were gone." He hiccupped a sob. "When I came home the next morning, my house was burning, and there was almost nothing left. I saw my mother laying in the yard, and my little brother beside her. There were two 'x's made of wood in the dirt beside them. I didn't even go into the clearing to see them; I knew they were dead. I just turned and walked to Balza. I hid in barns where I could."

The boy turned and looked to the woman. "This is the story I told you." He looked at Josef. "This is the story she heard."

Josef turned to the woman. "Who are you to this boy?"

"He is the son of my older sister. My friends and I wish for change in Kerek. The boy's father was a part of us. The boy walked to Balza over many days and found me. Now he helps me by walking as my protector."

Josef scoffed. "He's a boy."

"And yet, he fulfills the requirement of a Kereki male who must accompany me. My husband's family would make life difficult for those who would do me harm. My husband's father is the Justice of Balza. He is no friend to Vikland."

Josef raised an eyebrow. "And you think this makes you safe?"

"No one would be safer. Who would suspect the daughter-in-law of the Justice? A woman so frivolous, she spends a ship's fortune on shoes and dresses. So absentminded, she shows up for parties at her friends' on the wrong day. A sweet woman who has no children of her own, so she is always giving coins, and food, and clothes to children who follow her about and whisper their childish secrets."

Josef quirked a smile. "So much trust. How do you know I won't do you harm?"

The woman smiled back. "The boy said the woman in the toggery was a friend to us. So we looked to see who she spoke with. When the boy saw you with the rag and bone cart in Balza, he said you could be trusted. He would not tell us why, but he was insistent. The boy and I were only on our way to meet you this morning and ask you to join us, when we found the soldier and another in the roadway. Most of the blood had washed away in the rain—their dance with Trouble must have been during the night. The other was dead, this one was insensible. Now we are here.

"I am asking you again. Tomorrow night either the boy or I will come with a wagon. We will need you to dress as a man and take us to the encampment or to the fort at Earles. We are not known at either place. The boy's father was our contact, and we need a new one. Do you have friends in both places? Can you introduce us?"

"I will only tell you, I will take you close to the encampment. I will not introduce you. Anything else, you must ask the woman in the toggery. She will tell you what she wants you to know."

She gave him a long look as she considered his answer.

"We will talk with her before we come here again." She nodded at the boy. "We need to go, it's a long walk back to Balza."

You will learn more of Falan and Josef in Book 4 – *Exile: A New Beginning*, and Book 5 – *The Wrens Fly Away*

The adventure continues in

Exile: A New Beginning

Book 4 of *The Tales of Zren Janin*

Zren Janin has friends in high places. Through accident and adventure, he knows Ngahuru of the West Islands, Miyamoto Suki—a diplomat of Vikland, Bima Ritwik the Softfoot, Solkka Ulani—a man who is more than the son of a coffee farmer, and Vikland's prolific inventor and firemaster, Chul Swyler.

He is loyal to those he calls his family at Manumina, he respects the talents of the Wrens who came to fight for a chance at a better future than Kerek City had to offer, and he understands those who simply want a place to belong.

But not all of them will survive the war. Some will carry scars that will never fade.

During one of Ngahuru's long trips away from the others, the news comes to Manumina the Kerek King's son and heir has been murdered in the Sinner's District along with his friend, Primo Resoro. Without knowing who did it and why, the Kerek King and his wife flee the country with all the gold they can carry. Kerek City is a gift for the taking for any country who can get there first.

But there is no peace when the Matasi Navy sails in and the Triune Army takes over the port. Ngahuru's network collapses through betrayal and violence. The remaining Wrens fly to anywhere they think is safe. Vigilantes search for traitors, ragged soldiers look for someone to blame. Fire and death forces those survivors at Manumina to walk away from their home.

Who is still alive and who is not? What does the future look like when the people you love cannot be found? How can you search for someone when you don't know where to look?

What can a future in Vikland hold when the Wrens wear the faces of the enemy, and the Conrosans the voice of another language? As the world turns upside down, Zren Janin wonders what truths will remain, what promises will be kept?